To Karen
you are
best
yours

absolute

PRETTY LITTLE SAVAGE

SICK BOYS BOOK 1

LUCY SMOKE

Lucy Smoke

Copyright © 2020 by Lucy Smoke

All rights reserved.

This is a work of fiction. Any resemblance to persons, places, or events is purely coincidental. No part of this book may be reproduced in any form or by any electronic or mechanical means, including information storage and retrieval systems, without written permission from the author, except for the use of brief quotations in a book review.

Editing by Heather Long and Your Editing Lounge

Cover Design: Dee Garcia at Black Widows Designs

❦ Created with Vellum

AUTHORS NOTE

Hey there, awesome person who picked up this book!

Thank you for buying *Pretty Little Savage*. I just wanted you —the person with great book taste—to know that I both loved and hated writing this book. I rewrote the beginning more times than I can count—and I mean that quite literally. I lost count when I got up in the double digits. But now it's done and it's in your hands. Before we start Avalon's journey, however, I wanted to issue a quick warning.

Sick Boys is not a series for people who can't handle a little darkness. Both our hero and heroine have very human flaws and both will see a lot of bloodshed and pain before the end of this series. I do not consider this book to be a bully romance, though you may see some similarities. Because of my own experience in the past with bullying, I have elected not to label any of my present or potential works as bully romance. What I will say is that this is a college age, new adult, enemies to lovers MF romance.

This book deals with some darker themes. If

you are sensitive to or offended by any such themes that are common in dark romances or you are easily triggered, this book may not be the best fit for you. Please keep that in mind and read responsibly.

"If you expect nothing from anybody, you're never disappointed."
Silvia Plath, *The Bell Jar*

PROLOGUE

AVALON

I put my foot to the gas, and floor it. The wavering pointer on the speedometer jerks up and then inches over, slowly but surely making its way to the 100mph mark and then beyond. The headlights wash over the dark backwoods road. The longer I stare, the harder it is to see until I realize it isn't that the road is hard to see, I'm just crying.

Sobbing, actually. Big, heaving sobs wrack my frame as tears slide from my eyes. They slip down my cheeks, dirty little things, leaving me with a salty taste in my mouth that's tinged with a metallic edge. Tears and blood. How? Because I've bitten my lip so hard that I can feel where the skin has broken and blood seeps from the wound onto my tongue.

"Fuck him…" I whisper. I lift my fist from the steering wheel and bring it down hard. Hard enough that it sends a ricochet of pain up my arm. "Fuck *them*," I amend, because it wasn't just Dean Carter. It was all of them. All for one and one for fucking all. They would back him, I had no doubt. So fuck them all. "Fuck them. *Fuck them.* FUCK. THEM." I scream until my lungs hurt.

It hurts. Fuck, everything hurts. The worst pain imaginable. Like being shredded open and left, gasping, in a pile of trash. That's essentially what he'd done. Never in my life had I ever let anyone make me feel like I was just as dirty and disgusting as my mother—not even the bitch herself. But he'd done it. And why did I feel this way? Because I'd gone and gotten stupid. Oh, I told myself I was being smart but the second I gave in, the very moment I spread my legs, deep down, I'd known. I up and drank the dumb bitch juice he'd been handing out.

Had it been obvious? I wonder. *Had I just not seen the signs?* I didn't think it was fucking possible for a girl like me to be dickmatized, but I'm not stupid enough to believe that doesn't have any bearing on the betrayal I now feel. *God, I can't fucking* breathe!

The sex had been amazing. It'd been filthy and rotten and for some fucking reason, when I'd been in his arms, I hadn't been Avalon Manning, the girl from the wrong side of the tracks. I'd just been me without all of the past shit to ruin it. And he'd just been a guy—as annoying as he could be, as controlling and as much of an asshole as he was—that I liked.

Liked—as in past tense. Because, the fact is, I'm not in love with him. To love him would be to ruin everything that I am. Because I'm not a girl that loves. I'm a girl that fucking destroys, and oh, Dean doesn't know it yet, but he's made one of the biggest fucking mistakes of his life with me. The snake of pure, unfiltered wrath breaks free and slithers up and around my throat. It blurs my reality as I lift my foot off the gas and just let the stolen ride be.

Eventually, the Mustang comes to a slow stop in the middle of the road. Darkness in front of me and darkness behind—much like my past and like my probable future.

Here I am … sitting in a stolen car in the middle of

nowhere with blood and tears on my face. I laugh. It's fucking funny as shit. Stupidly funny.

I laugh so loud and long and hard that my stomach begins to cramp. Something feels loose in my brain. Like whatever had been keeping me semi-sane has snapped and broken. The barrier is gone now and it. Feels. Fucking. Satisfying.

My eyes slide to the side and I reach for the seatbelt as they land on the glove box. I unbuckle myself, moving slowly as if my limbs have minds of their own. I press the button and it opens. My fingers find the handle of the gun I'd seen stashed in here the first time I'd ridden in this car. It's easy to pick it up—too easy—and though the gun feels heavy in my grasp, it feels right too. I lift it and point towards the windshield. I picture the guys. One by one. Standing in a line in front of the twin beams of light pouring from the Mustang's headlights.

What would I do if given the chance to kill him? Could I do it? Could I pull the trigger?

Right now, I feel like it'd be all too easy to blow not just his but each of their fucking brains out—because if it wasn't for the other two, I might never have met Dean Carter in the first place. My finger finds the trigger in question and smooths over it, but I don't press down. Instead, I lower the weapon, and after a moment, I put the gun back in the glove compartment, close it, and snap my seatbelt back into place.

No, I'm not going to kill them. I've got better things planned for them. More torturous things. What I am going to do, however, is go back. Not to Eastpoint, but to the place where it all began. There have been far too many people in my life who seem to think they have power over me and it all starts there.

First the past. Then the present. Only then can I finally face the fucking future.

Rules to live by. To look forward, I have to go back. Just once. Just this once. I put my foot back on the gas and this time, when I floor it, I know exactly where I'm going.

Those boys—those sick, twisted, disgusting, perverted assholes—think they can sweep into my life and drag me through the carnage of hell. What they don't yet realize, though, is that I was born there and I know exactly how to not only survive, but to fucking rise.

1
DEAN

16 years old…

Money is the ultimate weapon. Money and power. What many people don't know is that all wealth is stained in blood. True power doesn't come without corruption. People fight, bleed, and die for money and power. No matter who you are or where you come from, it is the one undeniable factor of the future and what it holds. Because money is power and power is blood. And I want both.

Warm red liquid drips from my right nostril as I pant, my chest rising and falling. My father stands to the side, his cold eyes watching. Always fucking watching and waiting—either for me to prove myself his failure or his heir. There is only one choice. I refuse to be the first, so I must be the second.

Taking the other man's neck in my grip, my muscles contract in my biceps as I smash his face into the concrete ground. Once, twice, three times until he coughs out a groan beneath my grasp, the pain he must be feeling making the noise a broken imitation of what should be a long and labored sound. Only when it hits my ears do I release him and take a step back. I don't flinch when he coughs again and this time, blood spews from between his lips, landing on the top of my brand new shoes. White splattered with blood. That seems to be the symbol of my family—of all the families of Eastpoint.

Off to the side, Braxton and Abel stand alongside their fathers, their faces expressionless. They, too, will face their trials soon. This one, though, is mine. I've known the gruesome requirement and the expectations of me as the future leader of the Eastpoint heirs since I was a child. I will not fail and I will not falter.

A tooth lands next to my foot as the man on the ground hacks and moans, his pain a visceral thing that I can practically taste. A part of me wonders if I should like it as much as I do. Another part of me doesn't really give a shit.

"Dean." That single word from my father tells me that it's time. Time to stop playing with my prey. Time to end this. Reaching down, I lift the man by the front of his already torn shirt. If it's odd to anyone in the vicinity that a sixteen year old can be so much bigger or stronger than a grown ass man, no one—least of all the man himself—makes notice of it.

"You know what we want," I state. "All you have to do to stop this is give it to us."

The man shakes his head. "I don't—"

Never let him deny. The first thing my father taught me when dealing with traitors. Get their confession and then kill them. No chances to lie. No chances to grasp onto the sliver of their lives we owned and tear it back. Show nothing but complete lack of mercy. I slam my fist into his face and feel the breaking of cartilage against my knuckles. New blood pours freely from his nose where it only trickled from mine. The man whimpering in my fists had only managed to land one hit, but I can tell that that single hit has angered my father.

I'm doing everything right. I do not show hesitation. I pummel the man with my fists until sweat beads at my brow and slides down my face. I let blood coat my knuckles and stain my clothes. Yet, still, I can feel his disapproval radiating from across the room.

I don't have to look at him now to know that his arms are crossed over his chest and his dead gaze is piercing right through me.

"Please," the man gasps, his hands latching onto my shoulders as he tries to get his feet under him once more.

I kick his knee and send him sprawling. "Just say the words," I order.

He whimpers again as I grind my foot into his groin and press down. *Hard.*

"I'm sorry!" he bursts out, tears sliding from his eyes. "I'm sorry! I'm sorry! Okay? You want to hear me say it. I will! They offered me so much money. I c-couldn't … it wasn't because I'm not loyal. I am! I swear it! I'm working for you. I always work for you. They're nothing. I'm doubling for you—I'll bring you any information you want."

I look over my shoulder. Nicholas Carter nods once. There is nothing this man has that we want. Reaching back, I touch the cold metal of the gun strapped to the holster against my lower back. As soon as the man sees it, he scrambles back, looking from side to side as if anyone here can or even would help him. A part of me wants to look at Braxton and Abel—I want to know their reactions. But I don't. As soon as I do something like that, I know I won't be able to pull this off. I might enjoy a little bit of the violence. I might crave something to quell the rage inside me. But I don't particularly want to see what they think of me as a killer.

This is what we were born for, I tell myself. The words are an echo of my father's. We live the lifestyle of the rich and powerful and we need to pay for it. This is our restitution. Lest we never forget that we are on top for a reason. Not to become the chaos but to rule and control it.

I step forward and put the gun to the man's forehead. His cries and pleas are like white noise in my ears. There are no clear words. No comprehendible anything. Just static. I take a breath and without another thought, I pull the trigger.

2

AVALON

14 years old...

THE TRAILER SMELLS LIKE SHIT WHEN I WAKE UP. WITH mold in the walls and bugs crawling through the green carpet, it always does. I get up and change for school. Patricia's soft snores filter out from the living room as I brush my teeth and hair and hurry through the morning routine. Some people look at me and assume I'd be like any other teenager, more than happy to play hooky or get out of doing homework. But not me. I don't mind school. I'll do just about anything to get out of this hellhole and away from *her*.

Patricia is like a broken doll. Her face cracked or caved in. Her skin marked with age and from too much sex and drugs. Mother or not, she's dead inside. A rotting corpse that just doesn't know how to fucking quit. I've never believed in God a day in my life, no matter what the religious freaks at school preach—and there's always a horde of them down here in the South, well meaning churchgoers who want to save everyone—but sometimes, I pray that He'll fucking send a lightning bolt, a hurricane, *something* to strike her down. It never happens, though.

Other kids got moms who at least tried. Sure, they failed. Maybe they were mean. Maybe they hit their kids, but at least they acknowledged they had one. Sometimes, I wonder if Patricia even remembers that she gave birth to another human being. It's kind of difficult to reconcile the woman lying stretched out on our futon for a couch with her tits hanging out and stinking like last night's puke and booze with the traditional idea of motherhood.

I stop just inside the main hull of the trailer, and the scent of vomit and dust collecting in front of me makes me wrinkle my nose in disgust. She obviously never made it back to her room when she stumbled in the night before. Her emaciated hand hangs over the edge of the futon, her fingers brushing against one of the many liquor bottles that litter the floor. A white filmy dust coats the old, scarred coffee table.

A scowl forms over my face. *Where the hell had she gotten money for cocaine?*

I march across the living room and kick her hand, not caring if it hurts or leaves a bruise. She'd do the same to me if our situations were reversed. Actually, she'd do worse. "Hey!" I lean down and snap my fingers in front of her face. "Wake up."

A low moan leaves her dry parted lips as her snoring stops and her eyelids crack open the scantest bit. "Avalon?"

My scowl deepens. "Get up. I've got to go to school."

She doesn't so much as wave her hand as she lifts it and lets it flop back down in a useless gesture. "So go."

I clench my fists and kick her hand again. "No," I growl. "You have to come to my school today. We have parent teacher conferences. I told you about it last week." I don't necessarily want her there, but neither do I want the school to look into why my mother hasn't answered any calls or why she doesn't show up for scheduled meetings like the one we have today. Because she's too busy fucking around, being drunk off her ass, or high as hell.

She mumbles something under her breath that I can't hear and turns away from me. "Well, I'm fucking tired," she says loud enough for me to hear. "Maybe if *someone* had offered to help me out last night, I wouldn't be so exhausted. But no, one of us has to keep a roof over our heads." It's clear who this *someone* is supposed to be.

I resist the urge to yank her up by her hair and punch her teeth in, but just barely. "I'm not gonna fuck your friends for money," I say through clenched teeth.

She just shifts over. "You will eventually, Ava. Keep fighting it, but you were born to be like me." Her words are callous, not because they're said with any derision or intended meanness, but because they're so final. As if the idea of me fucking some old, smelly man for drugs or money is merely inevitable.

"You're a bitch," I snap, turning away and stalking towards the front door. It's no fucking use. She isn't going to get up and she's not coming to the conference.

Out of pure spite, I slam the screen door behind me and relish watching the faded crack that's been there for ages grow just a bit longer. I hope the noise sounded like needles in her ears. The selfish bitch.

"Avalon, looking good, li'l runt." Halfway down the concrete front steps, my whole body freezes at the unfortunately familiar voice.

I eye the man who'd spoken as he cracks the door to an older model Cadillac that I've seen far too many times and steps out. "What do you want?" I ask sharply, not really caring if I'm not showing him respect.

Roger Murphy is one of the biggest drug dealers in

Plexton and I've seen his ugly face—all puffy and red with an overgrown mustache and beard—all too often at my mother's trailer. She might claim she's nothing more than a stripper to the cops who bust her every once in a while, but I know the truth. There's no way she can afford Roger's shit from what she makes at the club.

Roger grins as he steps away from the Cadillac that's parked halfway on the grass. "Just stopped by to see yer momma," he says. His belly jiggles as he moves, the whole middle of him rounded like a pregnant woman. He's packing the same rot beneath his skin just like Patricia. His teeth are cracked and yellowed with age and drugs. His hair, straggly and limp. And as he gets closer, I can smell the sweet metallic odor that gives me an answer to my earlier unspoken question. Well, at least now I know where she got the cocaine.

"She's asleep," I state.

He strokes a grubby hand down his unkempt beard, fat fingers catching in the snarls and yanking free a moment later. "Well, that's too bad. Cuz you see, I came to pick up payment for my last … delivery for her."

Dread sinks into my guts, twisting something foul and sharp into my abdomen and making it bleed on the inside. "She's inside," I say without inflection, "wake her up if you want. I don't care." I finish my way down the concrete steps and take slow measured strides towards the end of the driveway. "I've gotta get to school."

Don't look at him, I tell myself. *Keep walking.*

Roger's hand reaches out and grabs ahold of my arm as I move to pass by him. My body stiffens. Rage seeps from my pores. He's touching me. Fucking touching me and I don't like it. I look down at where his hand rests against my bicep. "Actually," he starts, "I think we should go wake her up together, don't you? I want to make sure my other payment is cleared up."

I try to jerk my arm from his grasp, and when I fail to break his grip, something electric moves through me—a stinging sensation. *Fear.* I push it down. Shoving it deep into the recesses of my soul and stomping it into submission. *I'm Avalon Manning,* I tell myself. *I fear nothing and no one.* Doesn't matter if the words are a lie, they make my back straighten and my nerves stop jumping around beneath my skin. "No, I don't," I say through gritted teeth. "And I don't have any money. Patricia does. Figure it out with her."

He eyes me for a moment. "Ya know, li'l runt," he says, his fingers growing lax on my upper arm. "I ain't ever met another kid who talks 'bout their mom like that. Yer pretty grown, ain't ya. Ya actin' all womanly now. Telling me what to do and shit. Only bitches who ever do that are the ones suckin' my cock."

I grimace in disgust. *That will never be me,* I think.

"How old is you again?" he asks.

"Fourteen." Too fucking young for his old eyes to be looking at me the way that he is.

He uses his free hand to once again stroke his beard as he hums in his throat. I want nothing more than to rip myself away from him, but I'm not stupid enough to think that he didn't loosen his grip on purpose. He's waiting for something. Is he waiting for me to do exactly what I want to do? Pry myself from his grasp and run? The screen door behind me squeaks as it's pushed open. Against my will, relief pours through me. Hope. Patricia is a shit mom, but if she's here, maybe she'll make sure he doesn't force me back inside.

I look back, but her gaze isn't on me. It's on Roger and her eyes are alive with something grotesque. All at once, my relief shrivels into nothing along with my hope. She's not out here to fucking save me. She's here for what he can give her. And if he offered her enough drugs, she'd probably offer me up to him like a fat turkey on Thanksgiving Day. It's a wonder she hasn't forced the issue yet. Disgust whips through me.

"Roger?" Patricia's voice is a repulsive purr, but finally, Roger's hand drops away from me completely and I'm able to push back the urge to gouge his eyes out with my dull fingernails until it doesn't even register anymore. "Do you have what I need?"

Roger looks me over once more and slides his fat tongue along the length of his bottom lip before lifting his gaze to meet hers. "Yeah, baby," he says, striding forward. "I've got everything ya need."

"Avalon." I stop when my mother calls my name and look back. "No more crawling in through your window. If you're coming home tonight, use the front door. If you break the window, you're paying for it."

Come through the front door and see her in all her naked disgusting glory, she means, while Roger or one of his friends pounds into her dried out pussy. In response, I flip her off and keep walking. But even as Roger goes into the trailer and the door shuts behind both him and Patricia, my heart still beats rapidly, an unsteady tune in my chest. Fear is the presence of powerlessness, and for girls like me—without a single fucking person to give a shit if they live or die—it's always present.

I hate it. I hate it with every fiber of my being. It makes something sinister and disgusting curdle in my gut. A wrath unlike any other. It makes me want to walk into Patricia's trailer and take one of the knives from the kitchen block and slit Roger's throat when he snorts a line of cocaine off of the dirty glass of the coffee table. That's not exactly the image a fourteen-year-old girl is supposed to carry with her. It's not something that should make her smile—but smile I do.

Around these parts, Roger's a baller. He has the drugs. He has the money. He has the authority.

I have absolutely none.

But even in death, he and I are the same. Rich. Poor. Man. Woman. Doesn't matter.

Clenching my hand into a fist, my nails dig into the flesh of my palm. I wait for the moment that my nails break skin and blood coats my hand. I feel the pain. I suck it in and I let it blend into the other sensations creeping through my body. The pounding of my heart slows. The tingling prickle of numbing anger recedes into the darkest depths of my mind.

I lied. I *do* hate her. I hate her. I *hate* her. I. HATE. HER.

And I hate the fact that I do even more. Because kids aren't supposed to hate their parents, and parents aren't supposed to threaten to whore out their kids. There's so much hatred inside of me that it's burning me from the inside out. That's when I realize that I'm already so close to being just like Patricia. I'm standing on an edge of no return. One slip and I'll fall down the dark hole that she probably did years ago before she even had me, and ten years from now, I'll either be dead or still here—in this fucking town, sleeping in that fucking trailer. Except then, I'll have a kid of my own from a man who I won't even remember.

Bile coats my throat as I stop at the edge of the street, the bright yellow school bus passing across the road and turning down until it curves around to my stop. The image of myself is so real in my mind. And even though I look nothing like Patricia, I can see only her in everything I might do. My heart begins to race.

I can't let myself. Hot tears burn in the backs of my eyes, and I suck them back, refusing to let them fall. Refusing to be weak like her. I'm never going to let a man like Roger Murphy touch me again without my permission. If he tries, then I'll kill him. It's as simple as that.

3

AVALON

4 years later…

Rage pounds through my bloodstream as I slam through the front doors of the school building. Fueled by a healthy dose of *oh fucking hell no* and *what the fuck was this bitch thinking*, I stomp through the students collecting against the lockers of Plexton High School's main hall.

"Hey, Ava, mind if I stop by your corner tonight for some one-on-one action?" someone calls as I pass by.

I flip him my happy middle finger and keep walking. "Sorry, you must be this tall to ride the Avalon Express," I reply, dropping the finger and holding my hand up well over the idiot's height. "Oh, and a dick—gotta have one of those too."

"Fuck you!"

"Go fuck yourself," I snip back. "'Cause I sure as hell won't do it, pencil dick."

The guy fucking snarls at me, but I ignore him and continue on, ready for destruction.

Stopping just inside the cafeteria, my eyes scan the

room, halting when I spot my target. I crack my neck. This is about to get uglier than one of my mother's binge days.

"Looks like the whore's made her entrance." The comment comes from a short-haired blonde sitting at the end of the table that my eyes are locked on. My target. I march towards her and dumb bitch that she is, she smiles when I stop in front of her. I don't even give her a chance to react or see my fist coming. One second she's sitting there, her smug ass attitude making her cakey makeup crack as she tilts her head up at me and the next, my fist is flying towards her face.

"You bitch!" Her shriek of shock and horror is like music to my ears as she falls out of her chair and scrambles back on her hands and ass. A ripple goes through the room and all conversation stops as eyes turn to me. I'm used to being the center of unwanted attention. Patricia has fucked enough of these kids' dads to make me an unwanted outcast. It's been like that at each and every school. On a normal day, I don't give a shit. What they think of me doesn't matter. Today, I give even less of a shit than I normally do. Why? Because when I'm pissed, I tend to forget that there's no one in this damn school—and no one in this godforsaken town either—who gives a shit about me.

"What the hell do you think you're doing?" Brooke demands as she inches back another few steps while remaining on the floor.

Everyone at the bitch's table rises at the same time. Two of the guys from the football team start forward as if to stop me. I don't hesitate. I pick up the closest thing—a textbook resting on the ledge next to someone's backpack—and use it to silence the cunt screaming at me from the ground. I slam it into her throat, cutting her off and shoving my foot into her stomach.

"Are you really all that shocked to see me, Brooke?" I tilt my head to the side and stare at her as she chokes. "I mean, you practically begged for this."

"The fuck"—she breaks off, coughing, but I get the gist of what she's trying to say.

"Oh but you did," I say, pressing down with the sole of my shoe as I get in her face. "You're usually Miss Princess up at the top, but this time, you got real low and guess what—down here in the dirt? I'm the Queen Bitch."

She snarls, her hand rubbing against her throat as she tries to soothe the damage I did with the book. It's not going to work. And I'm going to fuck her up a hell of a lot more before we're done. Usually, I don't give a shit what people say. Caring gives them power. But there's a point when indifference is outweighed by the sheer disrespect.

Now, if her petty little rumors had kept to the fucking school then maybe—maybe—I might've let it go and ignored it. But they hadn't. She'd taken her preppy little ass down to my fucking neighborhood—dirty trailers, coke-head hookers, and all—and spread that shit there. I didn't know how she'd done it because looking at her, I didn't think she'd have the balls. But the memory of one of Roger's minions stopping by my mom's trailer last night asking about my prices makes my blood boil anew.

Brooke doesn't know it yet, but she's signed a fucking warrant to getting her ass kicked and I'm more than ready to deliver.

"Listen up, bitch," I hiss, dropping the book. I lean forward, wrap my hand around her throat, and squeeze. "You made a big fucking mistake coming after me."

She wheezes in my grasp, reaching up with weak hands as someone else comes up behind me and wraps their arms around my middle in a vain attempt to drag me away. Looks like the footballers have finally decided enough is enough. Yeah, as if I'll let that happen. Enough is enough when I fucking say it is. I slam my head back and catch the asshole by surprise. The arms around my waist drop away almost instantaneously as a masculine grunt sounds at my back and surprise, sur-fucking-prise, he doesn't touch me again.

My obvious anger doesn't appear to deter the girl in my grasp, however. "You're nothing but trash," she spits at me. "Just like your whore mother. Now everyone knows."

I roll my eyes. Patricia isn't a whore. Not by the traditional definition. She doesn't sell herself for cash. No. She likes drugs. She doesn't get high so much as she likes to get fucked up. Cocaine. Heroin. Ecstasy. You name it, she'd tried it at one point or another.

"Get your facts straight," I say through clenched teeth. "My mother's not a whore—just an addict. And you're nothing but a sad little bitch whose boyfriend couldn't keep it in his pants," I finish just before I slam my fist into her face once more. Something breaks under my knuckles and a warm wash of blood comes spurting out. The sight is fucking beautiful.

"So you *did* fuck him!" she screeches at the top of her lungs, even as she yanks a hand to her face to stop the onslaught of blood and mucus. "I knew it!"

"Not for his lack of trying," I say, taking a step back, "but for your information, no. I wouldn't touch your boyfriend if he was the last man on Earth. Wouldn't want to catch that frigid cunt syndrome he gets from you."

She gasps in outrage, the sound nasally as she struggles back to her feet before pointing a bloody finger my way. "It doesn't matter now," she sneers as blood drips over her lips. "You're fucking done for. My parents are going to sue you for everything—"

I laugh out loud. *Holy shit.* I knew stupid could be

funny, but that right there is pure comedy gold. She breaks off mid-sentence as I bend over and press my hands to my stomach. "You're fucking welcome to try." I continue to laugh through the words. I don't have two fucking pennies to rub together and this bitch thought she could sue me? It's more than laughable. It's ridiculous.

"I will!" she screams. "You thought the fucking rumors were bad? I'm going to *ruin you*."

Her? Ruin me? *Too fucking late*, I think snidely. "I'm not scared of your fucking rumors," I say. "They're annoying. That's all. But you and those rumors do have a few things in common—you're both fake and you both get around."

"You—" she gasps, stopping and looking past my shoulder as her mouth curves into a smug grin even as blood still flows freely from her nostrils.

I turn, looking back to see what she stopped for. *Well, shit.*

Principal Delaney stands just behind me, her thin arms crossed over her chest as she gives me her death glare. It's worse than the one I'd seen just yesterday—probably because I had seen it just yesterday and she didn't expect me to fuck up again so soon. Then again, I hadn't expected to walk home and be propositioned by one of the town drug dealers for tricks, so … I guess we both got unfortunate surprises this week. "Avalon Manning," Principal Delany's voice echoes through the cafeteria, loud even to my own ears—probably because it's near dead silent aside from Brooke's nasal panting and the principal's words.

She stares at me and I stare back, not bothering to lower my eyes or look the least bit remorseful. We both know I'm not. When it seems she has nothing more to say, or perhaps she's too shocked by my display to come up with anything suitable, I lift my hand in greeting and flash her a smile. "Morning, Principal Delaney."

Her eyes scan me before going to the girl behind me. "Are you alright, Brooke?" she asks.

A sniffle sounds from the bitch at my back and I can't help but feel my smile grow. I bet even faking that little sniffle has to hurt what with the broken nose she's now sporting. "No, Principal Delaney," Brooke cries. "Avalon attacked me! Look at my face!"

"Awww, don't worry, princess," I say sarcastically. "I promise my nose job was a lot better than your last one. And this one didn't cost your daddy anything. It was on the house." I turn and look back, centering her with my cold gaze. "Next time, however, you won't be so lucky." Brooke's mouth snaps shut.

Principal Delaney closes her eyes before reopening them and focusing her attention on me. "My office," she grits out. "Now."

I shrug and head back the way I came. Fifteen minutes later, Principal Delaney storms into her office, her eyes searching me out. As soon as she sees that I have, in fact, followed her directions, she calms somewhat enough to turn and close the door behind her without slamming it.

"I told you I never wanted to see you in here again, Avalon," she says after a beat of silence.

I cross my legs at the ankle before folding my hands over my stomach. "So you did." And to be honest, I didn't want to be in here again either. Life's full of fun little shitty surprises though.

There's a muscle beneath Principal Delaney's eye that jumps when she's mad. I watch as it pulses. She's a pretty woman, I'll admit—twitching eye muscles and all. Slender, with a nice olive skin tone, and almond-shaped eyes. She's smart and fair. In all of the schools I've been to in the last four years—five in total—she's been my favorite principal thus far. She actually seems like she gives a shit. If I were to feel bad about anything—though I really don't—it'd be giving her more work.

"Then why?" she asks as she reaches her desk and snatches her stress ball from the surface, squeezing it roughly. That stress ball and I have seen a lot of these episodes together—usually after I do something fun but a bit psychotic as some of my semi-friends like to tell me. They're not real friends, just people I hang with until I eventually fuck up and head off to the next school.

"Tell me, for what reason did you break that girl's nose in the school cafeteria not *twenty-four hours* after our last meeting?" The stress ball smooshes against the inside of her palm, bulging out between her fingers.

"Probably because, you know that little voice inside your head that tells you not to do something?" Her eyes narrow and I smile. "Yeah, mine does the opposite. It tells me 'fucking go for it, bitch.'"

"Is this about the rumor?" she asks. Of course, she's heard about it. I don't answer. She stares at me for another moment before closing her eyes and breathing slowly. In and out. In and out. I almost feel bad for her. Almost. "Avalon, you know that rumors are just rumors. They can't hurt you."

That's where she's wrong. Truth be told, Brooke had needed the ass whooping for a while. She's had it out for me since I arrived. Used tampons in my locker. Textbooks stolen and returned with nasty shit written in the interior. Missing homework. I'm not stupid. Day one, her boyfriend had hit on me, and instead of blaming the cheating, lying motherfucker, she chose to blame me. How's that for fucking girl power? But this latest stunt was the end of it for me. Delaney didn't think that rumors could hurt? Nah. They could do much fucking worse.

If the fuckers in my neighborhood thought a chick was for sale—something I'd worked hard at making sure they knew wasn't the case with me—then shit didn't end well when they found out she wasn't. I'm not a cock tease, but her threatening to turn me into one put a girl like me in danger, and that wouldn't fly.

"I told you yesterday that this school was your last chance, and I wasn't kidding," she finally manages to get out. "There's nowhere else you can go. There's no other school in the district that will take you—especially not with your record." She squeezes the stress ball some more, growing silent for a moment. Well, I can't say I didn't expect this. I close my eyes and sigh, waiting for the final statement. "You're so smart, Avalon," she says, sounding tired. I know she is. I also know she's hating herself for what she's about to say. I don't blame her—she's good at her job. But this is the end of the line for me. I knew it as soon as I'd made my decision. I accept it. "You're out of options." Her words come with no small amount of reluctance in her tone, but almost immediately following them is an answer from an unfamiliar and unexpected voice.

Both Principal Delaney and I jump as the door to her office swings open. "Perhaps I can help with that." We turn, in unison, towards a tall woman in sky high red stilettos and a pristine white pants suit when she steps into the doorway. Principal Delaney's secretary, Mrs. Blevins, hovers behind her.

"I'm sorry, Principal Delaney," Mrs. Blevins sputters as soon as she realizes I'm there. "I-I stepped out and didn't know you had a student back here. There was a commotion—"

"It's alright, Mrs. Blevins," Principal Delany says,

holding up the hand not currently crushing the stress ball. "And yes, I've got the commotion well under control." She shoots me a look.

The woman in white laughs and all of our eyes snap back to her. "I suspect your *commotion* has something to do with this young lady right here, Principal Delaney," she says, arching a brow as I frown her way. "Am I right?"

"Unfortunately," Principal Delaney replies with a sigh. "And I'm very sorry, but I do need to finish this, Ms…?"

"Bairns," the woman says, holding out a perfectly manicured hand.

"Well, Ms. Bairns, I'm sorry if we had some sort of appointment today, but as you can see I'm with a student and I'm afraid I'll be busy for at least another few hours." Principal Delaney's eyes glance back at me even as she takes the woman's outstretched palm, keeping her stress ball in her free hand.

"Actually," Ms. Bairns says, "I don't think that will be necessary. I'm a recruiter for Eastpoint University and I've actually come to speak with you about a student of yours that our Dual Enrollment program is highly interested in. I do believe I've come at the perfect time, too. This wouldn't happen to be Ms. Avalon Manning, would it?"

"We weren't expecting you until next week," Principal Delaney says, not bothering to mask her surprise. I shoot her a confused look, but she's too focused on the woman to see it.

Ms. Bairns smiles. "I was in the area."

"What the fuck is going on right now?" I demand, uncrossing my ankles as I stand up and face them both.

Principal Delaney drops the woman's hand and makes a noise that sounds suspiciously like a growl. I don't have to look at her to know that she's glaring at me—I can feel the burn of it on my skin but I don't care. I keep my gaze locked on the woman in white.

"What's going on, Avalon, is that you're being recruited," she replies. "Starting next week I would like to enroll you in Eastpoint University." I open my mouth, but she beats me to the punch. "Eastpoint offers a unique opportunity where select students who have yet to graduate high school can enroll and take credits towards a future degree and those same credits will count towards your high school diploma." She smiles at me, but my head is in a whirlwind of 'what the fucks.' "Since this is your last semester"—she pauses, looking to Principal Delaney as if to confirm and Principal Delaney gives her a nod in return—"you'll only be required to attend for a full semester, but it is very much Eastpoint's hope that after you graduate with your diploma, you'll be willing to stay and continue your education with us."

I open my mouth, but she jumps ahead. "And if you're worried about your parents, you needn't bother. I've just come from your mother's house. She's already signed off on the agreement."

My jaw drops. I can't imagine this woman—in her pristine white clothes—stepping even one centimeter into my 'mother's house.' Had she seen the streaks of dirt and grime nearly an inch thick on the cracked screen door? Or perhaps smelled the scent of days-old vomit and weed in the stale air of the trailer? And still, she came here to try and *recruit* me? I knew I was smart, but this was suspicious as fuck.

"Ava?" Principal Delaney's hesitant tone brings me back.

I shake my head. "You can't be serious."

"Oh, I'm completely serious, Avalon," Ms. Bairns

replies. "Eastpoint is an elite school and we only recruit those who are eligible for our programs."

I gesture down to my person. "Then there's obviously been some mistake," I say. "I'm not elite *anything*. Something you would know if you've been to my house as you say you have."

Ms. Bairns smirks as she looks down at me from the perch of her heels. I grit my teeth. A smirk like that makes me want to punch something. Again. "I think you'll find that, at a place like Eastpoint, elite means more than where you come from. Elite refers to where you're going. Everyone we recruit is going somewhere far better than anywhere they've ever been."

"That still doesn't explain why you want to recruit me," I say, narrowing my eyes. "I can't even afford college." And it doesn't make any sense for a college to try to recruit me. My record with schools isn't even close to being good. I've been kicked out of four schools—five if we're going to count the one I'm currently standing in. I'm not exactly prime fucking recruitment material and I know it.

"Eastpoint focuses on what's important," Ms. Bairns says with a knowing smile. Her ambiguity is not endearing. "And since you're being recruited, you must understand we're offering you a position on a scholarship. All program students are offered the same package. You come to Eastpoint, keep your grades at the level they are right now, and you'll also likely be offered a secondary scholarship to continue your education with us."

I snort. "Well, thanks, but no thanks," I say. "I've got a plan."

"Actually, I'm afraid you won't after today, Ava." Principal Delaney's words are ice cold water splashed over my head, reminding me why I'm in this office to begin with.

"With everything that's happened today, I have to take executive action."

Executive action meaning expulsion. *Fuck*.

"More than that," she continues, "you're looking at a possible assault charge. Brooke's parents aren't going to be happy about what happened today."

I'd known that, and this morning I'd been prepared for it. Now, though, with this woman's talk of college and diplomas—I'm reminded of the reason why I've kept my grades so high. I want to get the fuck out of here, and from the way the woman's smile widens, she knows it.

"I believe I can handle the student's parents," Ms. Bairns says, shocking me.

"Handle them?" I arch an eyebrow at her.

She shrugs. "Eastpoint—and therefore *I*—am willing to do whatever it takes to get you to our school, Avalon. If it takes a little money then that's what it takes. I assure you, I've gotten my charges out of worse situations." Ms. Bairns bends and meets my eyes head on. I don't jerk away or frown. I simply stare and wait, knowing she isn't done. "So, that begs the question, what will your choice be?"

Choice? With the way she's talking, she's not really leaving me much of one. The answer is pretty apparent. It's Eastpoint University, juvenile detention, or probably jail.

Eastpoint, it is.

4

AVALON

2 weeks later...

WELCOME TO RICH-PEOPLE-VILLE. POPULATION—TOP ONE percenters, their devilish offspring, and now me. To say I'm not exactly overjoyed is an understatement. The second I set sights on Eastpoint University, I know I'm going to fucking hate it here. The buildings look like mini-castles. Stacked brick. Spiked roofs. Tall archways. There's even a clock tower and statues placed in various positions around campus as we drive through the iron front gates.

"College semesters begin a little later than what you're used to, but I've arranged for your classes to start on Monday, so you'll have the weekend to take a look around campus and settle in," Ms. Bairns announces, breaking the blessed fucking silence I'd enjoyed for the last two hours—because it'd taken her nearly eight to shut the fuck up as she'd rattled on about Eastpoint this and Eastpoint that. "I have no doubt you'll be quick to catch up—especially with your academic transcripts." She chuckles. "I should let you know, though, there are just a few rules we should cover before we get to the dorm."

"Of course there are," I mutter, waving my hand for her to get on with it. I'll decide later whether or not I'll follow them. As far as I'm concerned there are only my personal rules that truly need to be followed. Everything else is mere suggestion.

"Since I'm your official sponsor, you'll be expected to keep in touch with me during your classes. You're eighteen, so you get a lot of freedom that some of the younger dual enrollment students don't. However, you will need to meet with me at least once or twice during the semester just so I can make sure you're keeping up with your studies and we can talk about your plans for the future—like you would have done with a guidance counselor at your last school," she says.

A yawn stretches my jaw as I turn my head towards the window to watch the passing scenery. "You'll be expected to perform well academically," she continues. "But after having a look at your transcripts, I've determined that you don't need extra tutors. If you were making those kinds of grades in AP classes, you'll settle in just fine here."

I resist the urge to roll my eyes. AP classes only seem hard because of the workload. The coursework itself isn't necessarily difficult. Nothing is if you have nothing better to do. There's no need for her to sound so fucking impressed.

"Since you'll be in the same dorm as the rest of those in the dual enrollment and scholarship programs, you should know that while the dorm itself is co-ed, your floor is all female. That means you may have friends over, but no boys will be allowed to stay overnight."

Saw that coming, I think. Not that it'd exactly be a problem. I've never trusted a guy enough to let him stay the night. In fact, I'm not looking forward to sharing a room either. The idea of trying to close my eyes mere feet away from a virtual stranger makes my knee start jumping. My sleep schedule is about to get all sorts of fucked up.

"Other than that, things will be simple. This isn't like high school. There will be no fighting permitted. Not with your roommate or with anyone else on campus. While I admire your ... erm ... passion, if I were you, I'd try to calm it down as much as possible while you're here."

I cut my eyes her way and narrow them when I see how tight-knuckled her grip on the steering wheel is. So much so that the skin stretched over her hands is quickly turning pale.

"Passion," I repeat the word with a quiet laugh. "*That's* what you're calling it?"

"I mean it, Avalon," she says as she turns the car around the side of a building that boasts tall windows and dark colored panes. Ms. Bairns pivots her head towards me and her eyes bore into mine, making me sit up straighter. "You were recruited and so, of course, we want you here, but make no mistake—if you make the same choices you made in your previous schools, there really will be nowhere else for you to go. Eastpoint is your last option and I'm glad you decided to accept it, but there are rules to be followed and violence on campus will not be tolerated. It's the end of the line."

End of the line, huh? I don't know why, but that sounds good to me. I like being on the end of a rope. Makes everything feel a little dangerous. My heartbeat picks up speed. Sweat collects beneath my arms and in the center of my palms. A dark craving blossoms in my chest. The stint against Brooke back at Plexton had curbed it somewhat, but ever since, I'd started feeling the need to cause a little chaos—perhaps the very same day Roger had let it be known that he wasn't above fucking one of his client's kids —it hadn't disappeared.

My gaze falls away from Ms. Bairns. "Yeah," I say absently as I let my mind wander. "I get it. Not to worry. No one fucks with me, I won't fuck with them."

When she doesn't respond immediately to my words, I glance her way and frown. Her muscles haven't loosened at all. In fact, with the way her hands are still gripping the steering wheel for dear life, it makes me think that my words put her more on edge than anything else. I think about saying something else, but I've got nothing more to offer. Instead, I refocus on the building in front of us as the car slows to a stop.

Havers Dormitory.

Of all the other buildings on campus, the Havers Dormitory is the least pristine, the least aesthetically pleasing. In fact, it looks like an architectural reject. Or just really poorly maintained. The roof slopes so much that it makes the whole building appear as though it's slanting into a new angle. The windows are dirty and the sidewalk in front of it—unlike what I'd seen the entire drive through the rest of campus—is riddled with cracks. The grass is overgrown around the face of the dorm and the plaque alongside the front doors is covered in so much grime that it's hardly readable.

Doesn't matter. It still looks better than the piece of shit trailer I'd grown up in. I follow Ms. Bairns in and wait somewhat impatiently as we go through the process of assigning me my room, key, and student identification. I half-listen as she explains the student allowance for food and other necessities, all of which can be purchased using my ID card.

By the time we finally climb up the steps to my floor—no fancy elevator for the program kids, I notice—I'm ready to jump out of my skin. I need to go for a run or something. I need a little bit of a release. My fingers tap out a rhythm against my thigh as I march behind the woman who's brought me here.

"Here we are," Ms. Bairns says as we stop in front of a plain white door with paint peeling in the top right hand corner. The dorm manager—i.e. the woman who'd likely been given the rundown on me and been told to keep an eye out—slides her gaze over her shoulder and scans my form. I arch a brow and tilt my head, staring right fucking back at her. Before I can say anything, however, a cell phone rings and Ms. Bairns jumps as she quickly retrieves the source of the noise from her purse and glances over the screen. "I'll have to leave you with Ms. Lowery, Avalon," Ms. Bairns announces. "I've got to take this." She swipes to answer her phone but doesn't put it to her ear immediately as she hurries through the rest of her explanation to me. "She'll get you introduced to your roommate. If you have any issues, I've written down the location of my office and my phone number on your papers."

I give her a nod and watch as she hurries back down the hall, her heels thumping sharply against the worn vinyl looking tiles. Ms. Lowery doesn't spare me another look as she takes a step forward and knocks on the door. After a moment, it swings open to reveal a short, skinny girl with faded purple hair. She scowls when she sees me.

"Good afternoon, Rylie, this is Avalon, your new roommate." Ms. Lowery gestures back to me. "Avalon, this is Rylie."

My arms are starting to ache as I continue to stand there and hold my bags, so when it doesn't look like the chick is going to move any time soon, I roll my eyes and without a word, shuffle forward and push my way past her into the room. I drop my shit at the end of the unmade bed that's obviously meant for me and turn back around. The girl—Rylie—continues to scowl at me before dropping her eyes and scanning me from head to toe. I'm used to it enough—being looked at like a threat. I appreciate the fact that she recognizes it as I return the favor. I know what Bairns is trying to do, stick me with a chick from a similar background and hope I make friends, and it seems her other victim is just as keen on the idea as I am.

Rylie is even skinnier than me. She looks like one strong wind might break her in half. Dark circles line the undersides of her eyes and they contrast directly with her pale skin and light lavender colored hair that's obviously in need of another dye job, her dark roots showing through. No expensive salon trips for this girl. If it wasn't clear enough by the dorm she's in and the fact that she's about to get me as a roommate, the threadbare cut off shorts and the oversized 80s band t-shirt that looks like some sort of thrift shop reject would do it. When it seems like she's finished with her perusal of me, I arch a brow in challenge and wait. Her hazel eyes roll back into her head as she pivots and reaches for a messenger bag I hadn't seen hanging from the back of the door.

"Wonderful," she says without inflection. "Just don't touch my shit and we'll be fine. I gotta get to class. Later."

I smirk after her as she practically sprints out of the room. "Nice chick," I comment dryly to no one in particular before turning back to my things.

I reach for one of my bags and unzip it, reaching inside for a bundle of clothes, getting ready to begin the unpacking process. As I do so, I wait to feel Ms. Lowery's presence disappear, but as I start pulling clothes from the duffle, I continue to feel her watchful eye on my back and it's starting to piss me off.

Lifting back up, I turn and meet her stare head on. "Got something to say?" I ask.

Her gaze hardens and in a movement that looks vaguely like one of protection, she crosses her arms over her ample chest and glares at me. "I'm sure Ms. Bairns warned you, Ms. Manning," she says slowly, "but I feel I should also extend my own word of caution."

I tilt my head to the side and wait. From the expression on her face—the twisted lips and the narrowed slits of her eyes—she expects me to respond. Silence unnerves a lot of people and it's clear, she doesn't like it much either. I blink slowly and continue to wait her out. I don't have a watch to accurately time how long it takes, but it feels like several long minutes pass before she finally speaks again.

"Eastpoint University is an old and respected institution, Ms. Manning," she begins. "And you would do well to remember that you are here by the grace of the founders and their families—who pay for your tuition, room, and board. It's in your best interest to keep your head down and your mouth shut about anything you may do, see, or hear here. Is that understood?"

Fighting back the smile that threatens to curve my lips upward is difficult. *Word of caution, indeed.* "Sure thing, Ms. Lowery," I tell her.

She continues to examine me as if trying to peel back the layers of my skin and see into my head. The thing about my head, though, is that no one has a key to that place but me. I'm not about to let some bitch with a warning on her tongue even glance inside—what she might see would shock and horrify her delicate sensibilities. And quite possibly send her running straight to Ms. Bairns, demanding that I be institutionalized and kept far away from the general, law-abiding, non-fucked up public.

She turns to go, but stops and glances back over her

shoulder. "Welcome to Eastpoint University, Avalon." For some reason, it sounds more like a threat than a real welcome, and that's just fine with me. I deal with threats the way I deal with everything in my life—in my own, savage way.

5

AVALON

I HOLD THE CIGARETTE TO MY LIPS AND INHALE AS THE smoke drifts up. Several students pass by, scowling my way. I ignore the looks and focus on what's right in front of me. This shit is the only thing keeping me chill right now when what I really want to do is something dangerous. My foot taps restlessly against the sidewalk as I glare at a girl who dares to scoff in my direction as she strides by. As if I'm beneath her.

The hierarchy of this place is laid out neatly. It doesn't take a genius to figure out who's on top. Their stain free, name brand clothes say it all. The Gucci belts and Chanel bags mark the students who wear them as above the average classes—their attitudes and how they carry themselves pretty much does the rest. They think they're invincible because they have wealth and wealth comes with power. I smirk at them as I let the ash on the end of my cigarette fall where it may. Inside my head, a pounding starts.

Then there are the ones like me. Program kids and scholarship students. They sink into the background in old jackets and torn up jeans that are frayed from use, not fashion. I see them too, much as they don't want me to.

This place fucking sucks. I hate to admit it but there was a small part of me on the drive here that contemplated the idea of a fresh start—a personality makeover. It looks like no matter where I go, though, appearing weak in any way is not a choice. The need to wreak a little havoc presses against my pulse like a goddamn chokehold—I want to get away.

I force my thoughts onto something else—trying, if only for a brief period, to distract the darker inner workings of my own mind.

Just in time, too, I think as a shadow falls across my front. "What the hell do you think you're doing?" a vaguely familiar voice snaps.

Lifting my head slowly, I meet a pair of glaring hazel green eyes. My roommate. "I'm not doing anything," I say, lounging back, feigning relaxation when all I feel is anything but. "Just hanging out. Taking in the scenery." I take another drag from my cigarette before snuffing it out against the pretty white brick sidewalk. A dark smudge marks the area, scarring it. I toss the butt into a nearby trash can.

She shakes her head. "No, I mean with that," she gestures to the black mark I'd left on the ground. "Marking your territory? What are you, a bitch?"

I shrug, casting a glance back to the surrounding walkways as more and more students spill out of their respective buildings and make their way across the campus. "I had a nicotine craving."

"Well, don't," she replies tersely. "Kick the habit. It'll kill you anyway."

I grow still and look at her again. "What the fuck do you care?" I say with an arched brow.

Instead of answering me right away, she seems to finally realize just how many people are watching us. Her shoulders tighten, lifting as she tries to sink into the far too skinny body—seriously, her metabolism must be through the roof. "Come with me," she says suddenly, taking a step back.

I stare at her in confused, albeit amused interest. When it becomes clear to her that I'm not going to get up and do as she says on my own, she reaches down, snagging my wrist in her hand, and pulls me along. Normally, I'd break someone's face just for touching me, but I find myself curious. So, I let her drag me behind her, interested to see what she'll do or say, when we turn a corner and she pushes me into a secret alcove so we're cut off from the prying eyes.

"Listen," she says, spinning back to me once she's made sure we're alone. "Normally, I wouldn't give a shit and I'd just let you learn the hard way, but you're my roommate and—"

I laugh, cutting her off. "Whatever you're gonna say, you can stow it," I scoff. "Don't go doing me any favors just because we got stuck living in the same room together."

She scowls at me, baring surprisingly straight white teeth. "Believe me, I'm not doing it for you," she replies. "It's for me. Roommates in Havers don't get switched. We're program students. We just have to deal with it—whatever comes. Which means if you get in trouble, I'll be stuck in the crosshairs. I don't fucking care about you at all. I'm doing this for me," she repeats.

"Well then," I say with mock seriousness. "Please, proceed." I gesture for her to continue, earning another whip sharp glare.

Rylie shakes her head, the waves of her purple hair sliding across her shoulders. "You can't smoke on campus.

Or drink. Or cause problems. Do what you want off campus, but unless you're given permission, you keep that shit away from Eastpoint."

I wave a hand. "If you're worried about the dorm lady, don't. She can't do shit outside—"

"I'm not talking about Lowery," she interrupts with a frustrated growl. "Jesus, you really don't fucking get it, do you?"

I pop my neck and give her my undivided attention. "Apparently not," I say with careful enunciation. "Why don't you spell it out for me?"

Rylie stares at me. Our eyes meet and hold, and I wait. This was one of those things people like us did. You face a monster and wait to see which of you breaks first. *Hint.* I never break first.

Finally, she glances away with clenched teeth. "Listen," she says again, beginning this time in a quieter, though no less frustrated tone. "I'm not trying to be an asshole."

I snort. "Could've fooled me. First time we met, I thought you wanted to cut me down to size. Not that I'd let you, of course, but you've got the perpetual resting bitch face under control, for sure."

Rylie's eyelashes flicker as she glares at me out of the corner of her eye. She blows out a quick breath. "That was for Lowery's sake," she snaps. "I don't know if you've noticed it yet, but she couldn't give a shit less about the students in her dorm. She's there to keep us in line and nothing more. She's a watchdog, not a friend."

I'd noticed, but I don't say anything, waiting, instead, for her to continue.

"Eastpoint is a private university," she says after a moment, "and the families that run it all have a stake in it. They accept only the elite of the elite." She pauses, looking at me fully once more. "Do you get that?"

I frown. None of this is new information. I've heard it all from Bairns, but coming from Rylie, it sounds less like a marketing ploy and more like disturbing intimidation. "I get that we're charity cases." I shrug. "Something to write off on their taxes or make them look good if they were up for any promotions or elections. Why does that matter?"

"We're not charity cases," Rylie says. "We're recruitments."

"Yeah," I reply flatly, "for the university. What? Does that mean their rich kids are too dumb to keep their grades up and they need smart poor kids to boost their general intelligence?"

Rylie inhales and then releases a breath. "No, we're recruited to come here and take classes with the children of the elite because after we all graduate, we're going to be offered an opportunity."

"What kind of opportunity?"

"The kind to work for the richest people in the world," she says. "They recruited people like us for a reason and it's not just because of our backgrounds. A lot of us in the program have nowhere else to go, it's true, but we're also not dumb. I don't know why you're here, but soon enough you'll realize that everyone in the program was selected for a reason."

Scoffing, I take a step back. I can only guess what their reason is for wanting me. Whatever the case, though, I'm not going to bow and scrape to their needs and wants. No matter what they expect, I don't blindly follow anyone. "Yeah, they can fuck off," I avow. "I'm here for the education and because, yeah, you're right, I don't have a place to go otherwise, but I'm not here to work for anybody."

I turn to go and Rylie reaches out once more, latching onto my arm. Pausing, I look back and give her hand a pointed glare. "That's fine," she says. "You can do that when you get out, but while you're here, you have to respect their authority."

The corner of my lips curl up. "I didn't see any authority figures out there," I point out. "There's no reason—"

"Just because you didn't see them doesn't mean they didn't see you," she says, cutting me off. "The Sick Boys know everything and if they think you're disrespecting them, you'll regret it. Trust me."

"The who?" I laugh as I brush her hand away from my arm. "Anyone who goes around calling themselves the 'Sick Boys' are probably just a bunch of preppy assholes playing at being badasses. I can handle dicks like that any day."

Rylie sighs. "They don't call themselves the Sick Boys," she says. "Everyone else does. Because they are sick. They're cruel. The last time someone got on their shit list, he left the university and hasn't been heard from since. They can make people disappear."

"What?" My smile drops away.

Rylie takes a step back, moving as if she's about to leave. "They're not just regular people," she says. "They're the richest of the rich and if you think they don't have connections to some bad people, you're wrong. Pretty much all of the wealthy in this country are corrupt in some way or another. These people are no different. If you're anything like me, then a shared room in a rundown dorm is probably one of the best places you've ever lived. If you don't want to lose that, if you don't want to lose your freedom, you'll be smart. Keep your head down and don't piss them off."

6

AVALON

Keep my head down and don't piss them off? What is it with people thinking they can tell me what to do? Rylie's words are still filtering through my head days later. I feel my lips curve upward as I shoulder my backpack and trek across campus to my first official class, drawing curious looks. *Don't piss them off?* It's laughable. Whoever these preppy rich boys are, they should be warned not to piss *me* off. Because I'm sure, unlike them, I'm the kinda psycho that goes bump in the night and they wake up with their house on fire.

As soon as I turn into the auditorium-like room, I feel eyes on me. New girl. New school. Same fucking bullshit. I pause and contemplate where to sit.

Strangely enough, though most of the class has already been filled, at the back of the room there's an entire row left empty. One that looks down on the rest. As much as I like the idea of sitting above these people and watching them, I like the idea of being able to put my back to the wall even more. I don't hesitate, taking the steps two at a time until I reach the row of desks and slide into the seat on the end, dumping my bag into the empty space next to me to ensure that if anyone thinks to come up and join me, they'll get the message. The message being *do not disturb*.

I steeple my fingers under my chin and yawn. It's only been three days since I arrived at Eastpoint, but I'm still getting used to the rooming arrangement. At the trailer, I'd just locked myself into my room, shoved a door stopper I'd stolen from the school beneath the wood, and turned on the piece of shit radio I'd kept in the corner of my bedroom before nodding off for a few hours at a time. With someone else in the room, however, sleep has become an elusive fucking bastard.

As I wait for the teacher to arrive, I let my eyes slide shut and listen to the bustle of the other students in the classroom with me. The sound of whispers hit my ears, making them prick with interest as I realize they're talking about me. I sigh. Things never change.

...think she's doing...
...new, she's got no clue...
...can't wait to see what they'll do...

The door opens and the whispers die. Not the normal natural slowing of conversation that announces the teacher's entrance and the beginning of class. No, instead, it goes from annoyingly loud and almost too obvious gossiping to dead silent. My eyes open. The teacher has arrived, yet for some reason, I get the feeling that the dead silence now perpetrating the room is not because of her, but the two guys who walk in immediately after her.

Without a word, the tall woman I presume to be the instructor steps up to the podium and begins to quietly unload her things from the satchel at her side. I feel the prickling burn of someone's awareness—the kind of feeling you get when you know someone is staring. My gaze follows the two guys who'd come in after the teacher as they stop at the bottom of the steps leading up to the desks, tilting their heads back as they look up and their eyes meet mine.

I arch a brow and settle into my seat. The room seems to hold its collective breath as the two of them begin to move. Curious, I follow the trail they make through the room—watching as girls ogle them with lustful eyes and guys either avoid looking directly at them or stare with worshipping expressions. As if these two aren't mere students but gods who've graced us with their presence.

The taller of the two men hangs back, letting his friend take the lead. Something about him makes me feel restless, though. By all appearances, he looks like an all-American jock—bright hazel-gray eyes, chiseled jaw, and even a little boyish curl of dark hair over his forehead. Perhaps he's fooled many people with his casual swagger and easy half-smile as he ignores the attention, but not me. I recognize a wildness to his movements. How? Well, chaos calls to chaos, right?

It's not hard to see savagery in someone else when you see it in the mirror every day.

They're halfway up the steps when I drop my gaze to the man in front. Although he's slightly shorter than the jock, and despite the fact that he doesn't have the hint of unhinged violence like his friend, he has a similar intensity. Instead of Mr. All-American, though, he looks more like a Rock God come straight from the silver screen. His body moves like a lithe panther, his ocean blue eyes piercing me with their careful consideration. The top of his hair is longer, a gleaming blond, but when he stops in front of me, I realize that the rest of his hair is slightly darker underneath.

My head falls back on my shoulders as they stop at the last row. *My* row. Right in front of me. Before he says a damn word, I know what's coming. I really hoped that this could be avoided, but it looks like that's not going to happen. I've been to too many schools to be ignorant of the fact that these two are clearly important—it's simply the way everyone in the room reacts to their presence.

The Sick Boys? I wonder absently as I meet the man's gaze. *Perhaps.* Guess I'm about to find out.

The frontman's lips twitch, one corner lifting into a smirk. "You must be new," he says.

I smile back and don't say a word, leaving him to make his own assumptions in utter fucking silence just because I know that it usually pisses people off.

He frowns when, after a few more moments, I still don't speak—which, of course, only serves to make my smile grow. His eyes flick over his shoulder to his friend, who shrugs, and then frontman is staring back at me. He huffs out a sigh. "Alright fine," he says. "Then lesson one. This is our row. No one else sits here unless we allow it." He slaps a hand down on the table. "Unless you're my flavor of the week, you're not invited. Get up and move. Now."

I shift, getting more comfortable in my seat. "I don't think so," I say. "I'm comfortable right where the fuck I am, and I don't see your name anywhere on the seat currently residing under my ass." A tingle slides through my spine and before I can stop that little whisper of chaos in the back of my mind, I blurt out my next words. "But you're welcome to try and *make me*."

Blue eyes widen and behind him, All-American chuckles. "Do you have a death wish?" frontman asks, dropping his hand from the table in front of me.

I lean back and cross my arms over my chest before shrugging. "Not particularly."

He grows silent and I take the reprieve as a chance to

glance around and gauge how the others in the room are reacting. The teacher remains turned away, obviously trying her best to act as if nothing is happening. It makes me curious as to who these guys really are if she's so willing to ignore what would have a high school teacher yelling at us to sit down and get ready for class. Ms. Bairns was right, this is certainly not high school, but I'm getting the feeling that neither is it a normal university. Everyone else in the room is not so subtly watching the exchange. Some with worried looks. Others with expressions that could only be described as bloodthirsty.

How very interesting…

I flip my attention back to the matter at hand—or rather the men at hand. "Listen," I say, waving my hand in their general direction, "you're welcome to sit at the opposite end of this row, but there's no way in hell I'm moving. If you wanted this seat, you should've gotten here first."

Frontman's hand lands back on the table, harder this time and he leans close—far closer than before. I still, forcing my body not to react. "I'll give you one last chance to get away without getting hurt," he says, his voice dark and low. "You should be grateful. We never give second chances, and maybe after you've recognized your place, I can show you a better one, eh? Maybe you'll actually get one of those invitations if you play your cards right."

I let my eyes trail down his body. He's hot——there's no denying that. It's obvious from the way his t-shirt stretches across his shoulders and pecs that he's packing a sinewy kind of muscle. He's got a swimmer's body and likely has a tapered waist with one of those sexy as fuck Vs that makes women lose their fucking minds. But I wouldn't be where I am or who I am if I let every guy with a gym membership tell me what to do. If he thinks I want to be his *flavor of the week* at any point in time, then he's got another thing coming.

"Tell me something," I droll. "Is your ass jealous of all the shit coming out of your mouth?"

His slightly stunned face morphs into one of devilish glee. "Well, we have ourselves a little fucking smartass, don't we?"

"Oh, honey." I shake my head. "I'm not a smartass. I'm a skilled and trained professional at stating the obvious. And it's obvious you think that I'm going to get up and move just because you tell me to. Except I'm not because I don't know you and I got here first. Therefore, my ass will be sitting right where I planted it. If you have a problem with that, you can take it up with someone who has a fuck to give. Here's a hint: It's not me."

The taller guy laughs, the sound so loud and booming it makes several girls in the room jump. Even the teacher, though I note that she still keeps her back turned. Plausible deniability. I shake my head again. Adults are such pansies. Frontman gets closer, slamming his other hand down on the back of my chair as he bends over me, that smile of his still in place despite my insult.

"It's been a while since I've been challenged like this," he admits. "You're turning me on, princess."

I scowl, baring my teeth. "Don't call me a fucking princess."

"Aww, don't you like the nickname?" he asks, grinning. "That's what you are, right? The Pauper Princess? One of our new program students, right? Well, let me tell you something, *princess*." I curl my lips back even more as he emphasizes the distasteful nickname just to be an ass. "The only reason you're even here is because of families like mine. We brought you here and we can send you back to whatever ghetto it is that you crawled out of. We hold the power and you hold nothing we don't fucking give you. Understand? Now get that gorgeous ass up, but don't worry, this time I won't ask you to move. I'll just slide beneath you and let you ride my cock while we learn about statistics, yeah? Your own personal welcome from the Kings of the fucking Eastpoint Castle."

My eyes flick to the man behind him and I consider my options. My tongue slides along the front of my teeth slowly before flicking out and licking across my bottom lip. Frontman's eyes follow the movement. There really is only one way to deal with guys like this.

Reaching forward, I curl my fingers into the soft cotton fabric of frontman's t-shirt. His eyes widen a fraction, but he doesn't resist as I use my hold to drag him closer.

"You want me to ride your cock?" I ask, keeping my voice low—just beneath a whisper so he has to lean in just to hear me. "You want me to fuck you? Put this pussy on your dick and slide down until I give you a taste of heaven?"

I can feel more than see his grin. "Yeah, princess." A husky note enters his voice—arousal. "I want you to show me what a girl like you can do."

"You sure about that?" I hedge, lifting my chest until my lips are just a hair's breadth away from his. "You really want to find out what a girl like me can do?"

"Fuck..." He hisses the word between his teeth. "Yeah, I fucking do."

I can't help my smile. It stretches my lips and when I part them to speak again, I can feel where his mouth brushes against mine. "Well, that's just too fucking bad," I whisper. "'Cause I don't fuck desperate assholes." With that, I stand up from my chair and shove him back so hard that, if it weren't for his friend catching him at the last second, he would've fallen on his ass. "And be careful what you ask for. A girl like me can cause a lot of fucking problems. I said it once and I'll say it again, I don't know you and I don't fucking care. You stay out of my way and I'll stay out of yours."

Silence stretches between us as I meet both his glare and his friend's—although his friend looks less angry and more amused. Strange effect, but his obvious pleasure makes my attention focus and my caution narrow. I shift on my feet, clenching my fist as I prepare for an outburst. If I get sent back to Plexton today, then it is what it is—but I'm not letting any rich fucking prick think he's got the best of me and certainly not over a stupid fucking chair.

Frontman's response begins with a slow chuckle. One that reverberates up his chest and out through his mouth. It hollows out his stomach with the sound as he places one palm on his abdomen and continues to laugh. Standing in a damn near quiet room listening to a maniac laugh has the hairs on my forearms rising. Anticipation has me licking over my teeth once more, clenching my fists at my sides.

"Oh you have no idea what you've done, do you, princess?" Frontman says through his laughter. "Absolutely none."

I shrug but don't say a word.

"What's your name?" he asks.

"None of your fucking business," I snap. He hasn't given me his. There's no way I would fucking offer mine first.

That doesn't wipe the smirk from his face, though. It just makes him shake his head. "Doesn't matter. We'll find out. As of right now, though, princess, you're on fucking lockdown."

Before I can ask what the fuck he's talking about, frontman turns to the rest of the class and points out across them. "Did everyone hear that?" he calls out. "This bitch is on lock. You know what that means." All eyes widen and then one by one each student turns and faces the front. As if they'd suddenly all found an interest in whatever the teacher is still writing on the board.

My fingers drum a beat against the edge of the desk as frontman pivots back to face me. "Not to worry, princess," he says with that eternally annoying grin, dropping his arm back to his side. "You can have this seat today and for the rest of them if you want."

"Great," I deadpan. "Thank you so much for your generosity."

"You'll be thankful for a lot more than that when we're through with you."

I narrow my eyes on him. "Do your fucking worst," I challenge.

He points at me. "That we will, princess," he replies. "That we fucking will. See ya later."

I don't bother with a response as he turns and walks away. His friend merely shakes his head and bounds after him as they both leave the classroom. I settle back into my seat as class finally gets started. Irritation begins to form and the itch at the back of my neck comes back with a vengeance.

7

DEAN

"I put a new bitch on lock," are the first words out of Abel's mouth.

I lift my head away from my phone just as Braxton throws himself into the seat next to me. "You should've seen her too, man," he says. "She was hot. Abel totally wanted to fuck her."

"Still do," Abel agrees. "I imagine having a mouth like that wrapped around my cock and..." He reaches down beneath the table and it doesn't take a fucking genius to figure out he's adjusting his dick.

I tear my eyes away from them and return to what I was doing before they showed up. Brax and Abel may be able to pretend, even only momentarily, that they're normal college students, but I know better. It's only a matter of time before the old men's rivals turn their eyes our way ... if they haven't already that is. I scowl as a text message comes through.

"The attitude, man," Braxton says, distracting me. "You should've fucking come to class to see it. She was a little firecracker."

"Think she'll be into sharing?" Abel asks.

Braxton laughs. "If you can even get her to spread her legs," he replies. "Hell, I'd love to just be a fly on the wall if you ever get her alone. She'd fucking massacre you."

"She's welcome to try," Abel says, scratching the side of his jaw. "I'd like to watch her try to tear me down. She's the type of girl who'll make you work for it, I bet."

I flick my gaze up to them but my phone screen lights up, drawing my attention right back. One glance at the name at the top and I turn it off and set it to the side. "Do the others know about the lock?" I ask.

"Announced it right there in class," Abel says. "Word will spread. She'll be a pariah in a few hours or less."

"What's the girl's name?"

Abel shrugs. "Don't know. She wouldn't give it. Pretty sure she's new and in one of the programs."

"She'll be in Havers then," I say with a nod. "Do what you need to."

"I'm gonna invite her to the party this weekend," Brax announces. "Think she'll come?"

Abel cackles, sounding far more amused than I've heard him in a while. "She will if she wants out of lockdown."

"I don't know, man." Braxton leans back and stretches his long ass legs out beneath the table, bumping into me. "She strikes me as the type who won't mind lockdown all that much."

"Well, regardless of whether she wants to come or not, if you're inviting her—make sure she comes. We can't let people think they have a choice when we demand their attention," Abel says.

"Oh, I'll test her alright," Brax replies with a wicked grin. "And I'll bet you a K that she'll fight it."

Abel whips out his phone. "You're on," he says,

tapping away. "There. A K on the line. Peanuts, but it's you and me, motherfucker." Brax just laughs. "What, don't think I'll win?" he challenges.

Brax doesn't get a chance to answer. "I don't care what you do with her," I say, interrupting them with a shake of my head. "If she threatens the balance—or our fucking authority—deal with her as you see fit."

"And what if we can't handle her?" Abel asks, sliding his phone back into his pocket.

I arch my brow at that. "You really think you can't?"

He rolls his eyes. "Of course not. I'm just saying … what if?"

I grin and put a hand under my jaw to crack my neck. "Then I'll be the one to fucking deal with her, and make no mistake, Abel." I turn and include Braxton in my look as well. "I won't be as nice as you two. So, you better get your rocks off with the girl first before I get ahold of her." I stand up from the table, shoving my chair back as I reach for my bag. "Invite her to the party," I tell them. "And I'll make sure she's fairly warned."

8

AVALON

"Are you out of your fucking mind?"

I slip the dollar store shades off my eyes and look up to the figure hovering over me as I lay stretched out on the front lawn of the dorm. "Nice to see you too, Ry," I say absently before sliding them back over my eyes and spreading back out. "But we really need to stop meeting like this. Can you move? You're blocking the sun."

In another second, her fingers brush against my temple as she rips my sunglasses from my eyes. "You have to be absolutely deranged," she continues, holding them above my head as she glares down at me. "Fucking insane. There's no other reason for you to piss off the worst of the worst mere days after I specifically told you not to!"

I sigh right before I kick my feet out, sending her legs collapsing out from beneath her and watch as she tumbles to the grass at my side. Snagging the dropped sunglasses, I settle them back over my eyes.

"If you've got something important to say, say it, or fuck off," I say around a yawn. "You're ruining my good mood."

Surprisingly, Rylie doesn't jump up and scream at me or try to hit me. She remains flat on the ground and throws an arm over her face to block out the bright rays of sunlight. "What the fuck did I do to deserve this?" she mutters. "Who did I kill in a past life? Were they really that important for me to receive this divine punishment?" I'm not unused to people referring to my presence as a punishment, but still, her dramatics make me chuckle. When I do, it earns me a dark glare as she lifts her forearm away from her face and growls at me. "I'm serious," she snaps. "If they moved people in the Havers dorm, I'd fucking ask for a transfer right fucking now because of you."

I shrug. "Don't know what you're talking about, but it sounds like a 'you' problem and not so much of a 'me' problem. Therefore, I don't really give a shit."

"You're on lockdown," she says.

Frowning, I lift up on my elbows and stare in her general direction. "What the fuck is that supposed to mean, anyway?"

"It means you're banned," she huffs out. "No one is allowed to talk to you. No one is allowed near you. And by now, everyone knows that the chick who rejected and tried to humiliate Abel Frazier is *my* roommate."

Ahhh, I think. *Social suicide. Or rather, social homicide courtesy of a fuckboy with nothing better to do. Oh well. Sucked to suck, I guess.* "I'm sure you'll be just fine," I offer placatingly, even though I'm kinda enjoying the growls of irritation coming from her. Fumbling absently for my bag, I reach inside and find the bottle I'd stored in there earlier. I take a sip and then toss it her way. "Here, this might help."

Face devoid of any emotion, she sits up, pops the cap of the water bottle, and puts it to her lips. One swallow later, her eyes widen and she spews every drop she still has in her mouth onto the grass, gasping as she stares from the crinkled plastic to me. "This is fucking vodka!" she shrieks.

I lift one shoulder and let it fall as I take the bottle back. "You looked like you could use something to help you chillax," I say with a grin.

"Are you really that unconcerned about what's happening to you?" She sounds shocked. "Like *really*?"

I stuff the now capped bottle into my bag and get to my feet. "The bigger question," I say pointedly, "is why do you seem to care?"

Rylie's cheeks tighten and she scrambles to get to her feet as well. The desire not to be on a lower standing is ingrained within her just as much as it is with me. "I don't care," she says through clenched teeth, "but whatever happens now is going to fall back on me."

I roll my eyes and slide my arms through the loops of my pack. "Don't worry about it," I say, grinning again when she growls at me. "Seriously. The more you give a shit about whatever fuckboy one and fuckboy two do, the more power you give them."

Her eyes widen and her jaw drops. "Did you just call Abel Frazier and Braxton Smalls … fuckboys?" she asks, astounded.

I shrug. "I call it like it is."

She shakes her head violently. "They're—"

I cut her off, irritated. I can only guess what her next words were about to be. "Just boys," I snap, "and they have no idea how the real world works. They don't get their hands dirty. They probably haven't ever had to make their own fucking beds a day in their life. They're pretty little princes who have no clue what it's like to fight and scrounge for a living."

The thought sparks an even deeper anger inside of me. I stride forward until I'm in her face.

"So, fuck them if they think they can just demand something and expect me to give it to them. I'm no one's bitch." I take a deep breath. "And I don't know about you, but they haven't earned my fucking respect and I'll be damned if I give it out like free candy. There's already enough this world expects to take from me."

She gapes at me, but I said what I said and I'm not taking that shit back. It's the truth.

Leaving her behind on the lawn, I turn and stomp towards the front of the dorm, swiping my card along the reader as I yank the door open and move towards the stairs. I drop my shit off in the room, kicking it under the bed as I grab my wallet, keys, and cell phone, depositing them all into my pockets and bra as I catch the door before it even fully closes, and pull it shut behind me on my way back out.

My feet hit the pavement, and I head for Ms. Bairns's office. Across campus, of course. It *would* be the furthest building. The walk, though, is long enough to calm the itch that still lingers in me. I really need to hit someone or go cliff diving—something to keep me from being too dangerous. It was easy enough to get rid of this feeling back in Plexton. Sex sometimes worked. So did getting into a fight with a random stranger. So did stealing my neighbor's dirt bike and driving it down through the mud of the local creek bed, getting as close to the edge of the ravine as possible without truly falling over.

Where some people avoid danger, I find that I don't just enjoy it, I *need* it. It's the rush of survival, plain and simple. Everyone's an addict—my mother, the students here at Eastpoint, and even me. Where they like drugs and money, I crave chaos. And if I don't take care of this hunger soon, it won't be good for anyone—least of all me.

I cut through the campus green where several groups

of students sprawl out under the sun. Some are studying, some are just enjoying the nice weather. Almost all of them look up when I pass. Their stares burn into my skin. In response, I break into a light jog and pick up the pace.

Just as I reach the front doors of the building that houses Ms. Bairns's office, the door is shoved open from the inside, and I swerve to the right, narrowly avoiding being hit. A dark figure emerges—tall enough that I have to crane my head back to meet his eyes.

I wait. Expectant. But instead of an apology, his lips curve into a facsimile of a smirk—not quite one and yet … at the same time, it feels like he's laughing at me and I don't fucking like it. He meets my eyes with a stare of his own. Eyes the color of dark molten honey, like burnished gold if it'd been mixed with chocolate—or they would've been had it not been for the hint of copper there. I glare up at him.

"Well?" I snap.

He arches a strong dark brow. "Well, what?" he inquires.

My hackles rise and try as I might to shove them back down, they remain up. The need to fuck something up pounds against the inside of my skull and I shove it down, but only barely. "You gonna apologize so I can be on my way?" I ask.

"You can be on your way whenever you fucking want. I'm not stopping you."

I roll my eyes, turn, and grab the door, yanking it open. "Asshole," I mutter as I slip inside. As the glass swings shut behind me, a deep chuckle from the man filters back to me and makes something unfurl in my stomach. I grit my teeth and continue walking.

Thankfully, this building—unlike the dorm—is equipped with an elevator. I ignore the girl who practically leaps out of the small space the second I enter and jam my finger at the button to take me to the correct floor. Seconds later, the elevator dings and the doors slide open to reveal a long tiled hallway.

Turning my head side to side, I take the first step off the elevator and scan my surroundings. With a low whistle, I march forward. I'm no expert in expensive shit—the most expensive thing I've ever owned is probably my cell phone—and it's a few years old, bought off the market with an already cracked screen. This hallway, though, I can tell is expensive. It's brightly lit—illuminating the marble white tiles underfoot. One side of the area is covered in a row of windows that stretch up to the ceiling and the other boasts large portraits of old white men in various forms of antiquated clothing, all of it formal.

It's kind of interesting seeing generations of rich assholes lined up one by one. I'm sure Rylie's right about the rich being corrupt. I wonder if any of these men ever killed for their money when they were alive. My guess is yes. Everyone kills—living with Patricia taught me that. Sometimes, it's the killing of childish dreams and sometimes it's just a fucking body. The end result is the same. Death and hopelessness.

Uncomfortable with the direction of my own thoughts, I press my lips together and stride forward, reaching the end of the hallway, and find Ms. Bairns's office. Pausing just outside of the slightly cracked door, I knock once and poke my head inside. Ms. Bairns's familiar face turns towards me.

"Avalon," she says, offering me a smile. "Come on in."

I push the door open even further, stepping into the lavish office. Hell, the place is larger than my dorm room. Doesn't seem all that fair since I have to fucking share it and live there, and she only has to be here likely eight hours a day or so, but I keep my mouth shut.

"You've been a busy girl," Ms. Bairns says as soon as my ass lands in the seat before her.

"Oh?" *Does she already know about the fucking pricks from class?* I wondered silently.

"Yes." She nods, opening a drawer and reaching inside. I watch as she withdraws a file. "You just moved in a mere few days ago, but you're already into your first classes. How are they going?"

My body automatically relaxes but only marginally. "They're fine."

Her eyes flick up to meet mine briefly as she palms the file and flips it open. "No problems?" she asks. "Are you making friends?"

I snort. When I don't answer, her head lifts again and she tilts it at me curiously. "You didn't bring me here to make friends," I say. "You brought me here to up your statistics and to look good on the college's tax receipts."

Her head's already shaking before I'm even done speaking. "That's absolutely not true, Avalon. You were brought here because of your potential."

"My grades?" I scoff. "They're good, but nothing's going to erase my rap sheet, Ms. B."

Ms. Bairns's face morphs, her smile growing warm even as a gleam enters her eyes. She lifts her arms up and props her elbows against the desk, settling her chin into her steepled fingers. "What if it could, though?" she asks.

"Excuse me?" I frown.

"What if your rap sheet could just"—she lifts one hand to flick her fingers out—"disappear." Ms. Bairns looks at me for a moment, waiting for some reaction but when she doesn't get one, she leans forward. "We can make that happen, you know?"

Here it is. I suck in a breath and let her see the unimpressed look in my eyes. *What Rylie warned me about. She was fucking right.* I lean my spine against the back of the chair and cross my arms and wait.

Ms. Bairns's must take that as her cue to continue, because she settles in and grins at me as she starts talking. "What if I told you that once you're finished with your high school credits here, we can transfer you in as a freshman?" she asks. "You could go to college here—a very prestigious university."

"I'm sure I can't afford it," I deadpan.

"Not right now," she agrees. "But with scholarships and—"

"Just tell me what the catch is," I say, cutting her off.

"No catch, Avalon," she says, her tone earnest as she reaches across the table and places her hand in front of me. I look from it back to her face. "It's a great opportunity. Yes, of course, the university will benefit from having students who bring up the general average of tests and scores, and if you do accept the scholarship, you'll be expected to finish all four years. Our retention rate is very important to us."

I'm not impressed. In fact, the more she talks, the itchier I feel—like a thousand tiny ants are crawling across my skin. It's disgusting "What else?" I snap, scratching at the back of my neck. I want nothing more than to stand up and leave this room, but at the same time I want her to be fucking honest. To open up and tell me what the fuck they really want from me. No one gives handouts. Those aren't real. People always want something in return.

She blinks as if surprised by my tone, but I don't really give a shit. Here she is, spouting off how great this opportunity is, but all I can see are strings. Strings hanging from the ceiling, encircling her arms and legs and pulling her movements. I wonder if they're tied so tight that they've cut off circulation to her brain—maybe that would explain why she seems to think I'm fucking dumb. I like Ms. Bairns well enough, but it's clear she's just another fucking puppet. And I hate people who let others dictate their movements.

"Well, after you graduate, we would love to offer you a position at one of our many generous benefactors' companies—"

That's it. I'm done. "No." I stand up. "I think that concludes this meeting. Thanks for the offer, Ms. B, but I'm good. I don't need a job."

Shock covers her face. "W-what about the scholarship?"

I shrug and head for the door. "I'll figure it out when I get there."

"Avalon!" The scraping of her chair behind me tells me she's not ready for this conversation to be over. I am, though. Her fingers encircle my arm as she pulls me to a stop. Stopping in my tracks, I turn my head and look down at where she's touching before looking pointedly back up at her. She quickly catches on and releases me. "You have to think about this," she urges. "This is your future we're talking about. Do you really want to go back home after you finish your dual enrollment credits?" Deep crevices begin to form between her brows.

"Why not?" I ask.

She sucks in a breath. "Avalon, you're smart," she says. "You're better than that place."

Oh, but that's where she's wrong. Seeing myself as better suddenly turns me into someone like the pricks from class—Abel Frazier. Or even the guy who'd refused to apologize after nearly plowing into me earlier. Once you start to see yourself as above everyone else, you start to think you're a god, and I'm no fucking god. If anything, I'm a devil.

"Thanks again for the offer," I say with a shake of my head as I reach for the doorknob. "But I've fulfilled my duty—I met with you. Told you my classes were fine. We're good."

I step out into the hallway, not all that surprised when she chooses to follow me. "At least think about it," she presses, her heels clicking against the tiles. She continues to trail me all the way back to the elevator, telling me what a great opportunity this will be, and the entire way, all I can think is that I really need something relaxing after a day like today.

The elevator doors slide open and I step inside, turning as she slaps a hand against the doors to hold them open, her eyes pleading. "Please, just promise me that much."

I frown at her curious reaction as I press the button for the bottom floor. "Sure, Ms. B, I'll think about it," I lie, but as the doors close all I can think about is her desperation.

Desperate people are often willing to forsake anything and everything to get what they want. What unnerves me most of all, though, is the fact that I can't pinpoint exactly why it is that Ms. Bairns wants me here. The franticness. The intensity of her plea.

What the fuck kind of school have I agreed to go to?

9

DEAN

I know who she is, and Abel's right about her. Not only is she a program girl with a bad attitude, she's also got a body made for fucking. She hides it under rough t-shirts and jeans, but it's not easy to conceal tits and an ass like that. It's also obvious that she has no clue who any of us are. Otherwise, she'd never have expected an apology from me. I chuckle darkly at the mere reminder. Those cold, cutting eyes. That fuck me mouth.

Poor thing. I watch her waltz into the building where my father and the other heads of the families hold their offices when they deign to come on campus. Her little muttered "asshole" just before the door swings shut behind her ass amuses me more than anything has in a while. Scratching the side of my jaw, I feel my lips pull up.

I don't normally get involved in games like the ones Brax and Abel play. As I watch her walk away though, the swinging of her ass draws my attention. Even from the back, her spine remains straight and rigid—defiant. For a man like me, she's nothing but utter temptation. She's a challenge, and I haven't felt the need to conquer something in quite a while—not when everything is already at my disposal. Almost everything anyway.

I scowl at the reminder, turning and stomping down the front steps of the building, and cut towards the parking lot. My phone beeps just as I reach the SUV and I pull it out—as if I've summoned the bitch from the depths of purgatory itself, Kate Coleman's name flashes over my screen. I delete her latest message and the rest along with the voicemails I haven't bothered to look at. She made her bed and I'll make her regret it. *Soon*, I promise myself. Soon her fucking bed will be on fire and I won't have to deal with Luc Kincaid either.

I scroll down to my email and then over to my access to student files. Within seconds, I've got an image of the girl from the office building and a file on one Avalon Manning downloaded to my phone. The list of her previous schools is damn near a full page long with the details of each transfer on the following sheets. I release a slow whistle as I pop the SUV door and get in, shoving the key into the ignition. Someone has been a very bad girl. Five schools. Numerous referrals. Suspensions for fighting, tardiness, smoking weed. I laugh. Man, public schools get so bent out of shape over the stupidest shit.

My phone rings just as I pull out of the parking lot, and I answer.

"Hey," Abel's voice filters in through the speakers. "I got the party all set up. Eli's on door duty and the rest are picking up chicks. You get anything?"

"Yeah. I got her file and I ran into the chick."

"You did?" He sounds excited. "What'd you think?"

"I think I'm taking this one on as a personal case," I say.

"Fuck you, man!" But the lightness of his tone doesn't disperse. My phone beeps again and I freeze up when I glance at the new call waiting. A blocked number. And only one blocked number ever calls my cell.

"Gotta go." I don't wait on a reply before pressing the end button and swiping green. "This is Dean," I answer the new caller.

"Warehouse 14. Friday night. Midnight. Do not be late." The line goes dead.

Fuck.

My hands clench the steering wheel and my pulse picks up. My lungs expand as I take a deep breath. The phone call can only mean one thing. We've got a fucking job to do.

10

AVALON

A yawn stretches my mouth. Damn, I'm so fucking tired. I can feel the individual grains of sleep still lingering even though I've been up for hours. The words in front of me blur into oblivion until all I can make out are dark lines on the pages of my textbook.

I mutter a curse beneath my breath and try to rub more life into my eyes.

"Avalon Manning?" I look up just as someone drops into the seat across from me.

I examine the girl before me, refocusing my gaze as I straighten my spine. Dark eyes, blonde hair, nice clothes, and an attitude that screams 'I don't care what you think.'

"Depends on who's asking," I say.

A card slaps onto the table and she taps her painted red nails over it. "This is for you." The girl slides it towards me.

I don't even have the mental energy to look at whatever it is she's trying to give me. Instead, I heave a breath and reach for my bag, stuffing my books and things into it as I rise from my seat. I thought the library would be a good place to get some shit done, but apparently not. "No thanks." I fight back a yawn as I finish packing.

If she's surprised by my lack of interest, she doesn't show it. In fact, she looks like she couldn't really give a shit less that I'm even standing there. "Not happening," she replies. "This is an order. You'll be at the Frazier House tonight. Party starts at nine. Be late or be early. I don't really care. But you'll be there."

"Highly unlikely," I say. "I don't take orders."

"It's from the Eastpoint heirs," she states.

"You mean the Sick Boys?" I inquire, clarifying. She nods and that only solidifies my answer. "Well then," I say, pulling a pen from my bag and reaching for the invitation. I scribble down a message and slide it back to the girl. "You can tell them that this is my answer." I leave the invitation on the table and make for the exit.

As I step out onto the sidewalk, another yawn catches me off guard. Scrubbing a hand down my face, I tilt my head up until I'm staring at the layer of clouds hovering above the buildings. This entire week has been a battle. The Sick Boys. The adjustment. Trying to sleep with a virtual stranger in the same room—impossible. I feel constantly watched, like a fish in a tank or a bug under a microscope. It only makes my internal cravings even worse.

I drag my dead tired ass back to the dorm, and some sort of fucking deity must be looking down on me favorably because for once, Rylie isn't here. Which can only mean one thing for me. Without a second thought, I drop my bag, snap the blinds shut, lock the door, and crawl beneath the covers of my bed. *Just a few hours*, I promise myself. My eyes close all on their own and now that I'm all alone, I fall into the best fucking sleep I've had in days.

Despite how tired I am, however, I'm a light sleeper—years of living with Patricia and her string of annoyingly persistent addict boyfriends has nailed that into me. When the lock on the door disengages, my eyes pop open and I sit up just as Rylie comes through with a square envelope in her hand. "Hey," she says, "this was poking out from under the door. It's got your name on it."

She tosses it onto the end of my bed and then goes to her desk. From the corner of my eyes, I watch her as she unloads her textbooks along with a fairly high quality laptop. That's one thing I've noticed about her—while the rest of her shit is old and often broken or fraying—she's got a bomb ass laptop. I'm curious as to why that is, but girls like us know one thing if we know anything at all—prying is a no go. Whatever she does—so long as it doesn't affect me—is her business.

I lift the card and a hiss of irritation escapes through my teeth when I realize what it is. The same fucking invitation the chick from the library had tried to give me. Interestingly enough, though, the note I wrote on it is gone. So, it's not exactly the same one. It's a brand new invitation.

Curiosity has me opening the envelope and pulling the card out of its confines.

You are hereby invited to the Frazier House
1400 Eastpoint Avenue
9 p.m.

I notice that as Rylie opens her laptop on her desk, she keeps her gaze glued to the screen and more specifically, away from me. I grin.

"You know what this is, don't you?" I ask, waving the card in her direction.

"N*ope*." The little pop she makes as she says the word is all it takes.

"Liar." I laugh, shaking my head and tossing the card and its envelope into the nearby trash can. "Doesn't matter, anyway. I'm not going."

Her fingers still against the keyboard and she bites down on her lower lip hard as if she's trying to convince herself not to say whatever it is she's thinking. I start a mental countdown in my head:

Five...
Four...
Three…
Two…

Just as the last number crosses my mind, she flips her body towards me. "You're going to make this a hell of a lot worse on yourself if you don't just go and get it over with," she snaps.

"Get what over with?" I ask innocently.

Her eyes narrow. "You're going to get yourself in so much fucking trouble," she says instead of answering.

"Good," I reply. "That's definitely something I excel at and it's been too long since I had a healthy dose of it." Maybe proving that I can't be fucking controlled by these Sick Boys will give me that rush of adrenaline I've been craving.

"Yeah, well, maybe it's fun for you, but not for me. I try to avoid trouble when it comes my way."

"Do you now?" I say, more than a little hint of sarcasm in my tone.

Before she has a chance to respond, my stomach rumbles, interrupting whatever she might have said, and I take that as my cue to end this conversation. I toss the covers off and reach for my shoes. It's dark outside now and one glance at my phone tells me that the cafeteria has long since closed. Only thing left to do is hit the gas station down the street and hope for a cheap, not yet stale prewrapped sandwich—a delicacy from my hometown.

"I'll be back later," I call out as I snatch my keys up and shove them into my pocket.

I'm already halfway out the door when I hear her muttered response. "Not likely."

I pause in the hallway, looking back. I wonder if she really thinks I'll go to their stupid party. *Because there's zero chance of that happening. At least, not willingly.*

My stomach rumbles again, making an uncomfortable whining noise, and I hightail it out of the building. The red and white neon sign of the gas station comes into view minutes later as I pick up the pace. *Hot dogs*, I think. I could really go for a fucking hot dog rather than a sandwich.

In the distance, a car engine rumbles and a loud mixture of rap and rock thump out of old speakers. It grows steadily closer until a red Mustang convertible speeds by and pulls into the gas station parking lot just as I hit the sidewalk in front of it. I freeze when the doors open and three familiar figures emerge.

With the top down, it's easy to see them, and I pause. The driver is none other than frontman—Abel Frazier—the dude from my class, and out of the back seat, his massively tall friend leaps over the side of the car—his shoes hitting the pavement hard as he bounces a little on his feet. But they're not the only reason for my pause. Unlike the other two, who simply crawled over the side of the vehicle, the passenger door swings open and a long booted foot hits the ground.

I should've known he'd be friends with the douches…

Abel's head turns and he stops, eyes locking on me for a brief moment before his lips spread into a grin. "Well, well, well, if it isn't our princess."

I cross my arms over my chest. "Well, well, well," I respond, "if it isn't dumb and dumber. Oh look, you brought a friend. Let me guess, his name is dumbest?"

He laughs at that. "Did you get the invitation to our little shindig tonight?" he asks.

I step off the curb and cut around the back of their car as I head for the front door of the gas station. "Sure did," I call back. "Hope you liked my reply."

As I reach the doors of the station, I look up and meet the eyes of the asshole who'd nearly smacked me with a door earlier that week. They're dark and watchful. Almost predatory. If Abel responds, I don't hear it. I'm too focused on this guy's expression. His smile is small, but fuck if it doesn't send shivers down my spine.

I shove those motherfuckers down and ignore the way my stomach clenches, grabbing a hold of the door handle and yanking it a bit too roughly as I enter the store.

I'm barely in the station for five minutes, perusing the bagged chip section when they follow me in. The attendant takes one look at their entrance—three broad-shouldered pricks in clothes that probably cost more than his weekly paycheck—and hightails it to the back, telling them to ring the bell when they're ready to check out.

I grunt and snatch a bag of chips—sour cream and onion flavor—and move towards the row of refrigerator doors for a drink. Footsteps sound to the right and left of me as I yank open a door and reach for a soda. A hand slaps the glass, and I jerk back as it bangs shut.

With a scowl, I turn to the source of my irritation. "Problem?" I ask, tilting my head to meet his eyes.

Abel stares at me with a grin, then props his shoulder against the very door I was standing in front of, crossing his arms over his chest. "Just wanted to introduce myself,

Avalon Manning," he says. "You know, since I have your name now, but you don't have mine."

My eyes cut to the side where his friends—particularly the one that makes me feel pinned under a microscope—stand. "I don't give a shit who you are," I state. "Name or not, you're just another asshole who thinks he can get away with anything and everything just because his daddy has money."

I turn to go and in the next second, the bag of chips in my hand falls out of my grasp as I'm suddenly grabbed and shoved against the cold glass of one of the refrigerator doors. His hands fall on either side of my head. "The name's Abel," he says as he leans into me, smiling. "Frazier."

"I never said I didn't know your name," I reply coolly. "I just don't care."

He arches a brow. "You should care," he replies. "A smart bitch would."

"Well, now, I think we've both established that I'm not necessarily smart," I start, giving him a smile as I reach for his shoulders, sliding my hands over them before yanking down and bringing my knee up right between his legs. His eyes widen and he falls to the side, cupping his junk and coughing through the pain. "I'm a fucking genius," I finish before lifting my head to eye the other two.

The taller one rears back and laughs. I feel my muscles tense at the sound, but he doesn't do anything to help his friend. Instead, he wipes his fingers under his eyes, looking down at his friend with a shake of his head, then gives me a wink before moving to help lift Abel onto his feet. "Take him back to the car, Brax," the third and final member of their posse orders.

"You got it, man," Brax says, lifting Abel up with one arm around his shoulder. He takes another look at me before leaving, shaking his head back and forth once more. "You're trouble, little girl." Though the words are an insult, coming from him, they sound more like an excited announcement, especially when he tacks on "I think I like it" at the end before turning and hauling his friend out. For some reason, I get the feeling that he likes my favorite kind of trouble, and I just bet it likes him right back. Too bad he's a rich asshole with shit taste in friends and I'm a program student from the wrong side of the tracks—if things were different we might've been friends.

As soon as they're out the door, and I'm left alone with the last guy, I shake off that thought and face the third man. For several long moments, neither of us say anything. His left brow quirks up as he slowly lowers his gaze, trailing those sharp eyes of his down over my ratty t-shirt and ripped jeans.

"Avalon Manning," he states, taking a step forward. I stiffen, pushing my back further against the door as I watch his every movement. Calculating what he'll do next. He surprises me when he lifts his gaze to meet mine head on and gives me the most dazzling fucking smile I've ever seen —filled with such predatory intensity that it makes me bite my tongue to keep from drooling. If I were any other girl, I'd likely have fallen to my knees at a smile like that. It's entrancing. It's dangerous. It gets my blood pumping.

But I'm not any other girl. I'm Avalon Fucking Manning and I fall to my knees for no one, especially not a prick who looks like he's used to having women throw themselves at him. "I know a lot about you," he says, breaking the silence.

"Oh?" My breath releases from my chest as I meet his stare, sliding through my teeth in a silent hiss.

"Eighteen years old. From Plexton, Georgia. No father. Druggy mother. Kicked out of five schools—"

"Four," I interrupt.

He arches a brow. "Considering you would've been kicked out of your last school before our recruiter found you, it would've been five."

I shrug. "You'd be wrong. I was never technically kicked out. I left voluntarily."

"Did you, though?" he challenges. "Or were you out of options?"

I hum, the sound vibrating in my chest. "Hmmmm," I say. "I wonder."

He steps closer and the sound of plastic crunching under booted feet reaches my ears as he kicks the bag of chips out of the way until he's mere inches from me. Though he's not as tall as Brax, he's wider. Fucking massive. His whole frame engulfs mine. A shiver chases down my spine. *It's not him I'm interested in,* I tell myself, *it's the hint of danger that lingers on him like a second skin.*

I lick my suddenly dry lips, unintentionally drawing his attention there. Dark brown eyes lower and stare as my tongue swipes from one side of my mouth to the other, slipping across my lower lip. We stay like that for several seconds, the pulse of tension ricocheting through the space between us. I grip my fingers against my jeans, feeling sweat beads pop up in the center of my palm. Excitement pulses in a steady rhythm against the inside of my ribcage.

I want to see what he'll do, I realize. I want to know why the others call him—them—the Sick Boys. I want to know just how fucked up they—he—can be.

And more importantly, *will messing with them give me the kind of high that I want?*

Unfortunately, after several beats of silence, he takes a step back. Disappointment rolls through me. I should've known better. Sick Boys? Ha. They're probably just pansies playing at being gangsters. They've probably never held a gun in their life, never seen the aftermath of an overdose, or had to be interviewed by cops simply because they lived in the same trash neighborhood as a gang leader. He slides me a smile as he heads for the front and just before he leaves entirely, he stops by the front desk and slaps his palm against the bell to ring for service. The sound echoes loud and high pitched up to the cheap, tiled ceiling.

"See you soon, Avalon," he calls back.

I open my mouth to tell him that he won't be seeing me at all if I can help it, but he's already walking out. The attendant must have been watching because it isn't until he's out of the store that the dude comes creeping back out. His eyes settle on me a little apprehensively.

"Are you ready to check out?" he asks.

A sound of disgust leaves my lips, and I ignore him as I stride towards the doors and shove them open. Abel, Brax, and the guy with eyes like the devil are already at the Mustang. He grips the driver's side door and leverages up and over until his legs slide to the floor before turning his head and meeting my eyes as the engine roars to life. Then his head lifts and he's looking at something past me.

I don't have even a split second to realize what's happening before a black bag is thrown over my head, obscuring my vision. I react violently, punching out. My fist connects with someone's side, and all I can feel is muscle. Then my arms are dragged behind me and quickly zip tied. Throwing my body against my attackers, I kick out, but there are too many arms, too many bodies grappling with me. I'm yanked off my feet and the sound of a car door opening reaches my ears just before I'm thrown into what I can only imagine is a wide backseat that smells faintly of sweat and leather. Unknown bodies climb in on either side of me, their arms pinning me in place to keep me from trying to escape.

My breath comes in ragged spurts as I continue to buck and fight. And even though I know I'm going to get these fuckers back for this, all I can think in this moment is *well fucking played, Sick Boys*.

Well motherfucking played.

11

AVALON

I don't have a conscience. I think only certain people get that luxury, and yes, I think having a moral compass is a luxury. When you're starving and exhausted and afraid to shut your eyes for fear of what—or who—you'll find crawling into bed with you when you wake, you start to lose sense of what's right and wrong. It becomes warped, twisted, and different from traditional views. It's clear that the Sick Boys have a twisted sense of what's right and wrong and I'd be a liar if I didn't say that doesn't interest me and make me curious.

My heart thumps rapidly in my chest, the smell of sweat and booze and tension shifting it into overdrive. To someone else, this smell might resemble fear, but to me, it's home. It's heady. It's addicting. It gets my adrenaline flowing. It makes that something dark inside me unfurl in my core. The only thing missing is a little bit of blood.

"What's Dean want with a new chick anyway?" someone towards the front of the vehicle asks.

So his name is Dean. I file that information away. Dean is the one that's going to pay for this. Sure, I'm having fun and yes, I'm more than a little curious about his methods, but that doesn't erase the fact that I now have to plan an appropriate payback for this little stunt.

"Don' know," someone else replies. "She's on lockdown though—Abel put her there. Heard she pissed him off."

"Did you see the way he came limping out of the station?" a third voice right next to me asks. "I think she kneed him in the balls."

The black bag over my head makes it so that I can't see a damn thing, but that doesn't mean I can't talk. "I did," I say.

There's the soft sound of movement as if someone in the front is turning around to look back at me. "Did we say you could talk?" he demands.

Even with my hands zip tied at my back, I manage to shrug. "You didn't say that I couldn't talk." Not that an order like that would stop me anyway.

Keeping myself as quiet and subtle as possible, I twist my wrists from side to side, feeling the hard plastic of the ties. These guys aren't professionals—if they were, they would've tied me a bit tighter. As it is, they've left me enough room to move my hands an inch or so away from each other, which means that I can probably get these cuffs off. As I'm debating on doing it now or waiting, the vehicle comes to an abrupt halt.

"Get her out," the first guy orders. Doors open and someone grabs onto my arm, yanking me from the car and onto hard pavement. The bag is removed from my head and I blink as I take in my new surroundings.

We can't be that far from campus—there just wasn't enough time in the car for us to be more than ten or fifteen minutes from where they'd picked me up—yet as I take a look around, I realize that we're in the middle of nowhere. Or at least, it seems like it since there are no other nearby buildings and everything is surrounded by a dense wood.

"Welcome to the Frazier House," someone says, pushing against my back. "Now, move."

I take a step forward, glancing up to the three-story building before me. House is putting it mildly. This place looks like a freaking hotel. Long vertical windows stretch up each of the floors and white pillars line the front. Golden light spills from inside as does music and laughter. The party, it seems, is in full swing.

Music pours outside, and though we get a few strange looks as we march through the crowd of people surrounding the property, no one stops to ask why there's a girl being led through a party in zip tied handcuffs. I start to wonder if this is, perhaps, a regular occurrence.

The guys lead me around the side of the house, through a massive area overwhelmed by plants and rocks and into what looks like a natural spring. It's not, though, because natural springs don't have heated pools or hot tubs bubbling out of perfectly cut rocks. A low whistle leaves my chest. These guys aren't just rich, I realize, they're fucking loaded.

Girls in low cut, barely there bikinis with martini glasses in hand—no Solo cups for these people—skirt around the edge of the water. Across from the glass back doors, a makeshift dance floor has been set up and unseen speakers radiate music out over the back lawn.

Someone pushes me towards the back doors, and they slide open just before I'm shoved inside. My thin soled Converse slap pure white tile and I stop and tilt my head back. A glittering chandelier hovers overhead, tinkling as the air conditioning kicks on and a wash of cold air brushes over my bare arms. Another door towards the front of the house is flung open and raucous laughter echoes up towards the massively tall ceilings as the three dickwads from the gas station come careening around the corner.

The place is packed, top to bottom. Several girls linger in the kitchen, giggling and reaching for Abel as soon as he stops inside the door.

"Abel!" one girl squeals, nearly leaping into his arms. Looking far less pale than he had at the gas station after round one with me, he grins at the girl and lifts her up until her legs spread wide and wrap around his waist. In the next second, his tongue is in her mouth and the sound of wet slopping groans follows.

I purse my lips and shift on my feet. The plastic around my wrists bites into the skin beneath my thumb as I slip my hand further out. Abel finally manages to pry his lips away from the girl humping his front. He whispers something in her ear that makes her giggle and drops her back onto her feet before slapping her ass and watching her walk away with a hungry look in his eyes.

Brax moves through the massive amount of people converging on the space now that the three of them are here with ease, and two of the guys who'd brought me in move to follow him. Together, they approach the island in the center of the kitchen that looks like the size of my mother's trailer and start unloading shot glasses and a tall bottle of clear liquid—tequila.

Abel crosses towards them, shooting me a dirty look. I smile his way. "Looks like I didn't completely ruin your night, frontman," I say.

"Not for lack of fucking trying," he snarls as Brax hands him a shot. He downs it in one breath before jerking his chin at the rest of the girls lingering about, not so subtly trying to catch their attention. "Give us the room," he commands, and just like that, they do.

Everyone in the vicinity, girls and guys alike—save for the two still standing at my back, the three assholes who orchestrated this kidnapping, and me—leave the room. I pry my attention away from Brax and Abel and meet the eyes of the most dangerous man in the room. Maybe he is and maybe he isn't, but I've got the feeling that he's the leader of this battalion of assholes. Therefore, he's the one that gets the focus of my attention.

"So, *Dean*," I say, emphasizing his name. I flex my arms. "Care to tell me why you thought it was necessary to bring me here? Do you *want* to piss me off?"

A cold smile filters across his face. "You and I both know you're not pissed off about this," he says. The blood in my veins freezes. I know that, but how does he know that? Dean folds his arms and stares at me as if he's waiting for something. I don't know what and I bide my time as I consider my response.

My gaze slides to the two guys remaining—keeping vigil at my sides as if they're bouncers in a club and they want to make sure no one can come near me … or rather, that I won't go near their bosses. *Too bad for them*, I think. They've got no clue what a little girl like me can do. They're obviously athletes of some kind—football if their size is anything to go by, but size has nothing on smarts.

I decide that now is as good a time as any to prove that. I twist one arm free of the zip ties, but hold onto the plastic ring, keeping both of my hands behind my back. Brax looks up and locks onto me, and my back straightens. A smile lifts his lips and he glances over to Dean, who shakes his head subtly. I narrow my eyes, but since neither of them say another word, I don't halt my plan. The green light is flashing and I'm feeling a heady mixture of anger and eagerness.

"So," I start casually, "which of you actually put the

bag over my head and zip tied me?" I ask the bodyguards. "Was it one of you or one of the others?" If luck is on my side, it'll be either one or both of them.

They glance at each other and then with a shrug that determines how very little they consider me a threat, the one on the right answers. "We did," he says. "Orders are orders."

I grin. *Ahhh, sweet lady luck. She did love me after all.* "No problem. Just wanted to make sure before I did this."

They frown and look down. "Did what?" the one on the left asks just a split second before I bring my hands around my front and punch him in the face before turning, grabbing the back of his friend's head and bringing it down just as I bring my knee up. There's a muffled crunch against my leg and then I'm shoved away.

"The fuck!"

"Bitch!"

I laugh, taking a step away from them and towards the butcher's block. Abel, Brax, and Dean—all three of them don't move a muscle as they watch me round the island and reach for one of the knives. Perhaps if I were more pissed off and less amused, they would have more reason to be concerned, but right now—I'm more curious than anything else. It takes a lot to get me to that kind of dangerous point. I use a sharper one to cut through the remaining zip tie and drop the plastic on the counter before reaching for one of the shots and downing it.

Red hot fire slides down my throat. Not as good without the lime and salt, but still … not bad. "Ahhh," I say on a sigh. "That's top notch shit."

Brax grins and takes a shot of his own before pushing another my way. This time, he hands me a cut lime and a salt shaker. "You're staying for the party then?" he asks.

"Nah." I pour salt on my hand, lick it, and take the

shot. The lime goes in my mouth as I slap the glass back onto the counter before turning and striding for the doorway. "But thanks for the fun."

As I pass, a hard hand grabs my arm. "You're not leaving, Avalon." Dean's words slide over my skin, making that unhealthy darkness that festers within me respond. I tip my head back and grin.

"Oh?" I ask. "And who's going to fucking stop me?"

His eyes glitter. Smoky and hazy with something unknown. Curiosity holds me bound. I don't even mind that he's grabbing me without my permission. For now … anyway.

"No one," he says, "but you'll stay."

"Oh? Why's that?"

Finally, he grins and releases me. I almost hate the feel of his skin leaving mine. He spreads his arms wide and takes a shot glass that Brax hands him. Swallowing, the workings of his throat mesmerize me for some reason. "Because you're curious," he replies.

With that, he nods to the others. Brax and Abel go for their guys—the ones who made the mistake of underestimating me—and they drag them out of the room. Just before Dean leaves, he turns and gives me a grin. "Enjoy the party, Avalon."

12

DEAN

"Think she'll stick around?" Braxton asks.

I honestly don't fucking know. She's a wild one, that much is clear. A challenge—just like I said I wanted. She'd sent the first invitation back with a big ol' *Fuck You* scribbled in red pen. Braxton had found it absolutely hilarious, but it had only made me want her here all the more. I want her to see it—the power we hold. I want to teach her a number of things—the first of which being that no one can tell me no, least of all a nobody like her.

Sitting back against the lounge chair on one of the rock platforms surrounding the pool, I tip my head back and stare at the top of the overhang. A deep sigh of irritation moves through me. The desire for something more, a distraction from what we're going to head into tonight pulses in me.

"Hey, she came," Abel says, refocusing my attention as I bring my head back down.

"Only because we forced the issue," I remind him. That, too, isn't surprising.

One of Eastpoint's cheerleaders passes by below,

throwing come hither glances up our way. Abel leans forward and gives her a wink. She giggles and turns her cheek away, but I know she'll likely be in his bed before the end of the night. That is, if she hasn't already been. Like the rest of us, he's got his own rules—one of which is to never fuck the same pussy twice.

"Well?" Brax presses. "You never answered me. Do you think she'll stick around?"

I shrug. "Maybe."

"Are we gonna drag her back if she does leave?" he asks.

I recline and pick up my beer, letting it dangle in my fingers. "Don't know yet. Whatever we do, we'll have to be careful. She's feisty."

Abel grunts in response. "That shit at the station was a fucking fluke. I didn't know she was going to go for my balls like that."

A laugh erupts from Braxton. He slaps a hand down on the table between us and shakes his head back and forth. "You should've fucking seen your face, man," he chortles. "You turned vomit green!"

Abel punches him in the side. "Shut the fuck up, motherfucker! Like you would've been any better if she shoved your balls up into your body cavity."

"She's got touchy points," I comment. "She didn't like you touching her."

He eyes me. "Yeah, well, she didn't seem to mind so much when it was you." That was true. My eyes narrow as the back door slides open and the object of our discussion makes her presence known. So she didn't leave yet. I watch her as she turns her head, scanning the yard before her gaze meets mine. My gut tightens. There's something about her that niggles at the back of my consciousness. I don't know what it is, but it's interesting. It's dangerous, too. Like ambrosia to my fucking need to control. I want to pin her down and watch her squirm.

"You still planning on fucking her?" I find myself asking.

Abel's head whips towards me, but he doesn't answer right away. When he does, his voice is contemplative. "Why? You wanna piece?"

I take a sip from my beer and set it back on the table. "Maybe."

"You did say it was personal now," he says.

That I did, but that'd been before the phone call. Whatever was about to go down tonight, whatever those motherfuckers are planning to demand from us—one thing we need to know for sure is that our rule here is solid. Regardless of whether or not I want her, I won't put that or Abel and Brax at risk. It's my one rule.

I wait a beat and then another, watching as she tips her chin up at me in challenge. I wonder if she thinks that makes her any less attractive. I don't move to give her any sort of response, and she merely turns her head away and disappears around the side of the house. Finally, I give my answer.

"Take her off lockdown," I say. "I wanna see what she does. We've brought her here to intimidate her, but as you can see—that's not fucking happening."

"You sure you trust her off lockdown?" Abel asks, curious.

I shake my head. I don't trust this chick a single fucking inch. "Have Elijah or Raz watch her. I want eyes on her 24/7."

Abel eyes me for a moment more before nodding. "Got it."

"It's eleven," Brax suddenly announces. I lift my head

and tilt it back, releasing a slow breath. "We've gotta go soon."

I hate that he's right. I hate not knowing what we're walking into tonight. The party will rage on here and if we're not back in a few hours, I know the team will start tossing people out. It's not like we crash here anyway. We've all got clothes and rooms at Abel's house, but this isn't home. It's a party palace. This is where we flex our fucking power over Eastpoint. It's where we reward our most loyal followers—letting them think they're close to us. And it's where we bring pretty little nobodies from Nowheresville and show them the truth. We show them that we hold the keys to the kingdom and if they're good little girls, then maybe … just fucking maybe … we'll let them look inside. But only if they fall in line—only if *she* caves to my authority.

Frankly, I just don't see it happening. Not yet, anyway. The issue with Avalon is that she really doesn't seem to give a shit. And damn if that doesn't irritate me and make me want to fuck her ass into a wall at the same time.

"Dean." Abel's tone makes my body stiffen. Rarely does he get that tone. Serious is not something he indulges in on the regular. "K.C. at twelve o'clock."

I don't immediately look, instead letting my eyes wander across the crowd below us until I find what he's talking about. Icy rage froths in my veins, and unlike with Avalon Manning, I feel my true devil rising to the surface. For this bitch, I have no problem letting my inner ruthlessness out to play.

"Well, boys," I say slowly. "It looks like a traitorous bird has made her way into the lion's den." I glance their way, noting their equal expressions of both coldness and brutality. "Let's play with it a bit before we kill it."

13

AVALON

I don't stay because they told me to. I stay because I'm still hungry as fuck and haven't gotten the chance to eat since the pricks ripped me away from my only opportunity at dinner. So, after they leave, I raid their kitchen. It's the least they can do for being assholes, and it's not like they can't afford it.

Now that the guys are out of the way, the kitchen is soon refilled with people. A lot of the girls from before come back, led by the blonde chick that'd practically ridden Abel's lap in front of everyone. They stand against the island, fancy drinks in hand and chat away, effectively ignoring me. Guess that means I'm still on lockdown.

I find some deli meat and the fixings for a nice BLT in the refrigerator and I go about making myself a sandwich. There's a shit ton of food in the fridge and cabinets, but this is a party, and people seem a little more preoccupied with the booze than the food. Whatever. More for me.

I shove the sandwich in my mouth and devour the thing, arching my brow as the blonde talking with her friends pauses and scoffs in disgust. One of her friends picks up the bottle of tequila Brax left behind and starts pouring shots. The blonde continues to shoot me hostile looks. Not my problem though, because the second I'm done eating, I'm out of here.

The sandwich disappears and I pat my stomach appreciatively before snatching the latest shot one of the girls pours. "Hey!" I suck it back without looking at her—no salt, no lime. I don't care.

"Thanks," I say with a grin, slapping the glass back onto the counter as I head for the back door.

"You can't do that," someone says behind me.

With my hand on the door handle, I look back, focusing on the speaker. Of course, it's the blonde. She steps forward and eyes me. "Yeah?" I reply. "Who's going to stop me? You?" I turn to face her and cross my arms over my chest. "You're welcome to try."

"You're on lockdown," she says as if that means anything to me. Here's a hint—it doesn't. But I know it does to her and the rest of her cronies. So, I uncross my arms and give her my full undivided attention.

My lips part and I slip my tongue between my teeth, swishing it back and forth as I stare at her hard. "And?" I challenge.

A flush rises to her cheeks, anger heating them until even under the dim lighting, they look pink. "That means you're nothing," she spits back. "You're gravel beneath our feet. You don't belong here. They're going to punish you. They'll make you wish you never set foot on our campus."

I take a few steps forward and push down a grin as I watch one of the girls behind her take a wary step back. *Smart girl*, I think. Unlike her friends. I stop a few feet away and lean forward. Her gaze meets mine and lets her see just how fucking apathetic I feel. Whether there's a dead look in my eyes or not, I know there's one thing that she doesn't have—complete and utter disdain. The kind that should make a person very cautious. Because the true form of darkness is indifference.

"Do I *look* punished to you?" I ask. "Or better yet, do I really look like I give a shit?" When she doesn't respond, I take a single step closer until our breasts brush against each other. She inhales sharply. "See, the thing is," I say, keeping my voice low and even, "*you* have to follow all of their little orders. You *choose* to do whatever they tell you. Know what that makes you?" Sheep. Little lost sheep. Lambs to the fucking slaughter. She narrows her eyes on me, waiting on me to say the words, but I don't. Instead, I wait to see her response. And it doesn't surprise me in the slightest.

"Whatever," she finally snaps, turning away. "It's only a matter of time before you're out. The Sick Boys own Eastpoint and if you don't line up and do what they say, sooner or later you'll be sent back to whatever whorehouse you crawled out of."

There was that ridiculous name again. They hadn't yet done anything to show me just how *sick* they were. I was starting to think it was just a moniker and nothing more. That there was no substance to these preppy rich boys with an attitude and control issues.

"Then you have nothing to worry about," I say, batting my eyelashes, but I'm also not done talking to her and she's being fucking rude. I grab her arm and spin her back to face me. An outraged squawk, like something a vulture might make, erupts from her throat. I roll my eyes and then shove her away. Shock cloaks her features as she stumbles back. I follow. Her friends scramble to get out of the way until it's just me and the bitch. With her back pressed against the counter and cabinets, I get real close—just as close as I'd gotten with Abel that day in class. I can smell the tequila on her breath.

"I'll give you the same warning I gave them," I offer. Her eyes widen when I reach up and tap my fingers against her cheek as I continue. If I wanted to, I could probably dig my fingers into her eye socket and pluck it out. I could wrap my hands around her neck and squeeze and I doubt any of her friends would save her. Instead, I shove those violent cravings down and settle on my smile. Her limbs tremble next to mine. "You stay out of my way and I'll stay out of yours."

Her throat moves around a swallow as I back up, letting her go. She practically sags in relief. At least, she should be relieved. She hasn't yet pissed me off enough for me to actually show her what I can do. No, we're just getting started here. I chuckle lightly, turning away and heading for the backyard. "Have fun!" I call back, stepping into the humid night air.

I PAUSE AND SCAN THE NEARBY AREA. PEOPLE PILE together on the dance floor, grinding against each other in a drunken stupor. A few girls send me scathing looks. I reply with a quirked brow and a silent dare. Unsurprisingly, none of them take me up on the unspoken challenge.

Steam wafts up from the pool into the cooler air as bikini clad women drop down beside it, dipping their dainty toes inside as nearby guys with beers in hand watch on. I turn my head and freeze when my gaze collides with the asshole's who brought me here. Dean's dark eyes glitter with some enigmatic emotion. Whatever it is, it stirs some of the lingering violence in me and makes me smile. I have to force my head away lest I fall into that gaze and drown in his darkness. I'm not quite sure how I know it, but I have this hankering suspicion that maybe… just maybe, I wasn't completely right about these boys. They're not boys at all, but men. And there's a predatory depth there that tells me I should use caution. At the very least with Dean. Of them all, he seems like the largest threat.

The heat from the hot tub and pool drifts into the air around me. As I take a step away from the back door, I realize just how big this party has gotten. There are people everywhere. In the pool. On the dance floor. I even spot a few couples doing a bit more behind a pair of shaded palms across the way. I roll my eyes. This is more or less what I expected of a college party. It's unfortunate that I came here unwillingly, otherwise I might stay to actually have some fun.

That's out of the question though. I don't trust these motherfuckers and I'm not really in the mood to try. I cut left back towards the path I'd been led down before, wondering just how far of a walk back to campus I should expect. I'm halfway there, too, when a heavy arm drops over my shoulder.

"Where do ya think you're going?" Brax asks, bending low so that his head is next to mine.

"Back to my dorm," I say, reaching up to pinch the top of his hand and quickly remove it from my person.

He laughs, grabbing onto my waist instead, and swings me around. "I don't think so," he says, grinding on my front.

I arch my brow as he bumps against me to the rhythm of the music. "What are *you* doing?" I ask.

A grin spreads across his face. "Distracting you for a moment," he whispers almost conspiratorially.

"Wha—"

"Braxton!" The familiar voice of his friend—Dean—stops my next question.

Brax's eyes light up with mischief. *I could've liked this guy*,

I think. Despite the slightly unhinged look on his face that I'm sure no one else can see. It's too fucking bad he's on the wrong side of this fight.

"Time's up," he says, giving me a wink. "Be good. Play the part and we'll lift your lockdown."

I roll my eyes. "Keep it or don't," I huff. "Makes no difference to me."

Brax looks at me and his lips twitch. "Funny," he says. "I think you mean that."

"I do," I reply.

He just smiles at me then turns me around and shoves me into a pair of waiting arms. I grunt as I land against a broad chest. Fighting back, I push against it until I can look up and see who it is. Abel.

He doesn't look down, but instead begins to herd me across the patio space, through the crowds of people until we're at a platform I noticed just as I stepped outside. Where Dean stands like a waiting King.

"The fuck do you think you're doing?" I ask as Abel palms my waist in much the same way Brax did. Abel doesn't answer as he lifts me up. Dean catches me and sets me next to him.

"Don't say a fucking word," Dean orders.

"I'll say whatever the hell I want." The words are out of my mouth, an automatic response, before I even have a chance to examine what's going on.

Dean growls and even I have to admit—albeit silently—it sends a thrilling tingle through my system. Instead of responding to me, he yanks me closer, drops an arm around my side and tightens his hold until I'm flush against his side. Awareness slips in like an unsuspecting drug. Invisible. Barely noticeable. And yet, the whole time, I can feel that something is … off. Something's not quite right. I take in his face. The hardness. The way he's not looking at me.

The way he appears to be holding me more like a prop than a person.

Curious, I think. *Very curious.*

It could be because he doesn't actually see me as a person. That's entirely plausible. It's happened too many times to count. Guys with money or guys who think they're better look at girls like me and they assume. They assume because of my background that I'm nothing but a cheap whore, a plaything. A girl like me will only look for attention because there's nothing else she can afford. Those guys are always dead wrong, and by the time they figure it out, it's too late for them.

So, normally, I'd throw Dean's arm off, punch him in the face, and walk away without a second thought, but my curiosity has me staying right where I am. Something tells me that Dean is thinking of something completely different than what those other dipshits would be thinking. He's not looking at me because he's not focused on me at all. His attention is somewhere else and I follow the direction of his gaze until I see that the crowd has parted to allow a single girl through and the music has dropped down to a whisper.

The girl's got long, thin wheat-blonde hair pulled back into a haphazard ponytail and eyes done up with dark eyeliner that smudges around making the thin slits appear bigger. With her red lipstick and narrowed eyes, she looks like a rich girl trying to appear tougher than she actually is. I glance down and note that both Brax and Abel have moved closer. They stand just below the platform, their arms crossed in an almost identical pose. They look like sentinels guarding their King. I can't help but silently chuckle at that thought.

Dean squeezes my side when he feels my amusement,

too, as if that will stop me. I huff out a breath, but I keep my lips shut, curious to see what he's planning.

Abel speaks first, his tone harsh and angry. "What the fuck are you doing here, Coleman?" he barks out.

She comes to a slow stop before them and stiffens under the eyes of everyone in attendance. Her head tips back, but she doesn't wilt under the silence or the glares. Instead, she seems to draw from it. Her shoulders push back, she thrusts out what little chest she has, taking a cue from a number of classic mean girl routines, and tosses her ponytail over one shoulder before crossing her arms and popping a hip out.

"I came to talk," she replies with just as harsh a tone.

"We have nothing to say to a Kincaid. Get lost," Abel says.

The girl's blue eyes narrow on him, her lips twisting in a way that doesn't exactly make her unattractive, but at the very least shows her displeasure. When her head lifts and she notices me, though, that's when it changes into something ugly. A snarl curls her perfectly painted red lips. She bares her teeth for a brief moment, kohl-lined eyes narrowing into slits.

This is why Dean is holding me the way he is, I realize with no small amount of continued amusement. I glance back up at him, taking in the stony expression on his face, and decide to do him a little favor. Sure, he's irritated me, but more than that, he's brought me to a place where I can have a little fun and I know before the night is through, I'll get some of that adrenaline rush I've been craving.

Rather than simply standing there, letting Dean hold me the way he is, I reach up and place my palm over his chest. His attention is diverted for the briefest of moments, glaring eyes flashing down to me as I plaster myself against him. I get what I want the second she sees it.

"Who the hell is that?" the girl demands, nodding her head at me.

"She's none of your business," Brax says, sounding just as amused as I am.

He gets it, I think. He's crazy enough to understand exactly what I'm trying to do without being told.

Slowly, I draw one single fingernail down the center of Dean's chest, relishing in the way his back muscles jump and stiffen under the palm I settle against his spine, just above his ass. I'm not exactly wearing seductive attire, but my shirt is low cut enough that a hint of cleavage can be seen and if this chick is what I think she is, I know it'll be driving her absolutely insane.

"I'm Avalon," I say, giving her a slow lazy smile. "Who are you?"

"I'm—"

"She's no one," Dean interrupts, snatching the hand slowly making its way down to the front of his pants. I chuckle quietly when he holds it and squeezes meaningfully.

"You and I both know that's not true," the girl states. Her lips tremble ever so slightly and she takes a quick breath before looking away and speaking again. "I'm sorry. I came to tell you—"

"It doesn't matter why you came, Kate," Dean says. "I don't give a shit. You're Kincaid's bitch now." The way he says Kincaid like a vile curse has me memorizing the name and stuffing it into a dark corner in the back of my mind. I'll come back to it later, I decide, because I just know it means something important. If anything, this Kincaid person is definitely his enemy and the enemy of my enemy is my friend—or so the old saying goes.

"I know you don't mean that," she says, taking a step forward. She doesn't get any further. In the next instant,

Abel and Brax have closed ranks and stand before her, closer than before and definitely blocking her path.

She releases a frustrated breath and snaps her gaze up. A cold, hard glare levels my way as if her position down there is my fault. Then her eyes cut to the man of the hour. "What the actual fuck, Dean?" she says through clenched teeth. "You're really going to play it this way? You're trying to get back at me with some cheap whore?"

I flick my tongue between my teeth, bearing them. Dean's hand tightens on my side as if he can sense the rising tide of anger inside me.

"I don't play your games, Kate," Dean replies lazily, and one by one, he pries his fingers from my waist and drops my hand still clutched in his. I'm subtly pushed back as he leans to the side and cracks his neck, as if he's physically preparing to tear into her. "You transfer to St. Augustine over the break and show up at the first party of the new year? Bold move, even for you."

Her mouth drops open. "I'm not playing a game," she says.

"Bullshit." Dean snorts. He takes a step forward and leaps off the platform with the agility of a panther. When he lands, he straightens, his shoulders spreading wide as he strides towards her. Dean gives her a cold smile, the kind of smile a man gives someone right before they slit their throat. My insides practically vibrate with the way it makes me feel. I frown. I don't like it. I don't like it at all.

In unison, Brax and Abel each take a step in the opposite direction, letting him through to his prey. Curious, I move to sit on the edge of the platform myself, letting my feet dangle as I take in the series of events unfolding in front of me. It's like watching a set of actors on stage. Each one plays a role, and right now, Dean's playing a wicked villain to this rich princess's damsel. I can see it in his movements, hear it in his words—he wants to make her hurt.

"You're pussy, baby," he says. "Hot pussy, I'll give you that, but pussy is still just pussy. You ain't anything special, no matter how much you want to believe so." Her breath catches at the insult and her cheeks darken. "Tell me something," he continues, reaching up and fingering a shoulder length strand of blonde hair. "How is Luc Kincaid these days? He fuck you yet? You let him have a nice ride in my sloppy seconds?"

The music is cut completely and nothing but silence reigns after that statement. I don't see the girl's face, but I can see it when her shoulders stiffen and push back. "You're a fucking asshole, Dean Carter," she says sharply. "You think I had a fucking choice? Our parents decided on the fucking merger. Not me. I didn't get a choice."

"No?" He shrugs absently, turning his head away. "Well, lucky you, you get a choice now—you can either leave willingly, or I can make you go. It's up to you, Coleman."

"This isn't how I wanted it to be, Dean." She reaches for him and, like a fat kid watching the ice cream truck get closer and closer, the movement has my complete rapt attention. Especially when he grabs her hand just before it touches him.

"Kincaid may be fine fucking my sloppy seconds, Kate," he says coldly, "but I don't fuck tainted pussy."

With that, Dean drops her hand and turns away. The music starts again and he digs his phone out of his pocket, looking down at the screen with a scowl before looking back up at me. I arch my brow in challenge.

"Dean—" Kate tries to move towards him again but suddenly there are two hulking behemoths—two of the same guys that had brought me to this backwoods party palace. She takes one look at them, snarls something under her breath, and storms off.

"Make sure she leaves," Dean orders. They nod and follow after her.

"Damn, man," Abel says, blowing out a breath through his teeth. "She was steaming tonight. I bet if you'd tried you could've fucked her. Fucking Luc Kincaid's fiancée might piss him off."

When he replies, Dean's head tilts up and back, his gaze meeting mine. "I meant what I said. I don't fuck pussy that isn't worth it."

My lips twitch. "What are we going to do about her?" Brax asks, noticing the direction of his gaze, and me still sitting here.

"Oh, don't mind me, boys," I say. I stand up and stretch, hopping off the rocky dais. "I'm just gonna go find a way home."

"Oh no you're not." Abel cuts me off, sliding in my path.

I don't slow. In fact, I keep going until my entire front is against his. "You going to stop me, frontman?" I ask.

Blue eyes narrow on me. "Why the fuck do you keep calling me that?" I shrug, but my nonanswer seems to piss him off. He growls and whips his head in his friend's direction. "We brought her here to teach her a lesson," he snaps. "It doesn't look like she's learned it."

"What lesson?" I ask curiously.

Brax chuckles, but it's Abel who answers. "We can do what the fuck we want whenever the fuck we want to, princess," he bites out, shoving his chest forward and bumping me. "Just like tonight, you could be walking along the street, and out of fucking nowhere, you've got a bag over your head and you're in our domain."

I laugh. "Is that what you think you accomplished

tonight?" The idea of them—all domineering, though they are—trying to put me in my place is ridiculous. "But sure, alright, fine. Say I follow your little rules." I flick my fingers their way. It won't fucking happen, but they don't know that. "What then?"

"You get to keep breathing," Abel says.

"Newsflash, cupcake," I reply. "I'm breathing right now in case you've missed it, but I'm not under your command at all."

His hand reaches out and snags my wrist. Bringing it up to his face, he licks a slow path up my palm, making my eyebrows shoot up towards my hairline. "Is that supposed to be sexy?" I deadpan.

"You're still here, aren't you?" he asks.

Before I have time to formulate a reply, Dean's voice barks out. "Enough," he grits, slicing his irritated gaze to Abel. "Release her," he snaps. "Now." Abel lets go immediately and backs up. "We have more important shit to deal with." Dean levels me with a look that dares me to challenge him. Little does this rich boy know, I love a good challenge.

14

AVALON

It's easy to tell when someone isn't really paying attention. I'd spent enough time in boring high school classes to recognize when a person's focus isn't on what it should be, and right now, I know that Dean Carter's attention—thank you mysterious, yet bitchy ex-girlfriend for that full name—is not on me. And whether he knows it yet or not, that's a mistake.

Because if he's not watching me closely enough—and hell, even if he is—I'm locked and loaded, ready to cause a little mischief simply as payback for forcing me to come to his stupid Sick Boys' party.

Perhaps he and his friends are far too used to having their every order followed. That's the only explanation I can think of. It's clear that he wants me to stay right where I am until he so deigns to address me, but I'm not the kind of girl that just sits around and waits for a guy to give her the time of day. No. I'm the exact opposite.

So, as soon as I'm sure he's more intent on whatever it is that his friend Brax is saying to him, I'm gone. Like a whisper in the wind.

Okay, not really, but I do find it all too easy to slip away as the music cranks back up and bodies start grinding on the dance floor again. As if sensing a predator in their mix, the partiers part for me, letting me through rather easily until I'm back in the house. *Smart little drunk lambs*, I think.

I make my way through the bottom floor of the Frazier House until I reach the front door. In the time I've been here, more cars have arrived. They pile out of the right side of one long driveway, one after another until there's really no viable space for anyone to get out, and that's where I see her. Interestingly enough, there's a second driveway that spans the opposite side of the house, but that one is empty.

Disregarding it, I prop myself against one of the pillars of the front porch of the mansion and eye the blonde as she scowls in frustrated fury at what looks to be a brand new Mercedes. A giant souped-up SUV is parked barely a few inches from her bumper. She turns back to the house as if ready to come back and ream someone a new asshole, but stops when she sees me, and I can't help but chuckle.

She might be rich, but it's clear that she's no better than I am in the eyes of the Kings hosting this party. I can't help but like that. Even if they're wrong to think that I'm a peasant to their royalty.

"What the fuck are you laughing at, bitch?" she snarls, stomping forward.

I cross my arms and arch a brow. "You," I say, nodding to the hot ride she's left in favor of coming to stand before me. "And your predicament."

Her pretty blue eyes narrow. "You think you're something special just because Dean Carter wants to fuck you?" she asks. "Just because you're a passing interest?"

I roll my eyes, but I don't correct her. "Not particularly," I say. Not that the King of Kings really has an interest in me. She doesn't seem to realize it yet, but I was merely a distraction for her—an annoyance. A tool and a pawn. Not something I let myself be too often, but when the mood strikes me—and I can find some amusement like I did tonight—I don't mind it.

"You're not," she says.

My nose twitches as the scent of strong alcohol, cigarettes, and vomit hit me when the front door crashes open and a guy comes stumbling out. He takes one look at us and mumbles something to himself, dropping a bottle of rum into the grass as he fumbles into his pocket. A second later, he finally finds his lighter and pulls a joint from the pocket of his button down collared shirt. I shake my head. Just goes to show, no matter where you are, there are degenerates.

"Want a hit?" he asks the girl on the steps—Kate. "You look like you could use it."

She sneers at him, so I speak up. "Yeah," I say. "I'll take one."

He shrugs and hands it over.

Kate's face snaps back to mine. "Wow, he really went and found himself a top class whore," she says, not even bothering to mask the disgust on her face as I inhale the weed. It's pretty strong shit too. I can already feel my head growing clearer.

"Not a whore," I say, handing the joint back to the guy as he plops down on the edge of the porch and leans his head back, closing his eyes and taking another hit. "Not Dean Carter's or anyone else's."

Kate narrows her eyes on me before striding up the stone steps until she's right alongside me. "You better watch your back here, new girl," she hisses as she passes by. "Your days are numbered. Dean Carter isn't the only one with power."

As soon as those words are spat my way, she marches past me and into the house to presumably find the owner of the SUV currently blocking her in. I hum low in my throat. "Not the only one with power, huh?" I wonder aloud. What is it that these rich kids think they know about power? Power is nothing but a game. Sex is about power. Intelligence is about power. Hell, money is about power too. Everyone has some sort of power. She just doesn't realize it yet.

"Don't worry 'bout Kate," the dude hanging out against the steps pipes up, distracting me from the direction of my thoughts. "She's just pissed that Carter won't give her the time of day anymore—not that I blame him."

I glance down. "Oh?"

His eyes crack open and he leans his head back to meet my gaze. "You're pretty ballsy, though," he continues. "I kinda like that. No one tells the Eastpoint heirs 'no.' I mean, sure, they're gonna make your life a living hell for it, but it'll be entertaining for me at least."

"Happy to be of service," I reply sarcastically.

He tips his head at me curiously, his gaze scanning me up and down as if he's searching for something. I don't know if he finds it or not, but he does speak again. "If I were you I'd try to conform. You don't seem the type, but it might make things easier on ya. No one overrules the Sick Boys."

My eyeball twitches at that nickname, but I don't comment on it. Instead, tipping my head back in the same fashion as him, I ask, "Not even you?"

He laughs, and the sound isn't unpleasant despite the drunken slur to his words. "Nah, man," he says. "I ain't got the kinda pull they got. My dad's got money but not Eastpoint money. I know I'm a lucky son of a bitch."

I roll my tongue inside my cheek as I let my eyes

wander down to the grass. When they light on the half filled bottle of rum still sitting there, an idea forms in my head. A beautifully wicked idea. My lips curve up.

"Hey," I say, "let me borrow your lighter."

The guy's eyebrows shoot up, but he doesn't say no. Instead, he reaches back into his pocket, retrieves the thing, and hands it over with a curious tilt to his head. I swoop down and pick up the bottle of rum. "Got a rag handy?" I ask, ever hopeful.

"Oh, shit," he says, his eyes widening and clearing of the cross-faded haze that's the result of the liquor and weed in his system. "What are you gonna do?"

I shrug, grinning, but not yet ready to give it away. "Rag or not?" I ask.

He digs into his pocket. "Got one of these," he says, holding out a…

I laugh, snatching the panties from his grasp. "Do I even want to know?"

A grin lights his face and while I wouldn't have considered him extremely attractive by any means, he's not bad looking. "I had a little fun before coming out here," he admits not at all sheepishly. "And it wasn't in private if you know what I mean. Thought I'd get those out of the way, was gonna throw 'em out when I got home."

"Sure you were, perv," I say with a laugh. I stuff one side of the panties—thank fuck they don't feel wet or dirty—into the top of the bottle, ensuring that the bottom portion of the cotton gets nice and soaked before I stride out into the middle of the lawn.

"You better fucking run after you throw that thing," he calls as he stands back. "'Cause whoever you're about to piss off is gonna fucking kill you."

An indelicate snort leaves me as I flick the lighter and hold the flame against the panties. It lights just as the front door opens and a scream rents the air. "What are you doing!"

I look back with a grin. "Just welcoming you to a Sick Boys party," I say as Kate rushes down the front steps and hauls ass towards me.

I don't stop or hesitate even when she's obviously intent on tackling me to the ground like a professional linebacker. I turn towards the Mercedes she'd been trying to get out of the driveway and toss my homemade Molotov cocktail. Glass shatters against the metal frame and an explosion of flames rockets up the side of the car, earning another ear-splitting shriek from Kate. I laugh.

"What the fuck is *wrong* with you!" Her skinny frame bolts towards her precious Mercedes only to stop short when she realizes she can't touch anything. "Ohmygod. Ohmygod." She turns around and races for the side of the house, stumbling in her haste, her high heels sinking into the ground. Clumps of dirt and mud trip her up as she finds the end of a hose along the side of the giant mansion and starts yanking it towards her car.

"Guess you shouldn't have called me a whore, huh?" I laugh—a full-bellied, can't stop myself, laugh. Watching her slip and slide in the dirt when she realizes she hasn't even turned on the water … it's too much, really. I fall to the ground and just lay there, staring up at the sky as the fire rages over her car. Tires pop under the pressure of the heat and the whole frame sags to one side.

She's got maybe twenty more minutes until the fire reaches the gas tank. I tossed it more towards the front anyway. Feminine cursing reaches my ears as water sprays out, shooting me in the face and chest before quickly diverting to the vehicle.

"You're insane!" she snarls as she tries to put out the fire.

I get up and look down at my soaked front. I don't even care. I pull my t-shirt away from my stomach, lifting it up and ringing out the water as I watch my handiwork.

"Yeah," I say, giving her a wink as she just stares at me. "You should remember that for next time."

Then a masculine voice interrupts. "What the fuck is going on here?"

15

DEAN

"Hey, where'd the girl go?"

No sooner has the question left Abel's mouth that I hear screaming over the music. Our heads turn towards the house as the back doors are flung open and Eli and Griffin come hauling ass out of the house. Eli looks up and calls my name. "Carter!" he yells, startling several people nearby. "We got a fuckin' problem, man." He gestures for me to follow him back into the house.

I take off, heading after him as Braxton and Abel follow. "What the hell is going on?" I demand. First, the girl up and disappears on her own and then—I come to a halt on the front step of Abel's house.

As if overwhelmed by his need to be a sarcastic asshole and point out the obvious, Abel snorts. "Never mind, found her."

"What the hell did she do?" Brax asks, his tone filled with—God, I really hope that's not admiration. That is not something I need right now.

"You're insane!" Kate says, her whole body trembling as she holds the hose—still spraying out water against her burnt Mercedes. There are black marks all along the side, and little fires still in the grass, mixed with...

"Is that a bottle of rum?" Abel asks absently.

"Did she make a fucking Molotov cocktail and chuck it at Kate's car?" someone else asks. I don't know who it is. All I know is that it's not Brax and it's not one of my team which means we've got too many fucking people bearing witness to a bitch who just took action on our property without our say so and that's a fucking problem.

"Eli," I snap. "Get everyone inside."

Without missing a beat, the big man turns and starts herding people. "Alright, motherfuckers, you heard the man. Nothing to see here. Return to the party."

"Awww, man, come on, I wanna see a catfight!" someone yells.

I don't need to do anything. Brax whips around and growls. "You want to fucking leave?" he snaps out. "'Cause you can leave willingly or in a body bag, your choice."

No one else says shit after that. I look at my watch. "We've got thirty minutes," I say. "We have to get this finished and we have to get out of here."

"On it," Abel says, disappearing back into the house.

I turn to Brax. "Can you—"

He laughs. "Nope," he says, shaking his head. "You deal with the bitches. I'm just back up."

"Fucker," I mutter, but there's no point and no time to argue. Kate's eyes lift and she looks at me over Avalon's head.

"Dean," she says, her bottom lip trembling—I can't tell, though, if it's anger or something else. To be honest, I don't really care. "Your psycho bitch just tried to blow up my car!"

The chick turns around, looking beyond me and Brax, as she scans the yard. She pauses and grins. I force myself not to turn the fuck around and see who she's smiling at. "Too bad she failed," Brax comments. "That would've been one hell of a show."

Kate flicks him a look of pure hatred—what do you know—it was anger after all. "*Do something*," she hisses at me as I stride down into the yard.

"I thought I told you to leave," I say, thinking over the events. A plan forms in my mind. This could actually work for me. Kate will keep sniffing around until Kincaid puts his own lock on her—and I don't see that happening any time soon. He'll want her to fucking annoy me as much as possible. What better way to make her move on faster than to make her think I've got someone new. I've already planted the seeds. I flick a glance Avalon's way to take in her reaction. Her eyes are on her shirt though, and I realize she's soaked straight down her front, the hard little points of her nipples standing at attention under the thin fabric of her t-shirt. I rip my eyes away and level them on Kate. "S'far as I see it, I told you to do something and you didn't do it."

"I was trying!" Kate says, gesturing to her car. "I'm blocked in."

"That sounds like your problem, Coleman," I say, hearing the telltale sound of a Mustang's engine revving as the twin headlight beams come careening around the opposite side of the house—down the path we don't let anyone take or park in. "Not mine."

I grab Avalon's arm and without looking down, I herd her towards the Mustang. Shockingly, she doesn't put up a fight. "Call a tow," I suggest, "but make sure you're not here when we get back." I pop open the passenger side door and push the chick towards the backseat.

Without a word, she climbs in. I hold it open and let Brax fold his big ass body in behind her.

Kate takes a step towards me. "Dean," she says, her tone placating, "please, don't do this. We were good together. I can break things off with Luc—I didn't even want the stupid engagement—"

"Don't care, Coleman," I say, reaching down and grabbing a cap from the car's floorboards. I slide it on and spin it so that the bill faces backwards. "You weren't ever anything special. It wasn't like I was going to propose. Have fun with Kincaid." I smile and I know it's mean. "Seriously, though, you might think about getting pregnant and rushing that wedding along before it's too late and he kicks you and your entire family to the side."

Her face slackens in shock. *Yeah, baby,* I think. *I know everything.* Not just about the engagement, but I know the reason for it too. Because without Kincaid, the Colemans are about to go from one of America's wealthiest families to insignificant and dead broke overnight. And even if we had fucked once or twice, I can't seem to find the sympathy in me to care. As far as I'm concerned, a disloyal bitch is just a dog who needs to be put down.

16

AVALON

I bite my twitching lips, not even bothering to resist the urge to look back and watch Kate's face as Abel puts the pedal to the metal and skids down the empty driveway, towards the road. She stands there, in the center of the lawn of the great big mansion—her eyes wide and mouth open as smoke still smolders on the ground next to her car. I don't know what Dean said to her before getting in the car, but whatever it was has obviously left an impression because she looks two seconds from breaking down right then and there.

I flip back around and settle into the back seat of the Mustang. Kind of a weird car for one of these guys to own. Although it's well maintained, it's an older vehicle, at least twenty years old. I debate on commenting but decide against it. Instead, I lean forward, poking my head between the twin front seats.

"Alright, we're far enough away," I say. "You can let me out now."

Abel doesn't look at me. "Sit down," he says.

PRETTY LITTLE SAVAGE

"No can do, frontman," I say. "I want out. I'm getting out."

"No, you're not," Dean says, his voice a deep growl.

"Wanna bet?" I pivot and look at him. Dean turns and fixes me with what can only be described as a look of deep warning. I ignore it. "Either you let me out now or I'll make you. Your choice, D-man."

His glare only intensifies, and yeah, okay, maybe if I was the type of girl to drop her panties for any guy who looked like a murderer in a thousand dollar hoodie, it'd make me sit my happy ass back down. But I'm not. I'm tougher than that.

"Do you really want to try me?" I ask.

He leans back, eyeing me, and I'm sure I've won—that is, until the right side of his mouth twitches and what comes out from between his lips is a very smug, "Brax."

Before I even realize what's happening, big, massive paws are gripping my sides and pulling me backwards. My spine slams into the seat and a hard, muscled arm as thick as one of my thighs comes across my front, gripping the seatbelt and strapping me into place. Rage boils up.

"Big. Fucking. Mistake," I say, just before I rear back and punch Brax right in the face as he hovers in front of me, still clipping the end of my seatbelt into place. And holy shit, his face is made of rock. I clench my teeth as pain radiates from my knuckles, but I don't show it. He stops, blinking as if he can't believe I just did that—but fuck yeah, I did. "Let me go," I snap, struggling in his grip.

Brax shakes his head and finally looks up at me. He doesn't even look mad about the punch. "Settle down, li'l psycho," he says, patting the top of my head. "We're just dropping you off."

"You're what?" I stop struggling and stare at the back

of his head. "Oh. Well, then. Why didn't you say so?" I catch Abel's glance in the rearview mirror.

"I can't believe you Molotov-cocktailed her car," he says with a snicker.

I shrug and relax more fully into the seat. Now that I know they're taking me exactly where I wanna go, I'm good. "It was dangerous," Brax agrees. "Had you hit closer to the gas tank and had she not been smart enough to grab the hose, the car would've gone up in flames."

"She had it coming," I say, unconcerned.

"Oh?" Brax leans forward and turns towards me. "How so?"

"She disrespected me."

There's a beat of silence in the car and then both Abel and Brax burst out laughing. I smile as I listen to the two of them. The only one who remains silent is Dean. And soon, as their chuckles taper off, he turns in his seat to look back at me.

"I don't care what you did," he says, "but you need to get one thing straight."

"Oh?" I tilt my head and grin. "And what would that be, D-man?"

He scowls at the nickname and just knowing that it irritates him only ensures I'm going to be using it every time I see him from now on. A charged feeling—an electric current—slides through the space between him and me.

"You need to keep stunts like that to a minimum," he says. "In fact, you need to erase the desire to commit them completely unless we order it."

An indelicate snort leaves my lips. "Okay, sure." The sarcasm is so heavy I can taste the sour tang on my tongue.

His scowl deepens. "You think I'm fucking playing with you?" he asks.

I shrug. "Doesn't matter if you are or not," I reply

honestly. "If you think you can control someone like me, you've got another thing coming."

He arches a brow. "Really?" Dean turns, leaning forward and pops open the glove compartment in front of him. I lean to the side and my eyes widen when I spot the familiar handle of a gun amidst a bunch of papers and other shit. My heart rate kicks up and I put my hand to the clip, my fight mode kicked into high drive. Another hand lands on mine, stopping me, and I jerk my head up and glare as Brax shakes his head.

Dean doesn't even touch the gun. He grabs a manila envelope beneath it and pries it loose before snapping the compartment closed. It takes a moment, but when he turns back and notices Brax's hand on mine, earning both of us a wicked glare, I start to relax.

"What's that?" I ask as Dean opens the envelope and starts removing papers. He flicks through them without looking up.

"Would you like to know?" he asks.

I roll my eyes. "No, I asked just for shits and giggles," I say snidely.

"They're a work up on you, little miss Ava," he replies, ignoring my comment.

"What?"

"Avalon Marie Manning. Born October 3rd. Eighteen years old. From Plexton, Georgia. No known father. Mother Patricia Manning. Arrested twice, once for shoplifting and another for possession of drugs."

I roll my eyes. "Weed's not really a drug," I say.

He shrugs absently, thumbing through another page. "Not many boyfriends here," he comments. "Five schools in the last four years. Numerous referrals."

"I thought we went over this already." I yawn. "It's only four schools."

"Not according to this." He taps his file, tsking. "Someone's been a very naughty girl."

"Only when I feel like it," I reply, batting my lashes as he flicks a quick look up before he returns to the papers in his hand.

I try not to let it show, but the more his eyes rove over the sheets, the more I feel my muscles tighten. He's got a fucking work up on me. A whole spreadsheet on my past. *It's fine*, I tell myself. *I don't give a fuck.* It's not like I'm trying to hide anything.

That's not what bothers me. What bothers me is that Dean Carter thinks he knows everything about me, and I still hardly know anything about him. That, I'll have to rectify.

"What else does your little worku*p*," I say, popping the last syllable of the word from my mouth as I do, "tell you about me?"

He looks back up at me. "Enough," he hedges.

"Yeah?" I smile. "Bet it doesn't have all the gory details of everything in my life that you think it does."

"You don't think so?" he asks. An underlying pressure fills up the car and I can sense the other two growing just as tense. Abel's hands grip the steering wheel tight enough to turn the skin over his knuckles white. Brax's eyes fixate on the windshield. Neither one of them says a word.

"No, I don't." I hold his gaze as I reach down and unclip my seatbelt. Brax reaches for it again without taking his eyes off the windshield.

"Let her," Dean orders and Brax jerks, finally tearing his gaze from the front to look at his friend in shock. But his hand falls away and I strip the seatbelt back as I lean forward, placing one foot on the floorboard between the seats and arching my whole upper body through the space between the front seats.

"What the fuck?" Abel snaps, his eyes sliding to the side.

"Keep fucking driving," Dean says as I angle my body so that I'm crawling through the space and land in the front seat with my back to the windshield and my thighs on either side of Dean's legs. He eyes me, and I know he's waiting to see what I'll do.

I grab the envelope and the papers with it and toss them into the backseat, letting them scatter across the floorboards. Dean's hands fist at his sides, refusing to touch me and it makes me smile. Abel's head turns repeatedly as he fights his need to watch the road and see what the fuck is going on. I can feel Brax's eyes on both of us. Putting my hand against the back of Dean's seat, I grip it as I hold myself precariously close to his body. I lean down.

"Doesn't matter how many people you pay, D-man," I whisper. "You'll never know my secrets unless I want you too."

"Everyone can be bought," he volleys back.

I laugh. That might be true for normal people, but I'm anything but normal. The car starts to slow and in my peripheral vision, I recognize the buildings we're passing. "Do you want to buy me?" I ask.

"I don't have to buy whores," he quips.

I tip my head back and tap my bottom lip with my finger. "Now, that's not the right word to use," I say. "That's exactly the kind of language that got your girlfriend in trouble." I grin. "You wouldn't want me to come after you the way I went after her, would you?"

He bares his teeth at me, his arm muscles straining as he grips the edges of his seat. From my position, I can smell the musk of his cologne, something dark and spicy. It fills my nostrils with a woodsy scent.

"You're playing a dangerous game," he says, his voice a deep growl as the Mustang turns down a side road.

"No, I'm not," I say. "Because I don't play games. *You do*."

One hand leaves the seat and grips my side as the car goes over a speed bump. The entire vehicle lifts and falls. Automatically, my hips lower and suddenly, I'm not hovering anymore—I'm plastered right up against him. And damn if I don't feel exactly what kind of weapon Dean Carter is packing.

He arches a brow and a smirk lifts his lips. "You might think you don't play games, sweetheart," he says, leaning forward until the warmth of his breath brushes against my lips. "But that looks exactly like what you're doing right now."

"Dean." Abel's voice is a warning.

The car slows and then stops completely. Dean's eyes center on mine as he ignores his friend, but Abel's not done. He throws the car into park, reaches out and grabs my arm, earning my attention.

"Tonight was a test," Abel tells me. I arch one brow. Like I didn't already figure that out.

I laugh lightly and shake off his hand as I reach towards the opposite side and pop open the Mustang's passenger door. I don't get out just yet, though. I let myself settle a little more firmly on Dean's cock, grinding just a smidge to see his reaction. His whole face turns to stone, his smirk vanishing in an instant, leaving only the cruel look in his eyes. The one that makes me want to be a little bit more than reckless—that look in his eyes makes me want to do something absolutely fucking savage.

"I know what you three were trying to pull," I inform them, turning my gaze to encompass the other two. "You rule Eastpoint, right?" I don't wait for them to respond.

"And I'm a new girl. I come in. I don't follow the rules. I don't bow down or ask 'how high' when you say 'jump.' That's a problem—but that's *your* problem, not mine. I'm not going to move when you tell me to. I'm not going to come when you call. I'm not one of your little minions. I'm here because I have nowhere else to go right now." I shrug. "And you could threaten to get me kicked out—hell, I have no doubts that you could follow through, but the thing is—it doesn't matter what you have in that little envelope of yours. There is nothing you could use against me—no blackmail material—to get me to fall in line. Do I want to stay? Maybe. But I don't follow anyone but myself."

"We don't need you causing problems," Abel says angrily. His brows are drawn down low over his face as he scowls at me and I know it's because he sees the truth in my eyes.

I shrug. "I'm not causing problems," I say.

"The hell you're not," he shoots back. "You defied us publicly. We can't let that slide."

"You're the ones who demanded obedience without respect," I say.

"Most people would be smart enough to realize when they're overpowered," Brax says quietly from the back. He watches me with eyes that are neither angry nor confused. Instead, there's a curiosity in his gaze. And a small amount of amusement.

I grin his way. "I'm not most people," I say, swinging my leg over Dean's thighs as I climb out of the vehicle. My foot lands on the sidewalk and I clamp a hand over the top of the door as I lean back in. "The sooner you realize that, the sooner you'll figure me out."

"There's nothing to figure out," Dean says, finally speaking up after what feels like a long ass silence. His eyes spit fire and determination. "I already know everything about you, little girl."

I bend lower, until my face is close to his. I don't say the words loud enough for the others to hear; instead, I whisper them right against his cheek. "If that were true, then you'd know that I'm no little girl, Dean Carter," I breathe. "I'm a goddamn weapon."

With a snap, I slam the door shut and walk away—feeling the cut of his eyes on my ass the entire way.

17

DEAN

"What the fuck is she—"

I cut Abel off before he can finish that goddamn thought. "Drive."

His mouth snaps shut, but I see the way he cuts a look to me out of the corner of his eye. He wants to say something, but he knows this tone. He knows what it fucking means. I stretch uncomfortably, reaching down to adjust my rock hard cock in my shorts. Avalon Manning is fucking dangerous.

When I first saw her, I thought she could be an amusement, but I never expected *this*. People are already talking about her. A body like that. A smirk like that. An attitude like that. It spells only one fucking thing.

Trouble.

And trouble is not something I need right now.

Abel and Braxton don't say a word for the rest of the drive. I try to think of ways to deal with Avalon. We can't have her running around doing whatever the fuck she wants, but if it's true that we can't control her, what else can we do? I sigh into the silent interior of the car. We'll just have to have her removed. Eastpoint is no longer an option for her. With her gone, things will return to normal. Even with that thought, however, I still can't help regretting it. It might've been nice, for a change, to keep a girl like her around. At the very least, she's not like the others—she's not conniving or boring. She lays it all out there. Reluctantly, I admit it. I admire her.

We pull up to the warehouse district—the district usually reserved for these kinds of meetings, not necessarily the kind of backroom deals the world expects people like us to make, but it's the actual reality of the rich and powerful, not the televised reality. Everyone's corrupt in some way. The richer you are, the dirtier you are.

"Did they say what this was about?" Abel asks as he puts the top of the car down and Brax immediately jumps out. We sit in the idling vehicle as we watch Brax run up to the metal doors. He locates the locking system, puts in his code, and the whir of locks disengaging hits my ears.

"They didn't say." I stare through the windshield, tapping my fingers along my thigh, feeling the muscle jump as my mind rolls back to the feeling of Avalon's body. Like fire and fucking more goddamn fire, she's a pistol ready to go off, and I find that I want to know what happens if I pull the trigger. "They never fucking do."

Abel grits his teeth and presses lightly down on the gas as the door slides open far enough. Brax waits until we're completely through before closing them. Only then does Abel shut off the engine and we both get out. I put the hood on my jacket up to ward off the chill inside the warehouse and pull out my keys.

The three of us make our way to the very back of the warehouse where I can already see the dim illuminating light coming from the row of grime encrusted windows. I put my keys back. There's no need. They're already here.

PRETTY LITTLE SAVAGE

No one makes a sound as we head up the creaky metal steps to the rust colored door marking the entrance to hell.

"Welcome, boys." I grit my teeth but don't comment on the fact that none of us are fucking boys anymore and haven't been since the first time we put a bullet in someone's head. Instead, I move to the round table in the center of the room. The three men across from us each mark the current head of the Eastpoint families.

Elric Smalls.

Lionel Frazier.

And the man in the middle, Nicholas fucking Carter. My father.

"Glad you could make it on time," Lionel says. It's less than five minutes to midnight and we're usually here fifteen minutes early, so I know by the sharp, caustic tone that he isn't happy about the change.

Had I not had to deal with a skinny little brat with a full mouth and even fuller ass, we might've kept to our usual schedule. But these three men are the very reason Avalon fucking Manning is now throwing our entire system out of whack. They're the ones who find and recruit the program students. The best of the best. To work for *us*. But whichever of these fuckers thought they could tame a wild chick like her, they really fucked up. Hell, I've only known her less than a week and I'm already doubting if she'll manage to stick around for the full semester. As things stand, I'll have to be very careful how I spin her actions against Kate.

We take our seats and for several long moments, nothing but silence greets us. Elric watches Braxton. Lionel watches Abel. And my father watches me. Round and round, here we fucking go. These circles never cease. They're always testing us, testing me.

"Do you know why you've been called here?" Elric is

the first to speak and as he does, his attention zeroes in on Braxton. I hesitate to look over. I don't want to see if Brax's gaze is growing hazy as it always does when he's faced with his father. An age-old anger that usually simmers deep beneath my surface when I think of Elric Smalls starts to boil up. Nicholas may be a shit dad, but Elric's the real monster and only the people in this room know the truth about him. Were he anybody else in the fucking world, he'd have been murdered long ago. But money is an interesting thing—some people say money can't buy you everything, but it can certainly buy you protection and that's what it's done for him.

I turn my cheek and stare at the man. "Why don't you inform us," I say.

Nothing but more silence and when I've about had enough, my father finally reaches into the briefcase he always carries around—always keeps somewhere just out of sight—and removes a file. "You pulled information on a new student at the school," he begins.

My spine goes rigid. "Yeah," I snap. "She's been causing issues, what about it?"

He arches his brow at my tone. "Can you handle the situation?" The question is an insult.

"Of course I can," is my immediate response. She'll be removed within a few days and on her way back to her bum fuck little town. "It's handled. What does that have to do with anything?"

"This student was specially recruited and we want to bring her in closer," Lionel says. "By any means necessary."

My whole body freezes. "What does that mean?" I clarify.

"It means," Lionel continues, "that this one is a bit different. She's currently finishing up her high school diploma and once she does, we'll be offering her a full ride. If she doesn't accept, we expect that you'll figure out a way to persuade her."

All of my plans to get rid of the girl go up in smoke. Lionel leans forward and fixes Abel with a meaningful look. "And when we say 'any means necessary' we mean it," he states.

Abel's back stiffens. Of all the people in the world, there are honestly no more than three people that I believe I would truly enjoy killing. And all three of them are in this room.

I know what they expect from us. They expect the worst.

Violence from Braxton.

Murder from me.

Sex from Abel.

Born, bred, and reared for these roles. Each man is a head of Hydra, herself. Cut one off and two more grow back. Each different. Each deadly. Though I want to bring a gun to their heads and pull the trigger, I know it'll never happen.

I lean forward, bringing my hand down on the table between Abel and Lionel. "*It's handled*," I repeat the words with more force.

I can feel my father's gaze on me. Even as Lionel turns his head and looks at me with mild surprise. "By you?" he inquires with a hum. "Well, that *is* unexpected."

"Not entirely," my father manages to say as he slides the file to the center of the table. I don't reach for it yet, though. For all I know, touching it could be the failure to whatever test this is.

"Why is the girl important?" Abel is the one to ask the question we're both wondering. Braxton, though, I doubt he cares. He has to be here for the meeting because he's one of the heirs—but women are not his specialty. Blood is.

"The why doesn't matter," Lionel answers. "It is for us to know and for you to find out when the time is right and that time is not now."

"Are we supposed to fuck her or protect her?" I demand.

If anyone's going to be fucking her, it won't be Abel. My dick still remembers the feel of her pussy pressed up against it through the fabric of our clothes. What strikes me stupid, though, is that she was even hotter standing on the lawn of our party house, soaked down after just having chucked a flaming bottle at Kate Coleman's Mercedes than any other woman I've ever seen in my life. That little bit of savage crazy is what makes the image of her rebound across my mind, stirring my shaft and making me more than a little itchy inside. She's like a train wreck when she walks by, and I can't help but stare and watch her burn. Deadly. Fatal. Full of sorrow. And yet, so fucking beautiful at the same time.

"Neither," my father says, answering my question. "For now, we want her under observation. If the only way to keep her there is by fucking her, then fine."

"Is she valuable?" Abel asks.

Instead of answering, Nicholas smiles and picks his briefcase up off the floor. He turns to me as he stands up. The three of us—Abel, Braxton, and I—all rise, too, when Lionel and Elric do as well. "It was good seeing you, son," he says, nodding down at the file on the table. "This is everything else your search missed. You're welcome to browse it."

With that, the three of them leave the room, one by one. Elric is the last one. He pauses alongside Braxton and looks down at him for a brief moment before turning his gaze to us. "I hope I'll see you three at the games this year," he says, and then he's gone.

The only thing that can be heard in the room after their departure is the turning of the ancient fan above us as it sways in time with the mechanism that keeps it going.

"What now?" Abel asks.

I reach over and pick up the folder. "Now," I say, striding forward and clamping a hand on Brax's shoulder. He doesn't react. "We get drunk."

"I mean about the girl," Abel presses.

There's really only one answer to that. We can't send her packing. We can't get rid of her. There's nothing else we can do but the impossible. I slide my tongue over my teeth, my fingers gripping the folder in my hand. "We claim her," I tell him. "From now on, she's Sick Boys' property."

18

AVALON

By the middle of the following week, it's clear that the majority of Eastpoint has heard about the party and the Molotov Cocktail incident. I can feel the stares or at least *someone* constantly watching me. The fact that I can't figure out who is slowly starting to drive me insane. Despite that, while the event itself hasn't exactly made me Miss Popular, I have noticed a distinct lack of violent glares from my classmates. They no longer go out of their way to ignore me, but neither does anyone seem too keen on sticking around me. Particularly, not Rylie.

"I'm not eating with you," she informs me as she packs her bag for class. "I need to keep my head down, and you," she pauses and points at me in accusation, "draw way too much fucking attention." Each sentence is said with a biting irritation. She says it, but a part of her doesn't mean it. I don't know how—considering her life has probably been just as fucked up as my own—but I know she's a bit softer than she should be. It's there in the way she nags me to keep my own head down. I won't ever do it, but it's cute that she thinks it's what's best for girls like us. It's almost ... nice to feel like someone gives a shit, if a bit unfamiliar.

I chuckle lightly as I thumb through a textbook and scan the contents, prepping for a quiz I know is coming up. "I mean it," she says.

"Sure," I say. "Ignore me all you want. Won't bother me."

She pauses just beside the door, her messenger bag slung over one shoulder. Her cool hazel eyes glare at me. Finally, she just throws her hands up and storms out. I wait a few more minutes to make sure she's not coming back for anything before I throw the textbook down and get up. I stretch up onto my toes, yawning and popping my joints.

My stomach growls as I debate what to do next and it solidifies my afternoon plans. Quickly changing into a pair of jeans and a new t-shirt, I snatch my keys and ID card and head for the student food court.

Halfway through the food court, I spot a familiar face that I haven't seen since the party and I stop dead, changing directions, and head for him. "Hey," I say, plopping down in front of him.

The guy lifts his head out of his cell phone and out from beneath the bill of his baseball cap. The second he sees my face, he grins and flips his hat around. "Well, look what the cat dragged in." He smirks. "Just the girl I've been hearing so much about."

I roll my eyes and wave my hand back and forth. "Oh, whatever."

"That stunt you pulled is all over school," he says.

"Yeah, well, I couldn't have done it without you," I say. "Thanks for the hand ... or should I say the panties?"

He laughs, throwing his head back, and slaps his hand on the table. "Please, no need to thank me, it was funny as shit to watch. Besides, I never really liked Kate."

"Awww." I fake a pout. "Too good for your dick?"

He doesn't even try to lie. "Yeah, pretty much."

"Thought all rich pricks were the same," I comment.

That gets me a huff of disbelief. "With Carter, Frazier, and Smalls in the pot?" he asks. "Not a chance in hell."

"Which is which?" I ask.

He pauses as if he's not sure if I'm being serious or not, but when I keep my face even he frowns. "Wow," he says. "You really don't give much of a shit about this place, do you? Been here, what? A few weeks? And not only have you pissed off the three richest and most powerful guys here, but you don't even know enough to know their last names?"

I shrug. "When it's important, I know it."

He shakes his head in disbelief.

"Besides," I continue, "I don't even know *your* name, and I can actually stand you."

"I'm so pleased," he says dryly. A beat passes and he grins. "The name's Jake, by the way. Jacob Hayes."

"Avalon," I say. "Just Avalon."

"Pretty name," he comments.

"It is what it is."

"Yeah, that seems like something you'd say." Jake shakes his head and pushes back from the table. "Well, I gotta head to class, but it was nice seeing you. Take care not to get into too much more trouble—word on the street is the shit you did to Kate's car got you off lockdown. Take advantage of that. Make some friends—something tells me a girl like you is gonna need them."

I'd laugh at that "girl like me" comment if I didn't know exactly what he was talking about. I stand too. "Wait," I say, catching him just as he pockets his phone, "I wanted to ask you something."

He tilts his head back and eyes me curiously. "What is it?"

"You seem like you know more about this place than I do," I hedge carefully. "I was just wondering if there's a place I can make some quick cash."

Jake shoves one hand into his pocket and lifts the other to scratch the underside of his jaw. "What kinda cash we talkin'?"

I stride forward slowly until we're chest to chest and then I reach up and tap the pocket against his chest, feeling the joint I knew would be there. "I think you know the kind I'm talkin' about."

He fights it. I see it. He fights it hard, but the longer I stand there, smirking up at him, the more I see him caving. He grins. "Alright, alright," he says, withdrawing his phone once more. "Gimme your number. I'll text you some times and locations. It's just some fun. If you wanna fight, I can introduce you to the bookie so you can get on the docket, but—"

I stop him right there. "I'm not a fighter."

He pauses and arches a brow as his finger swipes across the screen of his phone. "Bullshit," he says.

I shrug. "Alright then," I say. "Let me clarify. I don't fight for cash."

"Huh." His lips twitch. "Never would've figured that."

He's curious, but I don't say anything more and like the smart guy he is, he doesn't ask. We exchange phone numbers and I head off my way as he heads off his.

I grab a quick sandwich to go and start off around the campus, just walking aimlessly—not really ready to go back to the dorm and not really sure what else there is to do around here. I'm halfway down the row of buildings full of classrooms when I hear someone yelling.

"Hey! Hey, new girl!" Out of curiosity, I turn as a girl

with short, choppy hair comes sprinting down the sidewalk, a designer bookbag—holy shit, designer bookbags are a thing?—hanging over her shoulder. "Yeah! You!" She points and I turn again, wondering who the fuck this chick is trying to track down. When I realize she's not pointing at anyone behind me, but actually *at me*, my eyebrows shoot up into my hairline, and I slowly pivot back to face her as she comes to a startlingly abrupt halt before me.

She wheezes, one hand on her chest, "Sorry, just … give me like two seconds. God, I need to work out more."

"What do you need, rich bitch?" I ask.

She freezes but shockingly, instead of getting offended she gives me a sheepish smile. "It was the new girl comment, wasn't it?" she asks. "Sorry 'bout that," she says, straightening up. "I don't know your name or I would've used that instead." One perfectly manicured hand shoots out. "I'm Corina Harrison."

I flick my tongue between my teeth and narrow my eyes on her. "No thanks," I say, ignoring the outstretched hand. "I'm not interested."

The girl makes a noise somewhere between a gasp and a grunt as she reaches out and snags my arm as I turn to go. Once again, my brows go up. "Please wait!" she says.

"You wanna keep that hand?" I warn her.

She grimaces but remains locked on me. "I promise, I'm not here to do anything mean."

As if she could, I think. Still, her words come out in a rush of breath as she follows me when I try to take a step away. Short of shaking her off like a mangy mutt, there's not much I can do unless I want to get violent. I'm debating it, but looking at her big eyes and smooth face, it's kind of hard. Despite the fact that this girl obviously belongs at Eastpoint—the expensive backpack, the pound of perfect make-up on her face, the manicure, and the three inch wedges on her feet that probably cost more than my mom's rent—she's got this girl next door vibe about her. I know I called her a rich bitch, but what kind of girl would come chasing after somebody like me? My curiosity stays the violent tendencies telling me to break her fingers. If she pisses me off, though, it's still an option.

I huff out a breath. "What do you want?" I finally ask.

Her face brightens. "I was wondering if you would go out with me."

Shock ricochets through me. "Um … I'm flattered, but sorry, I am—unfortunately—purely a dick kinda bitch. It's unfortunate, but I like cock not pussy."

Confusion ripples over her features until she realizes what she said. "Oh, no!" she squeals. "No! I didn't mean it like that. I'm—oh my gosh—what I meant was that I'm going to Urban and I heard that you kinda had a thing going on with the Sick Boys so—"

"Stop." I hold a hand up, effectively silencing her display of word vomit. "Where the fuck did you hear that I have a thing going on with the Sick Boys?" I grimace as that stupid ass nickname comes out of my mouth. Sick Boys, my ass. But fine, whatever, if it's what everyone else calls them and everyone else understands them as, I'll say that shit. Doesn't mean it's true though.

Big brown eyes—that remind me of the little brats from my old neighborhood when the ice cream truck would come around—look up at me. "From them," she says.

I'm going to kill those fuckers, I think. I pry my arm out of her grip and as soon as she realizes that I'm not about to bounce, she releases me. "Well, sorry to break it to you"—I'm really fucking not sorry at all—"but your information's wrong. I ain't shit to them and they ain't shit to me."

She bites her lip. "So, you're not with them?" she clarifies.

"I'd rather be dropped off a cliff," I say brightly.

"Oh." She wavers on her wedges, chewing silently on her lower lip. "Well, I mean, do you still want to come?"

I snort. "You're really asking me that?"

Her shoulders move up and down. "Why not? You don't have many friends, do you? And have you ever been to Urban before? It's really fun."

I don't even know what Urban is. My answer is to cross my arms and eye her speculatively. "Is it dangerous?" I ask.

She shakes her head. "No, of course not."

"Then no thanks." I drop my arms and start off.

The clicking of her solid shoes hit the pavement as she follows after me. "Are you sure?" she beseeches. "There's dancing and—"

I groan but don't say anything as I make my strides longer, causing her to lag behind a bit as she struggles to catch up. That's what happens when you wear heels—anyone in Converse can outrun you.

"It's run by the Carter family, though!"

I stop dead, slowly turning back to face her and wincing when she finally catches up and ends up plowing right into me. Her backpack slips down one delicate shoulder. "Oomph, sorry," she mutters.

"Dean Carter?" I ask.

As if sensing my newfound interest, she smiles. "Yeah. The very one. If he's off from football practice and isn't throwing a party, he and the guys usually go. You can probably go clear things up with them if you want."

Yes, that sounds like a great idea. "Alright," I say, "but I'm bringing a friend."

She practically beams. "Awesome! I'll pick you guys up

in front of your dorm on Friday." Corina bounces away, lifting her backpack strap over her shoulder again.

"How do you know which—"

She giggles, looking back. "You're in the Havers Dorm," she answers before I'm even through with my question. "Everyone knows that program students live there."

With that, she whips around and struts off, her legs straightening as her heels clack on the ground. Sprinting in heels is pretty impressive, even I have to admit, but most girls wouldn't be able to, and why anyone would want to walk around like a clumsy deer is beyond me. I stand there, musing over that when her words actually hit me. Everyone knows that program students live in the Havers dorm and everyone knows that I'm a program student. Ergo, everyone on this campus knows where I live.

Fuck my life. Damn, I hope shit doesn't start stirring, or else I'm going to have to go off the deep end. And if that happens, it won't matter what threat those Sick Boys might throw my way—off the deep end Avalon is a bitch no one wants to mess with.

19

AVALON

Two days later, I get a text message from the rich girl who flagged me down. I'm not even going to ask how she got my phone number. I have my suspicions. Jake comes to mind. These people seem to get anything they want and I did tell him I was looking for a specific kind of trouble. As it stands, Eastpoint isn't that big of a school. Plus, I bet for these kids, if they've got the money—which they do—they can get any information they want. Dean certainly did.

I get off my bed and kick the end of Rylie's as I head to my closet. "Get up," I say. "We're going out."

She rips her headphones out. "What?"

Sliding my t-shirt over my head, I grab a tank and pull it on. "We're going out," I repeat.

Her eyes narrow. "Where?" she demands immediately.

I laugh and wiggle out of my pajama shorts, reaching for a pair of skinny cut jeans with holes cut out across the knees. "Out," I state.

Rylie rolls her eyes and plugs her headphones back into her ears. "Not happening," she says.

I finish dressing and yank my long hair out of its ponytail. Hanging down my back, it's nearly to my ass. Shit, I need to get it cut soon. Without even bothering to give her a chance to fight back, I grab Rylie's leg and yank her off the bed until her entire lower half slams into the floor.

"What the fuck?" she snaps.

"Oh look, you're up," I deadpan as she growls and struggles to get to her feet. I grab my phone and check the time. "Well, you better hurry—our ride will be here in less than twenty minutes."

"Ride?" she blurts. "Why didn't you tell me about this if you had it planned? And who the hell is picking us up?"

"I didn't tell you because I wanted to make sure you wouldn't run away." I smile. If looks could kill … Rylie would be figuring out a way to get rid of a body right about now.

For a full minute she stares at me, her hazel eyes narrowed and full of irritation. I blink slowly back at her, waiting and knowing I'll get my way. There's no way in hell I'm getting in Corina Harrison's car alone. I don't trust the chick and even if Rylie doesn't like me much, she's been far more honest than I suspect Corina has been. There's absolutely no way she didn't know my name if Dean's had his minions spreading shit.

"Where are we going?" she demands, finally caving as she slides the rest of the way off her bed and heads to her own closet.

I think back, trying to remember the name of the club Corina had told me about. "Urban."

She freezes and looks at me. "Urban?" She repeats the word as if it leaves a sour taste in her mouth. "Are you shitting me?"

"Not at the moment." I rake my fingers through my dark hair, trying to comb out the knots and snags as much as I can. My brush is somewhere in this room, but a quick survey doesn't turn it up. Oh well.

Rylie turns, leaning against the frame of her closet door as she watches me through slitted eyes. She crosses her arms over her chest. "And just where did you find the kind of money to go to Urban? Drinks aren't cheap, you know."

"I didn't say anything about money," I reply. I grab the bag of extra make-up samples and old dollar store eyeliner pencils and get to work. She remains with her side against the doorframe for several minutes, watching as I finish my make-up. It's not much, but then again, I'm only wearing it so I blend in rather than stick out. I'm on an information hunting mission tonight.

"I don't want to go to Urban," she states plainly.

"I don't really care what you want," I say. "You're going or else."

She bares her teeth at me. "Or else fucking what?" she bites back.

I grin, turning slowly to face her. Reaching back, I gather my hair into a fist—it's thick, and several strands slip out as I wrangle it up towards the back of my head. "Or else I'll tell Dean Carter you're on lockdown."

Her eyes widen and her arms drop to her sides. "Holy shit!" She gapes at me. "It's fucking true?" I don't say anything. It's a gamble, but I have a feeling that these rumors that have been trickling through Eastpoint have something to do with Dean and me. No one has come right out and said it—other than Corina, of course—but I have a feeling that he thinks staking a claim on me is his way of branding my ass and making everything I do somehow sanctioned by the Sick Boys—ergo, I can't fuck with their authority.

I shrug absently and quickly apply a layer of chapstick

to my mouth before popping the lid back on and heading for the door that leads to the hallway. "You coming or what?" I call over my shoulder.

"Shit—fuck!" I grin as her panicked words reach my ears. Stepping out into the hallway, I lean my back against the wall as I listen to the sounds of her scrambling to get changed. Not two minutes later, the door to our room flies open and she steps out, panting.

Rylie's chest heaves up and down beneath a mesh black top that covers a tank. Her long, pale legs gleam beneath the fluorescent hallway lighting and her combat boots make her look like she's on her way to kick some ass rather than go to a club. Her faded purple hair is pulled back and braided down her back. I smirk when she points a finger at me.

"You're a fucking bitch, you know that," she snaps. "And I swear to God if you pull me into any of your shit, I'm going to kill you in your sleep."

I step close to her until her breath is right against my chin, and she looks up with a glare. "You don't have the fucking balls, Ry," I say with a laugh.

She growls. "Try me."

I could. Oh, I really could. But despite how I kinda like to fuck with her, I think Ry's as real as it gets. My phone beeps and after a quick check, I gesture for her to go ahead. "Let's go," I tell her.

She huffs out one more breath and this time, when she speaks, her tone turns serious. "I hope you know what you're doing, Avalon," she says, "because if you're really fucking with the Sick Boys, it's not going to turn out well. There's a lot more to them that you don't know."

I pause at the top of the staircase and look back. "And you do?" I mean the question. Rylie does seem to be far more aware of things than I expect a girl who professes to want nothing more than to keep her head down to be. I don't know if it's simply because of her background—whatever that may be—or if it's something more.

Our eyes meet and for a second there's an understanding there. She *does* know something. Whatever it is, though, she won't say. Whether out of fear or self preservation, I don't know. I do know what it's like to want to protect yourself. An ancient memory surfaces in the back of my mind—something cold and sinister, something I thought I'd buried a long time ago. Unwilling to go there, I shove it down and slap on a smile.

"Never mind," I say. "Forget it."

Rylie doesn't say anything more—at least, not until we get outside, and together, we spot a red Ferrari parked at the curb. Corina looks up and waves as we approach. "What the fuck…" Rylie's words aren't loud enough for Corina to hear, but they make me glance her way.

I raise my brow when I notice how tight her hands get as she curls them into fists against the thin meshy fabric of the sleeves of her over shirt. "Hey!" Corina leans over and yells through the rolled down window. "Let's go! We're late!"

Yanking my attention away from Rylie's face, I turn to the girl in the car. "There's no time limit," I say as I crack the door open.

"Yeah, but I want to get there already," Corina whines.

I eye her. "You haven't been drinking yet, have you?"

She shakes her head. "No, but I'm planning on it. So, if we could *go*—oh is that your friend?"

"Yeah, she's—"

"I'll ride in the back," Rylie announces as she appears at my side.

"Sure…" I barely get the word out before she's shoving

the front passenger seat forward and climbing into the tiny back portion.

"Well, at least someone's smart enough to realize when Mama needs a margarita," Corina says. "Come on." She waves me in and I roll my eyes as I crawl into the incredibly small interior of what must be a million dollar car. The leather feels like fucking gold under my ass. Maybe more than a million dollars.

Corina grins as the door closes behind me and revs the engine. "Urban here we come!" she shouts excitedly.

My seatbelt clicks into place and as she puts her foot to the gas, I glance back. Rylie is staring at the back of Corina's head in a way that can only be described as pure fear. I'm not exactly sure why, but now is definitely not the time to ask. I flip back around just as the car slides into traffic and speeds forward, throwing me against the seat. Hopefully, we'll actually make it to the fucking club before we all perish.

20

AVALON

The lights in the club are dim, but what looks like paint is splattered across the floor, walls, and even the bar. Heavy rock-pop music echoes up towards the rafters. Corina pulls both Rylie and me through the crowd, heading straight for the long counter where two bartenders buzz back and forth, filling drink orders and passing out bills.

"Three rum and cokes," Corina calls from the end of the bar, lifting her hand high in the air. The bartender closest to us catches sight of her—or rather, her fucking massive tits as they nearly jiggle straight out of her tube top—and hurries over to collect her card.

I let my eyes wander. The place is massive. Three stories tall at least, but only the first floor has a full layout. The top two look like open balconies that line the perimeter. I can just barely make out people sitting on lounges and at tables that overlook the floor as they watch the rest of us below. Most eyes, though, are on the dance floor that acts as the centerpiece to the entire place. Even at this early hour, it's crowded with people.

"Here ya go!" A drink is shoved into my hand in one second and by the time I have the chance to look up, Corina's already downed half of hers.

"I don't drink," Rylie states, setting hers down on the counter. "But thanks anyway." She looks awkward and uncomfortable. For a brief moment, I regret forcing her to come, but truth be told, I didn't want to be here alone with Corina. I used her to get me here, but the fact is—I don't trust her. And Rylie, for all her claims that she doesn't like me, doesn't seem like the worst person to have at my back.

Not that I've ever had a friend at my back before, I think. *Shit. Maybe it really was a poor idea to bring her along.*

Before I can say anything, though, Rylie's head tips up and she looks past me. Her whole body stiffens up. "Hey, um, you need me around right now?" she asks.

I follow her gaze, but I can't see whatever it is she's looking at. So, I flip back to her and arch a brow. "Not really..."

"Cool, I'm gonna take off. Text me when you leave or if you need something and I'll catch up."

I blink and she's gone. "Well, that didn't last long," Corina says with a giggle as she slams back the rest of her drink before replacing it with Rylie's abandoned one. "Then again, I'm not surprised. She never comes to these kinds of places. It's not really her style."

My eyes settle on Corina. "What do you mean by that?"

She sips at her new drink and shrugs. "Oh, nothing really." Her gaze trails away and I have the distinct feeling that she's lying.

I set my own drink on the counter with a scowl. "I'm not here to have a good time," I state. "I'm just here to find those assholes and get some answers."

Corina looks up at me and smiles, her lips still sealed

around the straw in her glass. "Well, don't look now," she says around it, "but I think I've found them for you." She nods towards a place on the upper floors just behind me and I find myself turning and following her gaze. And she's right. There they are.

The two fuckboys I'd first had a run in with are sitting on either side of their King, laughing like hyenas as they let girls climb all over them. It's startling to see how friendly they are and then how empty the area surrounding him is. I can't say I don't like it.

"Don't wait up," I say absently as I leave the drink and Corina behind, making my way to a darkened staircase just beneath where they sit. Hopefully, it'll lead me straight to them.

I take the stairs two at a time and when I come up to the top, a familiar, broad-shouldered bozo steps in my path. I grin. "Well, hey there," I say, eyeing him up and down. "Long time no see."

The guy's eyes widen when he realizes who I am and I feel a sense of accomplishment when he subtly moves his lower body back a step. Smart move. "Let her through, Eli." Dean's voice echoes back to us. The behemoth looks at me once more, scanning me from head to toe as if he's expecting me to be decked out in weapons, and when he sees there's obviously nothing here but little, ol' me, he finally steps to the side.

"Thanks ... *Eli*," I say, patting the guy on the shoulder as I walk past. "Do me a favor and keep everyone else out for a hot minute, yeah?"

"He doesn't follow your orders, little girl," Dean says as I move forward. My eyes clash with his as I move onto the balcony. Though there's obviously other people on the second floor, as I glance around, I see they have this section roped off for their exclusive use. Perks of being the owner's son, I suppose. Corina did say that this was his family's club.

"I'm not little," I say as I step around a low table and come to stand right in front of him.

Those obscure eyes of his look up at me through long, equally dark lashes. Then he stands, towering over me enough that I have to tip my head back to look at him. "Want to correct that statement?" he asks.

"*Nope*." My hands settle on my hips and I smile, slow and evil as his eyes track their movements. "And you should be careful—just because you're taller doesn't exactly mean I'm little. Remember, I'm closer to hell and there's a whole lot of fury packed inside this tight body."

I choose my words carefully, specifically, and when his eyes widen a fraction, I know I've made the right decision. They dart down to the rest of me before coming back up to my face. He scowls. "What do you want?" he demands.

Without missing a beat, I take a small step back and sit down. Right on the surface of the table in front of the lounge. Smart choice too because just as I sink down, I see the realization that crosses his mind as I'm left eye level with his crotch. My head tilts back and my smile widens.

Dark eyes glare at me before he lifts his head. "Get out," he barks to the girls grinding on both Abel's and Brax's laps. Abel's responding groan of disappointment reaches my ears, but I don't dare tear my eyes away from the man in front of me. We've got a score to settle and it is by no means even yet.

They must have the girls well trained because I don't even hear a single peep from them as they slide off their prospective partners for the night and disappear down the stairs. Dean takes that moment to lift his eyes from mine. "Make sure no one else comes up or crosses over," he orders. If Eli answers, I don't hear. I simply wait for him to meet my gaze again. And when he does, it's like wildfire rippling through my system.

Sometimes, it's hard to see what's going on inside that controlling mind of his, but right now, I know. He's pissed.

"Well, are we going to get this over with or what?" Abel snaps when several more minutes go by without either one of us speaking. "I wanna get laid sometime tonight."

I arch a brow. "That's up to your boss," I reply. "What do you say, D-man, wanna get this over with?"

He sighs and takes a step back, removing his pants-covered cock from my face as he sinks back into his seat. "What the fuck do you want?"

What do I want? I want a lot of things. I want people to leave me the fuck alone. I want to be able to crawl into any ol' bed and sleep like a fucking log without thinking about what I could be waking up to. I want fucking freedom. But I settle for less because there's no other option.

"The truth," I state plainly.

He arches a brow, and for the first time since I came up here, I cut a glance side to side to see the others' reactions. Just like Dean, their faces are wiped clean of anything useful. No emotion. It's like they've trained to appear as the indomitable assholes that they portray. They probably are.

"What truth is that?" Dean asks.

My eyes meet his from beneath my lashes. "Don't act stupid now, Mr. Carter," I say. "If you're the one sitting in that middle seat," I nod towards him, "then, we both know you're not. I want to know why there's a rumor going around that I'm your property."

He doesn't hesitate. "Because you are."

My hands curl into fists and I have to will away the desire to punch him in his cruelly handsome face. You know, it's honestly not fair for pricks like him to look the way they do. "Well, look at that," I say, keeping my voice purposefully light and unassuming. "Not two minutes after I tell you that you aren't dumb, you prove me wrong. Good for you."

Out of the corner of my eye, I see movement. Turning my head, I watch as Brax leans forward, placing his elbows on his knees as he stares at me. He meets my gaze and reaches back with one hand, removing a cigarette pack from his back pocket. He slaps it against the palm of his hand once, twice, three times before ripping the plastic wrapping off and tossing it on the end of the table I'm currently sitting on. Sticking the end of one between full, masculine lips, he lights it.

A hand grasps my chin and Dean pulls me back around to meet his gaze. "You may not like it, little girl," he says, "but you're the reason we had to make it happen like this."

I narrow my eyes on his. "What the fuck is that supposed to mean?"

He doesn't smile. In fact, he looks more like he'd rather choke me out than put any sort of claim on me. "You refuse to fall in line," he says. "You don't follow our rules. You want the truth, baby? The truth is we don't trust you."

"So, why not kick me out then?" I ask. I'm not asking because I want it, but I am curious. It seems the easiest solution to all of his problems. Why hasn't he taken it?

He scowls and releases my chin. I blink. *Holy shit.* I hadn't even realized he'd touched me. Normally, I didn't let people—especially guys—touch me. *What the fuck is wrong with me?*

"You don't need to know why I do what I do," he grits out, sitting back. "All you need to know is that as long as you don't cause any more problems, we'll let you remain off lockdown. It's better for you this way. You should be grateful."

"Grateful…" I repeat the word with no small amount of skepticism. The only thing I've ever been grateful for in my entire life is my ability to adapt. Throw me to the wolves and I come back leading the pack. *That's just what this is*, I realize. *Another fucking test.* Well, I'm done playing things the Sick Boys' way. They want to play at being Kings, then I want to see how they react when a savage enters their midst. They have no clue what's about to happen now.

I smirk. "I get it," I say. "You've sanctioned my actions, haven't you?" I laugh. "You had to," I realize. "Because this way, if I do something that pisses someone off or gets me into trouble—it'll look like you gave the go ahead for it." I stand and their eyes follow me, but I only have my sights set on Dean. Leaning over, I run my hand down his chest as he stiffens and glares at me, unspeaking. I hook two fingers into the opening of his collar and drag him forward until my lips are just inches from his and I can smell the vodka on his breath. "All so you can remain in *control*." I chuckle darkly as I emphasize that last word.

If looks could kill…

If bodies could be made of stone…

If assholes who look like gods and acted like Kings could truly exist…

"I'll teach you to try and control me, Dean Carter," I whisper against his mouth. "And I don't think you're going to enjoy this lesson."

21

DEAN

Fuck, I think. Fuck. Fuck. FUCK! Damn her.

I stand against the balcony railing, my eyes glued to her ass below as she rocks that body against her newfound friend. I hate it. I hate her. And at the same time … I like it. She fucking called me out. Figured it out a lot faster than I expected. She's smarter than I gave her credit for and that's saying something since I've seen the inside of that file my father gave me. There's far more to Avalon Manning that likely even she knows. Otherwise, she wouldn't have grown up in that shithole trailer park in Plexton.

"What now?" Abel asks.

An unlit cigarette dangles from my lips. One glance back tells me Brax has already bailed for the night. "Nothing changes," I answer. "She's still under surveillance. They want her here, so she stays here." There's no doubt between us who *they* are, but just the reminder makes my muscles clench.

I don't like the people she's starting to surround herself with. She doesn't know it yet—perhaps she suspects—but we've had her in our sights since the Frazier House party. I know each and every person she's talked to. I know who brought her here tonight. My eyes trail to the woman in question. With ties like hers, I don't want Avalon anywhere near the bitch. Saying so, however, would reveal too much. And it's not like the girl is actually mine. It's all in name only. I don't look into how that makes me feel either. To do so would be bringing on more trouble than I need.

What does interest me, however, is the roommate. I wonder if Gloria planned that. If not her, then one of the old men certainly did. There's no doubt in my mind that the purple-haired chick knows more than she lets on. Poor Pauper Princess. She has absolutely no fucking idea that she's being herded. Even still, she's fighting it. Fighting it like a true queen would.

"Heard she contacted Hayes," Abel says as a waitress appears at his side. He takes the drink she offers and tips it against his lips. "Any idea where that's going? Do you think we should put a stop to it?"

"No," I say. "I wanna see what she does. If she's just out to make a quick buck, let it happen. If she gets into any of the harder stuff…" Well, then I'd know exactly what kind of person she is. Just like her mother. Trash. "We'll deal with it if it becomes an issue."

I can feel his gaze on my face as I stare down below. The way her ass sways in those jeans is doing things to my head. I try to tear my gaze away and find that I can't. Her shirt slips up as her arms raise. My eyes immediately go to the strip of skin she's revealed around her stomach. I can't help imagining what she'd let a man do to that shadow of a belly button. Would she protest if I licked it? Would she urge my head lower? Fuck. I should *not* be thinking about this. I shouldn't be thinking about her at all.

She's had a few drinks since she stomped down there

earlier. I imagine she's feeling the buzz about now. She'd be ripe for the taking. My mind takes that thought and supplies a scenario where she's laid out on my bed, hazy with the booze in her system—thick thighs spread wide. All for the taking.

"You're watching her awfully hard for someone who claims to not even like her," Abel comments. "You sure I can't take a hit off her? The old men did say 'by any means necessary.'" A snarl works its way up my throat. He chuckles, knocking my shoulder with his as he turns around and takes a step away from the railing. "Chill, bro. I'm just fucking with you. She's all yours. You called dibs."

"She's not mine," I snap. "She's a person of interest for the business. Nothing more."

"For them, maybe," he agrees before shooting me a look. "But not for you. What's the harm in fucking her?"

What's the harm indeed … something tells me that even two seconds in bed with Avalon Manning could cause a lot of fucking harm. She's the type of woman that topples hierarchies for fun. And though she doesn't know it, I know her dirty little secret. I know what gets her blood pumping. I know that parts of her records were expunged and I know why. Not even her mother can say she knows her daughter as well as I do. Then again, addicts don't know shit else but their drug of choice.

Now that I've found Avalon's, I wonder what'll become of us next.

I'm considering that when I chance another look down and watch as another man moves in behind her. His hands settle on those perfect hips of hers and his head tilts down until his lips graze her neck.

I see red.

22

AVALON

Sweat turns my hair into wet tendrils that stick to my flushed neck. Yet, still, there aren't enough shots and alcoholic drinks in the world that can dull the ache of fury in my veins. I dance next to Corina, my body moving easily to the beat of music that thrums beneath my feet and in the surrounding air.

"Now this is what I'm talking about," Corina yells over the music.

I ignore her. Fueled by rage and alcohol, I let my eyes close and I just move the way I want to. I arch my back and lift my hands to my hair, pulling the strands away from my skin. When my eyes reopen, I notice that Corina's gaze is zeroed above my head. I don't need to turn around to know who she's looking at. She grins when she looks back at me, her smile making a few guys to the left of us take notice. They move closer, making my spine stiffen. I'm fine as long as they keep their distance. A scowl overtakes my face as she leans forward, her lips grazing my earlobe when she says something in a voice barely a level above the music pounding in my ears. "He's watching."

Good, I think. *Let him.* Right now, the thing I want most in the word is Dean Carter's eyes on me. He might've put a claim on my ass to the rest of the school, but he and I both know the truth. He doesn't own me and he's going to regret pissing me off. No matter what I have to do to make that happen.

Feeling wicked and naughty, I lose myself in the dancing. I've been to backwoods parties with bonfire dances run by rednecks with jacked up monster trucks and radios blaring music meant to get people fucked up. A club is different. The beat of the music mimics the same pace of a good, hardcore fuck and the people seem to realize that.

Girls grind on girls. Guys watch. Guys with girls move slow—regardless of the pace that the music takes. Hard hands find my hips and I freeze. Corina's paying no mind; her own attention has been diverted to one of the lingering guys from earlier as he pulls her into a dance.

I stop dancing immediately. The desire to rip the guy's arms out of his sockets and beat him with them swells. "Get your fucking hands off me," I snap.

Mr. Idiot doesn't do that, though. No, he's not that smart. Instead, he leans closer, pressing an obvious erection against my ass as he dips his head and presses his mouth to my neck. "Come on, sweetheart. Don't be like that. I was watching you dance. You're pretty agile," he says. "Tell me something, you dance like that for a guy if you're all alone too?"

Cold rage spirals through me, but I don't even have the opportunity to react. All of a sudden, his hands are gone and I'm thrust forward. My palms hit the floor as I go down, my knees skidding against the rock hard surface of the dance floor where the sound of fists hitting flesh reaches my ears. I slowly get to my feet, turning back to see what the fuck just happened.

Dean stands there, his chest rising and falling rapidly—eyes wild and furious. What the fuck does he have to be furious about? That emotion should be solely reserved for me. Asshole. My thoughts are disrupted when he bends over, grabbing a guy on the ground up by the front of his ripped shirt, and drags him back to his feet as he throws yet another punch.

Mesmerizing.

I'm rooted to the spot as I watch him fight. Except, it's not really a fight because it's far too one-sided. Does it make me a pervert to admit, though, that watching Dean release his anger kind of...turns me on?

"You don't fucking touch her, do you understand me?" His words bring me back to the present.

"I'm sorry!"

My eyes fall to the guy in his grasp. His face is a bloody mess, and honestly, the only thing I don't like about it is the fact that I wasn't the one to make it like that.

"I didn't know she was yours."

"Well, now you fucking do, fucker," Dean snarls, slamming his closed fist into the guy's face one last time so hard that his eyes roll back into his head and the guy slumps onto the floor. He turns to me and looks over my shoulder as he speaks. "Get security to clean this fucking mess up. We're leaving," he snaps.

I scowl and back up as he reaches for me. "Don't fucking touch me."

Dean's eyes flash and instead of reaching for me again, he simply steps forward and bends down—shoving his shoulder into my stomach as he lifts and throws me right over it. "Hey!" I shriek. "Put me the fuck down!"

Instead of doing as I fucking said, though, Dean keeps walking, his movements making me bounce on his shoulder

PRETTY LITTLE SAVAGE

as I try to fight my way off. "Is this what you fucking wanted?" he growls.

"What are you talking about?" I reply, pushing against his spine even as his arm clamps around the backs of my legs.

I only know we've left the club by the way the air is suddenly not nearly as stifling and how the volume of people and music dissipates almost immediately. "Go get the car," he snaps to someone I can't see.

"I mean it," I say again, "put me the fuck down, Dean. Right now."

My whole world is upended once again as he finally releases me and swings me back to my feet. My legs buckle as my feet hit the ground, but it's obvious that we're not done because no sooner am I back on my feet and he's shoving my back against the brick exterior of the building, his angry brown eyes glaring down at me.

"Do you have any clue what that stunt of yours just did?" he asks.

I glare straight back at him. "I didn't fucking pull a stunt," I reply coldly. "But if you want, I can go back in right now and do something far worse—you've got it coming. If you think that—which was not my fault, by the way—was bad, you have no idea what I'm planning to do to you for those little rumors of yours."

"You listen to me, little girl." His face hovers in front of me. A lock of hair falls over his forehead as a shadow dances across his cheek from the nearby streetlight. "Your ass is mine—though in name only. You are a Sick Boy possession. Nothing more. But that means that no one is allowed to fucking touch you, do you understand. So, whatever fun you had planned, you can forget it. For the duration of your stay here at Eastpoint, expect a very cold bed. There will be no sex, no fucking, or *boyfriends*," he spits the word like it leaves a vile taste in his mouth. "Am I understood?"

"That right there," I say, nodding at him as I gaze up into his face. He's fucking delusional if he thinks I'm going to bow to any of his demands. "Making those little decrees of yours is what got you into this problem." I push up on my tiptoes until we're eye to eye. "I'm not one of your peasants and I'm certainly not one of your *possessions*."

The sound of a car pulling up makes both of us freeze, but when he lifts his head and looks back there's no concern on his face. In fact, there's no emotion at all as far as I can see. Dean's arm wraps around my middle and much like in the club, he picks me up without a single issue. I could be a sack of laundry for all the effort he puts into lifting me.

My back hits leather and as I scramble up onto my elbows, he gets into the backseat of whatever car we're in with me and pushes me back down. "What is your fucking deal!" I scream as I buck under him.

He curses and his hands fly to my wrists. Fingers wrap around my arms and pin them above my head and the world comes to a screeching halt when I feel it. My eyes widen and I glance down.

"You've got to be fucking joking," I snap, snarling at him. "Are you serious right now?"

He doesn't react, but I can still feel him there against my inner thigh. The most shocking thing, however, isn't that he's hard—it's that it's not pissing me off that he is. I shake my head. It's probably because I'm already pissed off.

I throw my hips up, trying to unseat him, and squirm against his grip. "If you don't stop fucking moving," he grits out. "I'm going to turn your ass over and spank it."

"Try it," I challenge. "And I'll slice your balls clean off."

He doesn't do anything and I chuckle darkly. A singular dark brow lifts over one of his eyes. "You seem to think you have some sort of decision in everything that's happening," he says, "but I've got news for you, sweetness." He leans down and I inhale sharply at the feel of his teeth grazing my earlobe. "Everything that's happening is because of you. This is all the result of your fucking childish actions. If you don't stop acting like a brat, I really will spank you. You can try to cut my balls off, but I promise you that you're going to want them for something else so I'd suggest you leave my man parts alone."

"I'm never going to fuck you."

When he lifts his head, the smile that overtakes his face is anything but kind. It's cruel and menacing. Dark and wicked. Had I really once told Rylie that these guys were nothing but preppy rich assholes? The look on his face says otherwise. It's that look and the blood still coating his knuckles from the guy he knocked out just for touching me that make me think that maybe ... just fucking maybe they've earned their ridiculous moniker as Sick Boys.

"Who said I was going to give you a choice?"

My blood runs cold. "Did you just threaten to rape me?"

Dean's lips part and his tongue swipes across his perfectly straight and perfectly white upper teeth as he looks down on me. That smile remains. The car stops and he backs off as the car door opens and he reaches back inside, grabbing me by my upper arms as he hauls me out of the car. My back hits the front lawn of the Havers dorm as he tosses me down.

"I never said I was a good man," he states, looking down on me. Abel was our driver, I realize, as he lowers the front window of the SUV—interesting that it wasn't the Mustang this time—and watches on. "In fact," Dean continues, "this is your official warning. Follow our rules, don't make any more noise, and you won't have to learn just how sick I can really be, Avalon."

With that, he turns around and gets back into the SUV. Abel takes one look at me, Braxton glancing over his shoulder from the passenger side, and rolls up the window before taking off.

I throw an arm over my face as I lay there on the wet, dewy grass. "Cowards," I spit out. The three of them are nothing but cowards. They think they're invincible. My arm lowers and my eyes lift to the night sky. Stars sparkle far above.

They may be powerful, but no one is invincible.

Even I know that.

23

AVALON

I'M BEING STARED AT. THE PRICKLY FEELING ONLY SERVES to irritate me even more than I already am. Turning my cheek, I fix the guy doing the staring—a grubby-handed man with a graying beard that looks more like a poodle's ass than an actual beard—with a dark glare. He blinks, dull blue eyes seeming surprised. He shouldn't be. He's been fucking staring at me for the last three stops. Finally, he ducks his head and looks away, shoving his hands into the pockets of his hoodie as he scoots along the bus seat towards the dirty window as far from me as possible without getting up and moving seats. I huff out a breath and pull out the map I'd grabbed from the bus station when I'd gotten on an hour before.

I'd left before Rylie got up this morning, but it's not like she would've cared. She's still kind of pissed at me for ditching her at Urban. Then again, it wasn't like I had a choice. A scowl forms across my face at the reminder, Dean Carter's features coming to my mind. I imagine reaching out and punching him in his perfectly straight nose. I want to see it crooked and broken. Blood in his teeth. I wonder if he'd still have that same callous look he had the last time I saw him.

Fucking prick. I bet he would.

I'm about five miles outside of Eastpoint—the city, not the university—and the farther away I get, the easier breathing feels. I hadn't even realized I was suffocating under their thumb. At first, it'd just been the party, but then with what happened at the club, it appears I'm no longer allowed to just have my anonymity.

If one more fucking bitch tries to cuddle up to me in class, I'm going to stab their eyes out with a pencil, I swear inwardly. I blame them for what I'm about to do. It's completely their fault. The Sick Boys.

Had it not been for Dean's proclamation, I wouldn't now be dealing with everyone on campus and their fucking brother trying to metaphorically climb into my pants. Oh, no. No one is allowed to touch me. To touch me would mean pissing off the King of the castle. But everyone wants to be my friend and they're not even attempting to hide their intentions. I fucking hate people.

The bus slows to a stop and I check the map once more before I get up and start to move towards the front. The stranger's eyes dart up and when he catches me glaring his way, he ducks once more.

"Hey!" the driver snaps. "No moving while the bus is still going." But the bus is already almost stopped. I flip him the bird, swipe the bus card I purchased earlier, and push the doors open before he has a chance to chastise me anymore. I really don't have the energy to deal with his shit today.

My legs move with purpose as I stride to the end of the street and hang a right, following the path I memorized earlier. There, at the end of the second road is the hiking trail I came all the way out here for. I'm not wearing the right shoes for hiking—hell, I don't have any. So halfway up the first hill, I can already feel it in the soles of my feet. I inhale the pain and let it rise up through my legs. It's all just a precursor to what I'm really here for.

Dean fucking Carter thinks he can control me. He and his friends think that because they have all the money in the world that everyone around them will fall to their knees and do what they want. But that's just not who I am.

I'm not the girl who lets anyone control her.

I'm the girl that you warn your children about.

Monsters don't go bump in the motherfucking night, Avalon Manning does.

I reach the top of the final hill, feeling the ache in my calves like a wave of anxiety right before a swimmer's dive. Despite the pain, though, the second I see what I've come for, everything else fades away.

A giant lake with waters that are green with age, moss, and algae. There's no telling what's beneath their depths. I take a step towards it, spotting a flat cliffy surface on the other side of the giant walls that surround it. It looks high. It looks dangerous. It looks *perfect*.

When I reach the flat cliff, I unload my bag, dropping it and my pants to the ground. I strip my shirt over my head until I'm clad in nothing but my underwear and bra. Scrubbing a hand down my face, I take a step towards the edge and look down. One wrong move and I could slip. I could fall. Hell, there's no telling what's beneath the surface. Could be rocks. Venomous snakes. My heart begins to race, and I shiver as a cool breeze drifts across my face while I pull my hair back and secure it into a ponytail.

Every time is like the first time. I close my eyes, thinking back to the very first time I realized I was just as fucked up as Patricia and the rest of the addicts that lived in my trashy trailer park. Everyone was an addict. She'd taught me that much. Even me.

My addiction was just different.

The itching. The craving. The feeling of needing a release. It's always with me. Just beneath the surface, wanting to get out. And I push it down. I hide it until I can't deny it anymore.

The rush.

The adrenaline pouring through my system.

In Plexton, there was always a plethora of ways to get my blood pumping. Dangers were around every corner. Drug addicts and dealers. Hookers and thieves. The thing about small towns is that everyone has something they want to hide. And the smaller the town, the more obvious it becomes.

I never wanted to touch the shit Patricia fucked for. What I crave isn't nearly as easy to come across. Several strands come loose from my ponytail, but I don't reach back to re-secure them. If I'm going to do this, then there's no more holding back.

Backing up several steps, I take a deep breath—feeling the rush of awareness as it slides through my veins. I bite my lip as my blood races. My heart jackhammers inside my rib cage. I guess there's a reason why a cage surrounds the organ that keeps me alive. If it weren't there, I doubt it'd stay still. As it stands, it's trembling inside me—knowing exactly what I'm about to do.

One step. Two. Three. Four. Five. My feet slap the ground as I race towards the edge. The second I leap, my feet leaving the ground, that's when it hits me. A burst of energy. Adrenaline. Shooting straight into my bloodstream, the headiest drug of all.

Wind whips through my hair, tearing the holder I'd had strapped at the back of my head free and suddenly, the mass of dark waves slap me in the eyes. Twisting in midair, I avoid the strands. I want to see it. I look down as the water comes rushing up to greet me. And it's only just moments before I land, that I close my eyes and take in the feeling of utter peace as it washes over me.

My head hits the water first and my body follows. It's like I'm being swallowed up. Surrounded. Encapsulated by something larger than myself. I don't fight it. Instead, I let it consume me as I sink into the grotesque black-green lake. Something catches on my arm and pain slices through me. My heart is still racing, like a trapped bird slamming against the inside of its cage, trying to get out. It can't. I can't.

I can never escape this twisted desire to get as close to death as possible and feel my body fight against it. I hold my breath for several more moments, staying submerged until my lungs start to scream for air. Only then do I kick out and swim upwards.

Breaking the surface, I gasp and suck in huge gaping lungfuls of oxygen, feeling tingles throughout my entire body. Like tiny little needles being jabbed into my skin. I laugh, spinning in a circle. If anyone were here right now, they'd likely think I'd gone insane. People believe that all forms of addiction are bad, but they're wrong.

I tread water as my mind supplies the reason.

It's dark and the heat is unbearable. Sweat builds under my armpits and in my asscrack as well as other places I don't want to think about. I turn over and shove my flat pillow over onto the opposite side right before I stuff my face against it. Within seconds, however, all of the coolness it holds is absorbed into my skin, and I'm stifling in the heat once again.

Somewhere in the trailer, I hear a door open. Sounds like Patri-

cia's home. I groan and close my eyes. Only when a floorboard creaks in the hallway outside of my bedroom do I notice that something's wrong. Patricia is usually loud when she comes in. The walls are thin and I can almost always hear her retching from the bathroom. But tonight, there's no puking sound. There's nothing but utter silence ... and that creaky floorboard.

Without even stopping to consider what's happening, I roll out of bed and bolt for the single window in my bedroom. I move the plank of wood that I keep it covered with and dig my little fingers beneath the bottom of the screen, popping it open, and climbing out. The second my bare feet hit the grass below, I hear the knob of my bedroom door jiggling. I've always felt safe so long as the lock was in place, but as I remain below my open window, hands over my mouth to keep my breathing quiet, I hear something sliding between the door jamb and the door, itself. Seconds later, my bedroom door opens.

I was never safe. No matter how many locks were in place.

I don't stop to think about that. I just take off.

Sticks and stones stab into the soft underside of my foot, but I don't feel the pain. My mind is racing. Where the hell is Patricia? Does she know that someone has broken into our trailer? I know where she usually is at this time of night. If it wasn't her in the house, then that's the place I'll look.

It takes forever to get to the place I'm thinking of. Finally, I'm standing outside of one of the drug dens of Plexton Trailer Park. I'm dirty and sweaty, tired, and trembling. I just want to go to sleep. My eyes hurt from how tired I am.

Striding up the rickety wooden steps, I stop just before I knock against the cheap plastic door with its triangle window a foot or so above my head. I stop because I hear her voice. Patricia's.

"—best stuff yet," she says, sighing in what sounds like relief.

"And you'll get more so long as my guy has his fun at your place," I hear someone else say.

Patricia groans and I flinch back at how sexual it sounds. "He'll have fun. She's just a little runt. S'not like she can fight back. Just hold her down and make sure you give me what you promised when you leave."

My arm drops to my side and I take a step back and another and another until I'm far enough away that I'm sure they didn't hear me. It's time, I realize. This is it. It's finally happened. She's finally cracked. Deep down, I knew it was coming, but I don't realize until that exact moment how much I'd hoped I was wrong.

Patricia knows. *The realization hits me like a shit ton of bricks. Slamming into me from all angles. She doesn't just know. She sent them.*

I start walking.

I don't know how far I walk or for how long. All I know is that by the time I stop, my feet are bloody and bruised and my head is sore and my stomach is growling. And all I can think of is how everything is spinning.

"Hey!" The world seems out of place. I'm dizzy. "Hey, kid!"

Spinning in circles. Out of control. I have no control. There's nothing here that's tying me down. I could just … forget it all. Pretend that I don't remember anything. That none of this exists. Where would I end up?

Before I can think to answer my own thoughts, an unfamiliar face appears before me. I jump back, yelping as feeling comes back to me, and I realize just how fucked up the soles of my feet are. I stumble and go down hard, landing on my ass on rough gravel and concrete. When I glance back up, I note that the person that approached me is a girl.

She stands there, with her hands on her hips, her white-blonde hair pulled back into a tight ponytail at the back of her head, and stares down at me. "Are you stupid or what?" she demands.

I don't even have the energy to be angry at the insult. I just stare, unblinking, up at her. Her green eyes flick down to my feet and they widen. "Holy shit, kid, your feet!"

"I'm not a kid." I hear the words come from my mouth, but it

sounds like they're from someone else because the voice is too hoarse and not at all like mine.

She crouches down and gently touches the top of one of my bare feet, making me flinch. "How old are you?" she asks, examining them.

I don't know why I let her or why I answer her question, but I can't think of a reason not to. "Fifteen," I say.

She looks back up at me and grins. "I'm eighteen," she admits. "So I trump you. You're a kid."

I frown but don't say anything. I'm too fucking tired. This chick, on the other hand, doesn't seem too keen on letting me sleep as I slump over and rest my head against an old shoe that's been left in the middle of the road.

"Hey!" she snaps, grabbing my wrists and pulling me back up into a sitting position. "None of that. At least tell me your name? I'm Micki. Where do you live? Are you lost?"

"Avalon," I answer her. "And no, I'm not lost. I'm fucking homeless." Because that place back there—the trailer with Patricia—it's not a home. It's never been a home.

Micki slowly looks down my body, taking in my clothes and shoeless feet. I avoid her knowing gaze. She's got that look about her—the one that tells me she can see right through me. I've had a couple of teachers like that but not another chick my age.

"Rough night, huh, kiddo?" she asks.

I grit my teeth. "Stop calling me that."

"Why?" Getting down on her knees, Micki urges one of my arms over her shoulder. "It's what you are."

"No, it isn't." I hiss as she forces me up onto my legs and my feet feel the pain of pushing against the pavement once more.

She laughs. "Come on, let's get you cleaned up. You're lucky I saw you—normally, I don't run this way in the mornings."

Micki starts chattering on and as I let her half carry, half push me to wherever we're going, I let my mind wander. Would foster care be better? *I think.* Should I tell a teacher about Patricia when I get back? They wouldn't give a shit themselves, but they could lose *their job if they don't inform someone, right? Then again, I've heard about some of the shit that happens in foster care. It likely wouldn't be any better there. At least, with Patty, I'd know what to expect.*

"Got a lot on your mind or something?" Micki asks when we reach a decrepit looking farmhouse with a back door that looks gray and brown from dirt and age. "You haven't said anything in a while."

"Thinking," I mutter as she pushes the door open and leads me into an older kitchen with vinyl tiles and blue countertops.

"About what?" she asks absently as she settles me in a chair and hurries to the sink, grabbing a washcloth from a hook alongside the stove as she goes.

I debate telling her the truth. I don't know this chick. What could she do? For shits and giggles, I do just that. I tell her exactly what I'm thinking.

I tell her about Patricia and why I was on the road. And as I do, Micki listens. Her eyes remain surprisingly calm as she soaks the washcloth in water and helps me clean my feet of the dirt and blood so she can take a look at my cuts more closely. The sun rises into the sky and the room heats up. Every once in a while, I'll stop and take a breath, but she never rushes me. She doesn't act concerned about someone coming down and wondering what the hell this girl with bloodied feet is doing in their kitchen. No one ever does either.

"So, what are you going to do then?" she asks after I'm done.

That's just the thing. I don't know. There's a piece inside of me that's always been there. An impulsive creature that says I should go back and prove to Patricia and her fuck buddies that I'm not to be trifled with. That to fuck with me is to die. That little part of me is the reason I see flashes of Patricia's face in my mind and a knife in my hand. I want to kill her. I want to stab out her guts and watch as she bleeds. I want to see her insides on her outsides and I want her to know who's the one doing it. That's what she should get for trying to sell me to some stranger. I want her to feel the pain that I feel, the betrayal.

When I tell Micki this, too, she doesn't say anything. Instead, she takes a step back and reaches for a roll of paper towels on the counter. She rips one off and hands it to me. "What the fuck am I supposed to do with this?" *I demand, my voice croaking out.*

She gives me a soft smile and rips a new one off. Then, without a word, she raises it to my cheek and begins wiping. Tears. She's wiping my tears off ... because I'm crying. No, not just crying. I'm sobbing. It's that one act from her that sends me over the edge. My whole body begins to shake as my shoulders cave inward. Micki's arms come around me and she pulls me against her.

I don't know how long it takes for me to stop crying, but when I do, I feel even more tired than before. My body sags into the chair. Micki tosses the soaked paper towels into the trash and then moves towards what I can only assume is a laundry room with the bloody washcloths in her hand.

"I'm never going to end up like her," I hear myself say aloud. If I fall down that rabbit hole, there will be no coming back.

"Want me to teach you how to avoid it?" Micki offers.

Startled, I lift my gaze to meet hers as she steps back into the room. "You?" *I ask doubtfully.*

She smirks and then reaches down, her fingers curling under the hem of her tank top and lifts. Bruises of every shade and every level of healing mark her skin. Along her ribs and down to her abdomen and it's then that I realize they're everywhere else too. I hadn't even noticed, but there are some lighter ones on her legs and arms.

"Yes," she says. "I can show you how to fight back if you want."

I gape at her. Why? *I think.* Why the fuck would she offer to help a stranger like me? *It isn't until she barks out a sharp laugh that I realize I said that out loud.*

"Because," she answers, "I believe in karma."

"Karma?"

"Yes." She nods. "A while back someone helped me out. If they hadn't, I probably wouldn't be here. And I think it's my turn to help you."

This girl is absolutely crazy. Certifiable. But as I sit there in her strange, empty kitchen with the leaky faucet and the blue countertops and white tiled floors, I can't help but think that maybe she's right.

For someone like Patricia, karma will likely be a bigger bitch than I'll ever need to be. But until the lazy cunt gets off her ass, what's the harm in taking matters into my own hands?

"Are you in?" Micki asks, holding out her hand.

I look up at her and though my muscles are sore and tired, I lift my arm towards hers. "I'm in," I say.

IN THE PRESENT, MY EYES OPEN AS I HEAR THAT OLD VOICE. I miss it. Micki had been a fucking light in my life, a true friend if ever there was one. She'd taken me to fight rings and taught me how to predict the movements of others. She'd even participated in some of my more insane adrenaline stunts. She'd recognized that I needed it, and she'd even accepted that as long as I remained in control of the danger, everything was fine. Thinking about her reminds me though … that she isn't around anymore. She'd been three years older after all and when high school was over for her, she'd moved on.

My throat clenches, and I realize that I've been in the water for too long, I can feel the ache of coldness in my bones. It's fucking freezing. Putting one arm in front of the other, I swim to the closest shore and climb out. Black and green gunk sticks to my skin, and as I climb back up the side of the cliff in my underwear, I know I'll need a bath when I get back to the dorm.

Regardless, it was worth it. Because as I climb, all I can hear in my head is blissful silence.

24

DEAN

There is a twisted part of me that likes pain. I like the fight. The feeling of blood on my skin and broken bones under my grip. That was why—when I had Avalon pinned in the back of Brax's SUV—I'd gotten hard. It had nothing to do with the feel of her soft figure beneath my harder one. Nothing at all to do with the way her tits had strained against her top as she'd fought against me. I close my eyes and hiss out a breath as the memory threatens to do exactly what it had the first time.

The lure of battle was it. That was why. *It's the blood and not the girl*—I repeat this in my mind until it becomes a mantra.

The desire to fight and feed the demon inside is part of me that I've always had to beat back into submission, only to let it out in brief spurts. Few people know what I'm truly capable of, two of which are watching me right now as I circle my opponent.

Troy Rodriguez has been mine and my brothers' trainer for years. Ex-military grunt turned bodyguard and personal trainer, he knows everything there is to know about self defense and attack maneuvers. He's more than trained, he's lethal, and right now I want him to release all of that dangerous skill on me. I need something to get me out of my fucking head so I can stop thinking about a bratty brunette that makes my cock pulse.

I dart forward and when I know he's expecting a punch, I spin on one foot and deliver a perfect roundhouse, catching him off guard. The look of shock that echoes across his face a split second before my foot connects with his jaw is enough of a rush that when he goes down, I bounce on the balls of my feet, but don't pounce. I don't want to truly hurt the guy. When I go off on someone, I want them to deserve the pain I give them.

Troy coughs and groans as he puts a tape-covered hand to his jaw and moves it up and down it as if making sure it still works. "You're getting more brutal," he comments. For a man who's not one to give compliments, it's high praise.

Across the room, Abel's snort makes its way to my ears. "He should be. He's had a rough few weeks."

I turn and shoot him a dark glare. "Oh?" Troy gets up and gives me the once over before he moves off the mats. "Well, next week when we meet, I expect you to be in top shape. You do seem distracted today."

That irritates me. "Distracted enough to kick your ass," I snap.

Troy freezes before turning slowly towards me. "Yes," he says without inflection. His eyes, like always, are cold. "However, when you got me on the floor, you should've followed through, but you didn't," he states. "I've warned you time and again." He takes a step back towards me. I stiffen. "You may be all grown up now and kidnappings and ransom calls less likely, but in your line of work—in the line of work you're bound to inherit—there will always be those wanting to tear you down." Troy steps right up to me, his chest brushing mine.

He's older than I am by a good twenty years, but the broadness of his shoulders, the lines of muscle carved in his chest along with the smattering of old scars—bullet holes and knife wounds alike—are warning enough. He is not a man to mess with.

The thing is, neither am I.

"Anyone who wishes to do so," I state, lifting my arms wide, "is welcome to try. I didn't follow through out of respect, but I'm in a shit mood today. If you want another round, I'm more than ready to demonstrate my abilities."

We lock eyes for a brief moment, and I wonder if he'll take me up on my offer. Of all the men my father's hired over the years, Troy is the most principled. He's also one of the very few I'd ever truly trust with my life. I have, time and again. I don't want to hurt *him*. I just want to hurt *something*.

Then Troy cracks a smile and clamps me on the shoulder. "Not today, kid," he says. "I've got errands to run for your father, but if you're still feeling like this next week, maybe I'll give you a go round."

"Oh, man," Abel says. "I was hoping to see some real action take place for a change."

"Be kind to the man," Troy says, slipping away as he reaches for his gym bag and hefts it up and over his shoulder. "Seems like he's having woman troubles."

I curse under my breath and snatch my water bottle off the ground before downing half its contents in a single gulp. Troy laughs, calling me out, the old bastard. "If getting laid will make you more focused, I encourage it."

Abel snorts. "That's not exactly in the cards. He seems to have suddenly gotten a hard on for a particular girl. One who'd sooner chop off his dick than ride it."

Plastic cracks as my fist clenches around my water bottle, but I wait until Troy has retrieved the rest of his shit and says goodbye as he heads out the door before I turn and fling it at Abel. "Don't bring her up," I snarl.

Abel jerks to his feet as the bottle hits his chest, splashing him with the remaining water. It falls to the ground and he glares at me before pointing a finger at my chest. "I fucking knew it!" he snaps. "You do want to fuck her."

I'd said as much, hadn't I? Yet instead of acknowledging it, I turn away. "She's my problem. Nicholas gave her file to me—"

"Yeah, and don't think we haven't noticed that you haven't shared a single shred of that file with us," Abel says.

"You've seen the file." I drag my fingers through the sweaty strands of hair at the top of my scalp.

Something hits me in the back of the head. My own fucking water bottle. I turn, baring my teeth, but Abel is right there. He stands toe to toe with me, face red with anger. If anyone else dared to get this close when I feel like ripping the world apart, I'd break their fucking neck. As it stands, I have to remind myself that this is Abel. My best fucking friend. My brother. Even if it's not blood, he's closer to me than any relative I've ever had.

"We've seen the file we had before the old men called us to the warehouse," he says through clenched teeth, glaring at me. "Not the one they gave you. We've let it slide because we know that you're on a tight rope, but since when have we kept secrets from each other?"

Never. That's the answer. These two had been there for my first kill just as I'd been there for theirs. We knew everything about each other. We knew which girls we'd fucked and left, and we knew which ones had almost gotten deeper. I inhale and hold my breath, letting the burn of it fill my lungs before pushing it out.

"If there was anything in that file that concerned you—that was a threat to you—you'd have it," I state.

"You don't think she's a threat?" Abel's eyes widen with incredulity. "If that were true then they would have no interest in her, but they do, and now, so do you." He shoves his hand against my chest. "If I were you, I'd just fuck her and get it over with. She's just a girl. Fuck her, make her fall for you, and then you'll have complete and utter control over her."

I grab his hand and throw it off me. "Oh, like you? I don't fucking prostitute myself. If and when I fuck her, it'll have nothing to do with the old men. They do *not* control me." The words come out before I can fully think of them and even as they fly from my lips, I can visually see the effect they have on him.

A cold mask falls over his expression, masking the small hint of damaged shock I'd barely gotten a glimpse of. He takes a step back.

Shit. Fuck. Why the fuck did I say that? "Abel—"

A fist flies towards my face and I don't even try to block it. Abel's knuckles knock against my cheek with enough force that I fall back several steps. The skin on my lower lip splits and blood fills my mouth. I look up and try again. "Abel, I'm—"

He doesn't wait to hear my apology. Abel turns around and leaves the room. I fall back on the mat and groan as I throw my arm over my eyes, blocking out the light. It isn't until the mat shudders as another steps on it that I recall Braxton.

"Not smart, man." I feel him hover over me before dropping to my side.

I lift my arm, but instead of looking at him, I stare at

the tiled ceiling of our personal gym. "I fucking know. I didn't mean it like that. I was just..." *What the hell am I doing?* "He's not a prostitute," I finish lamely.

Brax chuckles darkly. "Isn't he?" he asks. "Aren't we all? We sell ourselves to the orders of our fathers if only so we can overtake them one day."

I have nothing to say to that. I can't deny it. Clenching my teeth, I feel the burn as the cut on my lip widens and more blood hits my tongue.

"It's not forever," I say. "We do this to get power and we're almost there. People are already coming to us. They're getting old. They have more enemies than we do. They'll fall and when that happens … we'll be there."

Brax is quiet for a moment. I half expect him to answer, but when he merely gets up and silently leaves the room, I can't say I'm shocked. He never does. He wants to believe it as much as I do, but it's hard to think of freedom when you've been chained down for your entire life. My arm raises and I spread the fingers of my right hand out and hold it over my head.

Small scars dot my skin. My ring finger is too close to my middle one, the lingering reminder of a broken bone— one of dozens. All of us have suffered for this chance. Abel. Braxton. Me.

I'll see us on top even if it kills me.

25

AVALON

I LAY WITH MY FACE TO THE SUN, ENJOYING ITS WARMTH. When I first got to Eastpoint, the lingering chill of winter was still hanging over everything. But now, it's been weeks and I can feel spring trying to hurry her bitch ass up. Back in Plexton, summer seemed to stretch for nine months out of the year and the other seasons had to cram themselves into the remaining three.

A body drops down next to me on the grass, but I don't open my eyes. From the heaviness of the sound, I know it's not Rylie. Which leaves very few people who'd be brazen enough to approach me out in public like this.

I ignore him as I soak up the sun. Unlike the south, the heat here is far less humid. It's more enjoyable—bearable. It doesn't remind me at all of the cramped trailer parks and boarded up windows with no air circulation. As long as he's letting me be, he can bask in this fucking warmth right along with me. It's not like I really give a shit.

"You know you're causing a lot more trouble than you're worth," he says. And now I know exactly who it is.

Seriously, what is it with these Sick Boys? Do they have a tracker on my ass or are they just obsessed?

I crack my lids and look up at Abel. "And that's my problem, how?" I ask.

White blonde and dark brown locks slide across his upper forehead as his head dips and crystal blue eyes meet mine. "I can't say I know what it was like back wherever you fucking came from," he starts, causing me to laugh.

"You wanna know?" I ask, sitting up and brushing off a few stray pieces of grass. The landscapers recently cut it and there are chunks of it still sitting around. "It was cheap, it was dirty, and no one in my neck of the woods had anything like what I see here." I gesture around. Across the road, I can see the glimmer of sunlight shining off of someone's brand new Ferrari. I'm not ashamed to admit that I've had to get close to a few cars just to figure out what they are. I don't recognize half of the names and the ones I do recognize are only because they're well known for being unbelievably expensive. I'm far more used to broken down pickup trucks with more rust than paint and poorly maintained Cadillacs from the 60s.

"If I'm causing trouble, I'm not doing it on purpose. You're just seeing trouble where there is none." I get up.

He doesn't immediately follow. Instead, he chooses to sit there, staring up at me as he shakes his head. "You cause trouble wherever you go without even trying," he says.

I sigh. "Then what do you want from me?" What would it take for him and his friends to realize that I'm not exactly going to bend over backwards to please them?

Abel stares at me for a moment, but instead of an answer, he merely lifts himself off the ground and stands towering over me. Without Braxton at his side, it's easier to see how tall he actually is. He always appears smaller next to his friend; it makes me forget how formidable he is on his own.

"Come with me for a few hours," he says.

I blink in surprise. "I have class."

"Skip it."

My head tilts to the side and I snort. "That doesn't sound like something a program student should do," I say.

His lips press together, but this time I can see that he's fighting against a smile. "I'll cover for you," he offers, shocking me once more.

He can do that? Just how much power do these three guys hold with the University? I wonder idly. 'Cause even as unworldly as I am, I know that's not normal. Curiosity burns inside me and I find myself lifting my hand towards his when he holds it out.

"Fine," I say, "but if I go missing and end up dead in a ditch somewhere, I'm coming back to haunt the fuck outta your ass."

He barks out a laugh that seems to startle him more than me. Shaking his head, Abel pulls me along behind him. We cross the road towards the very same parking lot I'd been looking at earlier. Once again, I find myself sitting shotgun in his red Mustang convertible. Except, this time, I'm not riding on someone's lap. *Pity,* I think before I can help myself.

"Why drive a car like this?" I ask as he turns out of the parking lot and presses the gas.

"What do you mean?"

My fingers trail against the door as wind whips through my hair. "I mean, with as rich as you all are, you can probably afford something new. Something nice. This is the car a normal college student might have. Not one who's probably a millionaire. It's nice enough, but not old enough to be considered a classic or worth much."

He's quiet for several minutes and I let the sound of the wind and the traffic around us fill the space without commenting again. I wait to see if he'll answer. We drive for several more minutes and my brows rise as he pulls into what looks like an old school diner and parks the car.

Leaving the top down, he gets out and I follow behind him. We're halfway up the steps to the front door when he stops and turns towards me, causing me to come to a standstill as well. He doesn't look at me, but back at the Mustang as he speaks.

"It was my mom's," he says, and I can tell just by the way he says it that there's more to the story. But I don't ask. It's not my place. If I were to ask now, it'd break whatever truce we've come to. Because no one looks like that when talking about their parents unless their parents are dead or gone.

I merely nod towards the diner doors. "Got it," I say. "Are we going in there?"

He stares at me, frowning, and nods. "Yeah."

I go around him and start walking. "Then let's go," I call over my shoulder. "Since you brought me here, I assume you're paying and I'm hungry as shit."

"Why does that not surprise me," he comments dryly as he follows me inside.

The diner looks like it's been pulled straight from the 50s. Black and white tiles and red leather seats. One of the waitresses, an older woman with a gray and blonde bun at the back of her head, stops by, grabs a few menus, and leads us to a back booth, leaving only after we've placed our drink orders.

My eyes go immediately to the front page of the menu. I can feel the burn of his gaze on me as I peruse the possibilities. I shake my head and chuckle. "Say it," I command.

"Say what?" he asks.

"Whatever it is that you brought me here to say." I glance up. "I assume this is a business related date."

He smirks. "Who said this was a date?"

He's got me there. I shrug. "If it's not a date, then what is it?"

Abel doesn't answer and I watch as his fingers grip the menu, but his eyes don't fall to it. When the waitress comes back to take our orders, he orders a burger and fries without ever looking and I order a basket of the same.

"What?" he asks when she's left. "No salad?"

"Do I look like a rabbit food eater?" I snark back, taking a big gulp of the chocolate shake she'd dropped off. I shiver as the cold washes through me.

"No, you don't," he admits and we fall back into silence, not speaking again until our food arrives.

I'm only about halfway through my burger and he's finished his when he speaks. "How much do you know about the families that founded Eastpoint University?" he asks.

I shrug as I dip a fry in ketchup and shove it into my mouth. I chew and swallow before answering. "Not much."

"How much is not much?"

"Exactly what I said." I dip another fry, this time in my remaining chocolate shake. I bite the end of my fry with the chocolate on it and look him in the eye. "Why do you think I've done any sort of research on you? That I care enough to do so?"

"Because you're smart," he replies. "And you know as well as I do that the more info you have on your enemy, the better."

I laugh, setting the rest of my uneaten fry down in the basket. "Do we really look like enemies right now, Abel?" I gesture around. "Looks to me like we're just two college kids out to eat. Not exactly at each other's throats with guns and knives, now, are we?" I say the words, but the truth of the matter is they're not completely true. And he knows that. That's why there's a gun sitting in the glovebox of his Mustang. And it's also why I'm lying. Of course, I know more than I'm letting on.

He's right. I'm not stupid. I haven't seen Corina much since that night at Urban, but I had run into her a time or two and she'd been all too happy to spill the beans on what she knows of the Eastpoint families. I'm just waiting now to see what he's willing to tell me, and if he's just like me—a liar. Because that's what I am. A liar. A thief. But more than that, a survivor.

Abel pushes his basket aside and crosses his arms as he leans forward. "There are three families," he says. "And together, we hold more money than you can possibly imagine."

Again, he's right. I can't possibly imagine having enough money to pay for a regular car outright, much less the millions I accused him of having earlier. The thought of enough money in my bank account to never have to go back to Plexton again gives me a strange feeling inside. It's similar to the feeling I have just when I'm about to do something dangerous for that adrenaline high. The back of my neck begins to sweat. My chest tightens up. My heart gallops against the inside of my ribcage.

He leans closer. "Money is power," he says, eyeing me. "And you would do well to remember that we hold all of it."

I grin at his threat, crossing my own arms over my chest as I stare right back at him. "If you hold so much power," I challenge, "and you think I disrupt it, then why haven't you kicked me out, hmmm?" It's a risk to ask it, but it's also a dare.

Abel works his jaw, his teeth clenching and unclenching

as I watch thoughts filter over his face. The waitress returns and clears away his empty basket. I keep mine and order another milkshake—this one to go, since I have the sneaking suspicion our time here is almost up. I start eating again as I wait for his response.

After several more moments, he answers. "That's not in the cards for you," he says finally.

"Oh?" I finish off the last of my burger. "Why's that?"

He looks pained. As if the question itself—or perhaps the answer—goes against what he wants. That makes me even more curious. Instead of giving that answer, however, he gives me another question. "Is that what you want?" he asks. "You want to leave Eastpoint?"

I shrug, digging a now cold French fry into the Styrofoam container of my new milkshake before eating it. "Not really," I say around my food. "Just wondering, if I'm such a big problem, why not cut me loose. It'd solve all your problems, wouldn't it?"

"Perhaps," he concedes, but the way he's watching me doesn't really give me a clue to his actual thoughts. Like Dean, he has this way of closing off his feelings. Like a curtain coming down to shroud what he's thinking. It's quite annoying, if I'm being honest. I'm used to being able to read people—you need to have that ability if you're living in the ghetto. It's better to know who's out to get you and who's your ally. Ally or enemy, there were no friends. I wonder what the differences are in his world. I imagine among the rich there are just as many enemies, perhaps more. After all, he may say money is power—but where I come from, money is dangerous. Money breeds hostility and jealousy. Money is nothing but another drug.

The rich may think they're not addicted, but they're just like the rest of us. They only dress it up better.

"Are you finished?" he asks after another long silence.

I look down at my mostly empty basket and my nearly finished second shake and sigh, pushing them away. "Yeah."

We get up and he tosses down a hundred dollar bill on the Formica tabletop. I bet it's four times the cost of our actual meal, but he doesn't seem to give a shit about change as he gestures me towards the door. I go without comment.

Half an hour later, and through a lot more traffic than I expected this time of day, Abel's Mustang pulls up outside of the Havers Dorm. I unbuckle my seatbelt and reach for the door, only stopping when I hear the locking mechanism click. I glance back to where Abel's fingers are still on the button, but he's not looking at me.

"I'll make you a deal," he says. "You lay off my brother and I'll get him to back down."

I can feel the shock on my face. I couldn't have kept my eyebrows from shooting up towards my hairline if I'd tried. "How are you planning to accomplish that?"

His shoulders tighten as he draws in a breath and blows it out. "You let me deal with him," he replies before turning to look at me. "But if I do, will you honor it?"

I can feel something creeping up my spine. Though what it is, I'm not sure. I push down the urge to shiver and choose my words carefully. "What you do is none of my business," I say. "I don't care to get involved. The only reason I've done what I have is to protect myself. You leave me alone, I leave you alone. That's the best I got."

His blue eyes stare at me and the longer he looks, the more I feel like he's looking *through* me rather than *at* me. Abel never gives me a verbal response. Instead, his fingers hit the unlock button and he peels his eyes away, turning back to face the road. I climb out of the vehicle, shutting the door behind me, and watch as he pulls away from the curb.

I'm curious to see if he'll be able to pull it off. From what I've seen of Dean Carter, it doesn't seem like anything can stop him once he's on his warpath. That shiver I'd pushed down moments before comes barreling through me as the surface of my thoughts break free. *Do I even really want to see a normal Dean Carter or do I like the man when he's covered in blood and threatening to fuck me against my will?*

I don't stick around to find the answer.

26

DEAN

The sound of hard rock filters out through the open door of the garage. Abel's legs are splayed beneath the hood of one of his many cars. The Mustang sits in the shade, looking freshly washed. Shit. He just washed that thing last week. If he's doing it again, and working on the cars, it means he's in a mood, and I've got no one to blame but myself.

I kick out a foot, knocking one of the seats lined beneath his workbench out of place so I can sit on it. If he hears me over the wailing of Ronnie Radke, he doesn't show it. I wait, watching him work. His jeans are torn and dirty—hundred dollar fabric now stained with a collection from this very garage. Dirt. Motor oil. Probably other shit too.

My knee begins to bounce. I fucking hate waiting.

"Hey," I finally say as the song ends and another, less angsty one starts. Abel's movements still beneath the car he's working on, and his feet plant on either side of the creeper he's laying on before he slides out, looking up at me.

"What do you want?" he asks. He doesn't look mad, but he also doesn't look too interested in talking.

"To apologize," I admit. "About what I said."

He rolls his eyes and when he moves to slide back beneath the car, I get up, setting my foot on the ground between his legs. "You know I didn't mean it like that," I say.

Abel looks at me. "Yeah, I know, man."

I gesture around us. "If you know, then what's with all this? You only come out here when you're thinking."

He heaves a great sigh and when I remove my foot, he rolls completely out from beneath the vehicle before sitting up and pressing his back against the driver's side door. "I want to talk to you," he says, but when he doesn't elaborate, I take a step back and sit down.

"Alright," I reply. "Talk."

"It's about the girl." A wave of lust and irritation sweeps over me. Shit. Even the mere mention of her—not even her name—has an effect. It pisses me off.

I grit my teeth. "What about her?"

He eyes me. "I want to lay off her," he says.

"The fuck?" My muscles jump beneath my skin, the urge to pound something rising fast.

Abel looks away as he reaches for a nearby rag and begins to wipe off his hands. "She's a distraction and with Kate and Luc getting together, and the old men doing their usual..." He trails off for a moment before shaking his head. "We have more important things to worry about than a program girl. I think if we let it go, it'll resolve itself and she won't try anything else."

"She disrespects us at every turn," I snap. "She runs roughshod over us and our fucking authority and you think we should just *let it go*?" I'm fucking stunned. Is this the same Abel Frazier I've known my entire life? The one who doesn't understand the meaning of mercy?

"I think we can overlook it," he continues, still not looking at me. "We've made our point. You've staked your claim. If you're worried about her fucking someone from Eastpoint, well ... I don't think you really need to. There isn't a guy on our campus that'll touch her. Not with your name stamped on her ass."

Though I know he means it figuratively, there's a sick sense of pleasure in the idea of tattooing my name on Avalon Manning's ass. I reach down and scratch the bleeding roses I have tattooed on my side. It's been a long time since I've gone for a round in the chair. Maybe an appointment with the needle will help me settle.

"So, what do you think?" Abel asks, drawing me back from my thoughts.

I think giving Avalon any sort of leeway is asking her to fuck us over, but when Abel finally gets up, dropping the rag in a trash bin, and looks at me, I find it hard to tell him no. I press my lips together, thinking. I want to focus on something else. Something that's not *her*.

"What have you heard about Kate and Luc?" I demand.

Abel shoots me a look that tells me he knows exactly what I'm doing, but he answers my question regardless. "I know she's moved in with him. Not sure if he's realized the reason for their sudden engagement yet or not, but—"

"He knows," I say, cutting him off. "There's no way that fucker doesn't know. Yet, still, I have no clue what he's planning.

"You think so?" Abel asks as he starts picking up his tools.

"I know so," I reply. "He's a snake. He has to be planning something. He doesn't give a shit about her. He's just using Kate because he thinks she can hurt me."

"Can she?" Abel grins when he catches my look of irritation. "Just asking," he says.

"No," I answer. "She can't."

"But you used Avalon to hurt her," he points out.

I grimace. That hadn't been well planned on my part. Doing so had spiraled into the rumors and I'd fed them, letting people think that Avalon is my new fucktoy. Reality is, I haven't gotten laid since before she came. Maybe Abel's right. Maybe I do need to fuck her out of my system.

"About the girl," I start. Abel drops a wrench into the toolbox and looks up. "We can't just let her roam free."

He's quiet for a moment and then he nods. "No, you're right," he agrees, "but we don't have to keep antagonizing her."

I eye him. "Is there a reason you wanna let her off the hook?" He had, after all, wanted to fuck her the day he first met her. Maybe it's something more now? Fuck knows I can't seem to stop my reaction to her. No matter how hard I want to.

Abel sighs and turns, crossing his arms as he leans against the workbench. And then he shocks me. "Do you trust me?" he asks.

My head whips to the side and I stare at him. "What kind of fucking question is that?"

Cold blue eyes stare back. "Answer it."

Flashes of Abel and Brax carrying my half-conscious body through our house after meetings with my father. Them dumping me in showers to wash off the blood of the traitors I'd been forced to kill. Of bandaging broken bones when we were kids. Do I trust him?

I stand up and turn to him. "With my fucking life," I swear.

He nods as if the answer was expected. It should've been. "Then trust me when I say, laying off of her for the time being is a good plan. If you're worried, I'll have the three of us transferred to the rest of her classes to keep an eye on her, but I don't think we're going to find anything."

"You don't think she's working for the old men?" I ask. Maybe that's it, I wonder. Is that what she'd come here for? As a test? Those fuckers...

"No." Abel's already shaking his head. "I don't think she's ever even met them."

"Why would they be so interested in her then?" I point out, but I know the answer. The answer's in the file. It's because of who she might be. I curse and wave my hand. "Never mind," I say. "You're right. She's probably not working for them. Besides, she's still technically in high school. What would a high school girl do?"

Abel levels me with an exasperated look, his eyes dull and his lips pressed together before he heaves a sigh. "You know as well as I do, that anyone can cause damage. I'm not saying underestimate her. I'm just saying, she's probably not with them."

I think about it. "Fine," I say. "Transfer us. We've had Raz and Eli on duty, but she requires more personal attention. At least until she can be trusted."

His brows arch up. "You think that'll ever be the case?"

I don't know what to think when it comes to her. All I know is that my dick takes on a life of its own whenever she's in the room. *She thought I was threatening to rape her?* Ha. It wouldn't be rape. That's one thing I wouldn't do. She might say no, but her body would say yes. I'd make her beg for me even if she hated me.

Whether it's for my money or for what I can give them in the bedroom, they all do eventually.

To Abel, I say, "Just do it. We'll find out." Then I turn and leave the garage and let my thoughts overtake themselves. The funny thing is … they all revolve around a fat-assed brat with dark hair and eyes the color of a stormy sea.

27

AVALON

I'M BEING FOLLOWED, AND I CAN'T TELL WHAT'S MORE annoying—the fact that it's happening or the fact that they're not even trying to hide it. Had I known that this is what Abel meant when we made that deal three weeks ago, I might've turned it down. I've been doing my best to ignore it, but it's hard to completely pretend like Dean's eyes aren't trailing me everywhere I go. Half the time, I can't tell if he wants to fuck me or kill me. His expression rarely changes. I might not mind the idea of fucking him so much if he didn't act like he was so much better than me. Rich or not, I'm sure we both bleed red, and I'm more than willing to see if he does.

Every time I go to the cafeteria, I see either one or all of them—and if it's not them, it's one of their football buddies. Rylie has noticed as well, but she just shakes her head and doesn't comment. And since I'm unwilling to approach them, Corina seems to be the only one willing to give me some answers.

"Do an online search," she suggests as she stuffs a leaf

of dressing covered lettuce in her mouth. "I can promise you they're on there."

"Already have," I say, glancing over my shoulder.

"And?" She spears a tomato. "What'd you find?"

I shoot her a look. "You know exactly what I found," I snap. A fuck ton. A quick search on each of their names had brought up an extensive history. Old celebrity girlfriends. Net worth in the millions for each of them individually, and that's with the fact that none of them have even inherited their families' corporations yet. When that happens, it'll skyrocket even more, I'm sure. I knew they were loaded, but this ... is more than just wealthy. They're filthy, stinking rich. At least now I know why everyone at Eastpoint practically worships the ground they tread on.

"Then what do you want me to tell you?" she asks.

"Everything the search engine didn't," I reply.

She shrugs. "Well, they're on the football team. Have you gone to a game yet?"

"What information would that get me?" I ask with a scowl. I've never gone to a football game in my life and living in the South, it had definitely been difficult to avoid. To not like football in America is practically a sin.

Corina's laugh catches the attention of a few spare jocks lingering nearby. They pass us, carrying trays to the conveyor belt, eyeing her as they go. She flicks a strand of hair off her bare shoulder and gives me a sultry look. "Listen, sweetcheeks," she says, "if you really want information on them just do to them what they're doing to you." She leans forward and I can see the guys out of the corner of my eye, practically salivating as she almost bursts out of her tube top.

I stare blandly into her face. "And what's that?" I deadpan.

"Flip the script," she says. "Follow *them*."

I scoff, but it's not a bad idea. I'm still considering it when jock one and jock two finally decide to make their move.

"Hey, Corina." Jock number one moves in first, flashing a million watt smile as he hooks an arm over the back of Corina's chair.

She looks up. "Oh, hey, Chad," she says, fluttering her eyelashes.

I struggle to contain my eyeroll. Of course his name is Chad. Classic douche name for a classic douche looking guy.

"Been a while since we've seen you," Jock number two says, coming up on her other side.

She laughs delicately, and I watch as she turns towards one, her chest thrusting out as number two practically salivates into her cleavage. Some guys can be accused of being players, but if ever there were a girl player—she'd be it. "I've just been so busy with school lately," she says with a pout. "My professors are so mean this semester. None of them are willing to give me extensions on my papers."

"Awww, that sucks," Chad says, but he looks like he couldn't care less what she's saying and is more interested in other things her mouth could do.

Corina flicks a look my way and grins. "Have you guys met my friend, Avalon?"

Chad and Jock number two stiffen at the sound of my name and when Corina waves her hand my way, I watch their heads turn as if pivoting on spikes. "Uh, no, can't say we have," Chad says.

"Oh, well, let me introduce you. Avalon, this is Chad and Brock. They play on Eastpoint's basketball team."

I scowl at her.

"Hey," Jock number two—Brock—is the only one who manages to raise a hand and acknowledge my existence.

Chad, on the other hand, completely ignores me as he focuses on Corina. "We're going out to the warehouse district tonight," he tells her. "You thinking about going too?"

"The warehouse district?" She frowns and shakes her head. "No. I've got a test tomorrow and Professor Habersham is an ass. He's not even grading on a curve."

"Well, if you change your mind…" He lets his suggestive statement trail away as he slips his arm back from her shoulders and straightens up.

Curiosity forces me to confront him. "What's going on in the warehouse district?" I ask.

He stiffens. "Er … uh … nothing really."

Irritation forms. "Oh?" I slowly grab my tray and stand, pausing next to him as I round the table. "Then why would Corina be interested in going?"

"It's … I was just…"

Corina saves his ass by laughing. "Don't be such a prude," she says, reaching out and lightly slapping his arm. Personally, I'd like to do something a lot harder than slapping him for the boldfaced lie, but I'm being *good*. After all, I have a deal to uphold.

Chad glances at her before looking back to me. He rubs the back of his head, skimming his fingers across the near shaven underside as the longer part of his hair on top flops forward over one eye. "It's just where the guys, uh, host shit," he says lamely.

Corina leans forward. "I can't go, but you totally should," she says. "It's super fun."

"What kind of—"

"I'll see you later, Corina," Chad says, cutting me off as he slides away, tapping his buddy on the shoulder. "I gotta head out, but hit me up if you get some free time."

"Bye!" his friend says, hurrying after him.

I grit my teeth and glare after him. *Pansy*, I think. Corina merely chuckles. "You can't blame them," she says, grabbing up her tray as well and following me as we head to the conveyor belt. "You're kinda infamous now."

I lean back and crack my neck. "Lucky me." The sarcasm is heavy in my voice which only makes her laugh again as we grab our shit and head out.

"The Sick Boys pretty much hated you, then claimed you, and now they ignore you—"

My eyes slice her way, but I don't turn my head. "They're definitely not ignoring me," I comment. If that were the case then they wouldn't constantly be up my ass. In class, at least, I can pretend they don't exist. They become just another couple of faces in a sea of students. Everywhere else, though, it's hard to disregard their overbearing presence.

Our feet hit the sidewalk and I turn towards Havers with Corina following. "Yeah, well, no one has had this much of their attention or non-attention," she replies. "Not even Kate and she was practically Dean Carter's girlfriend."

"Practically?" I repeat. "I thought they were—"

"What?" she interrupts, eyeing me with amusement. "Official?"

I nod once.

Corina shakes her head. "N*ope*." She hops over a crack in the sidewalk as she pops the last part of that word. "Kate Coleman comes from wealthy stock, but even she wasn't good enough to be acknowledged as official. She got status for being one of Dean's most regular fuck buddies, but that was about it. She thought because they fucked enough that she could call herself a Sick Girl—not that there's ever actually been one of those. Regardless, as you can see now, she's nothing to them.

Even if Dean ever gave a shit about her, he certainly doesn't now."

"Did he have many fuck buddies then?" I find myself asking.

A glimmer of something mischievous enters her eyes as Corina whirls around, walking backwards with her thumbs tucked into her designer backpack. I scowl at it, waiting for her to comment, but thankfully she lets it go without a snarky remark.

"Not many," she says instead. When we make it to a crosswalk, she turns back around and watches the numbers across the street, counting down until we can make our way to the other side. "Dean's a private person. Kate was the most obvious of his sexual partners. I'm sure there's been more, but none that come to mind." She giggles as the countdown ends and signals to us to start across. "Actually, now that I think about it, if he's slept with anyone on campus, maybe he made them sign one of those NDAs."

"NDAs?" I look at her as we reach the other side.

"Non-disclosure agreements," she clarifies then shrugs. "It's pretty common for people like us."

'Like us' meaning the rich and powerful, I gather.

I find myself watching Corina as she moves ahead of me, walking faster in spite of the fact that she's wearing heels and I'm wearing Converse. She moves with ease as if there's nothing weighing her down. No darkness. No desire for the depraved. I've spent more time with her since that day she flagged me down and offered to take me to Urban, but as I stare at her now, I realize, I know nothing about this chick. We've spent several meals together—mostly for me to gather information—and all of it's been about *them*. None of our topics of conversation have ever had anything to do with her.

It's odd, I think. Don't most people like to talk about themselves? Especially girls like her?

"How do you know so much about Dean Carter and the Sick Boys?" I ask when we reach the front of Havers.

She pauses on the sidewalk, spinning back to face me. Her dull blue eyes crinkle at the corners as she looks at me. "I've grown up around families like the Eastpoint heirs," she admits. "I've been surrounded by them my entire life. I know who they are just as they know who I am."

I arch one brow. "And who are you?"

A grin spreads across her lips. "Just another rich bitch," she says, taking a step off the curb. "Have a good night, Avalon."

My eyes track her as she heads across the street to the commuter parking lot. She never looks back even once, and for some reason, that bothers me. That and what she said. I can't tell if it was meant to be as mocking as it sounded or if she was trying to be funny.

With a sigh, I turn around and head into the dorm, pulling out my phone as I go. Regardless of Corina's intentions, she's done me a few favors. There is one person who should've called and told me about the damn warehouse district, and luckily, Corina seems to know how to get a hold of everyone. If he could give out my number to girls like her, then I could certainly get his from the same source. I dial his number.

"Hayes," a familiar voice says a few moments later.

"Hi Jake," I say, "it's Avalon. I have a favor to ask, and I know how you love doing me favors, panty-boy."

28

AVALON

"Are you sure about this?" Jake's voice is tense as we step out of his car.

"Yeah," I say. "I'm sure. You should've told me about this place back when I asked."

He shrugs, unapologetic. "I wouldn't have told you about it now if you hadn't threatened to send your sick boys after me."

"Yeah..." I grin as I follow the crowd collecting outside of a tall, metal barn looking building. "About that," I say, "they're not exactly *my* boys."

He freezes, his hand reaching out and snagging my arm as he pulls me up short. "The fuck, man?" Jake's face is screwed up in confused shock. "You mean you're not dating Carter?"

"Not even if he begs," I reply, pinching the top of his hand between my thumb and forefinger until he winces and releases me.

"What the hell, Avalon!" He turns around and starts back to his car. "I'm fucking out of here."

"Hey!" I shout after him. "I still need a ride back."

"Oh, no," he calls over his shoulder. "Hell no, you're on your own."

God, he's being such a wuss. I roll my eyes and jog to catch up with him, grabbing his arm and immediately dropping it when he stops and glares down at me. "You owe me," I state.

He scoffs. "In what universe do I owe you anything, Ava?"

I arch a brow and cross my arms over my chest. His eyes dart down to my cleavage, but when I clear my throat with a meaningful growl they jump back up to my face. "You handed out my number, jackass," I snap. "To some rich bitch."

"Yeah, well, from what I hear, you two have been fast friends," he replies. "I fail to see how that means I owe you."

I shake my head. "The fact is, you sold me out. You also never texted me those locations you promised. I had to find out about this little district from Corina and her boy toys." He narrows his eyes at me, waiting, and I groan. "Fine," I snap. "Stay. Give me a ride back and I'll give you the earnings."

"What if you lose?"

I twist my tongue in my mouth and slide it through my teeth in the facsimile of a predatory smile before releasing it and grinning. "Do I really look like a loser to you?" I ask. Jake eyes me again, obviously doubtful. "And you might want to be careful in how you respond," I tack on. "I won't hesitate to take out your ride like I did Kate's and then where will we both be?"

"Rideless?" he guesses in a dry tone.

"Yup."

He sucks in a breath and shoves his hands through his hair, yanking at the strands, turning and stalking a few feet away before halting and pivoting back around. Jake jerks his hands out of his hair and points at me. "You're a goddamn siren," he accuses. "You've got a fucking hot ass and a gorgeous face, but you lead men to their deaths."

I ignore the ass comment. "Don't be such a drama queen," I scoff. "I didn't seduce you. Now, are you in or out?"

Jake storms towards me and then right past me as he follows the people heading into the building, cutting a glance my way when I reach his side. "You're really not fucking Carter?" he clarifies.

"Why the fuck does everyone think I am?" I snap back instead of answering. "Have they seen him with his tongue down my throat?" This question I do answer. "No, they haven't."

"What about you with yours down his?"

I punch him in the shoulder and shove past him into the door when we reach the main entrance. The warehouse is large and perfect for an illegal fight night. It's situated in the middle of bumfuck nowhere. Jake had driven even further than the day I'd taken the bus out of town for some lake cliff diving, but with how many people are currently crowding the interior space, it's clear that despite the location, it's popular and well known.

Already, there's a certain electricity in the air. It hovers over everyone, a building anticipation of the night's events to come.

"You know," Jake says absently as he finds his way back to my side, "you never answered my question."

"You never answered mine," I point out.

He shoves his hands into his pockets as we find a good spot towards the back—it looks like someone has carted out old bleachers and people are starting to claim their watching spots around what looks to be a large black fenced-in cage.

"People may not have seen the two of you sucking face," he finally says with a glance around—I assume to make sure the closest people are too absorbed in what they're seeing to eavesdrop on our conversation. "But everyone can sense the shit between you two."

"There is no shit," I insist.

Jake's dark eyes shoot down to me. I look away. "Bullshit." I stiffen. "Anyone with eyeballs can see the tension between you and Dean Carter. He's all but declared you his—something he's *never* done before. And if you're the type of girl I think you are, then you need to be real with me. You know it. Otherwise, you never would've used him as a threat to make me help you get here."

I inhale sharply and grit my teeth, hating that he's right. "Dean Carter," I start, feeling the venom on my tongue, "is an asshole."

Jake rolls his eyes. "That is nothing new," he states.

"Yeah, well, I'm new here. His level of assholery is still fresh to me."

"Does that mean you're not going to tell me what's going on?"

"Depends…" I let the word slide off my tongue as I scan the crowd, searching for a mass of people all circling one person. That's where I'll find the bookie.

"On what?" he presses.

"On if you can keep your trap shut and stop handing out any and all information I give you."

There. Across the room, a small head bobs up and down as people thrust cash out at him. I stand up. "I'll keep it a secret," Jake blurts. I jerk and look down with a frown.

I consider it for a moment, debating and searching for

any source of weakness in the information I possess. Pursing my lips, I glance back to the bookie before returning my focus to Jake. "There's nothing going on between us," I finally say. "Dean Carter is an enemy as far as I'm concerned. He staked a claim to prove a point. One that I do not like. So far, though, they've left me alone. As long as they continue to do so"—I step over one long bench and then completely off the bleachers—"I'll let them keep their thrones," I finish with a grin before turning around and disappearing into the crowd.

It's hot. Ungodly so, but after a quick conversation with the bookie to see who's lined up on the docket—not that I would recognize any of the names, but it's nice to familiarize oneself with the competition—I head back to Jake. Cutting my way through the crowd sideways, I avoid wandering hands and shove those who get too close.

A familiar tingle of excitement hits me in my core. A hungry monster making herself known. Which is the very reason I'm here tonight. I'm so exuberant that I don't even turn around and punch a guy in the face when he knocks into me and turns, cursing low beneath his breath. Doesn't matter. I'll get all this juice out one way or another tonight. I find Jake in the same place I left him with his phone in his hand and a frown on his face.

"Back," I say, popping a squat on the bench next to him and making him jump.

He slides his phone back into his pocket quickly—I narrow my eyes ... too quickly. "Where'd you go?" he demands.

"Bookie," I say, nodding back the way I'd come.

His head turns and I drop mine to the outline of the

phone in his pocket, but as he shoves his hands into them, I scowl. There's no way I'll be getting it to find out what the hell he's hiding. And I know he's hiding something. No one would jump like that if they weren't guilty of something.

"You should've told me," he says when he glances back at me. "I could've introduced you. Could've given you a better layout of who you should bet on."

"Not to worry." I shake my head. "I have it figured out."

"You do?"

Before I can reply, the lights dim and the crowd charges towards the cage as someone steps inside and a spotlight slowly comes to rest over him. It's the bookie— Danger, he'd introduced himself as earlier. He tosses back his ginger mane and though he's a skinny looking fucker, he's got tattoos etched across his knuckles as he fists pumps the air and brings a microphone to his lips.

"Lords and Ladies," he shouts, "are you people ready to see some bloodshed?" The crowd roars back and he chuckles, the sound deep and amused. "Well, then you've come to the right place. My name is Hanson Reed and I'll be your host for this evening."

I grin, standing up as I strip off my t-shirt. Jake's eyes widen when I reveal my sports bra. I leave my pants on. They're loose enough for what I need. "What the fuck are you doing?" he demands, his face paling.

I remove the tape I'd grabbed from one of the other fighters when I went to talk to the bookie from my pocket. "Getting your fee for the ride here," I say as I start to wind the white strips around my knuckles and through my fingers. I'd learned the hard way that un-taped knuckles in a fight can hurt like a bitch and I'm not about feeling pain, I'm about delivering it.

"I thought you said you didn't fight!"

I chuckle at the accusation in his tone as I finish one hand and move onto the next as Hanson continues to talk to the crowd. He's good at getting them riled. I'm half-paying attention, more focused on the task at hand as other people take notice and begin to stare. Jake looks around like he's afraid the boogeyman is about to pop out at any second.

"I said I don't fight for money," I reply. "And I'm not. The money is yours. The fight—" I cut myself off as I finish my second hand and clench my fingers up and down to make sure they're tight enough, but not so tight that they inhibit my ability to make a fist. Already that sick bitch known as addiction is clawing at my insides, ready to be let out of her cage. Or rather … into one. "The fight," I state again as I lift my head and take a step off the bleachers, tossing my unneeded shirt at Jake's face, "is all for me."

"This is such a bad idea," he says. "You can't do this."

"Wrong." I pause and turn back. "I can do whatever the fuck I want."

"You're just going to piss them off," he insists.

I laugh, a full bellied laugh. "I doubt they'd give a shit about me fighting either way." And even if they did, Abel never specified every action I could and couldn't take—then again, if he had, I wouldn't have accepted the deal. I need this. The rush in my veins. The feel of sweat coating the back of my neck as I pull my hair up into a ponytail. I anchor it at the back of my skull and swing it from side to side as I bounce on my toes. My desire for blood and adrenaline is already pouring through me. *Nothing can stop this*, I think. It's the best high in the world.

Controlling this feeling is better than any drug in the world.

"Ava!" Jake jumps off the bleachers and reaches for me

as I start off. I scowl when his hand closes around my upper arm.

"Remove. Your. Fucking. Hand." Already feeling the pulse of violence, I grit the words out. I don't want to hurt him, but every time someone touches me without my permission—as people seem to love doing at Eastpoint—it only serves to piss me off and make me that much more ready to break some bones.

Jake's hand is gone in a flash, but he still stands over me. "This is a bad idea," he repeats. "Please don't do this. I'm begging you. They're probably here. They'll see you."

I glance around but come up empty. "I don't see them," I say with an arched brow. "Besides why does it matter? Why would those pretty rich boys even be here?"

"Jesus fuck!" he snaps, staring down at me as though I've grown a second head. "Are you really that dense?" My shirt hangs between us, still clutched in his fist.

"Insults?" I huff. "Really?"

"Yeah, really." He shakes his head as if he truly can't believe me. I turn my head, noticing that Hanson is winding down his speech. He's getting ready to introduce me. I need to go. "Ava," Jake says, capturing my attention again, "they *own* this place. They own pretty much all of Eastpoint. You have no idea what kind of connections their kind of money has. They might seem like normal college students"—*they don't,* I admit silently. The Sick Boys are anything but normal. I don't say as much, however—"but they're beyond fucking powerful. And with power comes a lot of... " He bites his lip, his teeth a flash of white as his head tips back and his eyes dart around before coming back to me. "Power like the kind that they have is never one-hundred percent honest," he finishes.

He's being vague, but I get the point. They're wealthy. They're corrupt. They're powerful. The only problem with that is … I don't really give a shit. I made up my mind a long time ago. I'll never let anyone think they can control or use me again.

I take a step back. "Thanks for the warning," I say, softening my expression when Jake's panicked gaze reaches mine. "But don't worry about me. I can handle the Sick Boys."

"You say that..." Jake's face pinches up tight, "but I'm asking you not to."

"Why?" I challenge, taking another step back. I can hear Hanson announcing my opponent in the background, listing their accolades to get the crowd hungry for more.

Jake's eyes dart to the ground before lifting again. "I don't want to see you get hurt, Ava." It's nice. Honestly, it's amazing. Jake hardly knows me and yet he shows more consideration than half of the people I've met in my life, but I don't completely believe him. I think he doesn't want to be involved in my trouble, which I get. At the same time, though, for people like me, there's no hiding from the darkness. All I have left is to embrace it.

I give him a smile as I hear the speakers churn out Hanson's words. "And tonight, Lords and Ladies, we have a new contender. Please welcome Avalon Manning!"

"Watch a winner work," I say to Jake just before I turn and slide through the crowd, slicing my way to the fenced-in area where Hanson and another female fighter wait. I enter the ring, letting the black gate close behind me.

I'm ready for some bloodshed.

29

DEAN

No. She. Fucking. Isn't.

Those words are an echo in my mind, but as I step into the warehouse, dry sweat coating my throat, I see that she is exactly where that motherfucker said she would be in his last text. The dripping strands of my still wet hair hangs in my face, half obscuring my view, and I shake them out of the way. A few of the droplets land on a few people near me that haven't noticed my entrance.

One of them flinches as the cold water hits the side of his neck and he turns, face already morphed into an angry scowl, but one look at me and he hightails it as far from me as he can get. Smart dude. I storm through the crowd, circling the cage where Avalon fucking Manning stands.

The mass of people part to allow me through. It's as if they sense the predator in me; the barely restrained beast ready to tear someone apart. The only thing I am thankful for is the fact that she's not fighting a guy. Had I walked into that mess, I'd set this whole place on fire.

What the fuck is she thinking? I wonder as I track down the man who'd brought me here. Abel and Braxton are here too. I'm the only one who'd chosen not to show up tonight. At least, that'd been the plan. I growl when some already buzzed girl stumbles into my path. Without thought, I pick her up and toss her at the nearest guy and keep going, not even pausing to see if she'd been caught.

Anger rages through me.

Three weeks, I've stayed away from her, but it's clear that no matter what Abel says, she can't keep her end of the bargain. I've separated from her. I've left her alone when all I want to do is torment her. Of course, I've kept an eye on her. The three of us have been transferred to all of her classes, but now with my eyes firmly on her delicious ass as she delivers a perfect roundhouse kick to her opponent, I realize it hasn't been enough.

To look and not touch is fucking killing me. Whether she realizes it or not, Avalon Manning has just crossed a line. She's taken one step into my underworld and now there's no going back. I'm going to shove the pomegranate seeds down her throat and ensure that she can never leave.

I stalk further into the warehouse, spotting Jacob Hayes at the top of the bleachers, his eyes fixated on the fight as he clutches a dark swath of fabric in one hand and his cellphone in the other. Good. He'll be easy to spot and so will I when Abel and Braxton finally tear their eyes away from Avalon's ass long enough to find me. There's no doubt in my mind that those two are enjoying this far more than they should. The phone call I'd answered just before I'd left the house—and right after Hayes's text—had stated as much.

"Hayes." I growl out the man's name and even over the roaring excitement of the people crowding the warehouse floor and the old bleachers we'd had shipped here, he hears me. His eyes turn down and when he spots me, he gulps and waves me up. People scramble out of my way as I take the bleachers a step at a time, turning and using the benches as my stairs as I cut a faster path to the man at the top. "Why the fuck didn't you stop her?" I demand when I reach him.

"I tried, man," Hayes says quickly, "but she wouldn't listen."

"You should've made her listen," I hiss.

Someone screams and my head whips around to see the other chick deliver a punch to Avalon's face. It wasn't her scream, though, I realize when the girl backs up and all I see is Avalon's grinning sneer. Like she's enjoying being beaten on. *Interesting...*

She's a strong fighter. The punches hardly seem to faze her. In fact, they don't slow her down at all. She moves with speed, cutting around her opponent's body and kicking at her legs. When the other girl goes down, Avalon leaps on top of her and delivers blow after blow. I half expect the fight to end sooner than later, but then the opponent rears up and locks her legs around Avalon's body and suddenly the positions are reversed.

I clench my hands into fists at my sides. Blood and sweat. They're both covered in it. I can feel the buzz of the crowd as people push closer to the cage. In the next instant, Avalon has somehow worked her way out of the other girl's hold and they're both back on their feet. Circling.

The opponent turns her head and spits out a wad of blood. If I see Avalon do that, we're going to have issues. For some reason, there's a core piece inside of me that doesn't want to see her hurt. At least, not by anyone but me. I narrow my gaze when I spot a familiar head of white blond hair in the crowd next to a darker head that's nearly a foot taller.

Braxton and Abel.

They spot me a second later and nod as they make their way through the crowd, heading towards me.

"How did she even get here?" I demand as I wait for my brothers' arrival.

Jake shifts from side to side. "I brought her," he admits begrudgingly.

"You better have a good fucking reason—" I start.

"I thought you two were together," he says, lifting his hands in surrender, the shirt and phone still clutched in them. "That's why I brought her. She threatened me with you guys. I promise, I thought this was something you'd want, but I know better now, man. She set the record straight."

"She did, did she?"

"Who did what?" Abel asks as he reaches us, Braxton still climbing through the people sitting on the bleachers below us.

"Avalon said you two weren't anything," Hayes clarifies. "I swear, I won't give her shit if you don't want me to. I don't want any trouble."

My head turns back to the fight. Avalon's back slams into the latticework of the cage. Her opponent is bearing down on her, and honestly, it looks like the other girl is the better fighter. She's fit. She's fierce. But there's something about Avalon. A darker, more volatile edge.

I watch as she reaches up, linking her fingers through the holes of the cage. She uses her hold to lift her whole body and throw her legs over her opponent's head, effectively dodging the girl's next attack. She's impressive. Brutal. Savage.

The way she fights. The blood she wipes from her split lower lip. All of it is sexy as hell. And feeling that way about a girl like her disturbs me more than I'm willing to admit.

"What'd she say?" Abel inquires again when no one has answered him.

Braxton finally makes it to the top and towers over the rest of us as he turns and leans lightly against the back railing, watching the proceedings. He, of all of us, enjoys these kinds of fights. It's the violence. He soaks up the movements, watches carefully, precisely. He usually knows who the winner will be even before the fight has started, but none of us even knew Avalon could fight.

"What do you think?" I ask him instead of answering Abel's question.

"She's good," he says after a moment.

"How good?" I demand.

It takes a moment for him to answer, but when he does, he pivots his head so that his gaze meets mine. "Good enough to beat her," he says.

My eyes turn back to the fight as it winds down. He's right. Her opponent is tapering off, but as Avalon grins at the other girl, I realize that she's nowhere near finished. Her chest rises and falls in rapid movements but her legwork is precise. Careful. My eyes fall to her breasts and I have to grit my teeth at the realization that every fucking man in the room—my brothers included—are seeing her nearly bare up top. The little fucking strap of fabric holding her tits in place is barely acceptable. It's obviously worn from use and age. It's damn near a deep gray, but the hue tells me it hasn't always been. How fucking long has she had that thing? Not a split second after that thought occurs, her opponent punches her in the face and bloodstains join the fabric.

Without meaning to, a growl works its way up my throat, but fuck, the way she smiled when the blood was running down her lips … it should've been illegal. I spread my legs and anchor my feet to the tops of the bleachers, hoping that my hard on will go down soon.

"Dean," Abel calls, distracting me. I cut my gaze his way and he nods to Jake. "What do you want to do?"

I want to claim her ass in more than just name only, I think. But that's not what Abel is asking. I turn my body back towards Jacob Hayes and level him with a glare. "Listen up, Hayes," I begin, letting the unreleased growl fill my voice as I talk. "Regardless of what *she* says, we're the ones you fucking talk to when it comes to anything to do with her. As far as you and everyone else from Eastpoint is concerned, Avalon Manning is *mine*. Is that understood?"

His eyes widen but he nods quickly. "Understood," he agrees without argument.

"Good."

Before anyone can say anything else, a roar from the crowd grabs our attention, and I watch as Hanson, our bookie, makes his way back to the cage as a panting Avalon stands over her obviously unconscious opponent.

"Looks like you were right," I say to Braxton.

He shoots me a grin. "I always am."

30

AVALON

As soon as Hanson introduces me to the girl, I forget her name. It won't matter in the end. My blood is pumping. I shiver as I crouch down, waiting for Hanson to step out of the cage and lock it behind him. Sweat collects against the nape of my neck and slides down my spine. It's hot in the warehouse. The sheer amount of people they have crammed into the building rackets up the temperature.

"You're going down," the girl sneers.

Not likely. I don't say anything, though. That's not what this is about. While other fighters try to psych out their opponents, I never do. I don't care what they think of me. I don't care what anyone in this room thinks of me. All I care about is getting what I want. And what I want is to beat her into the ground.

The lock clicks into place and she wastes no more time on words but dives for me. I spin out of the way and grab the back of her head as I pass, sinking my fingers into her ponytail. Yanking her back, I deliver a punch to her stomach and then her face, sending her reeling.

The adrenaline makes my muscles feel lighter. It makes me feel like I'm floating. It makes me feel *powerful*.

My breath saws in and out of my chest. I could take her down now, but then that'll defeat the purpose. People scream in my ear, their chests pressed up against the cage as they yell at me to take her down. She's already down. Instead of doing that, though, I wait. It doesn't take her long to recover, thankfully, and when she does, she's even angrier.

"You bitch!" she shrieks and we're back to circling. I grin.

Everything in the room narrows down to the cage. Just her and me. Round and fucking round we go. Her feet move slowly, but her eyes remain on me. I'm careful—I have to be. Fighting like this is illegal. Unlike in television shows, this is real. It's not faked. No actors. And certainly no medics on standby. One wrong move and I could kill her. A thrill shoots through me, cooled only by the fact that the same goes for her. She could kill me.

I grin. It's not likely.

"The fuck are you smiling about?" she hisses, spitting out blood.

I shake my head and the next time she steps too close, I turn, arching my leg up and roundhouse kicking her in the side. She blocks it—but only just barely.

"Take her down!" someone yells.

"Hit her in the face," another commands. "Fuck her up!"

The only thing I don't like about doing this here is the fact that I recognize some of the people in the sea of faces surrounding us. They're students from Eastpoint. I don't, however, recognize the girl across from me. From the state of the still fading bruises on her arms and thighs and the ragged look of her clothes—she's just like me.

Guilt is an echo in my chest, but no one is making her do this. She chose to step into the ring with me, and that's her own fault. The tail end of that thought comes to an abrupt halt as she barrels towards me—all pretense of trying to stay away gone as she slams my back into the cage.

Hot breath hits my ear, slides against the side of my face. An irritating memory flashes behind my eyes when I squeeze them shut. I hear her chuckle and that only serves to piss me the fuck off.

Anchoring my hips, I reach up—sliding my fingers through the loops of the cage and I tighten my grip. She pulls back to punch me and I arch up, narrowly avoiding the hit as she slaps into the cage herself and I land on the other side of her and suddenly, we've switched places.

I punch her in the face. Blood hits the tape on my knuckles. A second punch snaps her head to the side and more blood shoots out of her mouth, landing against my face and upper chest, staining my sports bra. There's no better feeling than someone else's blood on your skin.

Rearing back, I deliver a head butt. My skull echoes with the agony that results from a stupid move, but it sends even more adrenaline pouring through me, numbing the pain. And we're back at it.

We fight for what feels like only seconds. Everything spins around me at supersonic speed, but I know it's longer than it seems. She's waning. Her hits slow down. Her body's unable to hold up under the pressure and the numerous hits. I don't want to stop. I'm not ready to let go of this feeling. The feeling of absolute authority.

I don't feel human anymore. I feel dangerous. I feel fucking weaponized. And it's glorious.

"You're done," I say, my chest heaving as she stumbles

under my latest hit. Blood hits my tongue. This time, it's my own. I lick at my lower lip, feeling a cut.

"I'm done..." she pants. "When I say so..."

I shake my head and punch her again, my taped knuckles slamming into her jaw. Despite her words, she goes down. The audience loses its shit. The roar of their excitement fills my head with nothing but annoyance, though. I don't care for nor do I want their approval. I stand still for a moment, staring down at the girl as I reach up and wipe my forearm along my hairline. Sweat collects against my skin, making me feel grimy and dirty.

I am dirty. Filthy. There's something wrong with me. Addicted to the adrenaline high. And as it falls down, so do I.

Back to reality.

I turn towards the exit gate as it swings open. A stack of hundreds is slapped into my hand. I look down at them with a scowl. A part of me wants to keep them—money like this would help me go a long way, but I made a promise to someone a long time ago. And when I make a promise, I keep it.

"Avalon..." Jake's voice is shaky, but it pulls me out of my thoughts.

I smile as I lift my head, ready to hand over the cash when I pause and the smile falls away. "You motherfucker," I snap in accusation, my eyes darting from the group of men who approach from behind him.

"I'm sorry," Jake says. "I—"

I growl and punch his chest with the hand holding the cash. "Your fucking fee," I grit out, storming past him as I release the money and he barely catches it.

"Not so fast, Ava." Dean's hand shoots out and he grabs my arm, halting any further movement. "You're not leaving just yet."

The high I had been feeling slowly creeps back into my veins as my blood boils and races faster and faster. It practically pounds beneath my skin. I shove down the excitement and look up at him with disdain. "Oh yeah?" I spit in his face. "And who's going to stop me?"

Those dark chocolate brown eyes of his flash with something dark and sinister, making my lips curl up in spite of myself.

"Avalon," Jake calls, "your shirt..." I rip my arm from Dean's grasp—hating the way his touch makes me feel—and yank my t-shirt from Jake's hand. Instead of putting it on right away, though, I use it to mop up the worst of the sweat and blood.

"That was some fight," Abel says, sidling closer.

"Fuck off," I snap.

Instead of taking offense, he merely laughs and slings an arm around my shoulders. "You should've told us you could fight like that, we could make some money, you and me," he offers.

My body stiffens against him. "No thanks."

Jake steps closer, earning a glare from Dean—well, well, well, looks like his betrayal didn't make anyone happy. I should've known better. With Dean's expression, my anger begins to cool. "Here," Jake says, trying to hand me the money back, "you earned this. I don't need a fee."

I grunt as I use my shirt to wipe around my middle. "Don't want it," I say, avoiding looking at the stack.

"Well, I'm not taking it," he insists.

I roll my eyes. "Then throw it away," I snap. "I told you, I don't fucking fight for money. It's yours if you want it."

"I don't."

Out of the corner of my eye, I see that my opponent has regained consciousness and a couple of guys are helping her out of the cage as she limps through the crowd. An idea pops into my head. I snatch the money from Jake. "Fine," I say.

"What are you—"

I don't stay to listen to his question as I pivot and head straight for the girl. Each guy supporting her has one arm over their shoulders. One narrows his eyes at me as I approach. "Sore winner?" he accuses, his eyes darkening as I stop in front of them.

"Not at all," I say. "I had fun." The girl lifts her head and I wince. Yeah, she's gonna feel this fight tomorrow. Hell, I might too, but there are still too many hormones flooding my system for me to feel anything right now.

"Then what do you want?" the other guy spits out.

"Nothing," I say and then reach forward, jerking the girl's elastic waistband of her shorts out and stuffing the stack of hundreds down into the side.

Her head lifts and confusion fills her eyes. "The fuck are you doing?" she asks, her words muffled as if she's still trying to get her bearings or stay awake—I'm not sure. Her eyes are hooded but it doesn't make it easy to tell if that's natural or because of me with how dark they both are.

"I don't need it," I say, turning back around as I finish the rest of my sentence over my shoulder. "And you look like you could use it. Thanks for a fun fight."

I walk away, but I don't get very far as a familiar masculine arm falls around my shoulders. "Come on, li'l fighter," Brax says with a grin. "Let's get out of here."

"I thought I was 'li'l psycho'," I say.

He shrugs. "Li'l psycho, li'l fighter—both are you, aren't they?"

Maybe. "Or little savage," I suggest.

Brax throws his head back and laughs. "You're right," he agrees. "That's what you are. A pretty little savage."

He steers me towards the exit and I see that Dean and Abel are already waiting there. Jake is nowhere to be seen. I guess they chased him off. My chest aches. I'm mad at him, but I'd at least hoped he'd stick around to give me a ride home after they laid into me. As the adrenaline begins to fade, soreness makes itself known. Walking back is going to be a bitch, I can already tell.

Shrugging Brax's arm off my shoulders as we stop at the far side of the parking lot, I lift my head and I meet Dean Carter's gaze head on. Might as well get this over with.

"Well," I state, crossing my arms over my chest, my shirt dangling from one hand, "go on." I gesture for him to say something.

Of course, being predictable isn't in Dean's nature. Instead of launching into the ridicule or scolding, he turns to his friends and nods. "Go ahead without me," he says. "I'll take care of this."

Abel hesitates. "You sure, man?" he asks.

Dean doesn't look at me. "Yeah, I'm sure."

Brax walks past me and heads for the familiar red Mustang parked alongside a black and chrome motorcycle. He claps Abel on the shoulder as he goes. "Just let it go," Brax says with a laugh. "Besides, I want some ice cream. I'm hungry."

Abel looks back once at Dean and then me before turning to his friend. I hear him complaining as they get into the car. "You're always hungry, asshole."

The tail lights illuminate as the engine turns over and both Dean and I watch in silence as they back up and drive off. Then, it's just him and me. Alone. For the first time in over a month, and I have no clue what's about to happen.

31

DEAN

Her eyes watch me with a caution that demonstrates her intelligence. She knows a dangerous man when she sees one. And tonight, I'm feeling particularly vicious. Watching her fight has done something to me, awoken the beast so to speak.

After Abel and Braxton leave, we stand in silence for several moments and my eyes eat up the expanse of flesh available to them. Her abdomen is curved, slightly rounded. Her ribs, however, are barely covered by a layer of fat. I can see them beneath the lower strap of her bra. And there, on one hip bone, I spot the edge of dark ink. A tattoo. I want to rip off her pants and see it for myself.

Instead, I force my eyes away as I turn to my bike and pick up the helmet. It's the only one I've got, but she'll use it. "Here," I snap, thrusting it into her arms. She doesn't have a choice but to take it.

"What the fuck is this?" she demands as I press the key into the slot and turn it. The growl of the bike's engine roars to life.

PRETTY LITTLE SAVAGE

"It's a helmet," I say, compelling myself to remain patient. "Put it on."

When I look back to make sure she's doing as I ordered, I'm not shocked to see that she hasn't. Her eyes jump from the black, full coverage helmet in her grasp to me before narrowing. She looks at the bike. "As much as I'd love a motorcycle, I don't think you're in the mood to give me one," she says. "Which can only mean that you want me to ride it … with you. And that's not gonna happen, D-man." Avalon steps forward and punches me in the gut with my own helmet. "No, thanks," she says sweetly before turning around and walking off.

Oh. Fuck. No. I let the helmet drop to the gravel coated ground of the warehouse parking lot and stalk after her. When I reach her, I grab onto her and spin her around. My mouth is open and words haven't even escaped yet when her fist comes flying at my face. Without thinking, I duck.

"The fuck?"

"Don't fucking touch me," she snarls, jerking herself out of my grasp. "You may think you own Eastpoint, but you don't own me. I can go where I want, when I want."

A growl works its way up my chest, but it stops when my eyes drop back down to her chest—which is heaving up and down. Then I look lower. Fuck … I wanna see that tattoo. I want to know what kind of image she's got on her body. If it's wicked and sinful or if it's the opposite of her personality, soft and girly.

I chuckle darkly, causing her to still when she would have moved a step back again. Like a deer caught in the beams of blinding headlights. I shake my head. "Get on the bike, Avalon."

She looks up at me, narrowing her eyes as her petite

little chin juts out. Her lips frame the word I know she's going to say. "No," she snaps.

We're barely ten feet from the bike, so I turn her gorgeous ass around and push her back towards it. She fights me every step of the way, but it's a little difficult for someone her size to truly overpower me. If it was about sheer determination, however, she might have a chance. Maybe.

But it's not. It's about my strength versus hers. And mine is so much greater.

When I've got her backed up to my motorcycle, I lean down, letting her smell the mint on my breath as I place one hand on the bike seat at her back and the other on the handlebars, caging her in. The vibrancy in her blue-gray eyes is lit with irritation and it only serves to turn me on even more. She's unpredictable like a fire—one strong gust of wind will blow her too far off course and she'll devour everything in her path.

"Get on the bike." I repeat the order, raising my voice above the sound of the engine's growl, watching her as I do. I can't help but grin as she shoves her hands against my chest. There's strength behind the movement, but between the two of us—I haven't used up most of mine in a fight yet tonight.

"Go. The. Fuck. To. Hell. Dean." She enunciates each word.

I close my eyes and inhale the crisp night air, smelling midnight flowers on the breeze. I can't tell if it's because spring is coming or if it's her scent. I kind of want it to be hers because then maybe I could bottle it and sleep with it. A thought forms and I can't help but chuckle again. Were I to do that, it'd turn the occasional morning chub into a fucking massive hard on every fucking day.

"Let me rephrase," I try again, opening my eyes and

meeting her furious gaze. "You've got two choices. You can get on my bike willingly…" I trail off, watching the movement of expression on her face as she waits for her second option. She's not going to like it. "Or," I continue, "I'll rip your fucking pants down your legs, spank your ass, and then strap you on—willing or not." I lean back, keeping my arms around her as the vibrations of the bike shake from me to her. "What will it be, baby? You want me to make that ass red before you ride my bike?"

She wants to hit me, I can tell. She even considers it. As unpredictable as she is, when I'm this close—when I can see the tiny flecks of gray clouds in her otherwise dark indigo and storm cloud colored eyes—it's easy to read what she's thinking.

"If you even try it," she hisses between pretty clenched teeth, "I'll make sure any children you have are adopted."

I laugh. It's impossible to stop it. Any other bitch would be too scared to defy me even once much less keep pushing like she does. It's refreshing. It's … addicting. I freeze at that thought, my laughter dying away. A dark realization occurs to me and it makes me look at her in a new light. When she doesn't move to make good on her threat, I shove away from the bike, grabbing her and pulling her with me until she's far enough that I can slide around her and sling one leg over the leather seat.

I reach for my gloves and strap them on, nodding to the helmet left discarded on the ground. "You might want to put that on," I suggest in a bored tone, reaching for the clutch.

Avalon glances down at the helmet and I keep my head turned away as I ready myself for a long ride. She struggles with herself, her bottom lip rolling back between her teeth as one canine bites down on it. Half her face is shadowed when she turns towards it and fuck me, but when she bends over to retrieve it, that perfectly rounded ass of hers is all but on display as the worn fabric of her work out pants is drawn tight over it.

I slam my eyes shut and suck in lungful after lungful of air, hoping to will my raging cock down. Seconds later, when I hear the telltale click of the helmet being secured and then her hands touch my shoulders as she slings her leg around the back end of my bike, I realize it's not going to go down. Not so long as she's near.

The bike has stalled out, so I turn the key back, remove it, and restart the thing again. The motorcycle roars to life.

"Hold on tight," I call over my shoulder.

There's hesitation in her movements—distrustfulness—but her hands move to my waist and her fabric covered breasts are pushed against my back. She must have put her shirt back on while my eyes were closed because when I reach back and press my hand to her side, I don't feel bare skin. A pity. I slide my hand down to the bag strapped to the side of the bike and retrieve some glasses for the ride.

With no need to back out of the spot, I reach for the handlebars and press down on the gas. We fly over the thin strip of grass separating the gravel parking lot from the road. Wind whips through me and I can't help but think...

Driving a motorcycle while being hard as hell fucking sucks, but with Avalon's tits smashed against me and her hands creeping close to my abdomen, I don't mind it so much.

32

AVALON

Goosebumps rise along the skin of my arms as we speed down a deserted highway. After being in the overheated warehouse for who knows how long, the sweat has dried pretty quickly. With my front pressed to Dean's back, I feel nothing but heat from him. But along my spine, as the wind blows up the back of my shirt, the chill of the air sweeps around us and makes me shiver. Unthinkingly, I press myself against him even harder, trying to ward off the feeling.

He stiffens but doesn't say anything. *I'm absolutely crazy to trust him.* Fucking certifiable. Then again, I've always known that about myself. Something about him, though, makes me do crazy shit. Just looking at his stupid face makes me want to jump off a cliff, if only to try to outrun the ridiculous feelings he causes within me.

Is he going to kill me? I wonder as the roads grow longer and emptier. Maybe. Though he looks like an all-American jock with a bad boy streak, something tells me that Dean has a violent side.

My insanity makes itself known in the fact that I can't really make myself care. I'm not scared of him.

I should've never gotten on the back of his bike. Especially not after his threat. I know better than to think he's taking me back to the dorms. No, he's taking me somewhere else, somewhere far from Eastpoint.

In fact, I don't know where the fuck we are. It's somewhere rural. The warehouse had been farther out of Eastpoint than I've been since I arrived, but now we're somewhere in the mountains and the air is even colder up here. Despite the protective glass covering my face, I lift my head as a smell slips through the cracks and crevices and under my chin strap. There's something salty in the air.

I sniff at it, wondering what it is until I turn my head and freeze as the motorcycle turns a corner and suddenly we're riding past a deep incline that opens up to the fucking ocean. Dark waters crash against the cliffs below. So vast, it looks like it goes on forever. I can see, in that moment, why some people think the Earth is flat. It's dumb, but the ocean makes it look like it's all one big fucking plain that stretches well into the distance. I can't imagine it ever ending.

Even growing up in Georgia as I had, I'd still been hours from the ocean. It'd been a fucking crime, I realize. Or it should've been. To be so close and yet so far from such a beautiful sight. Patricia had never owned a car. Her job had been walking distance and what few nights she worked the pole at the *Tiny Dancer* combined with her welfare check had gotten us by. There'd never been a need for one. I find myself wishing, though, that there'd at least been one time we'd gone to the ocean. I hate that I've wasted so many years without seeing it. A yearning starts up in my chest; the desire to fling myself off the back of

Dean's motorcycle and into the wicked waters below and sink as deep as possible, letting it swallow me whole.

The image is disrupted when Dean turns the handlebars of the bike and a copse of trees obscures my vision as we ride even higher. My hands sink into the fabric of his shirt as I try to quell the need to go back. To see it again. It's kind of amusing when I think about it; the fact that I'd only ever been a few hours away and yet it took moving up north to ever get the chance to see it.

Dean turns the bike even more inward until we're winding up a two lane path. Every few yards the line of trees opens up, revealing how steep the cliff along our side is getting. I don't mind, not when I can still catch glimpses of the sea and smell the cold salt on the air. The motorcycle decelerates as we come to a slow stop and Dean turns us both into a small alcove, driving about half a mile more before slowing to a complete stop and steering us to the side of the path.

When the bike is parked, I pull myself away from his back and remove the helmet—ignoring the shiver that finally courses through me when the cold air slaps me in the face. I drop the helmet to the ground and start to untangle the strands of my hair, yanking out my ponytail and braiding it back instead as I should've done before. The engine cuts off, and I stiffen as Dean gets off the bike. His stare is like needles against my skin as he removes his glasses and turns to lean against the seat. It's heated. It's piercing. It's fucking annoying is what it is.

We're all alone. Just Dean Carter and me. Electricity hovers in the air, charged with my irritation and his ... cryptic behavior. *What the hell is he thinking?* I wonder as I finish braiding my hair and straighten my spine to turn and meet his gaze.

"Well," I start, gesturing for him to get on with it, "did you bring me out here to kill me or what?"

He arches a brow and I scowl because I don't know if he's just doing it because of my words or because he's being obstinate. Probably both. "If I wanted you dead," he says, crossing his arms over his massive chest, "you would be. I wouldn't need to bring you out here to do it, either."

I mirror his stance, my arms moving over my own chest. His eyes drop down once as if he can't help it before lifting back to my face. "Then why did you bring me out here?" I demand.

Instead of answering, he merely smirks at me and says, "There are worse things I can do to you than murder."

My muscles tighten, pulling taut beneath my skin. I hate that expression on his face. It makes me want to punch him again. "You've already threatened to rape me once," I deadpan. "You haven't done it yet."

His eyes pull away from mine and he turns his head, gazing past the trees to yet another opening where the trees are thinner—their roots anchored into the side of the cliff as it overlooks the ocean. "Does it scare you?" he asks quietly.

"Rape?" I clarify, but before he answers I shake my head. "No."

Both of his brows shoot up this time as he looks back at me. "No?" I shake my head, keeping my expression even. My leg begins to tap against the soft dirt ground and his lips spread into a smile. "Little liar," he accuses softly. I bite the inside of my cheek to keep from saying anything. It doesn't work.

"You don't know anything about me that hasn't come from a fucking file," I snap. "So don't sit there and pretend. You threatening to rape me doesn't scare me. You won't do it."

Dean's in my face in a split second, his hand on my throat, and his eyes centimeters from mine as he leans down and presses against my windpipe. "Are you challenging me, Avalon?"

He loosens his hold long enough for me to speak. "No," I say, "just stating facts."

"*Facts.*" He spits the word. "Is that what you call it?"

I can feel the indentation of his fingertips alongside my neck. Warm and calloused. Not like a man who's spent his entire life in luxury, even though that's who he is … isn't it? I take a step forward, despite the hand on my throat, and when he doesn't move, I stomp on his foot. Dean doesn't even blink, but his hand does loosen a smidgen more, though he keeps his fingers against my skin as if he's trying to prove to me that he can.

"Just get on with whatever you're going to do and then take me back to the dorm. It's late, I'm tired, and I've got class tomorrow."

Silence stretches between us for a moment, and then he drops his hand away. "You're right," he finally admits. I narrow my eyes on him.

"What do you mean?"

Even as he invades my space and my lungs fill with the scent of him—something dark and sinister, like a forbidden spice—I can't help but watch him as one might a predator. When he stands in front of me as he does, towering over me like a monster ready to eat his prey, I just want to challenge him. Because I'm not like normal prey. I don't just roll over and take it. I bite back.

Instead of threatening me again, as I expect, his hands skid down my sides until they oh so carefully find my hips. His eyes flicker to mine and lock right before he pulls me against his body. Hot tingles of awareness pass through me. I can't move even if I want to. The press of him and the creeping awareness of danger has my blood pumping faster.

What the actual fuck is wrong with me? I think. I want to step away from him, but my body fights me. It loves his nearness, the heat he throws off like a goddamn furnace. And the sense of brutality that might be coming at me at any second.

"W-what am I right about?" I shove the words out, unwilling to let him think that I'm not letting him touch me of my own free will.

One corner of his lips stays up as his fingers hook into the waistband of my pants and pauses. "Everything I know about you came from a file," he answers. "And that's going to change."

I lean back, looking up into his face with suspicion. He looks like a fallen angel with those dark eyes and equally dark hair against a tanned face. The stubble growing across the lower half of his face throws shadows in the most dangerous of places, so that when he looks at me, all that's highlighted is the upper bridge of his nose and his cheekbones. There's no light other than that of the beam of the motorcycle's headlight—something I assume he left on—and the moon. It makes me realize just how far removed from civilization we are.

He claimed he didn't, but if he'd wanted to kill me, he could easily get away with it. Just toss my body over the edge of the cliff and be done with it. No muss. No fuss. I shake away those thoughts and glare up at him.

"What are you talking about?"

"I've made a decision," he says. "I know all about the bargain you and Abel struck, but it seems keeping an eye on you from a distance isn't enough. You and I are about to become *very* close, Avalon." When Dean emphasizes the

PRETTY LITTLE SAVAGE

word 'very,' he pulls me into him until I can feel the full rigid length of his cock in his pants.

My face remains passive as my heart begins to race in my chest. One of my hands glides up and I settle it on his chest, right between his pecs and beneath his sternum. "You think so?" I challenge with an arched brow.

"I know so," he replies coolly.

"Are you asking for a truce?" I inquire, curious.

He laughs, the sound low and vibrating. It stirs something wicked inside of me; a twisted desire for this man who acts like a King and looks like the devil. He *is* a devil, beautiful and cruel. I doubt there's a woman alive who could survive him, and I certainly know that if I tried, I'd be left as nothing more than a husk of a human afterwards. Because Dean Carter is a man that cannot be tamed.

"No, little girl," he replies. "No more truces. No more bargains. I'm done being nice."

I snort and he pulls back a little to look down at my face fully. A cloud of air expels from his mouth as he breathes out, small and barely there—but with how cold the mountain air is, it doesn't surprise me to see it.

"This was you being nice?" I counter with a smirk.

"Oh yes," he says, his voice so serious that it makes my lips turn downward once more. "I've been very nice to you, baby." He turns his face and nuzzles against the soft, whisper thin baby hairs at my hairline. This time, there's no repressing the shiver that comes from his nearness.

Fuck, I think. *I'm so fucking fucked. And not in the good way.*

"But that's all about to end," he continues, "because you can't be trusted."

"I don't trust you either," I point out. The masculine scent of him invades my nostrils and I try to back up, but his hands press down harder against my sides, anchoring me in place. After a moment, he drops his arms and takes a step back, turning towards his bike. My knees threaten to crumble beneath me, but I hold fast and steady, forcing myself to appear unaffected. Inside, though, my nerves are on red alert.

I feel alive. Like the moments right before a fight. Except I don't expect to defend myself against Dean the same way. He's cunning, sharp. Ruthless. I watch his movements carefully as he strides over to the bike and lifts one leg over the seat before reaching down and retrieving the helmet I'd carelessly dropped alongside it, not caring that it probably cost several hundred dollars.

"You never told me what you meant by what you said," I say as I take a step towards him.

He lifts the helmet in my general direction as he slides the glasses back over his eyes. "Guess you're going to find out, aren't you?" the asshole comments without remorse.

I sneer at him, stalking forward and ripping the helmet from his grasp. "This will be your only warning, Dean Carter," I state.

He leans back and slides both hands into his hair, pulling the strands back from his face so I can see him clearly—every chiseled and stubble-jawed inch of him. "Oh?" He smirks.

I scowl and lean into his face as I clutch the helmet. "You fuck with me and I will fuck with you ten times as hard," I hiss.

His lips part, his tongue coming out to slide across his lower lip as he bares his teeth. "I look forward to it, Avalon. If anyone can take me, I wanna see if you can."

He's playing with me. He has to be. But I don't give him the satisfaction of an answer. He can have the last word if he wants it. I've given him fair warning. Shoving my head back into the helmet, I strap it on and climb onto the back of his bike as it roars back to life.

"Don't forget to hold on," he says. "We've got a bumpy ride back."

Dean can't see the glower as my hands find the sides of his abdomen. Out of pure spite, I sink my nails into him, grinning when he grunts.

That tiny victory is short lived as he leans back and speaks again. "Be angry all you want, baby," he says. "Just remember I, too, give as good as I get."

My hold loosens, but only marginally, as we take off and I turn back, wanting to see the ocean one last time—the only good thing that came out of this night. Instead, all I see is the red glow of the taillight on the pavement beneath us like an ugly eye watching our every movement. The entire high from my adrenaline rush has seeped out of me within a few hours when usually it takes days or maybe even weeks for the need to build back up.

Dean is no good for me, but my one consolation is the fact that I'm not good for him either. If he tries to take me down completely, he'll find himself a King without a throne.

33

AVALON

Dean Carter is proof that not all demons live in hell. Some of them walk among us. He certainly does. With his head held high and an eternal smirk on his face like he can't help but laugh at the rest of the world. It pisses me off.

After our little foray at the warehouse and the midnight ride, I'm ready to just try and get back to a normal schedule the next day when I walk into class. But all my good intentions go up in smoke when I spot the object of my annoyance and persistent hatred sitting in my seat.

The girl behind me slams into my back when I come to an unexpected stop just inside the door, causing me to clench my teeth as she accidentally hits a few of the lingering bruises from the night before.

"Ugh, watch it," she grumbles.

I don't think, I just turn around and level her with a glare. "You fucking watch it, bitch," I snap back. Today is not the day to fuck with me.

She scoffs but turns her head away as she slides around me and hurries to her seat. Abel looks up from his spot and waves me over. I ignore him, taking the steps two at a time as I climb to the now unoccupied seats they've been using since they transferred into this class. The ones they used to watch me from afar. I can feel Dean's eyes following me.

I slam my bag down on the empty seat, take a deep breath and let it out before sliding into the chair and dropping my shit down by my feet.

They're just trying to elicit a reaction from me, I tell myself. *Remain calm.*

That, of course, is easier said than done when two minutes later, I watch as the three of them pack up their shit and move back with me. I stiffen as Braxton drops into the chair at the end of my row. My fingers twitch towards my bag, but I'm not even given the chance to avoid them because in the next instant, Abel bounds down the row in front of the one I'm currently sitting in, puts his hands on the table and lifts himself up and over and onto the other side, blocking me from exiting.

I turn accusing eyes on Dean who just stands behind Brax with his stupid grin.

"What the fuck do you think you're doing?" I demand.

Dean's eyes drop to Brax, who gets up and shuffles past me, dropping a hand on my shoulder as he goes. I shrug it off with an irritated huff before returning my scowl to the man still standing at the end of the row like he fucking owns the place. I mean, he does, but does he have to be so fucking smug about it?

Like the night before, Dean's hands come down and cage me in—one on the back of my chair and the other on the table in front of me. He leans close, my vision completely overtaken by his chest and the dangling chain hanging down in front of the loose band t-shirt he wears.

"I told you," he says, whispering the words so only I can hear. A shudder threatens to overtake me. I shove it down and jerk my chin up as he continues. "I'm going to be keeping a close eye on you, Avalon. Consider me your new best friend because we're going to be spending a lot of time together."

I recoil. "Excuse me?" He can't mean what I think he means. "You're not serious."

"Oh, I'm dead serious, baby." He licks his lips, drawing my eyes back to his full masculine mouth. A flash of silver between his lips startles me. How the hell had I never noticed it before?

"You're going to regret this," I say distractedly, watching his mouth even harder, trying to see the piercing again.

"This is a new kind of lockdown," he says by way of answer. His breath smells like mint and menthol. It makes me want a cigarette really fucking bad, if only to take a drag and blow it in his face. "It's you and me, Ava." His eyes bore into me, the different shades of brown and red in their depths mesmerizing. "And when it's not me, then it's you and them." He nods behind me, meaning Abel and Brax.

"Why?" I blurt. It doesn't make any sense. "Why me?"

He hums low in his throat. Eyes watch us. I don't know if it's just the other guys or if it's the whole class and I can't seem to drag my gaze away from Dean's to find out. "I don't know," he admits, reaching up and lifting one tendril of hair from my shoulder and smoothing the pad of his finger over the individual strands. "Maybe because you're special, baby." He grins. "And you just don't know it yet."

I pull my head back, tugging my hair with it. He releases the lock of hair easily enough and then slides into his seat as the teacher walks in and class begins.

I fume for the next hour and a half that I'm trapped in the room with them. The teacher goes over the material, his unusually attentive expression not even bothering to hide his curiosity as he catches a glimpse of the Sick Boys and me smack dab in the middle of all three of them. My annoyance intensifies into anger. He's provoking me. Pushing me. Wanting to see what I'll do, how I'll react.

Cutting a glance at the man in question out of the corner of my eye, I observe him silently. His head is turned towards the front like this is just another day in class. Yet, his body is facing me as he sits sideways in his seat, like he's unthinkingly blocking the exit route with his massive form. I wonder if he even realizes what he's doing.

When the class period is up and the professor dismisses us, his eyes still jumping up to us every few seconds, I quickly grab my bag and try to press my way out of the opposite side of the row. I'd rather take on both Braxton and Abel than Dean.

They don't stop me, but Dean's deep baritone does as he calls after me. "Be good, baby," he says loud enough for the whole class to hear.

If there was any question about the attention he's drawn to me, that one statement is the final nail in my coffin. My legs restart and I stomp out of the room. I'm so furious as I make my way out of the building that I don't even realize that I have a shadow until I turn a corner and spot him behind me.

"Jesus fuck!" I scream, rounding on him. "You scared the shit out of me."

Braxton rocks back on his feet, his hands in his pockets—and no book bag of any kind, I notice. "Sorry?" He smiles at me.

My brows lower as I stare at him for a moment. "How the fuck can someone as big as you make no noise?" I find myself asking.

His shoulders lift in a shrug, that smile remaining in

place. "Why are you following me?" I demand after that nonanswer.

"Just going to class, li'l savage," he says, that nickname reminding me of his reaction to my fighting. He, at least, hadn't acted like such an overgrown asshole.

Turning abruptly, I start off in the opposite direction of my next class, calling over my shoulder as I go, "Have fun! I'm skipping today."

Not even a minute goes by and he's right back at my side, striding along with me. I stop in the middle of the sidewalk, my fists clenching and unclenching at my sides. "Didn't you hear me?" I ask. "I said I'm skipping."

"I heard you." He nods. "And if you're skipping then so am I."

"What the fuck, Brax?" I demand. "Are you Dean's lapdog now?"

Braxton lifts one hand out of his pockets and scratches at the back of his inky dark hair; a floppy curl falls over one brow as he cocks his head to the side. "You heard the man, Ava," he says lightly. "You're on lockdown."

"So?" I gesture between us. "This is not your normal lockdown. I've been on lockdown before. Just put me on that again and leave me the fuck alone. This isn't necessary."

Brax drops his hand. "If Dean says it is, it is," is all he says in response.

I inhale through my nose until it hurts and I let out a short, frustrated scream. Flipping around, I don't stop walking until I'm standing in front of the building to my next class. "This is fucking ridiculous," I comment as Braxton stops alongside me.

"Want my advice?" he asks.

I tip my head back and gaze up at him—all six foot five inches of him. "Fine," I huff, "just spit it out."

"Accept it," he says, making my lip curl back in disdain. He chuckles. "I'm serious," he continues. "You're not going to make him stop by fighting it. Just let him feel like he's in control and he'll let you have some freedom."

My head rolls back and my eyes turn from Brax's face to the sky. Slowly, with great effort and a lot of breathing, I let the tension drain from my body. "He can't control me, Brax," I say. "He might control everyone and everything else, but nobody controls me."

"I don't know why you don't just give in," he replies as he steps forward, walking the ten steps it takes to get to the entrance. He reaches for the handle and holds the door for me. "Who knows? You might like it."

"That's not just doubtful," I say, taking a step towards him as I pass through and into the cooler interior, "it's fucking impossible."

34

AVALON

Murder. I'm honestly considering it. How to commit it and how to get away with it.

"Angry about something, princess?" Abel mocks as he walks behind me. I grit my teeth and ignore him, but he doesn't seem to mind all that much. He keeps talking. "I did warn you," he continues. "But you didn't listen."

"You never said he'd become this obsessive," I snap back, unable to stop myself.

Abel ambles forward, his longer legs easily overtaking mine even though I'm walking as fast as I can without breaking into a jog. He smirks down at me and it only makes me want to punch him in the face. "No one could have predicted *that*," he replies, "but you really only have yourself to blame. If you weren't so..."

I stop and turn on him, making him come to a halt as well or risk slamming into me. "If I weren't so *what*?" I challenge, venom in my tone.

He lifts his hands in surrender. "Nothing, never mind," he says, still smiling. "Just pretend I'm not even here."

I huff out a breath and turn around, heading up the

steps of the office building. "As far as I'm concerned," I mutter. "You shouldn't be."

We make our way into the building and up the elevator. The doors slide open when we reach Ms. Bairns's floor and I step out and storm past the long line of elaborate portraits. For some reason, today they seem like they, too, are staring smugly down at me. As it had been last time, Bairns's door is cracked. I don't even knock, I just shove through, causing the woman herself to start as she drops a sheaf of papers. They fall, scattering over the top of her desk.

"Avalon!" She stands up to welcome me but freezes halfway out of her seat when my shadow pushes the door open even further and strides in. Ms. B seems to catch herself staring and quickly shakes off the surprise. "W-welcome," she stutters out, throwing a hand towards the chairs in front of her desk. "Won't you take a seat?"

I drop into one of the overstuffed chairs and cross my arms over my chest as I lean back and glare over her head. She retakes her seat, eyes shooting to Abel. Unsurprisingly, she doesn't ask him to leave. Abel is, after all, practically the son of her bosses. Fucking rich people.

"Thank you for coming," Ms. Bairns's begins as she starts restacking the papers she'd dropped and shuffles a few of them to the side. "I was worried when you didn't show up for your last appointment, but I'm glad you're here now."

I don't comment, and she sighs as she pulls a small folder from beneath the mess even as she continues the attempt to tidy up. "Okay, well, let's just go ahead and jump into it, shall we?" This time, she's smart enough not to expect an answer. The only reason I'm even here today is because her last email had a more desperate edge concerning the possibility of me taking on a scholarship.

I'm honestly just waiting for her to bring that up again. My eyes cut to Abel. I wonder if she will with him in the room.

"I'm concerned about some missed classes," Ms. B states, glancing from the file in her hand to me. "How have you been? Adjusting well?"

"Everything's been just *peachy*," I say sarcastically, shooting Abel a glare as I do so. The corner of his mouth tips up, but other than that one small movement, it's as if he's pretending he's not even here. God, I really wish that were true. I'm getting tired of feeling like I constantly have a guard dog on me at all times.

"Right." Ms. B ignores my tone and continues on. "Well, I have to say that despite the few absences—your grades are impeccable. I'm not surprised. I was sure you'd be able to adapt well to the academic expectations here." She shoots me a beaming smile, but I feel like doing anything but smiling back.

"Is that it?" I ask. "You wanted to ask about the absences and tell me about my grades?"

Ms. Bairns's smile droops and, once again, her eyes dart to the man sitting to my right. She clears her throat. "Actually, no, I was wondering if you'd had a chance to think any more about that proposal I mentioned to you before," she says, lowering her voice and leaning forward.

My lips press together as I turn my head to the side, avoiding her gaze as I scan the room. Floor to ceiling bookshelves packed with volumes that look like they've been there since this building was built. Dust coats the front of the shelves, telling me they're just there for decoration. What a fucking pity.

"I'm still thinking," I say after a long moment.

"I honestly think it would be a great opportunity for you, Avalon," Ms. B presses.

When I glance back at her, I notice that Abel's head is

turned towards me. Oh, he pretends like he's looking at the bookshelf just as I was, but every few seconds, his eyes flick towards Ms. B and then to me. On the second pass, he realizes that I'm watching him and our eyes lock. I keep them like that as I reply to Ms. Bairns's words.

"I told you I'm still thinking," I say. "I haven't made a decision yet."

"But you promise to give it careful consideration?"

Abel arches a brow at me. I shake my head and pull my attention away, leveling it back on her. "Yeah, sure." I get up from the chair. "Are we done?"

"Um..." Ms. B hurries to rise from her chair as I don't wait for her to answer, instead, choosing to stride past Abel and head for the door. "Okay, well, don't forget, I won't be seeing you until after spring break, Avalon!"

I leave the room, Abel getting up and following me as I hit the hallway and storm past the portraits yet again. Getting to the elevator, I jam my finger against the button before turning around, ready to give Abel a piece of my mind for being such an intrusive dick when I find him paused in front of one of the many portraits. It isn't the look of concentration on his face, but the sheer vile hatred I see in his eyes that stops me.

Without even thinking about it, I turn my head, wondering what the hell could elicit such a reaction. The portrait he stands in front of is one of the newer ones. A tall man with a shock of white-blond hair similar to his stands there, clad in a suit that looks molded to the man's slender frame. There's a cruel beauty in the image before us. A coldness in the man's eyes speaks of something darker beneath the fabric he wears and the brush strokes that paint him.

"Abel?" The elevator dings just as I say his name and

he turns from the painting, heading straight for the doors as they slide open to reveal an empty compartment.

I don't get a chance to ask him what that was about because the second the doors are closed, Abel turns on me. "What opportunity was she talking about?" he demands.

A scowl forms over my lips. "Why do you need to know?" His stare never wavers and I growl. "It's nothing. Just a scholarship to come to Eastpoint as an official student rather than a dual enrollment student."

He blinks and then sinks back against the back wall with a nod. "Oh, okay," he says.

I eye him. "That's it?"

Abel waits until the doors open again and we stride out towards the exit. "You'll accept," is all he says.

My feet come to a stop at the edge of the stairs and he keeps walking, pausing only when he realizes I'm not with him. Abel's hair slides across the tops of his ears as he pivots back to me with an arched brow. The sun shines down, hotter than it's been these last few weeks. It soaks into my skin and makes me feel like I'm burning just as much on the outside as I am on the inside.

"What makes you think I'm going to accept?" I ask when I finally have his attention.

He shrugs. "You're a smart girl," he tells me. "It's a good deal for a girl like you."

I take one step down. "A girl like me?" I repeat his words with a shake of my head. "You would think that, wouldn't you?"

"Am I wrong?" he inquires.

If poverty was all that made me then no, he wouldn't be. But I was more than just poor. Blood and sweat and dirt coated hands reaching for me flashes in front of my field of vision, disrupting my current reality. I recall the memory I had the last time I went cliff diving. It hadn't been my mother's last attempt to sell me ... only the first. I swallow around a suddenly dry throat.

"The scholarship comes with strings," I say. "I don't like following other people's rules."

A bitter smile spreads Abel's lips, stretching them impossibly tight. So tight, I half expect the skin to split right open and blood to trickle down his teeth and chin. It's a barbaric expression. One I'm not used to seeing on him.

"Everything comes with strings," he says, his voice different from what I'm familiar with. Deeper. Darker. The clarity in his eyes fades as if he's gazing into a far off distance. "You may think that money frees you from some things, and maybe it does, but it ties you down in other ways." One of his hands comes up and rests against his chest as if he's stroking something beneath his shirt. I take another step down until I'm much closer to him and I catch a glimpse of the outline of something dangling around his neck, almost hidden by the crew neck of his t-shirt.

"Money might give you power, but even power comes with strings attached," he continues in that hollow tone. "Piss off the wrong people, make the wrong move, trust the wrong friends—and suddenly all of that money and power can disappear in a heartbeat. Money brings misery. Power brings nothing but bloodshed."

At that last comment, his eyes clear and he seems to realize where he is as I stand there, staring at him with curiosity, wondering where this had come from. I don't say anything and he doesn't offer any explanation.

Instead, the two of us head in the direction of my dorm, and when we get there, he leaves me at the door without another word.

35

AVALON

I haven't had this much attention in ... well, I've never had this much attention. Ever. At first, I think it's because of me, but as their stalker-tendencies become the norm over the next week or so, I begin to realize that they just naturally draw people's focus. Eyes follow them wherever they go. Girls go out of their way to try and capture their eye. Guys always raise their hands in greeting. It's like everyone wants to know them or wants to be known by them and they take it in stride, as if that's something they've grown up with their whole lives. For me, it's just another difference between us. While they might be used to being seen, I am used to being invisible and I don't like my new status.

"Hi, Avalon!" I nearly jump out of my skin when an unfamiliar girl walking down the hallway in Havers calls out to me, waving her hand.

Glancing over my shoulder, I scowl at her and shove my way into the dorm room where Rylie, thankfully, is not. I've had too much of this, I decide. I need another release. A break from this place.

I glance at the clock and realize I've only got a few hours left to pull it off. Buses in Eastpoint tend to stop running around nine so if I want to make it out to the lake, I've got to get my ass in gear. Dumping my bag of school supplies, I shovel in a new change of clothes and a few other things before changing into the only swimsuit I own —a token from the lost and found from one of my old schools. A lot of people don't like to reuse swimsuits, but for a girl like me, it's this or nothing.

I tie the top around my neck which, if I'm honest, is a bit too small before snagging a long t-shirt that looks more like a dress than just a shirt and slide it on over my head. My whole body perks up, my steps seemingly lighter and more energetic as I rush to get ready. It's like it can physically sense the release we're about to get.

Shoving my arms through the loops of my backpack, I cinch it tight and leave the room, taking the stairs two at a time, holding onto the railing so I don't slip and go flying down. When I get to the end, I practically leap off the last three as I make a beeline for the front entrance. I nearly stumble over my own two feet and go down in a heap when, as I push through the double doors, a tall figure turns towards me expectantly, a phone pressed to the side of his head.

"Yeah, I'll be there. Gotta go."

I straighten and glare at him. "Are you fucking kidding me?" I snap. "Do you literally just stand outside of my dorm all day, waiting for me?"

Dean arches one brow and stares down at me as he shoves his phone back into his pocket. For a moment, he doesn't say anything, but instead, lets his eyes rove down my body curiously. He doesn't answer my question. "You can't wear that," he says instead. "Go back and get changed, we're going to a party."

"Not just no, but hell fucking no," I tell him, crossing my arms over my chest. "I've already got plans."

He shrugs as if my words are a mere inconvenience. "Doesn't matter. They just changed."

"N*ope*." I stomp past him.

"What are these plans of yours?" he asks, following me.

"None of your business," I reply.

Just like Abel, he finds no issue keeping up with my pace. "If you don't tell me"—that deep baritone of his slides over my senses like audible porn and makes me want to stab my own eardrums out just to take back some of the power he's stolen from me—"then I'll just assume you want to go to this party and I'll carry your ass there as is."

I stop at the edge of the sidewalk. "Why?" I demand.

His lips turn down in a frown. "What do you mean why?"

"Why do you want me to go to some dumb party?" I ask.

"You're on lockdown, and therefore, where I go, you go."

My eyes roll back into my head and I snort, taking another few steps away. "Just go with the guys."

"They're already going." He reaches out and grabs me, halting any further movement. "Believe me, if I didn't have to go, I wouldn't be."

I debate what to do. I could still try to slip his grip and get away, but the likelihood is sinking by the second. Some guys are stronger than they look, and in Dean's case, he looks and acts just as strong as he actually is. The fingers circling my upper arm contract as he waits for me to make my decision.

"Let's make a deal," I suggest instead. "You take me where I need to go, no questions asked, and I'll go to your stupid party with you."

PRETTY LITTLE SAVAGE

His dark eyes narrow on me as if sensing for a weakness or a lie. "Why?" he demands, his grip becoming punishingly tight.

I glare at him. "I said no questions asked," I snap. "But I promise to go to your dumb college party as long as you fulfill your end of the bargain."

"I told you no more bargains," he says, but his grip loosens slightly and he doesn't sound as suspicious anymore. In fact, he sounds curious.

A part of me wants to know what the hell I'm thinking. The lake is one of the only secret places that's just mine. He knows where I live. He knows every class I take—hell if he's not in them, then one of the others is. He has my schedule down to a science and is constantly following me and steering me where he wants me to be. The lake is supposed to *mine*. Yet, the thought of letting him go, of letting him see that side of me doesn't leave a bad aftertaste in my mouth like I expected.

"It's either that or I fight you every step of the way," I comment.

When his eyes trail down my face a second time, I let him see the truth of my statement. He might be controlling, but I can be just as stubborn. His lips twist and he considers it for a moment. Finally, he drops his arm away from mine completely, scrubbing a hand down his face as he groans. "Fuck," he mutters. "Fine. Let's go."

And the excitement is back.

I don't hesitate to trail after him as he leads me to the side of the street where his motorcycle is parked beneath the large canopy of a red maple tree. "Where am I going?" he asks.

Instead of telling him, I demand his phone and smirk when he scowls at me as he slides it back out of his pocket and hands it over. It's a newer model, the screen perfect and uncracked. It takes me a moment to figure out how to use it, but once I do, I find the map app and plug in the coordinates before giving it back.

"That's where we're going," I say.

Dean turns and fixes the phone to the front of his bike so that he'll be able to follow the little blue arrow as he drives. One strong leg slides over the seat and he settles in, reaching back for his helmet. He hands me one and I pause when he lifts a second and slides it over his head, snapping the chin strap into place before backing out of the parking spot and turning the engine on. He brought two helmets this time…

I don't know why that thought lingers in my mind. If he wants me to go to a stupid party and he'd come to pick me up, it makes sense. At the same time, though … I turn the helmet over in my hand, noticing that—unlike the one he now wears—it's unscratched and pristine as if he just purchased it.

"You getting on?" His voice is muffled by the plastic covering his face and roar of the engine, but it still drives me out of my thoughts and I nod, sticking my head inside the fresh, clean smelling helmet and buckle it on before swinging my leg over the back of his bike.

I press myself against Dean's back and close my eyes as he presses the gas and together, the two of us go shooting forward, sliding dangerously across the pavement. Whenever I'm around him, my adrenaline seems to be ever present. As if she senses something more in the man in front of me that I still have yet to see.

It makes me curious and that's dangerous.

Dean doesn't say a word as he parks the motorcycle and lets me slide off the back. I wait for him to turn off the engine, stow the helmets, and pocket his keys so we can head up the path that leads towards the open ledge overlooking the lake.

Even though this is only my second time coming here, I remember the path well. He follows behind me, for once, letting me take the lead. I can sense his curiosity, but he doesn't ask any questions, letting the peace of the sounds of bugs screaming and animals scurrying around in the underbrush be. Halfway up, I pause and stare through a copse of trees at the mossy-green, still surface of the lake below.

"You know," I find myself saying, "when I was a kid, we didn't have places like this. Not in my hometown. We had trees and we had some mountains but no lakes where I was at."

Dean takes a step closer to me, his head lifting as he follows my gaze.

I turn and start the climb again, continuing as I walk, keeping my eyes on the ground in front of my shoes. "There was an old man that worked at the elementary school," I start. "I think he was a janitor or something. He worked for the school and the local church, but in the summer he'd drive out to the ocean—it was only a few hours away—and stay with his brother to teach deep sea diving classes."

"Did you know him well?" Dean's question startles me.

I bite my lip before answering. "I didn't know him at all," I admit. "I only know all that because when I was in second grade, there was a big announcement about an employee dying. They passed around a few papers in class and I read his obituary. Something happened during one of his last classes and he got caught underwater and he drowned."

We come to the ledge. "What does that have to do with us being out here?" Dean's voice deepens as I drop my bag and pull off my shoes. The sun dips below the tree line, but the sky remains awash with tones of reds, yellows, and oranges. "Ava?"

"Can you imagine?" I ask, staring across the open space the ledge presents us with.

"Imagine what?"

I pull off my clothes until I'm clad in nothing but the worn second hand, ill-fitting bathing suit. Dean's eyes track my movements as I step towards the ledge. I half expect him to reach for me, but he doesn't seem surprised at all.

Turning away from the water below, I face him with a smile. "Can you imagine the rush he must've felt before he died?"

"I doubt he would've felt any sort of rush," Dean replies quietly, no inflection in his voice. "Most people don't get excited by the prospect of dying."

My eyes find the ground once more as a smile comes to my lips. He's right. *Most people* don't. "I guess I'm not most people," I say, just before turning around and taking a step closer to the edge.

"Avalon..." His tone is a warning, but I don't care. "What are you doing?"

I laugh, spreading my arms wide. "It's called cliff diving," I say. A pebble slips out from beneath my bare feet and goes careening down the side of the ledge until it plops into the water below, causing a ripple to shudder over the once smooth surface.

"Why do you do it?" he asks.

I pause. *Why* do *I do it?* For the rush, of course. For the feeling of being in control of myself even when danger is so close. I like it—trailing that thin line between sanity and insanity. One wrong slip up could cost me. Yet, I keep coming back because I like the feel of my body rebelling against my mind and knowing that it has to do what I say anyway. The sweat that coats my skin. The heartbeat racing in my chest. It fights back with everything it has and yet nothing can stop it but me. *I'm* the one in control. Control that I've ceded time and time again—to school officials, to the fucking Patricias of the world, the Rogers, and even ... I'll admit ... the Sick Boys.

They have all the power. They have all the authority. Where I have none.

But here. Here, it's me. No one can control the things I do to myself but me. Not even my own body can stop me.

"It's dangerous," Dean says, bringing me back to the present.

"I know." I hear myself speak as if the words are coming down a long dark tunnel. My feet move beneath me as I turn to face him. His brows are creased and unlike earlier, he now looks like he's half a second away from grabbing me.

Dark brown eyes leap from where my feet are, the heels half over the edge already, to my face. "Are you sure you know what you're doing?" he asks.

I shake my head. "If I did, where would the fun in that be?"

"Aval—"

I don't hear the rest of what he's about to say because, without another second to think, I push off and leap back, sending myself flying over the edge. Wind whips at my hair, sending it all forward, shooting over my face and obscuring my view. *I should've leapt forward,* I think absently, but then, in a brief moment—my hair parts and I can see the molten sky above.

It looks like a cascade of fire over the ocean. And for a split second, the discomfort of the strands of my long hair that I'd forgotten to pull back before I'd jumped is forgotten. Then I crash into the water and the darkness swallows me up.

36

DEAN

I don't need to read her fucking file to know that Avalon Manning is fucked up. All I need to do is see her as she is right now.

For once, her eyes are clear and unclouded by thoughts or actions. She simply stands there, swaying back and forth as if she's dancing to music that only she can hear. I don't know if she even realizes it. I tell myself to act cool, to keep my hands down and not show her just how fucking freaked out she's making me.

I know she has a penchant for reckless behavior. That much *was* in the file. I never expected to experience it first hand, though. "Are you sure you know what you're doing?" I ask, tamping down on my nerves.

Her head twists from side to side, more of that swaying rippling through her body. I blink, realizing just how much of it I can actually see. Fuck, she's got curves. Her abdomen is almost completely flat—it would be if not for the lines along either side of her stomach and the small swell just above her bikini line. Her top is held tight against her frame, two small triangles of fabric all that stands between my eyes and those tits.

When she lifts her head, though, and smiles at me, all my thoughts of her smoking hot body recede. "Where would the fun in that be?" she asks me.

Fuck, she's gonna... "Aval—" I don't even get her name fully out before she jumps.

I shoot forward, leaping towards the ledge to stare over, watching as she falls the length of at least half a goddamn football field into the murky depths below. Her body hits, and a wave of water goes flying. I clench my teeth, hissing out my breath as I wait for her to resurface.

"Come on, come on, come on," I mutter. "Come up, damn it."

Thirty seconds go by. Then a minute. A minute and a half.

"Fuck this." I rip my shirt up and over my head, shuck my jeans and boxers, and toe off my boots in record time. My heart is jackhammering inside my chest. I swear to fuck if she drowns, I'm going to be so fucking pissed. Closing my eyes, I take the leap right after her.

Ice cold water closes over my head. I don't know how far I sink, but as soon as I gradually slow down, I swipe my arms up and swim for the top, popping up for a breath of air, only then realizing that she's finally resurfaced and she's laughing.

"Why did you jump too?" she chuckles, swimming first one way and then the other, her dark hair—which had been in tangles around her face earlier—is slicked back behind her ears.

"You didn't come up right away," I say, watching her body cut through the water like it's nothing. "I thought you'd..."

She spins in a circle, dipping her head back into the water again. "What? Thought I hit my head?"

I had. And the tightness that I feel in my chest now makes her amusement that much more irritating.

"What were you gonna do?" she asks, staring at me across the water. "Save me?"

Kicking my feet, I feel like an animal tracking its prey. "Of all the girls in the world," I say as I trail her through the water. "You act like there's nothing in the world you need saving from."

"Because there's not," she replies easily. "Anything I've ever needed saving from, I've always done myself."

She follows my movements with her eyes, backing up slowly as I advance. "Like what?" I press.

Her head shakes and when I'm only three feet away, she turns and dives deep—or at least she tries to. The attempt to get away is cut short when I reach out and wrap one arm around her waist, yanking her back against my chest. Ava's head comes popping back up out of the water, her hair flying in her face as she coughs.

"What the hell!" She gasps and sputters, spitting the gross lake water out as she yells at me. "Why are you naked?"

I smirk and lean down even closer. "You didn't answer my question." I whisper the words against her ear, causing her to stiffen. Her ass rubs against something else that's just a bit more stiff than she is.

Black hair slaps me in the face as she looks back. "Are you seriously hard right now?"

I ignore the question and instead, turn her completely around until we're both treading water, face to face. "What have you had to save yourself from, Avalon?"

Her lips part and I'm torn between wanting to stare

into her eyes and watching her tongue as it slips between her teeth. "Maybe I need saving from you," she counters.

I shake my head and smile. "Oh baby, there's nothing in the world that can save you from me."

For several long seconds, we're locked in a battle of wills, her and I. Our eyes center on one another, neither of us willing to look away. Bubbles pop up from the depths of the lake, reminding me that we're currently floating in a pool of algae and an unknown number of fish and other aquatic creatures.

This is not how I want to fuck her. For all I know, we'd both end up drowning. Yet, even though my mind agrees, my body pulses with need. My cock is rock hard as it presses against her lower abdomen.

I lean forward, until she's all I see. When she doesn't move back, her complete attention focused on me—making me feel like the most important thing in the world right now—I slowly touch my nose to hers. I want to kiss her. No. More than that. I want to fucking devour her. Consume all of her.

Avalon isn't the type of girl a man merely kisses. She's the type of girl a man gorges himself on until there's nothing left.

"You're so fucking dangerous, you know that?" I don't mean it as a question, but the words come out as one nonetheless.

One corner of those lush, fuckable lips of hers curves up. "If I'm so dangerous, then why do you insist on stalking me?" she quips.

My eyes flick between hers as I slowly kick my legs, driving us towards shore. She must realize what I'm doing too, because in the next moment her legs lift up and circle my waist. My cock fucking *pulses*.

I suck in a lungful of air. Down here, in the water, in

the woods, in the middle of fucking nowhere—everything feels humid and hot.

"Because," I say honestly, trying to drive my need to fuck her back, "I tried to leave you alone. Now, it's too late."

She tilts her head to the side, her smirk dipping into a frown of confusion as her brows draw down low over those gorgeous fucking eyes of hers. "Why is it too late?"

"You throw everything out of whack." Stroke. Kick. Stroke. With her strapped to my chest now, willingly clinging to me, it's easier to swim. "You go off on your own and do stupid shit."

She scoffs and when she would pull away, I stop swimming and press a hand to her back, spreading my fingers over her spine, stopping the movement.

"I don't do stupid shit," she argues anyway. "I just do shit that isn't sanctioned by the 'Sick Boys.'" When she says the stupid name Abel, Braxton, and I have grown up with, her arms come up out of the water alongside both of our heads and she curls her fingers into air quotes as she says the words.

I smile. "We didn't choose that name, you know," I tell her.

She blinks at me, her arms plopping down, splashing the side of my neck with water. "You didn't?"

Stroke. Stroke. Kick. "Of course, we didn't," I reply. "It's dumb. People have been calling us that since high school. First it was the Eastpoint heirs then it was the Sick Boys..." I trail off, meeting her eyes as my feet find the ground beneath the water and I stop swimming long enough to stand. "Does this feel boyish to you?" I ask, one hand cupping her under her ass and pressing her more fully against my raging hard on.

Avalon doesn't gasp. She doesn't blush. She doesn't do

anything another chick might. No, she just looks up at me, unblinking, and doesn't say a damn word. So, I answer for her. "I haven't been a boy since I was sixteen," I tell her.

Finally, a flicker of life in her eyes. "Why then?" she asks. "Why that age?"

Because that was the age I'd killed my first man, but I don't tell her that. I may want to fuck Avalon Manning, but I don't trust her. Not yet. Maybe not ever.

"Doesn't matter," I say instead, striding further until the water only reaches my hips before dropping her to walk on her own. She peels herself away from me without complaint, turns and heads for shore and I watch her go, hating the feeling of coldness sliding over my wet skin now that she's no longer clinging to me. "We're men. Not boys."

I watch as she turns and glances over her shoulder as she heads back towards the beginning of the path that leads back to the ledge where my clothes and her bag are. When her eyes dip below my abdomen as I walk the rest of the way out, it takes everything in me not to react. Her eyes widen and her lips part.

"Holy shit..."

I roll my tongue in my cheek, fighting a smile and failing. "Like what you see?" I ask. "Or are you hoping to start something?"

Her mouth gapes open like a fish. Closing once and reopening only to close again. Finally, she shakes her head as if clearing away the dirty thoughts I know are swimming through her mind right now. "Just didn't expect you to have..." She gestures to me. "That."

I shrug, swiping one hand up over my face and through my hair. The smell of sweat and something even more odorous hits my nostrils and I drop my arm once more. "Unless you want to give it a ride then let's get moving. We still have a party to get to, and now I need a shower."

Avalon shakes her head. "In your dreams," she mutters, turning away.

Little does she know, I intend to make my dreams come true. Every single, filthy one of them.

37

AVALON

He's fucking pierced. As in a sexy as fuck barbell straight through the head of his dick. I can't get the image out of my head. I'm still thinking about it as we drive back into Eastpoint, and he drops me back off at Havers with the order to get showered and changed and meet him downstairs in an hour. I don't argue. After all, I made a deal and now it's my turn to honor it.

So, when that hour is up and he pulls up in a black Escalade looking freshly showered, I get off the curb and open the passenger side door before sliding inside. I scan the interior of the car. It resembles a spaceship with its blinking lights and numerous buttons. Heated air pours out of the vents, sliding across the still wet tangles of my hair.

Dean glances over as the Escalade glides onto the road and does a double take. "What are you wearing?" he asks.

I glance down at the tattered t-shirt and cut offs I put on after my shower. "Uh, clothes?"

He laughs, shaking his head. "I told you we were going to a party," he says.

A scowl forms over my lips. "Yeah, and? Is there a dress code?"

"No." His twitching lips and sparkling eyes showcase his amusement and for some reason, that annoys me.

"Then why the fuck did you ask about my clothes?" I demand.

Dean turns his head back towards the road. "It's just interesting is all. Most girls would dress nice, especially if they know they're going to be seen in public with me."

An indelicate snort escapes me. "Yeah, probably because they care."

"And you don't?" I'm not sure if he meant it as a question or not, but it comes out as one so I answer it.

"No," I say. "I don't."

We pull to a stop at a red light and one of Dean's hands leaves the steering wheel, coming down hard on the back of my seat as he turns and leans closer, close enough that I can smell the mint on his breath and the spice of his aftershave. "And that, baby girl," he replies, "is why I can't leave you alone."

The light switches to green all too soon and he pulls away again, returning his attention to the road and leaving me feeling like I just ran a mile at full speed. *What the fuck is wrong with me?*

Several minutes later, the Escalade turns into the massive entrance to what looks like a private home. Unlike the Frazier House with its old school charm, this mansion is more modern with a sleek style frame. The top looks completely flat from where we park alongside a row of several other cars. Also unlike the Frazier House, this place has a parking lot of sorts—not a real one, but from the way other people have left their cars, it seems like it. No piling cars out the back of one lane, but all are lined neatly in a row on one side of the massive grass lawn.

"Where are we?" I ask as Dean leads me up to the double frosted glass doors at the front of the house.

Dean's expression is shuttered when he answers. "A party," he says.

I arch a brow. "Yeah, no shit, Sherlock. I mean, who's house is this?"

"Doesn't matter, we're not staying long." He doesn't bother to knock, just reaches for the handle, turns it, and gestures me inside with a hand on the small of my back. I don't have a second to recognize the intention behind his words because I'm too fucking confused by the feeling of his warm palm against my lower spine, reminding me of the burning feeling of his naked cock pressing against me in the water earlier.

"Where are Abel and Brax?" I ask. I wait until we're fully inside with the door closed behind us before I pull away from him, careful not to be obvious about it.

"They're here somewhere," Dean says, nodding towards a set of open doors. "This way."

I follow him through the house, noting that the people in attendance are all less lively than they were at the Frazier House. In fact, if I hadn't seen the effects of marijuana before and even used it a time or two myself, then I wouldn't now recognize that half of these people are stoned out of their minds. Cross-faded, I realize a second later when I spot several red solo cups along the surface of the coffee tables and fireplace mantle.

Dean pulls me into a kitchen that's easily larger than the entire trailer I'd lived in with Patricia. Strangely there's no one around, but it does have a great view out the back doors where I see a sea of other people—who all appear much more animated than those inside the house.

"Stay here," he orders. "I'm going to go find someone and then I'll be back and we can go."

Weird for him to insist on bringing me to a party like this, criticize my clothes for it, and then just drop me off and leave. I eye him curiously, but I don't say anything. Dean seems to realize my lack of answer and halfway to the door, he pauses and looks back.

"Stay," he orders again.

I flash him a grin, raising my hands in a movement of surrender. His lips press together into a scowl. "Say it," he snaps.

"Say what?" I challenge with an arched brow.

"Tell me that you're going to follow my orders and you'll stay right where I put you."

I roll my eyes. "I don't follow anyone's orders but my own," I reply. "But if it makes you feel better, yes, I'll wait here for you to get back. Just don't take too long or else I might get bored."

Dean's eyes slide over me and then, as if realizing that's the best he's going to get out of me, he nods once and disappears.

Huffing out a breath, I turn and press back against the counter of the unfamiliar kitchen. Girls in high heels and short glittery dresses that seem like overkill for a house party—this isn't some club, after all—stumble through and out the back doors. The noises that come from the open doors draw me forward. Curiosity sits in my chest as I glance out, scanning the crowd, but strangely enough, I don't recognize anyone at this party. I don't pay attention to most of my classmates, but I should remember some of these people, shouldn't I?

"Avalon?" I jerk around at the sound of my name being called. Corina stands in the doorway to the kitchen, a red Solo cup in hand as she blinks at me. "What are you doing here?"

I tilt my head at her and shrug. "Just hanging out," I

say. It's not technically a lie, but I don't necessarily want to tell her that I came with Dean.

Her eyes dart from side to side and she sets her cup on the counter before approaching. Corina gets close, sidling up to me with one hand on my arm. She leans in even further as her eyes widen as if she's still stunned by my mere presence here. I can feel my own eyebrows inching up towards my hairline. "Are you allowed to be here?" she whispers the question, making me jerk back with a scowl.

"I can go wherever I damn well please," I snap.

"No, I know," she says quickly. "I mean, do the—you know—do *they* know that you're here?"

Extracting my arm from her grip, I take several steps back. "Why does that matter?" I ask.

She groans. "Oh my god, they're here, aren't they?" Corina bites down on her lower lip, and surprisingly when she releases it, her teeth come away clean of her glossy lipstick. It must be some expensive shit.

"Why are you so concerned?" I ask.

Instead of answering, however, she just shakes her head and says, "You really shouldn't be here. Just..." Corina glances over her shoulder as if expecting someone to be behind her. I frown. "Just stay here for a moment," she continues. "I'll be right back."

She doesn't give me a second to ask what the hell is wrong with her before she practically sprints out of the room. After a moment of pure shock, I take the two steps it takes to get to the counter and lift her cup to sniff the contents. *How drunk must she be?* But all I smell is beer. And after watching her down shots like a professional that night at Urban, I know it takes a lot more than a few cups of beer to make her drunk.

Behind me, the sliding glass door opens. I set the cup down and glance back as a guy comes in, shaking his wet hair out as he tilts his head to the side and smacks the side that faces upward as if he's trying to get water out. When he notices my presence, he pauses and straightens.

"Well, hello there, beautiful," he says, an easy smile coming to his face.

I take one look at him and shake my head. "No thanks," I say. "Not interested."

His body freezes, mid-step, and I can tell that I've shocked him. I cross my arms and lean against the counter, wishing either Dean or Corina would hurry up and get their asses back. I'm getting bored just sitting around waiting, and nothing good ever happens when I get bored.

Instead of scoffing and calling me a bitch before walking out as I expect, the guy watches me as he strides to the refrigerator and retrieves a bottled water. He drains the water in one go, his throat muscles moving as he swallows, and then presses a button on the wall, causing one of the lower cabinets—or what had looked like the door to a cabinet—to come sliding out, revealing two neat little trash cans, side by side. He tosses the bottle into the one clearly marked for recycling and then looks back to me.

Since there's nothing else for me to look at or do, I stare right back at him. His jaw is defined, a shadow of stubble ghosting across the lower half of his face. His hair is slicked back, making it look darker than it probably is, but his eyes are a clear, almost ocean-blue.

"Haven't seen you around here before," he comments lightly.

"That's probably because I haven't been here before," I reply.

The corner of his mouth turns up and I have to admit, he's attractive. I'm just not interested. "What's your name?" he asks.

"Nunya," I say.

"Nunya?" He frowns as he repeats.

"Yeah, as in nunya damn business."

There's a beat of silence and then he barks out a laugh. Shaking his head, I wince when droplets of water from his hair hit my arm. With a scowl, I wipe the wetness off before backing up a step. "You're interesting," he says, laughter still in his voice.

"Oh?" I lift my hand and look at my nails, using it as an excuse not to meet his obviously very focused stare.

"Most girls don't try to hide their names from me; they want me to know," he says.

I drop my arm and level him with a glare. "I'm not hiding anything," I snap.

"No?" He takes a step closer and just from the way he walks, I can tell he's a fighter. His muscles bunch, constrict, and release like those of someone who's very aware of each and every movement. I stiffen and lift my chin to meet his gaze.

"No," I repeat.

One arm comes down on the cabinets behind me and he hovers over me. The scent of chlorine invades my nostrils. He's got at least half a foot on me, but hanging around Dean and the others, I've gotten used to it. I don't even flinch. "Then tell me your name, beautiful," he insists.

"I don't want to."

"Then how about I tell you mine?" he suggests.

"Shall I repeat? I'm not interested."

"It's Luc," he says. "Luc Kincaid." He says it and then backs up to watch my expression, as if waiting for some realization. It takes me a moment to remember where I recognize the name from. When I do, however, I keep my face impassive so as not to give it away. Luc Kincaid, Dean's ex-girlfriend's new fiancé.

PRETTY LITTLE SAVAGE

"Is that supposed to impress me?" I inquire after another beat of silence.

"Huh." Far from offended, Luc's eyes rove down my form, stopping on my long legs and ripped jean shorts. He smirks. "Usually it does."

"Well, sorry to disappoint."

"Oh, beautiful," he says, his gaze coming back to mine, "I don't think you could disappoint me if you tried."

"That's only because I haven't started trying yet."

Luc leans back and the smell of chlorine fades. "I know who you are now," he says.

I arch one brow. "You do?"

"You're the new girl, aren't you?"

I press my lips together. From what I recall, Luc Kincaid is not part of the Sick Boys' kingdom. "You don't go to Eastpoint," I reply.

"No." He shakes his head before backing off me completely. "But you do."

Something slides across his expression, something sinister and dark and not at all like the original surfer boy aura he'd exuded when he'd first stepped into the house. Before I can observe it further, however, the sound of heels clicking on the hardwood surface of the floor echoes through the room and Corina bursts back into the kitchen, her cheeks flushed. She comes to a sudden and abrupt halt when she spots me ... or more accurately, when she spots who I'm with.

"Luc..." She breathes his name like saying it too loud might offend him. "What are you doing here?" she blurts looking between him and me.

"It's my house, 'Rina," he says lazily, ambling around me and towards her.

"Yeah, I know, I-I just..." Her words trail off as he stops next to her in the entrance to the kitchen and he leans down. I don't hear what he says, but whatever it is has her nodding as he lifts his head and looks back at me once with that twisted smirk still on his face before he leaves the room.

Corina expels her breath in a rush and wobbles a bit. She looks at me and shakes her head. "Come on," she says. "Let's get out of here. I'll take you home."

I avoid her hand when she reaches for me. "I came with Dean," I finally tell her—there's no use in hiding it now. There's no doubt in my mind that he's made his presence here known somewhere. Besides if Luc Kincaid does, in fact, know who I am then he must know that Dean's here too.

Corina bites her lower lip again, worrying it with her teeth before releasing. "Fine," she huffs out, "then let's go find him."

I nod and follow her out of the kitchen. We walk through the rest of the massive mansion, passing several darkened rooms that smell of pot and alcohol. More than a few have couples mostly naked writhing on the floor. Rich people, it seems, are just like poor people when they're inebriated. Absolutely no shame and no inhibitions. I don't mind it. It just reminds me that regardless of what people think, only a thin veil of social status and wealth separates us as human beings.

"They're not going to be happy that you met Luc," Corina says as we cut through a back hallway, the sounds of loud sex coming from behind a few closed doors.

"Why?" I ask. She reaches for a side door and slides it open, revealing a path that looks like it leads around the back of the house. Her heels sink into the dirt as she starts down it with me at her back.

Corina shoots a look over her shoulder. "Surely you've

heard about Luc Kincaid by now? You've been at Eastpoint for nearly half a semester."

"I've heard of him, yeah, but I don't know why he's such a big deal."

Brows low, nose scrunched up, she flips around and stops, making me halt or risk slamming into her. "Luc Kincaid is the heir of St. Augustine," she says.

"Okay? Is that supposed to be something special to me? More rich people, who cares?"

"Everyone does," she says with a huff. "St. Augustine University is Eastpoint's primary rival and the founder of St. Augustine—*the Kincaids*"—she emphasizes the name again before continuing—"are in the same business as the Carter, Smalls, and Frazier families."

"And that means..." I shake my head. I seriously don't get rich people.

She groans and reaches out, smacking my arm. "They're corrupt," she hisses. "They manage huge corporations—we're talking international, Avalon. They bribe politicians to push through laws and projects that will benefit them. They recruit the best of the best and they have eyes and ears everywhere. Some people think that they're directly involved with organized crime but there's been no arrests of anyone in any of the main families. There's no evidence and any evidence that there might be is covered up pretty quickly." Corina sends me a pitying look.

"Honestly," she continues. "I don't know what Dean was thinking bringing you to Kincaid's house, much less leaving you alone."

"I can take care of myself," I say with a snort, but I can't deny my curiosity. Corruption, I expected. Organized crime, though? Just what else is Dean hiding? My heart rate picks up the pace. I want to know, I realize. He's like a dangerous stunt—like standing on the very tip of a mountain and looking down. I could jump and die or I could arm myself with the right tools to survive. And there's nothing more powerful than knowledge.

Corina shakes her head and turns back around. "Come on, I thought I heard someone say they were out back somewhere."

Questions and thoughts overflow in my mind. Anticipation thrums in my veins. Maybe it's not such a bad thing that Dean and the guys can't seem to leave me alone. Maybe Dean's obsession is an opportunity. I want to know more. I want to know everything about him. I want to know why ... I clench my hand and look down at where the skin over my knuckles stretches tightly. I want to know what it is about Dean Carter that disturbs me so much.

"Shit." Corina's hissed curse brings my head up and this time when she stops, it's too fast for me to avoid and I smack into her back.

"Fuck," I mutter, rubbing my nose. "What's—" My head lifts and my whole body stalls out at what I see before me.

A wave of cold so sharp it feels like glaciers in my arteries comes on so fast that it leaves me feeling like I've been frozen to the spot. Kate is wearing the lowest cut dress I've ever fucking seen in my life, the neckline so far down that it dips below her naval, showing off the darkened hollow of her belly button. The only thing keeping the sorry excuse for fabric from opening and revealing her entire front is the crisscrossing of golden chains between her breasts and around her neck.

Something dark slithers into my throat. My eyes and nose burn. The urge to commit a violent act worse than anything she's ever experienced rises like a tidal wave. She twines her arms around Dean's neck and plasters her front to his chest. That's not what gets me. What gets me is the fact that he's not. Fucking. Removing. Her.

Without stopping to think, I turn around and start walking. If I stay I'm going to do something like set *her* on fire this time. I know I should stop and think about why I'm so angry, I should examine these feelings, but I don't want to. I can't.

Corina follows me and only when we reach the front of the house do I speak. "I could use that ride now," I say.

Thankfully, she doesn't respond. She just leads me to her car. As I climb into the passenger side and settle against the crisp leather seats, I close my eyes and try to call upon the same numbness that I'd used many times before. I just want to drown myself in it right now. I want to forget. I want to fucking hurt somebody.

38

DEAN

Sweat slicks down my spine as I finish up my work on the second floor and then head back to the first. A headache pounds at the back of my skull, slow, but persistent. I'd love nothing more than to take Avalon back to my place or hell just get her back in my Escalade, strip her bare and fuck her to within an inch of her life. It's either that or kill something, because honestly, those are the only two things that can calm me right now.

I search the house first and when I don't find either Brax or Abel amidst the stoned out and sex-crazed crowd, I take the side path and head around to the back. As soon as he spots me, Abel lifts a hand and waves it my way. Brax turns and lifts his head. Curiously, however, I've yet to see Kincaid. Odd considering this mansion is his father's.

"Where's Avalon?" Abel asks as I approach.

"She's here. Inside. I don't want to stay long." I scan the crowd gathered outside. Smoke lingers in the air. The smell of weed and sex is on the breeze. It's always like this at Kincaid's parties. Something about his deviancy just turns the people around him into raging nymphomaniacs and fucking addicts.

"You came because of the rumors, right?" Abel asks. "Are you going to talk to him?"

I snort. "I'm going to fucking make sure he stays where he's supposed to."

"So, it's true then?" Brax leans forward. "He's coming to Eastpoint?"

"No." It can't be true. I won't let it. Besides, of all the people in the world, my father would never let a Kincaid attend Eastpoint University. The only thing he cares about more than his damn revenge on Kincaid is the money in his pocket and the power in his possession. It's also the only reason he hasn't had the head Kincaid killed.

"Are you sure, man?" Abel's tone suggests his doubt. "I've heard some pretty disturbing shit. The Colemans are lobbying for him to transfer. They don't like that Kate was forced to because of Luc's engagement to her."

My upper lip curls back. "The Colemans are fucking destitute," I snarl. "They have no say."

"There's more, though," Abel says. "I spoke with Lionel's secretary the other day about the charity ball at the end of the year. She wants us all to make an appearance—"

"You're still calling your father's wife his secretary?" I ask, raising a brow.

Abel stiffens and glares at me, continuing even as he ignores the question. "She also mentioned him meeting with someone from St. Augustine," he spits.

"Kincaid?" Fury eats away at my logical thought. "No, it can't be. He'd rather die than…"

"Do you think it has anything to do with—" Brax starts.

I don't let him finish that statement. My eyes shoot to

the backdoors. I can't see through the curtains covering the glass, but I know Avalon's on the other side. Sucking in a breath, I turn back to the guys. "Even if they're meeting, hopefully it's just for business. That's not out of the realm of possibilities," I say. "Kincaid would be a fucking idiot to come to Eastpoint. All of his power is at St. Augustine. If he transfers..."

"We'll eat him the fuck alive," Abel finishes with a nod.

"Still." Brax's head comes down as he speaks, his eyes shifting side to side as he shrinks down into himself, trying to appear smaller. I tilt my head at the movement. It's so unlike him. "Nicholas should know about the Colemans now, shouldn't he? So should Kincaid." He shakes his head. "There's something else going on and I don't like not knowing what."

"Maybe they really are in love or some shit?" Abel offers, but even I can tell by his tone that he doesn't fucking believe it.

"Doubtful," I say, "but that's something we should probably discuss at home. Not here."

"So, what then? You just came to find him and threaten him?" Abel arches a brow at me. "How are you going to fucking do that if you can't find him?"

I smile then. A slow movement as I roll my tongue into my cheek and glance up once to both of them and shake my head. "The threat's been taken care of," I say quietly. "Don't worry about that."

Brax's head jerks up and his eyes narrow. "What did you do?"

"Just left a reminder of sorts," I say. "Or a warning, depends on how you look at it."

His face remains serious for a moment before he breaks out into a smile that matches mine. Before he can say whatever fucked up shit I know he's thinking, however, a small body slams into me and nearly sends me flying to the ground.

"The fuck?" I look down, but my entire field of vision is obscured by a face full of makeup and flat tits beneath a gold swath of fabric. "Kate?"

"You came," she says, nuzzling against my chest.

"Get the fuck off me," I snap. "Now."

Her head backs up and it's then I see what she's wearing. A dress that looks more like a bathing suit except the bottom most certainly does not cover her ass. I recoil when the tequila on her breath hits my face. "Someone said you were here, but I did—did—didn't believe them," she says, stuttering her words out.

I drop my arms, unwilling to hold her any longer, then grimace when her snake-like limbs coil around me on their own. "Kate, I swear to God, if you don't fucking—" She sniffs and presses her mouth to my neck, cutting me off. I shoot a glare over my head at the two fuckheads currently watching with barely repressed amusement. "Fucking help me, assholes," I grit out.

"Oh, no, looks like you've got that one all figured out, buddy," Abel says, taking a step back. "Who am I to come between you and the she-witch."

Kate's head whips around and she levels him with a wavering glare that would have more power if she didn't teeter on her three inch fucking heels. "You're such a fucking dick, Abel," she complains. "You never liked me."

Abel arches a brow. "Still don't," he agrees.

Kate jerks her chin up before returning her face to my neck. Putting my hands on her shoulders, I don't even hesitate to shove her back. "Dean?" Wide, hurt eyes look up at me.

"What the fuck do you want, Kate?" I demand.

"I-I just wanted to see you," she whimpers. "I m-miss

you. You don't know what it's like being at St. Augustine now. No one understands me like you do." Resisting my grip, she fights to plaster herself against my chest once more.

"That's your own fucking problem, Kate," I say through clenched teeth. "You made your fucking choice."

With that, I pick her up, take two steps, and fling her into the pool. Her shocked gasp reaches my ears a split second before the actual sound of the splash she makes. I can't even stay to relish the feeling of dumping her ass and likely all the expensive shit Kincaid's bought her into the pool because now I want to fucking leave.

I shoot a glare to the guys who are standing by, laughing their asses off. "Nice one," Braxton chuckles. I flip both him and Abel my happy as fuck middle finger and head for the house.

When I check the kitchen and come up empty, something prickles at the back of my mind, but I'd honestly half-expected Avalon to go snooping anyway. I check the rooms with people and then the ones without. I even go back to the second floor, but there's no fucking sign of her. The more I search, the more furious I become.

"What's wrong?" Braxton asks as I come storming down the stairs.

"I can't fucking find her." I slide a hand through my hair and clench my teeth, trying to think of where the fuck she could've gone.

A girl passes by the two of us, a glass of what looks like wine in her hand. Without thinking, I reach out and grab her. "Hey," I say, "have you seen a chick about this tall"—I pause and lift my hand to the appropriate height before continuing—"long dark hair, dressed in a t-shirt and pair of jean shorts?"

She blinks at me for a moment. Brax steps forward. "She doesn't—" he starts, only to be interrupted.

"Actually, yeah," the girl says, capturing both of our attention. "Thought it was a little weird for someone to come here looking like that," she scoffs, and I resist the urge to tell her that her fake tits probably wouldn't look half as good in the second hand shit Avalon wears. "But yeah, she left a little while ago with a friend."

She left? I drop the girl's arm and back away. *She fucking left?* Dimly, I hear Braxton talking to the girl, but I don't hear whatever it is that they say. All I know is that Avalon fucking left.

"Hey, man," Braxton's voice comes back to me as he clamps a hand on my shoulder and urges me out the front door. "I asked a little bit more. Sounds like Corina was here. It's okay. She probably just took her back to the dorms."

It didn't fucking matter if she left with Pope fucking Francis. The fact is that she fucking left—after I'd told her to stay put. *This,* I think. *This is what I fucking meant by her going off and doing stupid shit.* I shake Brax off and head for my Escalade.

"Where are you going?" he calls after me.

"Havers," I yell.

39

AVALON

I slam the flat of my palm against the wood of the door, pissed that I even forgot my key in the first place. "I'm fucking coming!" I hear Rylie curse on the other side and then the door is opening.

I don't wait for her to finish; I shove it in and storm past her, yanking my t-shirt off and dropping it to the floor as I sit on the edge of my mattress and reach for my boots.

"What's your problem?" she mutters, closing the door behind her.

One boot goes flying towards the closet—barely missing her as she crosses back to her side of the room—then the other follows. I don't answer her, and though I can feel her curious gaze on my back as she settles back beneath the covers of her bed, she doesn't ask again. For which I'm grateful. Even I don't know why I'm so mad.

I strip my shorts off and reach for an oversized t-shirt meant for sleep. Pulling it over my head, I crawl beneath the comforter, resting back and staring at the ceiling. It takes a while, but as the silence continues, it's not long until I hear Rylie's soft snores drifting over to me.

My muscles are tense, refusing to relax. I ball my hands into fists and wish I had my old principal's stress ball. That damn thing would get a work out with me. My anger simmers below the surface of my skin, and I can't seem to stop the carousel that my thoughts have jumped on. I close my eyes to escape the feeling, but it only gets worse. The problem is, once I've closed my eyes, it's almost impossible to open them back up again. So, I just lay there, stewing in my own furious confusion. Eyes closed. Body taut and mind a disorganized mess.

An image of Kate with her body against Dean's pops into my mind's eye. I repress a growl of irritation and roll onto my side, away from Rylie's soft sleep noises. *How the fuck can she sleep with someone else in the room?* I wonder absently. I've grown used to her enough that I can catch a few hours here and there, but it's been a while since I've had a truly full night's sleep and I doubt tonight will be that night.

Probably because I can't stop thinking about it. About him. About her. *Fuck him,* I think. I rear up without opening my eyes and punch at my pillow, mashing it under my head before slamming the side of my skull back into it.

Dean Carter can go to hell, and I'd be happy to send him there.

Several minutes go by—stretching into an unending cavern of time—and despite my resolute belief that I wouldn't sleep, the longer my eyes stay shut, the more my thoughts begin to drift out. My cheek presses into the fabric of my pillow and I turn into it, inhaling the scent. It's dry in the room. Too hot. It reminds me of another time and place where a different heat had settled over me, and maybe that's the reason why, when I do actually fall asleep, I'm thrust into an old memory that I'd hoped to never relive again.

. . .

"Pretty little thing, isn't she?" I come awake to the sound of voices in the house and my first thought is, not again. I don't think. I just scramble out of bed and head for the window, digging my fingers beneath the dirty frame. I freeze when the window doesn't budge but instead pinches down on my hands. That's when I realize something's different. "The pictures are certainly something, but you know I want the real thing, Patty."

"You can have it," she says, her voice growing closer to my bedroom door.

Hurry, hurry, hurry, *I urge myself, yanking at the window. Again, though, it doesn't move. I scan the outer edges and my eyes widen when I see what's making it stick. Long, thick nails are jammed into the outside of the frame, pinning it in place. As drunk and high as Patricia is ... she figured it out. She must really be desperate for the cash.*

Sweat collects at the base of my neck and slides down my spine, pooling in the small of my back beneath my tank top. Don't panic, *I tell myself.* Just think. *But thinking becomes difficult when I hear the sounds of two sets of footsteps quietly approaching my bedroom door.*

"She always keeps her door locked," I hear Patricia whisper.

That's right, you dirty cunt, *I think.* Just for times like these.

The man with her scoffs, the noise disrupted when he coughs and the sound of phlegm choking in his throat filters through the thin wooden door. "Don't worry 'bout that, Patty," the man says after he's finished clearing his throat. "I think I can handle one little door. Is she a screamer?"

No, *I think.* But I am a fighter. *I dash across the room and stand at the door, debating. There's nothing in the room to block it. Nothing save for the twin sized mattress and the rickety bed frame, but that's light—I should know since I carried it home after someone tossed it to the side of the road. It works better than the mattress on the floor since the roaches crawl under it now rather than over my feet while I'm sleeping.*

"She's never home when I send people in," Patty says quietly, replying to the man. "So, I don't know. But I know she'll be here this time. I nailed her window shut. She should still be sleeping, and even if she's not, there's only one way out and you're looking at it."

"So she's a virgin then?" I close my eyes and lean my head against the doorframe. The excitement in his tone is repulsive. I can't see him, but he sounds old. Much older than a man like him has any right to be. Men who buy little girls, even teenagers, should die as soon as they're born. There's no place for filth like him. Then again ... maybe I should be grateful because there's no place for me either. I curl my hands into fists. But I don't care if there's not a place for me. I'm going to fight anyway. No one will take from me what I don't want to give.

And unfortunately for him, I'm not a virgin. I'd lost that shit not long after the first night I'd caught one of Patty's friends trying to sneak into my room. I'd known she'd do it again. I just hadn't expected her to catch onto my escape hatch. I hadn't thought her that smart. But I had given up my virginity to one of the boys from school —a nice nerdy guy who'd been far too fast, but at least it'd been my choice. *That's what mattered. My choice. My body. My control.*

My heart is pumping. My chest feels like a vise is being squeezed around it. My mind begins running in circles. There's no other way out, though. Patty's right. It's the door or I break the window. And if I break the window there's no fixing it. I'll be sleeping with a broken window and I'm not stupid enough to believe that these stupid motherfuckers won't try to get in any way they can.

No, I have to stand my ground. I have to fight back. I have to prove to these assholes that if they think they can come in and treat me like my mother then they're in for a big surprise. I take a deep breath and step back.

My eyes lock on the doorknob and I watch as it turns, stopping only momentarily when the locking mechanism kicks into place. Then it starts turning again, the man doesn't even try to finesse it. He just turns until I can hear the flimsy lock inside the knob crack and break and then the door creeps open.

Game on, motherfucker.

The second he steps into the room, I fly at him. My fists hit a flabby stomach and a shaggy face. The man grunts under the surprise of my assault, his arms coming around to lift my much smaller frame. He slams me down on the floor and the musk of his breath hits me in the face a split second later.

I should be terrified, *I think to myself. And yet, as I rake my dull nails down the side of his face and kick at any place I can reach, all I can really focus on is my anger. It's a boiling volcano inside of me, overflowing, and the moment the man rears back and I'm given an opening, I take it with no qualms. I punch him straight in the throat and grab his head with both hands when he's choking on his own partially crushed airway.*

Yanking his head back, I slam it into mine and wince when stars dance in front of my eyes, but it does the trick. The man falls off me with a grunt and for good measure, when I get to my feet, I kick him in the balls. What is left of the oxygen in the man's lungs expels, and I turn to see a shocked Patricia still standing in the hallway.

She gathers herself and gives me a look of contempt. "You couldn't just lay down and take it?" she snarls. "After all I do for you—" I'm not going to let her finish. I take two steps towards her and watch with dispassionate indifference as my fist flies at her face. It's almost like watching a movie because I don't even feel it when my knuckles connect with her cheek and slide up into her eye socket. But she goes down. I step over her prone form on the floor and I'm halfway to the front door when I hear her mutter something behind me. I don't stop to respond, I just storm out of the trailer in nothing but the tank top and flannel shorts that I went to sleep in.

I'm shaking—both on the inside and on the outside. When I take off and just start running, I don't know if the shaking will ever stop. My body is alight with energy, full of it. It's all consuming. It makes me feel powerful. It's adrenaline. And as much as I like it, I know it's a lie.

There's nothing powerful about me, but maybe if I act like there is—maybe after tonight—word will spread and the desperate motherfuckers of this stupid town will get the message. Mess with Avalon Manning and you'll regret it.

I don't know how long I run, but the sky is starting to turn a lighter blue with red and orange hues staining its edges when I finally stop. Only then do I think about what Patricia said to me just before I left.

"You're just like me, Ava," she had whispered. "Nothing but a dirty, cheap whore."

40

AVALON

Nothing but a dirty, cheap whore...

A lock clicks and I sit upright as the bedroom door swings open and the lights are flipped on, momentarily blinding me. Breathing hard, I cover my eyes once I see who's standing there—like a barely repressed violent statue in the doorframe of my dorm room. Sweat slides from beneath my eyes ... no, not sweat. *Fuck. Am I crying?* I wipe the evidence away and inhale hard before looking back at the man who's been the bane of my existence for the last two months.

"What the fuck?" Rylie's groggy voice drifts over to me as she pokes her purple head out from beneath the sheets. As soon as she sees who our late night visitor is, her eyes widen and then narrow when they swing my way. "What did you do?" she snaps.

I ignore her.

"Get out." Dean's command leaves no room for argument and it's perfectly clear that he's not talking to me.

With an irritated huff, Rylie throws back her sheets and reaches for her shower caddy.

"No, fine. I'll just take a shower," she mutters, glaring between us as she shoves her way around him—as tired as she likely is, she's far more brazen right now than she normally acts. "A long one," she calls back.

Dean steps further into the room and the door closes behind him.

"How the hell did you get in here?" I ask.

He arches a brow before striding further into the room until he hovers over where I still sit in my bed. One hand lands on the mattress and the other on the headboard. He leans in close. "I go where I want, when I want, little girl. Did you really think you could keep me out?" It's a rhetorical question, I know. So I don't answer. Dean shakes his head and levels his heated gaze on me. "You and I have a chat coming."

"No." I shove him back and swing my legs out from beneath the cheap comforter.

"No?" The surprise in his tone might be funny if I felt like stopping to think about it. But I don't stop and I don't want to think about it.

"Looks like your hearing isn't impaired," I say in a dry tone as I dig through my drawers for workout clothes. "Congratulations."

"You don't tell me no," he growls. "No one tells me no."

I find what I'm looking for and without looking back, I whip my shirt over my head and snatch my sports bra and wrangle it on. "I just did," I reply. Leaving the shirt off, I find my running shorts and socks. The effects of the old memory still linger over my mind and I hate it. I feel weak, a mass of trembling fire. Anger and confusion and old hatred all combining into one body—mine.

"Why the fuck did you leave?" he demands, his voice tight as he watches me change. His eyes trail down the ratty sports bra—not all of the stains from my last fight came out even after I ran them through the wash on the first floor a few times, but at least now they look more like dirt stains than someone's blood.

"I left because I wanted to," I state.

"I told you to stay. You said you would."

He takes a step closer, and I move one back. Push and pull. That's what this feels like between us. Like we're both choking on leashes with each end in the other's hand. He pulls me and I yank him. He pushes me and I do the same. My fingers curl into my palm and I stab the blades of my nails into the fleshy padding beneath my thumb. Too much. He's too fucking much. I feel trapped by him, by this room, by this whole fucking university.

My body whirls towards his, and without considering my words, I blurt the first thing that comes to my mind. "Why the fuck did you bring me there?" I snap. "What was the point?"

Dean leans back, his hooded gaze turning his eyes into slits. I feel like I'm being watched by a snake. The only difference between Dean Carter and a serpent ready to strike is their pupils. In every other way that matters, he's a dangerous creature. One that I've let get far too close, far too often.

"I already told you," he starts. "I can't trust you—"

"Bullshit!" I yell, cutting him off. "Don't fucking play that. You don't trust me. I don't trust you. We've been over it. What's the real reason you took me to Luc Kincaid's house?" His eyes shoot open in surprise and I smile a cold mean smile. "Oh, what? You thought I didn't know? Were you trying to hide it? What else are you trying to hide? The fact that you're using me for some stupid, corrupt game you've got going on?" That's the only thing that makes sense to me right now. There's no way Dean Carter could be genuinely interested in a girl like me—I'm poor, I'm foul mouthed, and the things I've seen and done in the last eighteen years of my life are probably darker than he could possibly imagine.

There's blood on my hands. Rage in my veins. And so much hatred, I don't know if I'm sucking it in or exhaling it with every fucking breath I take.

"You're King of the fucking castle," I continue, unable to stop myself as I take two steps towards him and shove him back against the door. "You rule the roost, right? You have everything you've ever wanted. Just a snap of your fingers"—I stop and make the snapping motion with my hand right in front of his stupid, handsome face just to make a point—"and it's yours, right?" I shake my head and lower my arm. "But then I come along and what? Suddenly, you don't get everything you want." And what does that make me to a man like Dean? A challenge. A real one. That's all I've ever been and all I'll ever be.

Bile that's been sitting in my stomach since I first saw Kate and Dean plastered against one another comes rushing up my throat like liquid fire. By the sheer force of my will, I tamp it down. "When will you fucking get it?" I glare up at him, spitting the words through gritted teeth as he stares down at me. His jaw is hard, the muscles beneath his shirt like stone. My chest pumps up and down with exertion. "I'm not going to be controlled by you. *Ever.*"

Cold, brown eyes meet my gaze. "Are you done?" he asks after a beat.

"Yeah," I say. "I'm fucking done." I shove away from him and the door, turning my back to him.

One step is all it takes. One step and then I feel his hard hands on my waist, his chest against my spine, and his breath in my ear as he whispers against the side of my face. "Good," he says. "Then it's my turn."

Dean lifts me up, spins me around, and in reaction, I kick out, knocking him back. The lights go out when his back slams into the switch, but he's not done. Not even close. A low growl leaves his lips as he palms my waist, hefting me into his arms once more before tossing me back onto the mattress of my bed, his body coming down hard over mine a split second later. His hands grip my wrists, yanking them up above my head and holding them tight. Warm breath filters over my face and I turn away, bucking beneath his heavy body.

"Get the fuck off me, Dean!"

"Oh, no. You had your turn, baby. I let you yell and I let you question me, but now it's my turn to start asking the questions. It's my turn to get some answers." He grunts when my knee slams up against his thigh, nearly unmanning him. Quickly adjusting, I curse when his whole body —all six foot three inches of masculine anger—sinks down on me, effectively pinning me in place.

"You drive me absolutely insane, Avalon," he confesses when my struggles are smothered. I jerk my head around and glare up at him.

"The feeling's mutual," I snap.

With how close he is, I can see the individual strokes of his eyelashes. They frame his brown eyes perfectly, darkening the edges and making him look like a dangerous monster in the darkness of my dorm room. Fuck him for looking so good when I'm so fucking pissed at him.

"I didn't say that I didn't like it," he replies, startling me into silence. I don't know what to say to that, so I merely stare up at him, waiting for him to say whatever it is that he so obviously feels is his right to. Carefully, with a focused gaze centered on my face as if watching for a tell that might predict my next move, he transfers both of my wrists into one of his hands. Fingers trail down my cheek as he brushes a few stray strands of my hair out of my face before he grips my chin and lifts it.

"You seem to think that there's a choice left for both of us," he whispers into the darkness, his breath fanning across my lips. I swallow around a dry throat and glare up at him. "There's not." His head comes down and just before his mouth brushes mine, he turns his cheek the slightest bit to the side and skims his lips up the side of my face until his nose is buried in my hair. "We're locked in this, you and I," he says. "There's no getting away. You keep fighting and, baby, I have to admit, it turns me on"—he stops and pushes his hips into mine to demonstrate just how much, and the memory of his hardened cock after we got out of the lake comes to mind. The thick length of him, the flash of silver at the tip. Any saliva I had in my mouth is gone in the next instant and my mouth tastes drier than a desert. "But it's time to stop," he continues. "No more fighting me. No more going off. No leaving. You've been caught, Avalon. Accept it."

His head pulls back slowly, in small increments, but when it does, I grit my teeth and hiss out my response. "Never." I am not something that can be tamed. I am not someone who can be controlled. I won't allow myself to be.

Dean tilts his chin to the side, examining my expression as if he's trying to unlock a particularly difficult puzzle. "Do you think it's going to go away?" he asks.

"I don't know what you're talking about."

He snorts. The sound is so boyish it surprises me. A smile cracks his lips and he leans down until his nose is against mine, his fingers still latched onto my jaw as he holds me in place. Unconsciously, my thighs press together. The fucker feels it—I know he does—because as soon as I make that movement, his hand leaves my chin and moves down my body and it's then that I realize just how bare I am compared to him.

Dean's warm palm skims across my stomach and I can feel my muscles jump and leap to his touch. "Let me ask you something," he says. "If I were to put my hand down your underwear, would you be soaking wet for me?"

I shake my head, in part trying to drive away the thoughts and feelings he arouses in me and also to deny him. "You'll never find out." I expect the words to come out strong, sure, and certainly not as breathy as they do.

Without warning, Dean lifts up suddenly and curls his fingers beneath my thighs, lifting and spreading them without remorse as he moves in and presses his jean-clad cock between my legs. I gasp and arch up, squirming away from the sensation. My hands, now freed, shoot down and press against his hard abdomen.

Dean nuzzles his face into the side of mine, until his nose is back in my hair. *Is he … smelling me?* "Oh, Ava," he whispers. I shiver at the feeling of his words said so quietly, so intimately against the skin of my scalp. "You asked me when will I fucking get it, but the thing is … I do get it. You don't trust anyone. I knew that even before I read your file. Anyone can see it from the way you carry yourself."

My legs are hooked around the outside of his rock-like thighs as he kneels over me on the bed. He pushes forward, miming what would be happening between us if we were naked. A groan bubbles up in my throat and I shove it down, but every time he thrusts forward the outline of his zipper brushes against my clit through my underwear. Sparks dance behind my eyelids. *Shit, when did I close them?* They fly open in the next instant, and I realize that's not the only thing I didn't realize. My hands are no longer pressing against him, trying to hold him off, but instead, my fingers are sunk in the fabric of his t-shirt against his back as I cling to him and he whispers the words into my hair.

Dangerous. So fucking dangerous. He makes me feel unstable, like I'm trying to walk in a straight line during an Earthquake. "What will it take for *you* to realize that I'm not giving you a choice, baby?" A strong hand delves into the strands at the back of my head as Dean leans back, his eyes lit with something cruel and dark as he grips onto my hair and yanks my head back, baring my throat. A shiver skates down my back.

Shit, this is so not good.

"You drive me absolutely insane," he growls, leaning down, breathing against the column of my throat. He's so close that I can feel the tickle of his stubble against my skin. I hold my breath, unwilling to do anything that might bring me any closer to that mouth of his. He accused me of being dangerous? That was like the pot calling the kettle black. Dean Carter is the dangerous one. If I let myself, I could let him slip beneath the surface of my guard; I've only ever let one person beneath.

"We're not doing this," I finally manage to choke out, resisting with my words since it seems like my body won't do it for me. "We can't."

He chuckles, the sound a wicked vibration in his throat that makes his chest shake against me. "Can't?" Dean's head turns from side to side as he shakes it, making his stubble scrape precariously close to my neck. It disrupts the fucking logical thoughts in my brain and makes me think of nothing but what it would feel like if he put all of that sexy as fuck energy and prickly sensation lower—between my thighs. Unconsciously, I clench them again and fight against the urge to suggest it.

I am not ruled by my pussy, I tell myself. *I don't trust Dean Carter ... but do I really have to trust him to want to fuck him?*

"I can do anything I fucking want, Avalon," Dean says, pushing his hips into mine. My lower spine arches and I clench my teeth to keep from screaming at how good it feels. "I can get the key to your dorm room and wake you up in the middle of the night by sliding beneath your covers and spreading your legs. How would you like that? If you woke up to a screaming orgasm? I can give you that, you know."

"Ha." I push the sound out and against his grip, I shake my head. "You wouldn't be able to get in without waking me up, D-man, but nice try."

His hips begin slow back and forth movements as he grinds his cock against me. It scrambles my brain and I hate him for it. I hate his words. I hate the way he makes me feel. I hate the thought that he might've just come from Kate straight to me. That reminder sends a wash of cold, prickling awareness through me.

What the fuck am I doing? I delve my fingers beneath his shirt and sink my nails into his skin until I feel the thinness of his flesh, until I'm two seconds away from breaking the surface.

He curses and his hand leaves my hair as he reaches down to grab my wrists. "Fucking—"

"If you really want someone to fuck," I hear myself saying as if from a long distance away, "why don't you go find Kate?"

Dean rears back, confusion and surprise marring his perfectly handsome face. I stare up at him, unblinking. "What the fuck is that supposed to mean?" he asks.

Ripping my hands from his grasp—he lets me—I shove against his chest until I can fucking breathe again. "It means exactly what I said," I say. "If you're wanting a bitch to be at your beck and call, then you're in the wrong dorm room, D-man. I'm not here for a good time. I'm here because I've got nowhere else to go."

"Are you saying no then?" He arches a brow.

"Yes." I untangle one of my legs from around his thigh and shove my foot into his chest, pushing him back even further. He goes without resistance, but still, his eyes watch me with a careful curiosity that sets me on edge. "I'm saying no and I'll continue to say no. Touch me again and I'll shove your metal-head cock so far into your body cavity that you'll have to see a fucking gynecologist to get it removed."

He surprises me when he asks, "Is that why you left?" I blink, and he continues. "Because you saw me and Kate? You thought I was going to fuck her?"

I scowl, hating the tight feeling of irritation in my chest. "Wouldn't matter if you did."

A grin spreads across his face. "You think not? What if I want to fuck you?"

I jerk my other leg away from him and get off the bed. "No," I snap, turning away and reaching for a pair of pants lying across the floor. I yank them on, not caring if they're mine or Rylie's. All that matters is that they fit and they're another barrier against the sinful man in my bedroom that makes me want to taste violence and blood on my tongue.

"I'm not a toy, Dean," I say, facing the door. "And I also don't follow anyone's rules but my own. You should remember that." At the sound of movement behind me, I glance over my shoulder.

Dean gets off the bed and as he nears me, I can feel my muscles contracting, growing tight and tense as if preparing for an attack. But all he does is step around and reach for the door handle. He turns the knob and a wash of light spills into the darkened interior of my dorm room, partially blinding me after so long in the shadows. I lift a hand to ward off the initial brightness.

He stops in the doorway, his back turned towards me, shoulders slightly inward as if he's thinking deeply. Then, in a rough, almost hoarse voice, he speaks. "I wouldn't touch Kate fucking Coleman again even if I were riddled with disease and she was the only cure," he spits out, sounding furious—with me or himself, I'm not sure. Dean stops and turns his head, his eyes finding mine over his shoulder. It looks like he wants to say more, but instead, his eyes turn to the floor of my open closet door. "While you're getting dressed, you should pack a bag too. spring break starts tomorrow."

Startled by the abrupt shift in conversation, I gape at him. "Why the fuck would I pack a bag?"

He smirks, turning sideways as he steps out of the room, leaving the door hanging open. "Because unless you've cleared it with your dorm manager you can't stay in Havers over break."

My jaw drops. No one had fucking told me that. "You're lying!"

A barked laugh escapes his mouth. "No, I'm not."

I take two steps forward, curling my fingers around the edge of the door frame as I glare up at him. "Then I guess I'll just have to clear it with her," I snap. Because there's no way I'll be going back to Plexton.

Dean's lids lower as he smiles down at me. "You might find that a little difficult," he says with a wink. "After all, I did tell you that I can get whatever I want, baby."

Down the hall, the bathroom door opens and Rylie appears, pink-faced and scrubbed clean, carrying her caddy. She stops when she sees that Dean's still here and her mouth twists down in an irritated scowl. I can fully relate to what she's likely feeling right now.

I lift onto my toes until I'm as close to Dean's height as I can get. "Well," I say quietly, letting my eyes drift down to his lips before meeting his gaze once more, "you're not getting me."

Dean tilts his head to the side and I watch as that silver barbell I'd noticed before flashes behind his teeth. "We'll see, Avalon," he says, before taking a step back. "We'll see."

41

AVALON

When the sun rises the next day, I'm unceremoniously booted from the Havers dorm just like Dean had predicted. Rylie steps out onto the front steps alongside me and sighs, casting a look my way without turning her head like she doesn't want me to know.

"Don't say it," I warn her, sliding my cheap ass shades over my face and looking up into the clear sky. It's going to be a scorcher and the heat only makes my scowl deepen.

"Maybe you should call—"

"There's no need," I say, cutting her off as I readjust my backpack. And I'm proven right when, after a minute the low, thumping sound of rock blasting through classic speakers comes around the corner and a cherry red Mustang pulls up in front of us. Dean is such a fucking enigma sometimes, and yet so predictable at others, it drives me insane, but at least this time I'm right. I glance back at Rylie and arch a brow. "Wanna come along?"

She scrunches her face up and takes a step back, the sunlight glinting off her hair and making it appear more blonde than lavender. It's been a while since she's given it a touch up, and it's fading back to its original color. "Not a chance in hell," she says with a firm shake of her head. "You might be crazy enough to spend a week with the Sick Boys, but I'll take my chances with where I'm heading."

The passenger side door opens and Dean steps out, aviators centered on the bridge of his nose as he leans against the back of the car with his arms crossed over his chest as he watches us from several feet away, waiting for me to make my move—and I will … in a moment.

"Where are you heading?" I ask, cutting a look to Rylie.

Her shoulders stiffen and she hefts her bag up further on her shoulder. "I don't ask about your time with him," she says, nodding to the man currently watching and waiting for me. "You don't ask me about what I do on my own."

I purse my lips, but she's got a point. "Alright, well…" I head down the front steps. "See you in a week," I call over my shoulder.

"If they don't kill you!" she calls back.

I laugh. As if that would happen…

My legs carry me towards the Mustang and Braxton grins from the back, waving my way. Abel, on the other hand, fiddles with the radio, turning the knobs until the rock cuts off, shooting into static before he gives up and smacks the off switch. I stop in front of Dean and look up.

"Well?" I say.

One side of his mouth curls up and he reaches for my bag, taking it off my shoulder, and then pops the trunk to toss it in among a few other bags I catch a glimpse of before he slams it shut again. "Let's go," he says, slinging an arm over my shoulder and leading me to the passenger side.

"Not so fast," I say, stopping him as I dive out from

under his arm. "I think I got this myself, D-man, but good to know you can be a gentleman when you want something."

I don't give him a chance to respond but curl my hands around the edge of the rolled down back window and heave myself up and over until I land in the backseat next to Brax. I reach for the seat belt and clip it into place as Dean looks down at me with one arched brow visible over his sunglasses. "Problem?" I ask.

He shakes his head, reaching for the door and popping it open. It isn't until he's inside, slamming the door behind him that I hear him mutter, "Not yet."

"Woohoo!" Brax shouts, jiggling the back of Abel's seat as he hops up and down in his seat, laughing and making the whole car shake. "Let's get this baby on the fucking road! I'm ready to go!"

"Jesus fuck, cool it!" Abel snaps.

"You're liable to make the car flip," I comment dryly.

Brax shoots me a grin. "Nah, Abel's sweetheart can handle a lot more than my big ass," he says with a wink.

I roll my eyes, crossing my arms, but it's hard to keep the smile off my face—not when he's so obviously excited. "Yeah, speaking of big asses, why the hell are you back here?" I ask. "Is this like some sort of punishment? Stick the smallest person in the back with the giant?"

Braxton laughs again and wiggles his brows. "Would you rather be back here with D?"

That's a no brainer. "On second thought," I say, "strap in and let's go."

Dean reaches for the radio and turns it back on, and this time, an older Tupac song starts blaring. Abel puts the car in drive and we cruise away from the curb as the sun burns down on my forehead and the smell of gas and wind slaps me in the face.

"It's gonna be a long ride," Abel calls. "I hope you've got something to entertain you."

"You're here, aren't you?" I snark back.

He doesn't reply, but I notice the corner of his mouth tipped up. It's almost as satisfying as the scowl now on Dean's face in the side rearview mirror. Almost.

A BEACH HOUSE. THAT'S WHERE THEY TAKE ME. OR rather, it's more of a fucking compound than a mere "house." As Abel slows the Mustang and turns down a short lane, I realize dozens of cars have already arrived. Porsches, Ferraris, Lamborghinis, and dark SUVs line up in the circle driveway of a gray brick mansion with white shutters. I can smell the salty ocean on the wind. Closing my eyes, I inhale, letting the scent fill my lungs.

"Welcome to the Eastpoint Estate," Braxton says, leaning back and sliding his shades over his eyes when someone waves to the car as it cruises through. I'm supposed to spend seven days in this place. Locked up with Dean the dick, the Sick Boys, and their equally rich and annoying friends. *Maybe I should've slept on a bench on campus instead*, I think a bit belatedly as the car comes to a stop.

Brax places his hands on the side of the car and hops out. Everyone else is a bit slower to move, including me. My body feels itchy—that sensation I get right before I feel the need for a good adrenaline high. I can feel the stares already starting. It's not just Dean's football buddies but their girlfriends too. Dozens of blonde-haired, blue-eyed model-thin girls already sporting their first bikini of the spring break season.

"Is the whole fucking school staying here?" I ask sarcastically as I scowl at a bitch walking by. Don't need the fucking looks of disdain to know I'm not welcome. It's not like I would've chosen to be here anyway if I had another choice.

Abel rounds the back of the Mustang and pops the trunk. "Most people have their own private residences along the beach," he says as Dean grabs a duffle bag and slides it over his shoulder before reaching in and lifting mine up. He tosses it to me, his eyes obscured by his aviators. "But for those who live a bit farther down, they usually stay here. Don't worry, we have our own wing. No one will bother you."

A thought occurs to me. "You said this is the Eastpoint Estate," I repeat, curiously. "So, who owns it?"

Dean and Abel exchange a look, and this time, Dean answers. "All of us," he states. "It's a bit complicated, but technically all the Eastpoint families have a stake in everyone's property. The families co-own this one."

"Complicated how?" I press. "Seems pretty simple to me."

Dean slams the trunk closed after Abel retrieves the rest of the bags. "Just complicated," he says in the way that means he wants me to drop the subject. I do, but I file his reaction away for future reference. As much as he likes picking me apart, it's only fair for me to return the favor. Unfolding the layers that make up the man known as Dean Carter is liable to send me down a dark and twisted path. After all, they're not called the Sick Boys for their saintly behavior.

"Come on," Dean grunts as he leads me towards the front entrance. "I'll show you to your room and leave you to unpack."

"Ain't much to unpack," I reply with a shrug but follow him nonetheless.

Abel disappears when we enter the house, but Dean

doesn't say a word as he guides me through a series of twists and turns that make my head spin. There are so many side hallways and so many doors that I swear the building is never ending. The only way I know we're ever actually moving is because the farther we go, the fainter the sound of people and party music gets.

We descend to a deeper level of the house until the sunlight wanes and there are fewer windows. "Here," Dean says, as we hit a final floor and he stops and gestures me forward.

There are four doors and he nods towards the last one on the right. "This will be your room," he states. "Braxton's there and Abel's there." He points to each prospective room before leveling me with a look. "I'm across from you, and I'll know if you try to sneak out, so don't try anything."

I laugh. The thought is fucking ridiculous. "How are you going to know if I sneak out?" I challenge. "You're going to be half-drunk all week, aren't you?" For all the emotion he shows at that question, his face could've been carved from stone. I roll my eyes. "What if I have to use the bathroom?" I ask, changing the subject as I turn and look up and down the hallway. "I don't see any other rooms and I doubt I'll be able to find one in that fucking maze you call a—"

"There's one in your room," he says, cutting me off. "We each have a private room, so no need to go anywhere."

"Oh?" I arch a brow and cross my arms over my chest. "Do you expect me to just sit in my room all week like a good little girl?"

"Yes, that'd be preferable."

A part of me is shocked by his statement. Not by the words themselves, but by the fact that I think he's actually being honest with me. Nonetheless, I answer with a snort of derision. "Not happening," I state, shaking my head.

He doesn't say anything to that, which, once again, is a shock. I go to turn the knob of the door that's mine when I realize something. Pausing, I turn back to him. "There are three Eastpoint families," I say. "Three heirs. Why are there four bedrooms down here?"

Dean's face darkens and instead of answering, he turns around and storms across the hall to his door. He cracks it and then tosses his bag inside before turning around and facing me. "I had some stuff delivered for you," he tells me. "Get settled in and I'll come back for you later." He steps forward and I back into the door, looking up at the underside of his jaw as he glares down at me threateningly. "Do. Not. Leave. Until I come back," he orders.

With that, he turns and strides off, his legs carrying him away from me as fast as he can walk without seeming like he's running away. I smirk at his back but wait to say what I'm thinking until he's out of earshot.

"Pussy."

42

DEAN

I stalk through the house feeling angry and dangerous. *Was this such a good idea?* I wonder. Having her in such close quarters for a full fucking week. Right across the hall. Available. Waiting. Ready for me.

She wants me, that much I know is true. The lake. Her fucking dorm room. The jealousy in her tone when she mentioned Kate. Oh, I know she won't admit it, but that doesn't make it disappear. The only problem I'm having is this desire I feel for her.

Avalon is trouble. Not only are the old men interested in her—for reasons I still haven't figured out—she's a wild card. Untamable. And that only makes me want to control her even more. Every word I spoke to her while I was there in her bed, between those lush thighs of hers, had been true. She's not the kind of girl that'll let a man inside her without trust. It's not like I want her trust. I don't give a shit about that. I just want her to stop fucking with my head. Every time I get near her, my cock pounds and I want nothing more than to rip off her cheap clothes and spread her across my bed like a meal fit for the King I fucking am.

How long has it been since I've gotten laid? Maybe that's it. Maybe all I need is to get some head or some easy pussy and then all of this desire will disappear. Perhaps it's not really her that I desire.

With my thoughts running in circles through my head, I make my way back up the stairs to the main floors and go in search of Abel. I find him—and Brax—in the media room, their bags dumped haphazardly to the side, already in spring break mode.

Both have stripped off their shirts, the air in the room hot with so many bodies piled into it. At least eight guys sit across the giant horseshoe shaped couch, their eyes zeroed in on the flat screen TV that spans more than half of the wall in front of them. Half of the screen is replaying an old football game and the other half is a split top and bottom with two players racing cars around an unending track.

I shake my head as the top car on the screen skids and flips, wrecking and causing half of the couch's occupants to scream angrily, and make my way over to where Abel and Brax stand against the windows, watching the pool game taking place.

"I need you to help me look after the girl this week," are the first words out of my mouth.

Abel's head lifts in surprise while Brax merely ignores my comment in favor of taking a pool cue and moving into position. I switch the full brunt of my focus onto Abel.

"Why?" he asks.

"I just need to make sure she doesn't do anything stupid while she's here," I say.

Before Abel can respond, the side door opens and two

of Eastpoint's top cheerleaders enter in string bikinis that could probably double for tooth floss. "Hi, Dean," one says, waving at me as she passes.

The muscles in my back stiffen as she runs a hand across the upper part of my spine. I almost tell her to get her fucking fingers off me before I break them. Almost. Instead, I keep the comment to myself and give her a brief nod of acknowledgment before turning back to Abel. "Can you do this for me?" I ask, meeting his gaze.

Abel frowns. "You wanted her here, man," he says with a shake of his head. "You're on your own with that girl."

"We need to keep her close. The—"

"Yeah, yeah, they want us to keep an eye on her," Abel says, cutting me off. I grit my teeth and resist the urge to snap at him. "The thing is," he continues. "We could've done that with a PI or something. Hell, I bet we could've let her stay in the dorms and had one of the managers or even her roommate watch her for us, but no. *You* wanted her as close as possible. Close enough to put her in the extra room." He lifts his eyebrows as if making a point. And a fucking good one at that.

What else was I supposed to do, though? I couldn't trust anyone else to watch her; she'd only sneak through their grasp as she's done repeatedly with us. I open my mouth to say just that when a small figure appears at my side—the cheerleader's back. She smiles up at me and holds up a brown bottle.

"Thought you might be thirsty," she says in a soft voice. The sides of her arms press inward, plumping her chest up. It's obvious what she's doing.

"Dean?" Abel's tone is deeper, a warning. I jerk my head up and look at his stony face. What the hell does he think I'm going to—oh. My eyes return to the girl. Yes, this could work. This is exactly what I need. As if he can read my mind, Abel's hand snaps out and he grabs my arm. "Don't."

I shake him off. "Don't worry about it," I say. "Just do me that favor and keep an eye on her this week."

I try to remember the cheerleader's name—Megan or Michelle or something like that. "No," Abel shakes his head. "I'm not watching her and if you think this won't piss her off, you're wrong."

A snarl builds in my throat. "Avalon Manning doesn't fucking control me," I growl. "Her wants or desires have nothing to do with me. She's just here so we can keep an eye on her."

"So, you two aren't dating?" Megan-Michelle asks, looking up at me hopefully.

"You two need to fuck, that's all," Abel says, ignoring her.

"I'm okay with that," the girl pipes up, misunderstanding as she presses against me more insistently. I take the beer from her and set it on the ledge of the window.

Abel bears his teeth at the girl. "Get. Fucking. Lost," he orders. Her eyes widen and she squeaks, looking from me to him before backing away, turning, and scuttling out of the room.

"Was that really necessary?" I ask blandly. I didn't want her, but I did want to use her.

Abel nods towards the side door and heads for it; I take his lead and follow. As soon as we're out of the house, away from the public eye of everyone else partying it up inside, he turns and slams me back against the building. "I tried," he snaps, getting in my face. "I tried to get you to stay the fuck away from her, but like goddamn magnets, you're attracted to one another. *You* brought her here. *You* set her up in *our* side of the house—right fucking across from you. Are you really going to pretend you don't want her? We all know what you did when you went to her dorm last—"

"I didn't fuck her!" I shout, pushing him back.

"That's fucking clear, asshole, or you wouldn't be acting like this." Abel sneers at me, throwing his hands up. "I'm done. I'm over this. Fuck her, get her out of your system or hell, fucking date her. I don't care at this point. It's obvious you're obsessed with her, why the hell can't you just admit it?"

"Because we don't know who she is yet!" I yell. How the fuck can he think like this? "She's a fucking enigma." I turn and storm two feet away before pivoting back and pointing at him. "Why the fuck are they so interested in her? Does she know?"

"I don't think so," he replies, cooling visibly. He runs his hands through his hair, grabbing at a good sized chunk of it and gripping tightly as he thinks. "No, she can't know. If she knew then..." Then what? That is the question. How could we tell? We haven't been around her long enough. Two months—most of it spent watching her from afar—is not enough time.

"And that's my point," I state. "You can't be sure. None of us can."

He groans. "Fuck's sake, why the hell do you have to make everything in life so goddamn difficult?" he asks. "If you want her, take her. End of story. Who the fuck cares if she knows about them? Tie her ass down, spank her until she gives you the answers you want and then fuck her into a wall. If she betrays you, we'll make her pay. Don't fucking worry about that, but man, you've got to stop with this bullshit. Brax is pretty done with it. He likes her. Hell, I like her. I respect the fuck outta her. Knowing where she came from, the shit in her file. She shouldn't be nearly as strong as she acts. If anyone deserves a good fucking time, it's that girl."

Everything he says is true. She's far stronger than she should be. There's a core of steel that's kept her sane throughout her years with Patricia Manning. The file on *that* woman had been twice as thick and even worse than what my own mind could've imagined, and that ... that was a scary fucking reality. Because I could, without a doubt, come up with some fucked up scenarios myself. The fact that she came through all of the shit in her childhood and not only is she brave and smart, but willing to stand up to guys like us, is more than worthy of respect. It's downright problematic. I'm not used to strong women. None of us are.

Gold diggers? Yeah, sure. They're a dime a dozen. Rich little princesses without a fucking brain in their heads? We see them every fucking day. But girls—women—like Avalon? They're a rarity.

I hate to admit it, but I don't want her for a good fucking time. If that were it, I would've fucked her ages ago. No, with her, I'm half fucking terrified that one night isn't going to cut it. I doubt it'll be enough.

While I'm arguing with myself, hating the truth in Abel's words, he takes a step towards me and clasps me on the shoulder with a shake of his head. "Just don't do anything stupid, man," he tells me. "Like it or not, we're in this house with her for a week and I don't want to have to deal with shit hitting the fan if she gets pissed off at you. I'll always back you, you have to know that—but when it comes to her ... things are a little bit different."

He leaves me like that, with those parting words, as he trudges back inside. And all I'm left with is a cavernous hole in my chest and confusion in my brain. To fuck her or not, that's the question. The answer, I have a feeling, will soon reveal itself, because no man—not even me—can resist temptation for long.

43

AVALON

My room in the Eastpoint Estate is the largest bedroom I've ever seen. Easily twice the size of my dorm room if not larger. The entire back wall is covered in a row of windows that overlook the ocean. I take a step towards it and pause when I notice the black plastic bags sitting on the king-sized bed that dominates one half of the room.

Curiosity has me walking towards it rather than immediately going to the windows, dumping my backpack on the floor, and reaching for the first bag. Inside is a collection of fabric. I reach into the mouth and pull out something silky; it takes my brain a moment to play catch up. It's not silk. It's a bathing suit. A dark navy blue one that might be conservative if it weren't for the fact that the entire back is missing, made up of only enough fabric to cover my ass and a string to keep the front in place. I dig back into the bag and find three more just like it—in varying styles and colors.

In bag number two, I find soft, beachy dresses and cover ups, and in bags three and four, I find more clothes

—shorts, tank tops, and t-shirts. Funny enough, they're all perfectly matched to my size. *That sneaky bastard,* I think with a shake of my head.

I change out of my clothes and select a black and gray two piece with crisscrossing straps across my chest and back. After, I spend the next hour roaming the room and opening everything I can get my hands on. It still blows my mind that there are people in this world that have enough money not just for one nice home but dozens. Homes that they don't even use but one week out of a year. The closet is barren save for a few hangers, and the drawers are full of extra sheets, towels, and blankets. The bathroom has a deep jacuzzi tub and a separate walk in shower with white marble tiles across all three walls.

After an hour and no sign of Dean returning, I decide to give up on playing the good girl and head out. After all, I never promised that I'd stick around and wait for him. It's not my fault if he comes looking for me and I'm not there. I find my way back to the main floors of the mansion by following the sounds of people, and when I step back onto the main foyer, I realize that even more people have arrived.

Day one and spring break appears to be in full swing. Girls in bikinis much more risqué than my own and guys in board shorts race through the house, beers and Solo cups in hand. I don't know where the alcohol came from, but it seems like whoever planned for this knew they would need it in abundance. Interestingly enough, I don't spot a single staff member. No cooks. No maids. No butlers. Just a bunch of college kids wrecking some millionaire's vacation home as they get drunk and fuck on the banister of the upper stairwell.

I roll my eyes and head towards the back of the house.

Stepping out into the sunlight is a wash of hot air and that same salty sea breeze, and if I ignore the people crowding around the pool and the guys to the side of it playing beer pong, the scene, alone, is quite beautiful. I'm drawn to the half wall of stones cutting the pool area off from the ocean and beach.

Glancing over, I see that it's actually not a half wall at all, but an extension of a cliff and beyond it is a full drop off. "Beautiful, isn't it?" A shadow falls over my side as an unfamiliar voice speaks.

Turning my head, I meet a pair of ice blue eyes. "Yeah, it is," I agree.

He sticks out a hand. "I'm Jeremy."

I look down at his hand and then back at his face. "Avalon."

When he realizes I'm not going to take his hand, he lowers it and grins sheepishly. "Sorry, didn't mean to bother you," he says. "Just thought it'd be nice to admire the view with somebody."

Tilting my head at the guy, I scan him from head to toe. He's not bad looking, with a fit physique and classic washboard abs, but it's clear he's not from Eastpoint. No one else from Eastpoint has had the balls to approach me, and I doubt any of them would risk the Sick Boys' wrath just to look at a view with me.

"No one saying you can't admire it," I state, glancing back to the sea.

"Ah, but I don't think we're admiring the same thing now, are we?"

My lips twitch against my better judgment, and I shoot him a reproachful look. "That's an absolutely awful pick up line."

He laughs but takes a seat against the wall anyway. "Yeah, I know, but you cracked a smile, didn't you?"

I shake my head. "What school are you from?" I ask.

His eyes widen. "How do you know I'm not from your school?"

"I just know." I flick a pebble off the top of the wall and watch as it disappears into the churning waters below.

"Fair enough." He nods. "I go to Hazelwood U."

"That's on the West Coast, isn't it?" I ask curiously with a raised brow. "What are you doing so far from home?"

He puts both hands against the wall and crosses his legs at the ankles. For a brief moment, I think that it's an awful choice. Someone could come up and just grab his legs in one go and tip him over the edge and then it'd be too late. Poof. He'd be gone, his body washed away in the ocean. I keep my feet firmly planted on the ground.

Jeremy laughs, unaware of my thoughts. "I'm actually here with my step sister," he admits. "She goes to Eastpoint."

"I see."

A few moments later, a second, more familiar figure appears at the edge of the crowd and makes his way over. "Avalon." I tip my head back until my eyes meet Jake's. He darts a glance to the guy at my side and then frowns. "Hey..."

Jeremy uncrosses his legs and stands. "Jeremy," he introduces himself.

"Jake, uh, can I have a moment alone with Avalon?"

"Sure." Jeremy looks back at me as if to make sure I'm cool with it. I shrug. It's not like I was asking for the presence of either of them. He nods to me. "Guess, I'll see you later, beautiful."

Jake's lips part in shock, but I merely shake my head as Jeremy moves away and Jake darts a look at me. Might as well get this shit over with. "What do you want?" I ask.

"I came to say sorry," he tells me, pressing his lips

together before taking a step closer and dipping his head. "For the fight. I know you didn't want me to call them, but I—"

Holding up a hand to stop his pathetic excuse of an apology, I huff out a breath. "Save it," I say. "I don't need an apology. I hate them anyway. I didn't expect loyalty or anything. You're good."

"You're sure?" Jake eyes me as if he's uncertain of my words, as if they're hiding a deeper meaning.

"Yeah." I roll my shoulders back and stretch as I hop off the wall and take a step away from the ledge. "Like I said, you didn't owe me shit. Still don't. Can't blame you for covering your ass."

"I still feel bad about it," he admits.

"Why?" I ask. "It's not like you did any damage."

"Yeah, but—"

"Forget it," I interrupt. "Seriously. I have."

A beat passes. First one, then two, and by the third, he's grinning. "You were really something in the ring," he says. I smile when he grins at me.

"'Course I was, I learned from the best." I head off to the side and when he follows, I don't stop him.

"Where'd you learn to fight like that?" he asks.

"Backroads, high schools, and parking lots," I reply. "Pretty much wherever there was a fight." And I remember the first girl that I'd fought. Big eyes that felt like she could see through my fucking soul and an even bigger roundhouse. Every skill I'd picked up in future fights had been because of her, and how bad she'd kicked my ass that first time around.

I make it back to the pool and then head up into the air-conditioned mansion with Jake trailing me. "I know you said you didn't expect any loyalty or anything, but I want you to know that I do like you." When I shoot him a scowl, he rushes to correct himself. "I mean, as a friend. You're pretty cool and I like hanging with you. Maybe if you're cool with it, we could grab a few drinks and go down to the beach? I promise, I'd be a fucking idiot if I tried hitting on Dean's girl."

My hand shoots out and my knuckles punch into the wall right where he was about to walk through and Jake freezes, eyes jumping from my arm to my face. "I'm not Dean's *anything*," I snap, dropping my arm and turning to face him. "If you wanna hang, that's fine, but don't say shit like that again. Dean is not my keeper."

"I-I'm sorry, man, I just thought since you were here—I mean, after the fight, when he—"

"Dean is a controlling dick," I say, cutting his bumbling tirade off. "He wants to keep me in his sights so I don't do anything stupid by his standards. If we're going to be friends—fine—then we're going to lay out the facts right here and now. You're not loyal to me."

He blinks as if shocked and I arch a brow. Jake's eyes find the ground and he shoves his hands into the pockets of his board shorts. "It's not that I don't *want* to be loyal, you know..."

"I get it." Hell, of all the people here, I think I'm the only one that really truly understands that loyalty is nothing more than a pendulum. It swings one way and then another. "Loyalty is about survival, and at Eastpoint, the Sick Boys are the biggest predators. You chose them and you'll choose them again. I'm not mad about it," I tell him. At least, not anymore. "I just want to make sure that we're on the same page. The one thing I fucking hate is people trying to get close to me and lying."

Jake grits his teeth and one hand shoots out of his

pocket as he scrubs it down his face and nods. "Yeah, okay, I get it. No lies."

"And no pretending," I confirm.

He nods.

"Then we're good."

I turn away and head to the kitchen; I'm pulling two beers out of the fridge there when he finally makes his way into the room.

"You know," he begins, taking one of the beers from my hand and twisting the top off, "if anyone could challenge them for Eastpoint's loyalty, I think it could be you."

I laugh, shaking my head as I twist the top off my beer as well and toss it into a nearby recycling bin. "Nah. I don't want that kind of loyalty," I say. "These people"—I stop and gesture to the crowd we're watching just out of the kitchen doors—"are loyal to the top dog and that can change at any moment. It's fake and I don't do fake loyalty."

Jake's head bobs up and down and he puts the mouth of his beer bottle to his lips, sucking down half the bottle before lowering it once more. "I get what you're saying," he replies, his eyes centered on the windows. "I do, but I think they're different."

I don't have to ask to know who he means. *Them.* The Sick Boys. Dean, Abel, and Braxton.

"I think," he continues, "even if one or more of them lost everything tomorrow, they'd still stick by each other." A cold wave of air shoots out of a vent somewhere in the room, dropping the temperature, and I fight back the urge to shiver as it slides over my skin. "I don't know why I think that. There's just something about them..."

As he trails off, I spot one of the men in question. Braxton lifts a girl in a white bikini and tosses her into the pool before launching in after her. My lips twitch. He looks so young and carefree as he dive bombs into the pool, making a huge wave that has several of the current occupants slipping off their floats into the water. He comes up, laughing, bright teeth, sparkling eyes, and dark curls flopping against his forehead.

Jake's right. I can't imagine Braxton without Abel or Dean at his back and vice versa for the others. There's an invisible bond between them. It was there in the warnings from Abel. There in the way Braxton never approached me without them unless he was asked to. They back each other up. They support each other. The only thought that comes to mind is that they resemble a family. Like brothers rather than best friends.

"The blood of the covenant is thicker than the water of the womb," I mutter absently.

Jake looks at me, his brows drawn down. "What?"

I sigh, shaking my head. "Nothing," I tell him. "It's stupid, just an old Bible verse."

"Didn't take you for the religious type." I can tell I've shocked him, but when you grow up in the southern backwoods, the religious fanatics ran supreme and though I'd never gone to church myself—I certainly doubted Patricia ever had either—it was hard to get out of a place like that without a few notes from the doctrine.

"I'm not." I stare out into the sun and ocean scenery, frowning as my mind tells me to move. To walk away. To make a joke and distract him from his curiosity. I don't do any of those things, though. Instead, I tell him the truth. "It's a common saying," I tell him. "But it's usually misquoted. Are you familiar with the phrase 'blood is thicker than water'?" I ask.

He nods, curious eyes watching me.

"The real quote is 'the blood of the covenant is thicker than the water of the womb,'" I say.

And it means the exact opposite of what people assume. It means that the family they choose, the bonds a person makes in life is stronger than that of the connection of blood relatives. Because in the end, the family that a person is born with doesn't always necessarily see you as anything more than a possession or a meal ticket.

44

AVALON

Two days into spring break and I think, maybe the Sick Boys aren't so bad. Most people are too afraid to talk to me. I would like to think it's because they heard about what I did to Kate's car or they've heard about the fight at the warehouse and recognize that I'm a badass bitch. In actuality, however, I'm pretty sure it's because of the guys. People are terrified of coming near me because the Sick Boys have made me both desired and untouchable.

I don't like people as a general rule—the only ones I can seem to stand are Dean and the guys, Rylie, sometimes Corina, and Jake. Suffice it to say, I'm not disappointed by the lack of well wishers and friendship making. I'm perfectly content to drink beer and tan by the ocean.

On the second day, Jake tells me he found a staircase leading down to the actual beach and we gather our shit and practically camp on the sand for the entire day. "Corina's here," he comments, tipping back his fourth beer of the day and draining it down his throat.

"Yeah?" I should've expected that. "I haven't seen her."

He shrugs. "She's probably off with her new guy

friend. Heard she brought some dude with her. They're probably fucking in one of the spare bedrooms nonstop."

I snort at that comment. "Jealous?" I ask.

He drops his bottle into the pile we've collected between us before grabbing a new one out of the cooler and cracking it open. "Not really. Corina's ... well, let's just say she's not the kind of girl I'd stick my dick in more than once."

That bothers me for some reason, but I don't reply. Instead, I rest back and stare up at the massive cliff as a hoard of guys from the party above come down the staircase we'd found earlier with giant surfboards at their sides. They make carrying the heavy boards look easy, but I'm sure it's anything but. They're big and clunky and professional grade if the glossy sheen of their surfaces is anything to go by.

I look up when a shadow falls over me. "Hey, Brax."

Braxton's body may be hovering over mine, but his eyes are zeroed in on my friend. "Having fun?" he asks, glaring at Jake.

Reaching up, I slap his washboard abs. "Leave him alone," I snap. "I need someone to hang with since y'all ditched me at the first opportunity and no one else is willing to fucking entertain me."

"Dean hasn't come to see you yet?" I jump when Abel's voice sounds right behind me as well.

Sitting up, I strain around Brax's big ass body and gape when Abel comes striding up, carrying one of the surfboards. Body cut like a fucking Olympic swimmer, the upper half of his wetsuit hangs down revealing the deep grooves along the sides of his abdomen. Curious, my eyes cut back to Brax. Unlike Abel, he's wearing fairly plain board shorts, but they do nothing to diminish the deep v cut of his body that seems like it's pointing straight down to the front of his pants.

Jesus fuck. I whip back around, snatch my beer up and drain it in one go.

"Nope," I answer quickly.

Abel comes around the side and I try as hard as I can to not watch as he bends over the cooler to grab a beer for himself. "Stubborn asshole," he mutters.

"What?"

He shakes his head, popping the top. "Nothing. Don't worry about it. Are you enjoying yourself?"

I nod and peel my eyes away from his fine ass muscles to look back out to the sea as the waves come crashing in. Two of the others who'd come down with them start out with boards already flat on the water, their bodies pressed down as they paddle into the waves.

"For a prison, it's pretty nice," I comment, lifting my beer again.

Just before Brax lets out a snort, his hand comes down on my head, rubbing awkwardly like one might do to a kid sister. "As if we could keep you here if you didn't want it," he replies.

I can feel Jake's shock like little pinpricks along my skin as he watches the exchange. I ignore both and keep talking to Abel. "So, you surf?"

Abel shoots me a grin and sticks his beer in the sand so it doesn't fall before using two arms to lift his sturdy board and shove the end into the ground. It's at least a foot or more taller than his frame. "Nah, this here's just for decoration," he says sardonically before shaking his head. "Yeah, I've been surfing since I was a kid. My mom liked to do it."

"Hmmmm." I watch him with interest. "Do you look like her?" I ask.

He pauses, half-bent over as he reaches for his beer. There's a moment of silence and then he stands up and turns away. "No," he says quietly, "I don't look anything like her." Then without another word he drains his beer, dumps it in our pile, and grabs his surfboard, heading out.

I cock an eyebrow up at Brax questioningly. "It's not you," he says, shaking his head. "His mom's just a sore subject."

"He seems to care about her a lot," I comment. "The Mustang's hers, and now surfing..."

"Yeah." Brax nods, but he doesn't elaborate. It doesn't take a rocket scientist to figure out that I've stumbled over something that's just between the three of them. So, I just lie back down on my towel and finish my beer.

Night falls rather quickly when you have nothing better to do than lay under the sun, watch hot guys surf, and drink. Hours later, I've changed out of my swimsuit and into one of the beach dresses Dean had left in my room. It's a dark blue one that ties at the back of my neck and hangs around my thighs, and it's probably the most expensive thing I've ever worn. I'm a little peeved that Dean isn't around to see me in it, but if he wants to buy me shit and then disappear into the fucking wind like a coward, I guess I'll let him.

My cheeks are flushed and I know for damn sure that I'm not completely sober as I make my way back to the beach. In the time since this afternoon, someone has built three giant structures of wood spaced out along the sand and lit them aflame. It seems everyone from the mansion has come down here for this—a bonfire party or whatever it is, because unlike earlier, the sand is crowded with college kids. Music plays from somewhere amidst the masses and couples bump and grind as they dance to the beats.

"Fancy meeting you here."

I nearly jump a fucking mile when a semi-familiar voice speaks in my ear. Whipping around, I jerk my hand up and back and stop when I catch a glance of a smiling face. "Jeremy." I'd nearly punched him out. Slowly, I lower my arm back to my side. "Don't sneak up on me," I snap.

His eyes widen and he takes a step back as his smile slips a little. "Sorry about that," he says, ducking his head.

"It's fine, just … don't do it again."

"Here." He lifts another brown bottle and waves it towards me. "An apology."

I take the beer, but don't open it. I should've heard him come up. Normally, I would've. How many drinks had I had? I'm not drunk by any means, but I know I'm not completely clear headed either. I set the beer down in the sand.

"Forgiven," I tell him and he grins.

"Want to dance?" he asks, offering me his hand, palm up. I look from him to the crowd as they slide against one another. I haven't danced since the club and though I could really use the relaxing time, I'm hesitant to agree. When he sees the indecision on my face, Jeremy's hand drops. "We don't have to dance if you don't want to, we can just hang."

"Avalon!" I see it. That split-second between when I hear Jake's voice call out my name and Jeremy's disappointment, there's a sliver of irritation. He backs up.

"Wait," I blurt.

Dean's not around, I hear my inner voice say. He hasn't been around since he dropped me off in my bedroom and booked it like his ass was on fire. Everyone's been acting like I'm something special to him and even now, I know Jake's coming up because he sees me talking with Jeremy and somehow, he thinks that I don't have a say. Dean put a claim on my ass. No one at Eastpoint will even fucking come near me and yeah, I'm fine with it being like that. But maybe I don't want everyone to think that I'm under Dean Carter's thumb.

He may have brought me here, but he doesn't own my ass.

Jeremy looks up and meets my gaze as I reach out and take his hand. "Yeah," I say, making the decision even as I hear Jake panting as he tries to get to me through the crowd. "Let's dance."

A smile lights his face and without a second thought, he grips my hand back and leads me into the throng of grinding bodies. The music is louder here. We're so close to the fire that the heat is sweltering. Beneath my dress, sweat coats my body and beads begin to form, making my skin glisten. Jeremy's hands find my hips and together we sway, moving to the rhythm of the music coming out of invisible speakers.

"I'm really glad I found you tonight," he says, leaning forward and whispering the words in my ear.

"Oh yeah?" I say when really, I want to tell him to shut up and let me dance. I don't care what he has to say. Already two seconds into the middle of the dance area, and I want to leave, but I don't. I stay. I let him move with me.

Maybe I do it because I know I shouldn't. Everyone's been warning me not to take things too far. Everyone's been urging caution. But I'm fucking tired of playing by another's rules. I'm tired of following in Dean's footsteps and being swept along by his fucking wants and desires. Just for tonight, I want to close my eyes and pretend that

I'm just another girl—a normal fucking college girl—dancing at a beach party.

"Yeah," Jeremy says, one of his hands reaching around and sliding to the small of my back. One of his legs presses forward, between both of mine. I sigh and my hands find his chest. *This was a bad fucking idea*, I think. He's ruining it. "I want to take you up to the house and show you the meaning of a good time," he says. My eyes open just as his head dips down. *No fucking way.*

My neck snaps back and I'm two seconds from shoving him straight into the bonfire when he doesn't release me but pulls me even closer. I don't need to, though, because Jeremy is no longer my main problem, I realize as he disappears and I stumble, nearly falling on my ass.

It takes me a second to recognize what happened, but the sound of fists hitting flesh draws my attention and then I see. "Dean!" I snap, racing forward. I catch his arm when he goes to hit the guy again and Dean's head jerks to the side. The music comes to a sudden halt like a record scratching against a disc and everyone in the nearby vicinity stops what they're doing to watch the scene unfold.

"What the fuck were you doing?" Dean yells at me. "You let this motherfucker touch you when you're mine?"

"Yours?" I repeat, releasing his arm. "Since fucking when? I'm not fucking yours."

Dean storms up to me and grabs my elbows. "The hell you're not!" His head lifts and he glares at the people around us as I struggle in his grasp, turning my arms so that I twist out of his embrace. "Everybody listen the fuck up!" he yells.

No, I think. *He wouldn't. He's not that stupid.*

Oh, but he is, I realize a second later as he keeps talking.

"As far as everyone here is concerned, Avalon Manning is Sick Boys property!" he calls out. "If any of you fuckers touch her, come near her, or so much as look at her the wrong way—your ass is dead."

Fury pounds through my system. Absolute fucking rage. And all of it is centered on the man standing before me. "You don't fucking own me!" I yell at him.

Dean's head snaps around and he narrows his eyes on me. "You think not, baby?"

"I *know* not, asshole!"

Then, he takes a step towards me and before I can scramble out of his reach, he bends over, slides one arm around the backs of both of my thighs, and tosses me up and over his shoulder.

"Dean!" I snap, rearing up as he turns, not waiting for anyone to respond as he heads for the stairs. "I swear to fuck, Dean, if you don't put me down right fucking now—" I cut off when I catch a glimpse of Jake standing next to Abel and Braxton. Traitor! Though, again, I shouldn't be shocked.

"Take care of that," Dean orders the guys, nodding to where Jeremy lies, groaning with a hand covering his bloodied nose. He doesn't let them get another word in before we're both moving past them. Dean ignores me and my struggles until we're halfway up the stairs. "Stop it," he growls out. "Or you're liable to send both of us over the edge."

He's right. My head lifts and I see just how far up he's taken us. If he drops me like this, it's not going to end well. That and that alone, is the only reason I finally settle, waiting until we get to the top of the fucking stairs and away from the cliffs before I redouble my efforts to get out of his arms. But it isn't until we're inside and down in the guys' personal wing of the mansion that he releases me.

"What *the fuck* was that about?" I demand, punching his chest the second my feet hit the floor.

"I told you," he growls, slamming his hands on the wall behind me. "I fucking warned you not to pull stupid shit. Then I see you grinding on some guy in the middle of one of our fucking parties—"

"I was *not* grinding on him," I snarl. "We were dancing, and what the fuck do you care? You've been MIA for the last two days. You can't just waltz back up to me and act like you didn't run like a scared little bitch."

"Yes, I fucking can." Dean reaches around me, turns the knob of my bedroom door, and a moment later, the wood is slamming into the wall as he backs me into the room and shuts it.

45

DEAN

I stare down into her furious blue-gray eyes and wonder—not for the first time since I met this girl—if I've lost my goddamn mind. She makes me feel like I have. Backing her further into the room, I turn her away from the light switch, leaving everything in the shadows.

"What?" she snaps as she moves away from me only to have me step right back into her personal space.

She looks good. Tan. Pink cheeked. Sexy as fuck. It's been a fucking nightmare trying to stay the fuck away from her since we got here. Now, I have to wonder why I even fucking bothered.

"I don't fucking do this," I say, staring into her eyes.

"Do what?" she replies, scowling at me.

My hands find her hips and I jerk her forward until she can feel what she does to me. Even through our clothes, my cock throbs at her nearness. But, of course, she doesn't even blink. No, not this girl. Her eyes stay on mine and even if they widen a fraction, she still doesn't do what I expect. She remains completely impassive other than that one, singular movement.

No, impassive is the wrong word. She's not impassive. She's fucking raging inside. Angry. Wrathful. Like a war goddess that has yet to be unleashed. *I give up,* I think. I can't do it anymore. I can't stay away. Abel was right. There's no point in even trying. If she's working with my father and the others, then so be it. I'll risk it. I'd risk fucking life and limb just to feel all of her fucking fiery heat on my dick.

"You're going to have to use your big boy words if you want me to understand your meaning, D-man," she says, bringing me back to reality.

My fingers clench on her sides and I sweep them upward. I graze the outside of her breasts, where the low cut halter dress I bought for her ends and my fingers meet sweet, smooth skin. I keep going until my hands make it all the way up and wrap around either side of her neck. The feel of her pulse pounding, racing against my palms turns me on in a new way I've never experienced. "I'm tired of this," I tell her. "I'm done."

"*You're* done?" She narrows her cold gaze on me. "That should be my line. I'm tired of your goddamn hot and cold act. You bring me here. You ditch me. You tell everyone I'm yours—which I'm not, by the way—and then you—"

"I want you to be," I cut in.

Pink lips part and I watch as her tongue slides behind her straight white teeth. "You … want me to be what?" she repeats. As if it's un-fucking-clear. As if it's not obvious how much I want her even when my cock is straining against my zipper and pressed to her stomach.

I grit my teeth and tilt my head down. "Mine." I whisper the word. She's so close, I can smell the salt on her skin. My mouth waters. "I want you to be mine and I want to hear you admit it from your own lips."

Silence stretches between us. "Why?" she finally asks. Isn't that the million dollar question?

"Because you're annoying," I say, closing my eyes as I press my forehead to hers, holding her still. No longer does she try to back away from me. "Because you fight me. Because you're not afraid of me."

She snorts, the sound derisive and amused at the same time. "Not to burst your masculine bubble, D-man," she says, "but you're not that scary."

I open my eyes. "Not to you apparently," I reply.

"But you find me annoying," she says.

"Yes," I admit. "And sometimes, I also want to choke the fuck out of you." As I say the words, I tighten my grip on her throat.

A dark glimmer of something only I can name enters her eyes. "Careful," she whispers back. "I might be into it."

"Oh, baby girl," I say, grinning as I look down at her. "There's no 'might' about it. If I do it, you'll be into it."

"Oh yeah?" Avalon arches one brow. "Then why don't you show me?"

"How can I resist an invitation like that?" I ask absently. The answer is: I can't. I don't give the little smartass time to answer. Instead, I lower my head and crush my mouth against hers.

My tongue pushes her lips apart and for the first fucking time in my life, I find true heaven. People say that hell is frozen over, but that isn't true with her. She's perfection and so much filthy wickedness, it's a wonder neither of us burst into flames the second our lips touch.

I clench my hands on the back of her neck, angling her head the way I like as I lick at her lips. I want to consume this girl. Devour everything she is and take it into myself. I let my tongue tangle with hers, let her feel the piercing centered there. Oh, what I wouldn't have given to be wearing a different one right now. I can just imagine how she'd come apart for me if I had a vibrating tongue ring in. I could press it right against her little clit and hold it there for eternity and feel her juices coat my face.

Electricity races through me as I slide one palm up into the dark inky blackness of her hair and I tighten my grip—pulling it as I yank her head all the way back. She gasps as her mouth pops away from mine.

"Dean…" My cock fucking throbs at the sound of my name on her lips. I press an open mouthed kiss to the pulse point of her throat. *Mine.* I want to stamp my name all over her ass and make sure every fucker who looks at her knows that she belongs to someone—not just any someone. Me. Her fucking *King*. I want her—the girl who refuses to bow to anyone. I want her to do so for me. And there's only one way I know of, to make that happen. If I want her to bow then I've got to bend. Something I've never done before in my life.

It's not a hard decision.

Groaning into my mouth, when my palms leave her neck and move down to the backs of her thighs, Avalon doesn't fight me. In fact, she jumps, her legs opening, spreading as she catches the back of my neck with her arms and I lift her against my chest.

One step. Her tongue enters my mouth. Two steps. I can feel the heat of her pussy through our clothes. Three steps. I press her down into the surface of the bed and lay her out.

"Dean?" She frowns at me when I don't come down on top of her like she expects.

Because no, that's not how I'm going to start with this woman. I want Avalon Manning to be more than a body in my bed. I want her to fucking want me as much as I crave her. I want her to think about me the way I think of her—all the fucking time in an all consuming cycle.

I lower myself. When my knees hit the floor, her hands sink into my hair. Shivers chase down my spine as her nails scrape my scalp. I lift her dress and press a kiss to the softness of her stomach. My lips stretch and I smile as I feel her inhale sharply, her belly sucking in and her chest rising beneath the dark fabric that will soon enough be crumpled on the floor along with her panties. She knows exactly where this is going. My mouth on her little pussy. My tongue deep inside her walls. I can't wait to fucking see her come apart.

46

AVALON

AM I DOING THIS? FOR REAL? WITH HIM?

The answer is yes. I am. And if I'm being honest with myself, we've been riding a bullet train straight to this moment since I first realized who he was. His hands move beneath my dress, pushing it up as he kisses my stomach and then nuzzles further down until his face is centered right over my panties, so close I can feel the heat of his breath on my pussy.

My eyes slide shut and when his palms spread my thighs open, pushing them up and out until my feet are planted on the edge of the mattress and he's staring at the crotch of my thong. One thick finger strokes down the center and I have to bite my lip to keep from screaming. I'm wet, soaked as fuck. Ready.

"Dean," I say his name through gritted teeth, "either do something or let me get the fuck up and go get someone who will."

His finger freezes, his hands retract, and I think, *well shit, I pushed too far too fast.* Then something cold touches my skin. I jump and his hand lands back on my thigh, holding me down. "I wouldn't move if I were you," he warns.

My head arches up and I see a flash of silver. A pocket knife. My heart starts pounding faster, harder, echoing in my ears. My breath shudders out as my chest expands. Dean's fingers hook into one side of my thong and he cuts it away before doing the same to the other and then he takes the bottom of my dress and glances up, those dark eyes of his meeting mine as he begins to slice upward. The back of the metal blade presses against my skin, making my heartbeat leap as he cuts a perfect path up past the swell of my breasts until the fabric is laying open, revealing everything that my bra doesn't cover. That, too, though, is no match for him and soon I'm laying bare and naked beneath Dean Carter.

His eyes never leave mine as he presses the back of the weapon against his jaw and closes it with one hand and drops it next to my head. "You and I both know there's no way I'm letting you out of this room until I've had you in every position I've imagined you in since I met you," he says, dipping down and licking the dried sweat from my throat.

I clench my whole body as I feel the ball of his tongue piercing against my skin. My eyes close once more and I have to resist moaning at the feel of his fingers as they make their way back down to the place between my thighs. One stretches into my opening, pressing inside and curving up in a come here movement. Dean's lips move from the tip of one breast to the next as his stubble scrapes my flesh raw.

I can't catch my breath. I'm in sensory overload. The feel of his fingers—first the one and then two and then three pushing into my core. The sound of my pussy growing wetter and wetter as he gets me off. The loudness of my own moans as I stop resisting them and let them out, meeting his growling satisfaction as he bites down on one nipple, sending me straight up and over the edge into a fiery fast orgasm.

Panting, I tighten down on his hand as Dean withdraws his fingers and lifts them up for me to see. He grins, and I have to admit, wickedness is a good look for him. He presses his hand to my mouth, stroking my lips with my own wetness. I don't even have to be told. I lick the cream from his fingers, staring straight into his eyes as I do, daring him to help me. He doesn't disappoint. Dean leans forward and licks the opposite side of his own hand; the only thing keeping our mouths from fusing together.

As if a chain has been cut and he's unleashed, Dean pulls back and rips his shirt over his head, tossing it away. He helps me remove the scraps of the shredded dress and throws it as well. Dean's hands fall to his waist and I bite my lip, watching as he unbuttons the top of his jeans and then lowers the zipper. The base of his cock makes an appearance, and when he shucks his pants and boxers the rest of the way off, stepping out of them before coming down over me, I grin.

"Nice to see I didn't imagine that piercing," I say.

Dean arches a brow and then reaches down, cupping himself and guiding the head of his cock to my entrance. He rubs that piercing against my clit, ever the tormentor. He pauses. "Birth control?" he asks, eyes shooting to mine.

I laugh. "Dean, I've been on birth control since I was twelve. You're good." I arch a brow. "Unless you have something to tell me."

"I've been checked," he assures me, resuming his torture. The metal of his piercing feels warmer than I expect it and I imagine exactly where it will soon be—in my pussy, scraping my G-spot. "Have to get regular physicals with the team."

"Right," I say absently, nodding. Football. I forgot, he's a player. It occurs to me that I've never actually been to a game, but I guess football doesn't happen in the winter and spring. My thoughts are completely erased a moment later when he lowers his knees and then brings the head of his cock to my opening and presses inside and fucking hell, he's thicker than his fingers. Way thicker. Deliciously so.

I groan as he starts with shallow thrusts, working the first half of his length inside. "Fuck," he hisses through his teeth. "You really are gonna fucking kill me."

I whimper when he hits something particularly deep and my nails sink into the skin of his back. He groans.

"God, those fucking sounds." His breath hits my ear—hot and humid—a split second before he leans down and his teeth scrape my earlobe. He bites down. *Hard*. I moan as a shot of adrenaline pours through me. "Louder," he orders. "I want them to hear you come on my cock."

Shit fuck. I don't think anything could sound hotter than the confidence in his tone. There's no question of whether or not I'll come on his cock—only the inevitability. He's going to be the death of me. He's going to wreck me from the inside out and I'm perfectly okay with it as long as it feels this fucking good. I gasp as he pulls back and thrusts into me, his cock spearing through my pussy and hitting a point inside my core that almost hurts.

Dean arches up, doing it again and again. Moving faster and faster, slamming into me so hard that the bed moves and the headboard smacks into the wall with every thrust. His hand comes down, gripping my breast, and squeezing roughly. I love it. The roughness. The aggressive feeling of being fucked by him. I've had guys do it before—grab my tit when they fuck me, but for some reason—

coming from him, it's different. Perhaps because he doesn't just squeeze and release like they had. Instead, he squeezes harder—hard enough to hurt—before he lets go and then feathers his fingers over the tip again. His thumbs and forefingers move over my nipples. Gently. A tease. A whisper right before he fucking grips the peaks and twists.

"Fuck!" I scream as an orgasm lashes through me. It barrels through my body, white hot, unexpected. Faster than I'd ever imagined. It wipes out all rational thought and completely consumes me, overwhelms my logical brain and drowns out all else until I'm riding on a wave of pure ecstasy. It's then that I realize, Dean Carter is a fucking drug. Dangerous. Deadly. Addictive.

I pant, gasping for air. Shocked at how hard it is just to fucking breathe. But he isn't done. Far from it, in fact. He withdraws his cock, sliding through my folds, coated in the remains of my orgasm, and smiles down at me. "Good girl," he whispers, bending towards me and pressing a fast kiss to my mouth. Then he powers forward again, and as sensitive as I am after my last orgasm, I feel the movement ten times harder. My nails scrape down his back, dragging down his sides, over his ribs, and I know without seeing them that I've left my mark on him.

Dean hisses, arching into the pain of my grip. I know it has to hurt, but from the way he's acting—grinding into me, fucking me harder than ever—it's clear he doesn't give a shit. *Dirty asshole*, I think, even as I cling to his much larger frame, letting him overwhelm me. It takes only minutes of his thrusting before I feel the flutterings of another orgasm.

What the actual fuck? I just came. It's not possible. "Dean," I gasp.

"That's right, baby," he urges, thrusting faster, hitting

against that spot inside me—pounding it into oblivion. "Say my name."

He's unhinged. Powerful. Hungry. Unstoppable. I open my mouth to scream again, but nothing comes out. The pleasure ricochets up through me, and my chest collapses. My heart slams against the confines of my ribcage. My eyes roll back into my head.

I'm going to die like this, I think just before the peak overcomes me. *In the throes of some ridiculously delicious sex.*

Hands grip my wrists and yank them away from his flesh. My eyes slam open. I hadn't even noticed when they closed. He shoves my arms up the bed, beneath the pillows, holding them down as his hips rise and fall. We're connected, now, only by the place where he's pounding his cock into me and where our hands clasp together. Dean's eyes meet mine—dark and heated.

"Look at me," he commands. There's no denying him. I already am. "You're gonna come again, aren't you?" he asks with an evil smile.

I can't respond. Trying to inhale and exhale is still too much of a chore. I open my mouth, but instead of speaking, I moan when he pushes into me at the same moment. He grinds down until I can feel nothing else but my skin against his. I groan, tossing my head back into the pillows at my back as he chuckles, the sound reverberating through his chest. I gasp, inhaling sharply as he hits that spot again —the one pulsing deep inside. And then he hits it again … and again. *Fuck!*

"Scream," he whispers in my ear, his fingers releasing my hands and trailing down to my breasts once more. He circles my nipples. I know what's coming, and I can't fucking wait for it. "Scream for me." He pinches down, eliciting such pain and yet, such pleasure as well, I can't help but give him what he wants. Another scream rips through me as I come, and I come *hard*. White light blinds me. Pleasure wraps around my throat and squeezes. No. Not pleasure. His hands. I open my eyes—mid-orgasm—and see that he's released my nipples and moved to my neck. He squeezes with both hands, clamping down on either side—cutting off the blood flow, but never my oxygen as his face contorts.

"Fuck yes!" he yells. "Milk me, baby. I want this pussy to take all I have to give." The dirty words coming from his lips spur me on. He was right. If he's the one doing it, I *do* like it. I arch against his grip, against his cock as he thrusts into me relentlessly.

I feel him lean back, pulling his cock from me and spurting the rest of his cum against the outside of my pussy and over the curve of my stomach. He groans as I catch my breath—still entrapped in the high of feeling like I just jumped off a goddamn cliff.

And it's only when he groans and releases my throat—when dots of black and white appear in my vision—that I realize just how fucked I really am. Because sex like this has only one path—straight to fucking hell.

47

AVALON

I HAD SEX WITH DEAN CARTER. AND ... I LIKED IT. It's a new thing for me, liking sex. It's always been more or less about release. Not an activity that I want to spend all night doing or even all day. But that's what happens. I wake the next morning with his face already buried back between my thighs. Thighs that he makes tremble and shake as he sucks my clit into his mouth and rubs the metal rod in his tongue up and down it. He makes me want it. Over and over. All that explosiveness between us, the hatred, the frustration, we take it out on each other and it's the hottest thing I've ever felt in my life.

Sex with Dean is like getting the biggest adrenaline high I've ever had. We do it more times than I can count. Against the wall with his face next to mine as he pounds into me. In the shower with me bent damn near in half as he fucks my pussy with his chest pressed to my spine. On the bed. In front of the windows overlooking the ocean. When I think I can't do it anymore, when I'm too fucking sore that I feel like my pussy can't possibly get wet ever again, his arm will curl around me while I'm exhausted beyond belief, and then suddenly his fingers are between my legs and the floodgates are open once more. He pushes me onto my back, shoves that pierced cock of his right into my pussy until I'm screaming out yet another orgasm.

It's mind blowing, and worse, it's confusing.

I lay there, my head pillowed on his bicep as I count the individual hairs on his arm. Outside, the sun is starting to set. An array of various colors reflecting against the surface of the ocean. I'm in a beautiful bedroom in a beautiful place with a man who's spent the last day and a half proving to me the meaning of dickmatized, yet all I can think of now is how fucking exhausted I am and how far from reality this all is.

Dean's breath blows out against my ear as he sighs, his chest moving up and down against my back. "What are you thinking?" he asks as if sensing the darkening turn of my thoughts. I wish he'd just remained silent, but speaking has ruined the whole atmosphere I was enjoying.

I reach up and yank an arm hair out in retaliation. "Shit!" He retracts his arm and my head lands against the mattress, bouncing once, twice, and a final third time as I laugh. "What the hell was that for?" he asks.

"I was enjoying the moment," I state. "You ruined it. That was punishment."

The covers slip away as he shifts over me, pressing his bare chest against mine, the prickling hairs on his pecs rubbing against my nipples, making them tingle. I glance down, over the small pale scars that mar different parts of his body. Some of them surprise me because I recognize them. I know a knife wound when I see one. But I don't ask. We may have given in to the sexual chemistry, but neither of us trusts the other. Not yet.

"You never answered my question." He presses a kiss to my shoulder, one palm coming up to cup my breast.

I sigh as I relax into the mattress. "I was just thinking about my hometown," I say. Though his eyes flick up to scan my face, he doesn't reply. Instead, Dean spends the next several minutes working his way back down my body with light kisses and hard sucks until I'm writhing in his grasp.

His broad hands touch my thighs, spreading them wide and then he dives between them like a starving man. How he can do this again when he's already done it so many times, I don't know. I release a groan as his tongue circles my clit. My fingers tangle in his hair, scratching against the back of his skull. I press down, urging him to go faster, to make me come. He obliges and not long after, I'm gasping out yet another fast release as he arches up over me, cock hard, and mouth wet with my essence.

I don't turn away from him when he kisses me. Instead, I open my mouth to it. He moans against me, sucking my tongue in and tangling it with his own. It's dirty and raw, the sex between us. Not exactly what I expected—but in a good way. I'm happy to know that all of his swagger and confidence isn't unearned. At least, not in the bedroom.

My fingers touch his side, stroking over the dark inked lines of the tattoo of thorny roses etched into his skin. There's more on his back. The whole of his spine is nearly covered from his shoulder blades to the top of his ass, but I haven't gotten more than a few glimpses here and there. Nothing concrete to say for sure if it's just a bunch of little pieces or an entire masterpiece put together on the canvas of his flesh.

He groans and pulls his mouth from mine, resting his forehead between my breasts as he collapses. "I'm going to die from sex," he complains as I sift my fingers through his hair.

I chuckle. It's probably the most childlike he's ever

sounded in front of me. Complaining about sex. "What a way to go, though," I reply absently.

He mumbles something, turning his cheek and nuzzling one of my breasts. Weirdo. We end up lying there for so long, I almost lose track of time. But it's long enough that the sunset fades into night and darkness creeps into the room, leaving the two of us in shadows. I used to hate the darkness. A lot of bad things happen in the darkness. It was Micki that changed that for me. She taught me that everyone forgets that a lot of good things happen in the darkness too.

Darkness breeds intimacy.

In the early morning hours, there are more booty calls and deaths than any other time. Why? Because those are the prime hours of the dark. When vulnerability is at its peak. When—if death doesn't come knocking—you crave the feeling of another body alongside your own.

Right here. Right now. I feel vulnerable. It's not something I'm used to and unlike what I expected, it doesn't make me uncomfortable. Because I don't feel alone in my vulnerability. Whether he'll admit it or not, Dean showed me a side of himself that I doubt many others get to see. The jealousy. The possessiveness. The sharp desire and will to control another human. They're all a part of him, making up who he is as a person and there's a reason behind it all. Just like I know there's a reason behind my need for adrenaline. I'm not an idiot. I know it's not natural, not normal. I know that the things my mind comes up with and the sick need for that rush of life right before I do something dangerous isn't exactly a healthy coping mechanism. I just don't fucking care.

"Tell me about your mom." My fingers still as Dean speaks, making that request in a voice that sounds half asleep. His lower body is heavy, trapping mine to the bed, and when I don't immediately respond, his hands come up and stroke my sides. "Please."

"Dean Carter..." I say, forcing a light chuckle into my tone, "are you actually using manners for once?"

"I know how to get what I want," he replies.

My response is a hum in my throat.

"Avalon." He lifts his head, soil-rich eyes the color of a burning sun meeting mine. "I'm serious."

My lips part, and I resume combing my hands through his hair, needing the movement to stay sane as I recall things about my life and Patricia that I'd honestly rather not.

"My mom's a stripper," I admit. "Has been since before I can remember." The words are halting as they scrape out of my throat. I hate talking about Patricia. Hate the fact that just the sound of her name on my lips makes my body tense and makes me remember things that are better left in the dark. "From what I understand, she used to be really pretty," I admit.

Dean's head lifts, but I don't look down. "She's not anymore?"

I shake my head. "Not really, her skin sags and she's got these pockmarks in her face. Years of alcohol and drug abuse eventually take their toll. She doesn't look anything like me, now that I think about it." Where I have dark hair, she has fair. Where I have pale skin, hers is tanned. Where I'm short, she's tall and willowy.

"Hmmmm." His hand clenches on my side, the rough coarseness of his palm against my smooth skin makes a shiver skate down my spine. "Maybe you get your looks from your dad," he suggests.

"Dunno," I say. "Never met the guy."

"Then you're probably lucky," he mutters. Before I can ask why, he blows out a breath, arches up and turns over, dragging my body until I'm plopped on top of him as his head rests back against the pillows. He grunts, flinging an arm over his head, covering the upper part of his face. I prop my chin on his chest, between his pecs. *How can I still want him?* I wonder. I should be all sexed out and ready for a long nap, but just staring at his face, tracing his tattoos, it makes me want to jump his bones for the millionth time in a row.

He lifts his arm and looks down at me, a grin flicking across his face. "Penny for your thoughts?" Before I can say more, however, a loud banging noise sounds from the hallway.

"Hey! Dean! Get your ass out here!" Abel shouts, his words slurring, and then something slams into my bedroom door. "He's not in here," Abel says, sounding like he's talking to someone else. "Where the fuck did they go?"

Dean groans and I roll off of him, popping off the bed and reaching for a swath of fabric laying across the floor—his shirt I realize when I yank it over my head to cover myself and it falls down to mid thigh. "Fuck." Whipping around at the rough curse from him, I stop and laugh when I see Dean's eyes eating up the expanse of leg still visible beneath the hem. "You look so fucking good in my clothes, baby."

I roll my eyes, and just as I predicted, a split second later, the door to my room comes slamming open. "Ava!" Abel stumbles into the room. "Oh shit." He stops as Dean grabs a handful of covers and yanks it up over his junk.

"Should've locked the door," I say smugly before turning to Abel as Braxton follows him through into the room. Unlike Abel—who is so obviously and clearly smashed—Braxton doesn't show his drunkenness until he moves to take a seat on the edge of the bed, misses the mattress completely, and hits the floor. I choke back a laugh when Abel launches himself onto the mattress and rolls against a naked Dean without preamble or reserve.

"I'm going to take a shower," I announce, "and when I get out, I expect all guys out of my damn room."

"Have y'all been in here all day and night?" Abel asks, his head popping up and eyes widening when he sees what I'm wearing. "Go you. Finally!" He throws his arms back, smacking Dean in the face and making his friend growl and shove him over the side of the bed.

"Get off me, motherfucker," Dean says, but he doesn't have a single ounce of anger in his tone. When he looks back to me, his eyes fasten right back on my legs. "And you," he says, "hurry it up. We're throwing another party tonight and you're going."

I take two steps to the side of the bed and bend over. His hand comes up and locks onto the back of my head. "Oh, I am, am I?" I ask in challenge.

"Yes, you are." His lips touch the corner of my mouth and he growls when I pull away before I can fall into another lip lock with him. I know if I do, then there's no way he won't join me for a shower and I remember quite clearly how the last one had gone.

"Then you better leave me alone to get ready," I say, sliding away and heading for the bathroom. I let the door close behind me and sag against it the second I'm out of his sight. I thought there was no way Dean could control me, but if I'm not careful then that damn pierced cock of his might very well accomplish what he couldn't and I'm not sure how I feel about that.

48

AVALON

Unsurprisingly, Dean is gone when I emerge from the shower and so are the guys. I roll my shoulders back, trying to work out the kinks in my neck. Despite the hours of nonstop sex, our last conversation has me feeling tense. I quickly change into a new swimsuit and yank on a pair of shorts and a t-shirt over it.

I know Dean said something about wanting me at the party, but I'm suddenly not so much in the partying mood. So, instead of going in search of him, when I hit the main floor, I turn towards the backdoors and find my way outside. The bonfires have been snuffed out and it seems that the majority of the party is now taking place at an embankment a little bit farther down.

Good, I think, as I head down the stone staircase.

My feet hit the sand and a shiver courses through me. Without the bonfires lit, the beach is cold at night. *Who would've known?* Not me, that's for sure, but now that I'm sitting here right in front of it, I can see the appeal. I plop down on the ground and sigh. Despite the stickiness of the sand and how irritating it is on the backs of my thighs, the endless appearance of the dark waters makes me want to stand up and walk towards it ... and then keep walking until I'm completely submerged in it.

"Hey." I jump as something cold touches my shoulder. I jerk my eyes up and meet Dean's enigmatic gaze, and I realize he's holding out an opened beer bottle. His fingers brush mine as I take it. I force back a shiver and raise the mouth of the bottle to my lips, taking a long, slow drink. My muscles tense as he stands beside me and the dying bonfire a moment more before sinking to the sand, letting me know he's not just here to deliver a drink.

"How'd you find me so fast?" I ask.

He shakes his head but doesn't answer. With his body next to mine, close enough for me to feel the warmth of his skin, but not so close that we're touching, it seems a little odd to not be touching after the last twenty-four hours. I don't know what we are, though, or if we even are anything.

"Truth," he says suddenly.

A sigh slips from my lips. "I'm not playing a stupid game," I reply, lifting the bottle and taking a swig.

"I'm not asking you to. Just tell me a truth."

I analyze him from the corner of my eyes. "A truth for a truth?" I clarify.

He doesn't look my way but keeps his face turned towards the water. "Sure, if that's what it takes to get inside that devious mind of yours."

My lips twitch. Asshole. "Fine," I say, "you first."

"I hate my dad."

I blink. I hadn't exactly expected him to be so forthright, especially so quickly. "I hate my mom," I reply, taking another sip. After a moment of silence, when he doesn't say anything more, I feel the unusual need to elaborate and words start spilling out. "I used to say I didn't. I didn't like the idea of hating her, but … she's a pretty shit person."

"No need to justify it to me," he says.

A soft breeze that smells like salt hits my face as a wave washes in against the shore several feet away. Turning, I stare at his profile. He sits on his ass with both feet on the ground, legs bent, and his shoulders rolled forward. My eyes are immediately drawn to lines of black peeking out from beneath his shirt and I'm transported back to a moment when he was driving into me that his tattoos were all I could see. That and a white light as my orgasm crashed over me.

I want to ask what the meaning of his tattoos are, if they have a meaning anyway—for all I know, they could be pure decoration—but something tells me they're not. Dean Carter does not strike me as the type of man who does anything for the fun of it.

"It's your turn again," I point out, tipping my beer in his direction. His drink remains dangling from his fingers, the bottom resting against the sand.

After a moment of silence, his head tilts and he turns to look at me. "I went first," he says. "I think that earns me a second round where you take a leap of faith and just tell me something about you that no one else knows."

My lips part. "No one knows that I hate my mom."

"Maybe not," he says. "But anyone can guess. Give me something else. Something more meaningful."

"Why?" I ask.

"What?" he replies. "I've been inside your pussy, but you can't tell me a secret?"

I groan and bare my teeth in irritation. "I hate that you're such a fucking control freak," I snap.

Finally, there's a crack in his mask. His lips twitch and

the corner of his mouth lifts until he's smiling—actually smiling, teeth and everything—at me. "No, you don't," he challenges.

"Excuse me?"

He shakes his head and chuckles. "I think that's the furthest thing from the truth and that's not how this exchange works. No lies in this game."

One arm hangs over his knee and I have the urge to knock it off and then knock his ass to the ground. "What do you know about me?" I say, but my words don't carry their usual acerbic-ness.

"A lot," is his immediate response. He sets his beer down in the sand and lifts his hand up until his fingers graze my cheek. I freeze at the feel of skin on skin contact. Which is fucking ridiculous. I've felt his skin on mine before. Hell, I just got done having a day and night long fuck fest with the dude, but this time is different. This feels like something more. And I don't know how to react to it.

"I know the reason that you're so fucking hostile and stubborn is because you've had to be. Let me guess … you grew up in a house with a revolving door? Did your mom date a lot of guys? Did they ever look at you the way adults shouldn't look at children?"

With every word he speaks, the colder I become. A prickle of something sinister slithers up my spine. I grab his wrist and hold it away from my face. "Did you learn that from your fucking *research*?" I spit. "How nice for you to think you can figure out everything about someone just by paying people off. Well, do you want to know what I know about you, D-man?"

He looks at me and I hate how I can't fucking tell what he's thinking right now. "Yes." I might have missed the word if I hadn't been listening for it. As it is, the whisper is so quiet, so quickly swallowed by the wind and the sound of crashing waves that I almost think I imagined it. But in his eyes, I see the truth. I know I haven't.

"You're such a control freak because you feel out of control most of the time," I accuse. He doesn't blink or react, and I think back to all the times before. The gas station. The Frazier House party. The warehouse fight. The lake. *He hates his dad...*

"What else?" he asks when I don't keep going.

"You're an asshole," I state.

The corner of his mouth twitches. "That's not a secret." No, it's not, but the reason for it is. I just haven't figured that reason out yet. He moves closer until I can smell more than just the beach breeze and saltwater. My lips part. He's so close and so fucking annoying. "Avalon..." My name is a whisper on his breath right before he leans forward and his bottom lip brushes mine.

But we never kiss. We don't get the chance. "Hey, yo, Dean!" a deep baritone calls out.

Pulling back, Dean glances over his shoulder at the sound and his eyes widen. "Marcus." And like a little kid on Christmas morning, his face brightens and he gets off the sand, forgetting me as he greets the new man coming up with Abel and Braxton. He's tall, not as tall as Braxton —but I'm beginning to believe that there never will be any that can match him in size—with sandy blond hair shaved completely at the sides, leaving only the waves of longer strands on the top as they flop sideways in deference to the wind.

"Where the hell have you been?" My eyes track their movements, watching as they embrace in a manly hug with a few back claps and then Dean leans back, smiling at the man. A familiar form appears behind them.

I get up. "Corina?"

"Hey." She waves and skirts around the guys, eyeing them as if they might bite her. I frown but don't comment as she approaches. "I heard you were here."

"Yeah..." I cut a look to Dean out of the corner of my eye. "I kinda didn't have a choice."

She smirks. "Sounds like it."

"Heard you came with a guy," I say.

Her smile freezes but then comes back full force as she giggles. Corina taps her perfectly painted nails against her lips and winks. "I don't kiss and tell." Bullshit. I roll my eyes, but let her have it. She glances back at the guys again. "Actually, I was wondering if you wanted to sneak off."

"You were?" A loud bark of laughter has me looking back at the guys. Dean's got the new guy's head in a lock and they're fucking around, light wrestling like they're nothing more than normal college students. It's kind of cute, but I still can't help but feel that maybe ... they're pulling me into that image of them that's not real. Normal college students ... I don't know what they are, but I know they're not that. Dean and I may have fucked, but it's not like we're dating.

I gave in. I gave it up. But I'm still not his. No lies between us, my ass. I scowl. "Yeah," I say, turning back to Corina. "Sure. Let's go."

"Do you want to let them know?" She nods towards them.

"No." I start walking. "No need."

She doesn't say anything to that, just shrugs and turns and starts walking. Instead of heading towards the fires and music down the beach, however, Corina moves back to the stairs. We leave the beach and the sea breeze behind and return to the house, which as I glance around, I realize has been deserted in favor of the party down below.

"Where are we going?" I ask as she heads through the main floor to the front steps.

Pulling out a key ring, she swings it around on one finger and winks back at me. "Only the hottest house on the block," she says. "My place."

49

AVALON

Of course, Corina's place would be like a mini replica of the Eastpoint Estate. The only difference is, instead of gray brick, hers has bright blue siding. But it, too, is built like a mini hotel.

"Why were you staying at the Sick Boys' place if you have a house on the beach?" I ask as we head up the front steps.

Corina pauses at the door and looks back, the blonde and brown locks of her hair falling over her shoulder. "Well," she says, biting her lip nervously, "my cousin's actually staying here this week."

"Okay?" I arch a brow and look pointedly up. "I'm sure this place has enough rooms for you and your cousin."

She shakes her head. "He's ... private," she replies. "It's difficult to explain, but what he wants—he gets and he wanted the house to himself. He said we could come over tonight and I thought you might wanna get away for a bit."

Ugh, rich pricks. "Sounds like an asshole if you ask me."

"Heh, yeah, I guess..." She turns back and opens the

door, leading me through the main hall and into a massive media space.

The room is filled with a sickly sweet smoke. The only lights on are dim glowing ones that pulse to the beat of the slow, rocking music coming out of the television speakers. Apparently, we're not the only people her cousin invited. Everywhere I look, I see couples. Couples making out on the couches. Girls and guys sitting around, drinking and smoking and ... I pause when I see pills exchange hands as a guy I don't recognize hands over a little white baggy to a couple of girls in exchange for a wad of cash.

Corina giggles, distracting me from the sight, when a guy steps towards her and wraps his arms around her waist. He plants a kiss on her mouth so consuming that it looks like he wants to devour her. *So much for not kissing and telling*, I think. More like kissing and publicly declaring herself ready to go.

Whatever. It's not like I didn't just fuck my own bad-for-me asshole. I've got no room to judge.

"This is Avalon," Corina introduces after a moment, pulling back and wiping the corner of her mouth, but surprisingly enough, despite how hot and heavy the kiss was, her lipstick remains unsmudged. That's gotta be some good shit.

The guy lifts his head and I blink, noting the different colors—blue and brown eyes stare at me. "Seth," he says, introducing himself by holding out a hand. I take it, but instead of shaking mine, he pulls me towards him and presses a kiss to my knuckles. "And if you ever need a little love, don't hesitate to ask for it."

My eyes jerk to Corina, but she doesn't appear offended at all. Instead, she slaps his arm with a laugh. "Knock it off," she urges. "She's taken."

"Oh?" He releases me. "My bad, lady."

"Taken?" I repeat, cutting a glare her way.

She eyes me. "Everyone's heard," she tells me.

"Heard what?"

She looks down. "About what Dean did on the beach. It's official *now* right?"

I'm not even going to bother with a response, just thinking about one pisses me off. So what if Dean lost his cool on the beach and carried me off like some dumbass caveman. That doesn't prove shit. Corina sighs as Seth nuzzles her neck and whispers something in her ear.

"Okay, okay," she laughs, replying to whatever he said before turning to me. "I'm gonna go … um, show Seth something real quick. Can you—Seth, stop it!" Another girly giggle escapes her lips.

I wanna fucking groan. This was not what I signed up for. I should've never come. "Yeah fine, whatever," I say. "Just leave me your keys in case I wanna go." She doesn't even hesitate. I stuff her keys into the pocket of my shorts as Seth whisks her out of the room and there's no doubt in my mind what exactly she wants to *show* him.

I don't mind being abandoned; what I mind is being left in a strange place with people I don't know, and even if I did, I doubt I'd like them. But I'm also not the clingy type. I wander through the house, moving away from the moans of people fucking and the sounds of others getting high and cackling like hyenas at nothing particularly funny. It's like walking through a museum. It kind of resembles one. At least, from what I know of museums and shit from online pictures and movies and TV shows. Fact is, I'd never been to one. But I imagined they'd all be something like this—with a cold atmosphere and impersonal pictures that could be in anyone else's house.

This really was a mistake, I think. I should leave. I make the decision to do exactly that when I turn and slam into a massive body and nearly go down on my ass. The only thing that saves me is said massive body's arm shooting out and catching me behind the shoulders. I blink up. "Thanks—" My words are cut off when I recognize the calculating gaze of the man holding me. Without hesitation, I yank myself out of his grip and straighten myself. "What are you doing here?"

"Nice to see you, too, beautiful," Luc Kincaid responds, flashing me a smile.

"I'd like to say the same, but I'm not much for lying."

He grins. "Oh no?" He moves closer. "Then tell me the truth, did your boyfriend send you here?"

"Boyfriend?" I scowl at him. "I don't know who the fuck you're talking about. I don't have a boyfriend."

I try to move past him, but his arm—the same one that had just been around me—comes down, his palm slapping the wall with a resounding clap that hurts my ears. "I thought you said you weren't much for lying?"

My tongue slides across my bottom teeth as I glare up at him. "I was just leaving," I say.

"No, stay, why don't you?" Luc's other arm comes up, his fingers grazing my side and making my spine stiffen.

"Don't fucking touch me," I snap. And asshole that he is, he doesn't—but he gets damn close. So close I can smell the alcohol on his breath and the sea on his skin.

"Why are you so mean, beautiful?" he asks, the words little puffs of air that shift over my throat.

"'Cause being a bitch is so easy," I reply.

He chuckles, the sound vibrating through the otherwise empty hallway. "You know," he starts, "I've done more research on you since we last left off. How lucky am I that I run into you here—at my house."

"Your house?" I tip my head back as he leans up. "You're Corina's cousin?"

Luc's only answer is a mischievous grin. "Want to know what I found out about you, Avalon Manning?"

I breathe through my nose, the muscles in my leg jumping as I try to think of a way to get out of his hold without touching him or him touching me. Irritation fans the flames inside of me. "No, I don't."

He ignores me and keeps talking as if he hadn't heard it at all. "I took a little trip a while back. Met an interesting woman."

"What the hell does that have to do with me?" I demand, shifting from one foot to the other. I might just have to fucking chance it. I'm ready to go and this dick is blocking my way.

"I find it fascinating that a woman as disgustingly ugly as that made you," he answers. Cold washes through my body. *No,* I think. He couldn't have. I meet his eyes, but there's no hint of a lie there. He could just be really good at lying, but something tells me he's serious. "I almost didn't believe you were related," he continues. "But I saw a few similarities." I flinch as if he struck me. That's one thing I've always prided myself on—how I don't look a thing like Patricia. "Your eyes for example." He stares at me. "They're a similar shape, though yours are more perfectly aligned and hers a bit too wide for my taste. Your chin, too. Everything else, though, I think is all you, beautiful."

"What the fuck do you want?" I snap. "Is this some kind of threat?"

He shakes his head. "Not at all," he says. "It's an offer."

"An offer?"

Luc leans back down into my space. My skin heats up, but it's not from embarrassment. It's from anger. I can feel it underneath my skin. Getting hotter and hotter. "She asked me to fuck her, you know," he whispers against my skin, "when I went to that club she works at. I wouldn't touch that drugged out cunt, but you, darling … you, I could do all. Night. Long."

I'm done. I've had it. Grabbing each of his wrists in my hands, I lean up into his face and spit my reply. "Not a chance in hell," I say, right before I slam my knee into his balls.

The sweet sound of a groan choking in his throat reaches my ears and I smile as I shove him to the side and step over his body, looking up when I catch Kate gaping at me from the end of the hallway, a cell phone clutched in one hand. She scowls as I draw nearer. "Maybe you should keep an eye on that fiancé of yours," I say as I pass by.

"No need," she calls back. "You'll be out of here soon enough."

If she means out of this house then she's one-hundred percent correct. It's probably the most right she's ever been in her life because I don't even hesitate to leave Corina without even trying to find her slutty ass. I'm fucking out of here.

50

DEAN

Cold beer. Cool breeze. Warm bodies. Life can't get any better than this, I think for a moment, except it could. I could be back in bed with a fiery little fucking brat who drives me insane and always pops off with an insult. Twenty-four hours hadn't been nearly enough time to explore every inch of her. From her small, dainty little feet, to her toned legs, and that ass that I most certainly wanted to fuck into a wall. Again.

"So, where's this chick I've been hearing so much about?" Marcus asks, distracting me from my less than PG thoughts.

"Pretty sure I saw her heading off with Corina earlier," Abel answers, tipping back his own beer and draining it before tossing the empty bottle towards a nearby black trash bag already laden down with them.

I scowl but Marcus beats me to the punch with a confused look. "You let her hang with Kincaid's cousin?"

Braxton snorts. "There's no *letting* that girl do anything," he says. "Dean's been trying to lay down the law with her since she arrived."

"Ahhh." Marcus shoots me a knowing look—the prick. "One of those, is she?"

"You have no idea, man." I drink the rest of my beer and toss it towards the same trash bag as earlier before stepping away. "I'm gonna go see if she's up at the house."

"And if she is?" Marcus calls after me.

"I'll drag her ass back so you can fucking meet her, asshole," I say over my shoulder. "But be warned, it might be a while."

The three of them laugh as I head up the staircase. I'm halfway up when I feel my phone vibrate in my pocket. *Fuckers*, I think. They probably want me to get more beer. Well, they'll just have to wait until after I'm done with Avalon.

I wait until I get to the kitchen before I pull my cell out and double check, but it's not any of the guys. It's fucking Kate. I almost don't open it, but then I see the little paper clip attached to the text and click on it.

It's Avalon. But that's not what has me shaking in rage. It's the man that's got her pinned against the wall. I can't see her face, but even with his face in her neck—I can see exactly who *he* is. Luc motherfucking Kincaid. And she's with him. *What the fuck is she doing with him?*

My thoughts spiral. *Does she know who he is? Is she fucking him? Or is this ... something more?*

The rumors about Kincaid possibly transferring come to the surface of my mind, but now they seem like a much bigger threat. Could she have something to do with it?

No, it can't be, I think, but the denial is full of doubt. There'd been no obvious connection between the two even amidst the extra file we'd been given. *Could that fucker be using her? To what end? Does he know what she is to us?*

I look back at the text and see that Kate's left a little message below the image.

Thought you should know that your new girl isn't everything she seems.

My arms tremble with rage and before I can even comprehend what I'm doing, I turn and throw the phone as hard as I can. It slams into a mirror hanging across the room and the loud crack that echoes sounds like a gun shooting through glass. Mirror fragments rain down against the floor and as if she's been pulled from my very thoughts, Avalon steps into the room holding a set of keys that most certainly aren't hers.

"What the fuck?" She stares at me, looking from the shattered mirror to my enraged expression.

I advance on her. "Where the hell have you been?" I demand.

"What?" she blinks and unlike anyone else, she doesn't act scared as I stalk across the room.

"I said." Step. "Where." Step. "The fuck." I push her back, against the wall, right next to the broken frame of the now trashed mirror. "Have you been?" My shoes crunch against the glass and I look down, thankful that she, too, has shoes on. Then I shake my head. No. I shouldn't give a fuck if she gets cut up because that's what's happening to me right now. I feel deep slices ripping through my organs as I stare into her storm-cloud eyes.

"I was with a friend," she says, looking away. "But I got bored so I came back."

"Corina?" I clarify. I reach for the keys clutched in her fist. I know I'm about to piss her off and I don't give a shit —but I wouldn't put it past her not to try and shank me with one or all of them. At first, she holds onto them, but when I press down on a particularly sensitive nerve in her hand, she releases with a sharp inhale.

That's right, baby. I know a lot of things you don't know yet.

She lifts her head and eyes me. "Yeah."

"Was she with you the whole time or did you sneak off, Avalon?"

Her lips curve down into a deep scowl. "What the fuck are you talking about?"

She tries to shift away from me, but I grab her and press myself fully against her chest, pinning her to the wall. "Don't fucking walk away from me," I snarl. "Tell me—were you with your little friend this entire time or were you with Luc Kincaid—fucking him?"

A beat of silence passes between us and her head sinks back on her shoulders. Her eyes narrow into tiny little slivers. For several moments, she doesn't say a damn thing, and that's it. That's when I fucking know. I've been fucking played by her. Avalon Manning is no pauper princess. She's a gold digging whore. Just like everything the file says her mother is.

And my fucking father—he and the other heads of the family. They knew. Why would they give me her file then? We were supposed to watch her. Was this it? Just to make sure she didn't fuck up? If that was the case then I'd fucking ruined that plan, because I did fuck it up. I let her get under my skin.

"I'm going to give you three seconds to let me go," she says in a voice so quiet I almost don't catch the words.

I stare at her face—the smooth, creaminess of her skin. The dark lashes that frame her eyes. The small smattering of freckles so light they only really reveal themselves when she's lying out in the sun. And I want to fucking ruin it. I want to wreck this face. Put my hands around her throat and squeeze. I can feel the heat inside me build, like a volcano ready to erupt.

"Dean." She says my name and I hate the way I love it

on her tongue. "Get your fucking hands off me now, before I make you. I've had a shit night and I really don't want to fucking do this right now."

"Just tell me the truth then," I insist.

I want to hear her say it. I need to hear her say it. I want either her confirmation or her denial—either one will tell me what kind of person she really is, but in true Avalon fashion, she gives me neither. When I don't move, she places two hands on my chest and shoves me back before turning away.

"I didn't fucking say you could leave!" I reach for her arm, but as soon as I feel my fingers lock on her bicep, she's twisting out of my grip and throwing a right hook towards my face.

"And I didn't fucking say you could touch me, asshole!" she yells back. "I'm fucking sick and tired of you dicks thinking you can just grab me and throw me around like a goddamn ragdoll! You think just because I fucked you that I belong to you? Well, I don't. I belong to no one but myself. So, you can go fuck off for all I care."

Red colors the corners of my vision. Even sitting alone in his giant fucking houses with wounds all over my body from nightly 'training' sessions. Even after I'd killed my first traitor. Even through the worst of my adolescence and childhood, I'd never felt this angry. And before I can stop to think or ask myself why it's like this with her it's already too late.

More broken glass crunches under my shoes as I snatch her up and slam her back into another wall, shoving my body against her, letting one of my legs between her thighs. "You do belong to me," I tell her in the coldest of tones. "I can do whatever I want with you and there's nothing you can do to stop me. You're not going to run away. I'm not going to let you run back to him—he only wants to fuck whores anyway ... or wait, is that what you want? You want me to fuck you like a whore? I thought I pleased you enough already, but if that's what you want, baby..." I move back, dropping her back to the floor so that I can see her reaction.

Big fucking mistake. Avalon shoots away from me and when I move to follow her she turns back around and punches me in the nose. "Shit!" I stumble back as blood pours down over my upper lip, but she's not done yet. Oh no, not my girl. She rears back and delivers what I might've called the perfect full frontal kick if it hadn't been aimed directly for my balls.

I go down in a heap, wheezing as pain ricochets through me. The glass on the floor cuts through my fucking jeans and I can feel the stings of each wound. None are greater, though, than the thought that I've been well, and truly fucking fucked by her.

A small feminine hand sifts through my hair, yanking my head back as I try to catch my breath and keep from throwing up. Her other hand grabs my throat as she leans down and hisses in my ear—and even through the agony in my body and the fury I'm feeling, I can't help but find her fucking magnificent in her own wrathful animosity.

"I am not any man's property, Dean. Least of all yours."

I cough and glare up at her. "You think not?" I ask. I try shaking my head, but it's difficult with her nails scratching my scalp, holding me there. To think, just hours ago, those nails had been in different places and for much different reasons. "That's all your pussy's ever meant to be, baby," I spit out. "Property. And I think that's what kills you inside. So, regardless of how I might look to you now, Ava.

I win and I will always win. You fucked with the wrong man."

She laughs. An honest to God, fucking laugh. "You think you've won? Oh no, Dean." She shakes her head. "You didn't win. You opened Pandora's box, and my demons are coming for you."

With that, she drops my head and walks away. I don't hear or see where she goes and I can't seem to make myself get up off the cold tiled floor. Droplets of red continue to drip from my face and I don't know how long it takes for me to get back on my feet, but when I do, I have to use the wall for support.

Goddamn her.

"Dean!" Abel's half panicked voice reaches my ears, and I wince at how sharp it sounds. He comes barreling around the corner, panting, sweating, eyes blown wide and shaking.

Shit. Tonight is not the fucking night for this, I think, but he's my fucking brother, so I straighten away from the wall and head towards him even as I snatch up a hand towel and start wiping my face.

"What is it?"

"Where the fuck is Avalon?" he demands, but before I can say anything, he shoves the screen of his phone in my face which clearly depicts Avalon in our garage, grabbing a key from one of the hooks on the wall. I watch in utter shock as she waltzes right over to where Abel's Mustang is parked, gets in, and peels out. "She stole my fucking car!"

I take a deep breath and release it. Braxton comes around the corner and stops when he sees us. While Abel is too freaked out to notice, I know Brax sees the cuts of my jeans and the blood staining my clothes, and it doesn't even surprise me when he crosses his arms over his massive chest and waits for me.

"Pull up the tracking," I say coldly. "We're going after her."

"Damn right we are," Abel snaps. "What the fuck is she thinking?"

I know what she's thinking. She's thinking she can run from me. But no. That's not fucking happening.

51

AVALON

I put my foot to the gas, and floor it. The wavering pointer on the speedometer jerks up and then inches over, slowly but surely making its way to the 100mph mark and then beyond. The headlights wash over the dark backwoods road. The longer I stare, the harder it is to see until I realize it isn't that the road is hard to see, I'm just crying.

Sobbing actually. Big, heaving sobs wrack my frame as tears slide from my eyes. They slip down my cheeks, dirty little things, leaving me with a salty taste in my mouth that's tinged with a metallic edge. Tears and blood. How? Because I've bitten my lip so hard that I can feel where the skin has broken and blood seeps from the wound onto my tongue.

"Fuck him…" I whisper. I lift my fist from the steering wheel and bring it down hard. Hard enough that it sends a ricochet of pain up my arm. "Fuck *them*," I amend, because it wasn't just Dean Carter. It was all of them. All for one and one for fucking all. They would back him, I had no doubt. So fuck them all. "Fuck them. *Fuck them.* FUCK. THEM!" I scream until my lungs hurt.

It hurts. Fuck, everything hurt. The worst pain imaginable. Like being shredded open and left, gasping, in a pile of trash. That's essentially what he's done. Never in my life have I ever let anyone make me feel like I was just as dirty and disgusting as my mother—not even the bitch herself. But he'd done it. And why do I feel this way? Because I'd gone and gotten stupid. Oh, I told myself I was being smart, but the second I gave in, the very moment I spread my legs, deep down, I'd known. I'd up and drank the dumb bitch juice he'd been handing out.

Had it been obvious? I wonder. *Had I just not seen the signs?* I didn't think it was fucking possible for a girl like me to be dickmatized, but I'm not stupid enough to believe that doesn't have any bearing on the betrayal I now feel. *God, I can't fucking* breathe!

The sex had been amazing. It'd been filthy and rotten and for some fucking reason, when I'd been in his arms, I hadn't been Avalon Manning, the girl from the wrong side of the tracks. I'd just been me without all of the past shit to ruin it. And he'd just been a guy—as annoying as he could be, as controlling and as much of an asshole as he was— that I liked.

Liked—as in past tense. Because, the fact is, I'm not in love with him. To love him would be to ruin everything that I am. Because I'm not a girl that loves. I'm a girl that fucking destroys and oh, Dean doesn't know it yet, but he's made one of the biggest fucking mistakes of his life with me. The snake of pure, unfiltered wrath breaks free and slithers up and around my throat. It blurs my reality as I lift my foot off the gas and just let the stolen ride be.

Eventually, the Mustang comes to a slow stop in the middle of the road. Darkness in front of me and darkness behind—much like my past and my probable future.

Here I am ... sitting in a stolen car in the middle of

nowhere with blood and tears on my face. I laugh. It's fucking funny as shit. Stupidly funny.

I laugh so loud and long and hard that my stomach begins to cramp. Something feels loose in my brain. Like whatever had been keeping me semi-sane has snapped and broken. The barrier is gone now and it. Feels. Fucking. Satisfying.

My eyes slide to the side and I reach for the seatbelt as they land on the glove box. I unbuckle myself, moving slowly as if my limbs have a mind of their own. I press the button and it opens. My fingers find the handle of the gun I'd seen stashed in here the first time I rode in this car. It's easy to pick it up—too easy—and though the gun feels heavy in my grasp, it feels right too. I lift it and point towards the windshield. I picture the guys. One by one. Standing in a line in front of the twin beams of light pouring from the Mustang's headlights.

What would I do if given the chance to kill him? Could I do it? Could I pull the trigger?

Right now, I feel like it'd be all too easy to blow not just his but each of their fucking brains out—because if it wasn't for the other two, I might never have met Dean Carter in the first place. My finger finds the trigger in question and smooths over it, but I don't press down. Instead, I lower the weapon, and after a moment, I put the gun back in the glove compartment, close it, and snap my seatbelt back into place.

No, I'm not going to kill them. I've got better things planned for them. More torturous things. What I am going to do, however, is go back. Not to Eastpoint, but to the place where it all began. There have been far too many people in my life who seem to think they have power over me, and it all starts there.

First the past. Then the present. Only then can I finally face the fucking future.

Rules to live by. In order to look forward, I have to go back. Just once. Just this once. I put my foot back on the gas and this time, when I floor it, I know exactly where I'm going.

Those boys—those sick, twisted, disgusting, perverted assholes—think they can sweep into my life and drag me through the carnage of hell. What they don't yet realize, is that I was born there and I know exactly how to not only survive, but to fucking rise.

WHEN I PULL UP TO PATRICIA'S TRAILER, ALL OF THE lights are out and the street is empty. She's either not home or dead asleep, and I'm not in the mood to let her sleep. I get out of the car, slamming the door behind me and clicking the button on the keyring to lock it. I bet Abel is flipping his shit right now. After all, I had stolen his precious car. Yet, I can't find it in me to give a shit. All of the fucks I had to give are suddenly gone. *I'm all out. Try again tomorrow, assholes.*

I walk up the concrete steps and yank open the cracked screen door. The door, of course, is unlocked. *Dumb bitch,* I think, pushing it open and stepping into the dark interior.

"Hey!" I bark out, my hand sliding along the wall for the light switch. My fingers hit it and the yellow bulbs in the ancient ceiling fan flare to life, casting the rest of the room in a hazy filtered light. My feet freeze. My breath leaves my chest in a rush.

What the fuck? I can't reconcile what I'm seeing in front of me.

There's blood everywhere. Something wet squishes

under my sandals. I look down and realize that it's not just the futon and coffee table, but the carpet is fucking drenched in it. In some places on the green fuzzy surface of the floor, blood has dried into a crusty brown, but not where I'm standing. No, instead, I'm in a pool of it. The liquid squeezes out of every fiber of the fabric beneath my feet as I press down and stumble to the side.

"Patricia?" I call out her name, but there's no response. "Mom!" There's no body. No evidence of anything else amiss save for all of the blood. If some of it's fresh and some of it's old, does that mean it's hers or not? Everything else looks exactly as it had the day I left—glass coffee table covered in old, empty liquor bottles, an overfull ashtray, and the white coating of cocaine dust. The entire room smells of rust and something else. I wrinkle my nose and cover my face with my palm. It smells like something's not burning, but has been previously and was only recently put out.

"I can't believe it." I'm so focused on the scene before me, confusion swimming through my mind, evaporating all of the anger I'd just been feeling, that it takes a moment for me to realize that the words spoken are not my own, but in fact the words of an intruder. And by the time I do, it's too late.

I half turn towards the voice, recognizing the deep, craggy sound just as a needle presses against my upper arm and fire shoots into my skin. Jerking away from the device, I punch out, slamming the man holding the syringe. Roger.

"The fuck—" My words cut off as the whole room tilts. He shakes the hit off and looks at me with a grin before stepping further into the trailer and closing the door—the door that I'd stupidly left open—behind him.

"Didn't know what to think 'bout that fancy 'Stang in the yard, but I'm glad to know it's you, li'l runt," he says.

I stumble back, my chest hurting. My legs feel like they weigh hundreds of pounds. "What the fuck's … what did you do?" I mumble, my words slurring.

He takes a step towards me, his big belly jiggling and he grins—his yellow stained teeth appearing even dirtier in this light. "Oh that?" he asks. I move back and fall, my spine slamming into the floor, halfway between the living room carpet and over the crease onto the vinyl tile of the kitchen. "That ain't nothin' fer you to worry yer pretty li'l head about, runt," he says. "'S just something to make you a bit more agreeable. I came prepared this time."

"This time?" His words are hard to follow. My head hurts. The room spins, blurring as the light flickers in and out. Then I realize, it's not the light flickering—I'm blinking, trying to get a handle on my senses, but whatever was in that syringe … the syringe! My eyes shoot to where it's fallen on the floor, but it looks eons away. Too far beyond my reach. Drugs. He shot me up with drugs. Heroin? Something else? What is it?

Rough fingers grab at the back of my head, yanking on my hair as Roger grins down at me. "Couldn't have you fight'n back like ya did my boys," he says. His boys … the guys Patricia had tried to sell me to. They were his guys.

With one hand on the back of my head, Roger's free hand reaches down to the zipper of his pants and lowers it. I jerk back. Holy fuck. No. Not this. "Damn," he says, "that mouth of yers, girl. Been dreamin' bout it for years."

His zipper is down and the button is undone and out flops his dick. Short and thin, it's a pathetic excuse for equipment. Whatever he shot into my system makes every movement I make seem slower and weaker. Like my body weighs ten times its normal amount. It's a struggle to rear back, but I manage it. Casting a scowling glare so full of disgust, I can taste the emotion on my tongue, I look up at him.

I bare my teeth at him. "You try to put that thing in my mouth," I hiss. "And I swear I'll bite it off, Roger."

He scrapes his fingernails against my scalp, locking onto my hair once more before shaking it in my face. "You do that," he growls, "and I'll punch out all yer fuckin' teeth, bitch, and face fuck you."

I laugh, my head sinking back on my shoulders. "Try it," I warn him, forcing myself to enunciate past the throbbing in my head and body. My throat feels like it's on fire as the words come up. Shivers skate down my spine and I blink hard. *Fuck, this isn't good.* My stomach cramps. I'm gonna puke. But it's been hours since I ate, so even if I do all that will come up is bile. I hadn't once stopped except to get gas using the cash I'd found alongside the gun in Abel's glovebox. The gun. I wish I'd brought it in with me now.

Roger looks down at me with a frown and suddenly, his hand is gone. "Maybe you need another dose, eh?"

What? I think dumbly. He turns and leaves me where I am, striding back to where he dropped the syringe and then—as if I'm watching a character in a movie—he withdraws a small glass vile from the back pocket of his sagging jeans. My eyes follow the movement of his hands as he sticks the needle into the top and withdraws more of the murky liquid.

No. Nonononono. NO! Then it hits me. This is really happening. I'm really well and truly fucked. *What have I done?*

"Don't worry 'bout nothin', li'l runt," Roger coos as he comes nearer. I slide back, my hand shooting out from beneath me and my head cracking into the tiled floor. Stars dance in front of my vision as the needle presses back into my arm and more fire coats my throat as I let out a scream

—except it only echoes in my head. Loud. Too loud. And then silent. As if my eardrums have ruptured. The sound in the room cuts in and out just like the light as a second wave of the drugs hitting my veins overcomes me. Nausea curls in my stomach—a stomach that I turn over on as I try to get away.

My breath saws in and out of my chest as I scramble to find something to hold onto. My fingers lock around the table's leg and I grip it, using my hold to pull myself towards it. I can't let this happen. But my body remains where it is. I'm not *fucking* moving. My arms and legs are limp, useless. And my grip? It isn't even tight. I hardly feel the wood beneath my palm. In fact, I hardly feel anything. Not the cold of the vinyl floor against my cheek. Not the heat of his hands as they grab my hips and drag them upward. It feels as though there's a wave of water surrounding me and I'm only brushing against things rather than touching them. I'm floating.

A harsh bark of laughter ricochets in my eardrums, sounding louder than anything should when you're underwater. It hurts. It pisses me off. Red drips in front of my vision and I realize that despite my inability to feel it, I've ripped a nail back as I claw at the table in an effort to get away. Blood pools against the bed of my nail and slides down my finger, dripping onto the back of my knuckles.

A laugh sounds in my ears as I'm flipped over onto my back. The ceiling light is too bright for my eyes. I slide them shut, trying to think, but it's hard to wade out of the fog that's clinging to my thoughts. I grit my teeth as fat, beefy fingers find the collar of my shirt and rip it straight down the middle. My arm burns from where the needle came out of my skin.

My skin … it feels like it's melting. It's too hot. It's too much. Everything is too much. I open my mouth as fire races along my nerve endings, burning me from the inside out. What the fuck is happening to me?

My head snaps to the side and I only realize in a belated moment of clarity that I've been struck. My eyes open again and I look up into the old, pockmarked face of Roger. "Stop yelling, bitch," he snarls. "You'll like it if you just … open … yer … damn … legs."

I was yelling? I think. *Why hadn't I heard it?* He struggles, breathing hard as he pries my thighs apart. Bile rushes up my throat. Jesus fuck. He's going to rape me.

Fight, I snap at myself. *Fight, you dumb bitch.* I can't let this happen. *I won't!*

"You're just like your fucking mother," Roger says, licking his lips as he reaches for the waist of my pants, peeling them down. I urge my arms to move. To stop being so fucking useless, but it's as if every muscle I've ever possessed has been stripped away. I have no strength in my limbs and my body isn't listening to my mind as it screams for everything to *just fucking stop!* "There we go, darlin'." Roger's voice makes my stomach curdle as if there's spoiled milk inside me. He licks his dirty fingers and pushes them down, between my legs.

This is what hell is. It isn't a little red man dancing amidst the flames. It isn't an ice cold monster struggling to free himself from his own personal prison as he freezes everyone around him. Hell is human. It is this man. This place. Right here. Right now. And after all the fighting and rage and cold, hard struggles I've gone through, I've finally fallen victim.

I gasp out, hating the pain of knowing he's pushing his fingers inside me. I can't feel it, but I know they're there. Stretching me on the inside to prepare for him. There's vomit in my throat, stopping me from saying a damn word. Silence echoes in my mind and all around.

I don't want this. This isn't me. This isn't happening. Why is this happening?

My head turns to the side as the nausea overwhelms me and yellow acid purges from my stomach, coming up my throat—burning my esophagus, leaking out of the corner of my mouth. My arm flops up, weakly. I push against Roger's face, shoving him back in an attempt to fight. It takes everything I have, every decibel of will, every fucking ounce of rage in me, to accomplish even that much.

"Oh, no, you don't." My ears ring when he scowls at me, pulling his hand back and balling it into a fist before letting it fly. It hits my jaw and my head goes flying back. "I've been waiting years to do this, you little cunt, and nothing's going to stop me from finally getting what I deserve."

Spots dance in front of my vision, shades of black and white and reds and blues. I can't … my head weighs a hundred pounds. It's a struggle to lift it. My eyes connect with the dirty popcorn ceiling and the water stains around the light fixture. In the edge of my vision, I can see Roger's head bobbing. My legs are shoved wider, wide enough that I can finally feel the pangs of it as feeling begins to slowly make its way back into my limbs.

Too late, though. It's too late.

The blunt head of his dick rubs against my folds.

Kill him, I think. *I'm going to fucking kill him.* Rip his intestines out and string him up. I'm going to watch him fucking suffer. God doesn't exist, not in this place, but if He did, then He should know—He did this. He created this monster on top of me and I'm going to burn everything He made down.

I clench my teeth as Roger pushes into me and moans.

"Fuck, yer so fuck'n tight, ya bitch." He slaps my face. "Loosen up!"

A laugh bubbles out of my throat. I can't fucking move. I can't fucking lift my own head, but the moment is funny to me. I laugh and laugh and laugh.

"The fuck are you laughing at, bitch!" Another slap snaps my head to the opposite side.

My chest rumbles with my amusement even as he fucks me. He has no idea what he's done. My mother was right. I've become a whore just like her. I hope he enjoys this pussy because I'm going to make sure he pays for it with every liter of blood in his body. There's no escaping me anymore. If he doesn't kill me before the drugs are finished running through my system then there's only one end left for him. Death. By my hands.

Something sounds in the distance. Wood splintering. Glass breaking. "Who the fuck are—"

There are no words from the new person. There's nothing but a tension so cold, I can feel it like a wave over my flesh. Suddenly, Roger's body is ripped away. His pathetic excuse for a cock falls out of me and he's gone.

My mind drifts, dreams of blood and rape and death echoing in the background. Somehow, I think I can even hear Roger screaming now. And it's a lovely soundtrack to listen to as I finally pass the fuck out.

52

DEAN

THE SOUND OF A GROWN MAN SOBBING REACHES MY EARS and I scowl. I want nothing more than to turn around and go back out there and take off another one of the man's fingernails or hell, maybe this time, I'll just remove the whole finger. I hadn't been shocked to learn that Avalon was going home. What I had been shocked about was to walk in and see … that.

Even Abel, as angry as he'd been—as fucked up as we all were—had frozen at the sight of Avalon on the ground under some dirty, fat fuck with his dick pushing between her thighs. Sickness sits in my gut as I finish washing the evidence of blood from Avalon's face, her hands, and her thighs. She's been out for hours. Long enough that I'd contacted a local doctor and had them drive out to check on her. With connections like ours, we have people in every corner of the world and Plexton isn't but a few hours from a few major cities.

I touch her forehead but there's no fever. The man's sobbing turns into high pitched screams of agony. I don't want to think about what Braxton's doing to him—all I know is that it hurts and I hope he keeps going.

The first few hours had been nothing but blubbering as we strapped him down. There had been no stopping that. Even Abel participated. And no matter how loud the man we now know as local drug dealer, Roger Murphy, had gotten, Avalon hadn't once woken. It was only after Brax had dipped the motherfucker's balls in water with a jumper attached to a car battery, that we had finally gotten more than crying and screaming.

No, we'd gotten something I hadn't expected.

Information.

Blue-gray eyes crack open and meet mine. I jerk to my feet, leaning over her. "Avalon?" She doesn't respond to the sound of her name. Not even a flicker of recognition. Dark bruises underline her eyes and an even darker one mars the side of her face. She's been slapped, punched, raped—fuck —and it's because of me.

She ran because I'd been too fucking angry, too blinded and possessive. I'd wanted to make her hurt, but not like this. Never like this. "Avalon, can you hear me?" I try again.

Her dry, cracked lips part. "Why the fuck are you here?" she croaks out.

Should've expected that. I drop the washcloth into the basin of the bowl that I'd brought to her bedside and reach for a bottle of water. "Are you thirsty?" I lift it up and shake it at her.

She stares at it for a moment as if uncomprehending and then she nods. I help her sit up and touch the opening to her mouth. She drains it in less than a minute, sucking back every drop like she's been traveling the Sahara for years. "I came to bring you back," I say quietly.

A low, pained groan echoes through the door, drawing

her attention. Avalon turns and looks over my shoulder. I'm in here with her, but she should know that I'm not alone. I'm never alone. "They're out there," I tell her and then grit my teeth as a burning violence beats a steady drum in my head.

"The Mustang," she mutters, the random word making me blink as I glance at her. I touch the back of her head and it's like she doesn't even notice. She doesn't flinch away or even spare me a glance as her eyes remain fixed on the door.

"What about the Mustang?" I ask.

"There's a gun in the glove compartment," she says, finally turning to meet my gaze. "I need you to go get it for me."

I stare at her. This is what makes her different, I realize. She's not cowering, not afraid of the man she knows is in the other room. She's not doing what any other woman would be. She's far too cold for that, like a perfectly cut blade. I can see it in her eyes. She doesn't care. All she wants is retribution.

There's a turbulent need in me to give that to her. She deserves it. She *should* do it. And even if she doesn't, I will. Because whether she realizes it or not, this whole situation reeks of a setup. Though there's blood on the floor of the trailer, obviously not from her or her rapist—her mother is nowhere to be found. Not only that, but it's still bothering me—the way she left. I'd been too wrapped up in my anger and the feeling of betrayal to see it.

"No need," I say, reaching back and retrieving the gun inside my back holster. I pull it out, flick the safety off and hand it to her. "You have this."

The low groaning on the other side of the door turns into a high-pitched scream. She fingers the gun. "What are they doing?" she asks, knowing exactly who they are. Brax and Abel—most likely Brax. Even if I'd wanted to, I couldn't stop him, and I don't want to make them stop. I'm relishing in those sounds of torture.

"You know what they're doing," I state. "They're making sure your prey stays right where he's supposed to." I pause and finger the frayed edge of the paper thin mattress she's lying on. I don't even want to think of the things it's soiled with—it looks like it's damn near twenty years old and it smells like piss and vomit. "Until you're ready."

"I'm ready." As she says it, she slides her legs out from under the covers and stands up. She doesn't look stable and her eyes are far colder than I've ever seen before.

I stop her before she reaches the door. "Avalon," I place a hand against the doorframe and stare down at her, "this changes nothing between us."

Her head tilts back and she stares at me unblinking, and she says four words that prove just how much of a savage my girl is. "Open the door, Dean."

53

AVALON

I don't feel like myself, and yet, at the same time, I feel more like myself than I've ever fucking felt in my life. There are whispers in my mind. Ice in my skin. Hatred in my veins.

I feel fucking wrathful.

There's still nausea in my system. I can feel the need to puke like a goddamn anchor around my neck, tugging me down, down and even further down into a dark pit that I refuse to let myself sink into. My skin is cold and clammy and every step forward feels like I'm dragging chains behind me. *How long have I been out?* I'd been given two doses of whatever that shit was Roger had shot me up with. Sweat coats the back of my neck and the top of my forehead, but I clench my hand around the handle of the gun and that, surprisingly, makes me feel better.

As if he senses the thoughts in my head, Dean's hand falls on the knob and he holds it a moment after I tell him to open it. "I had a doctor check you out," he says. "You'll be a little more lethargic and you might have some memory issues, but—"

My memory is perfectly fine. If I try to think too hard, my head starts hurting, but otherwise, I remember everything clearly. *Oh, how I wish I didn't.*

"You'll make a full recovery," he finishes.

I don't respond, and when he still doesn't open the door, I realize he's waiting for that. So I nod, and then he takes a deep breath and the door swings open. Dean takes a step to the side, allowing me just enough room to see through into the dirty, grimy kitchen and living room of the trailer I'd spent the first eighteen years of my life in. All the blood has dried, staining the floor in dark shitty, brown colors. It smells like rust and sweat and puke. Abel stands back, arms crossed, but when we step out, his head lifts and his eyes widen.

"Ava…" He looks from me to Dean. "She doesn't need to be here for this," he snaps.

I don't look at Dean to see his expression, his words are enough. "It's her fucking right," he says.

If I hadn't already suspected, if I hadn't already known, I would've known it in that moment—they're not ordinary rich college kids. Corina's right. They're corrupt. Everyone else is right to call them Sick because that's what they are. That's what this is before me—a deep, dark sickness of violence that it's clear they're very familiar with. There's no other explanation for the scene before me now. For the unbothered look in their eyes as I take in the sight of Roger strapped to one of the lattice covered chairs from the kitchen table, his head bowed and bloody. Broken. He's naked all the way down and there are lines of cuts along his upper chest and back and sides and arms, oozing blood. Lines that most certainly hadn't been there before. Brax stands in front of him, his hands covered in black gloves. A little bucket of water sits beneath Roger and next to it, is a car battery with a jumper cable attached to it.

PRETTY LITTLE SAVAGE

"This is your choice," I hear Dean say behind me. "He'll die. You can decide—either we kill him or you do."

It's not a question, but there is an answer, and I already know it. I look at Brax as Dean talks. He looks like I feel. Cold. Dead. Full of a desire to maim and destroy. There's a smudge of blood on his cheek. When he looks back at me, he smiles, and even for someone as fucked up as me—for someone who already knows what she's going to do about the man sitting in that chair—the look of Brax's smile scares me. His eyes don't look like they normally do. There's a cruel, sick, twisted glint in them, and I'm reminded of the first day I met him. He smiles like this not just for enjoyment, but something else…

My eyes go down, down, down to the front of his pants and they widen. "Are you fucking hard?" I ask.

Braxton's smile droops but only a smidge. Instead of answering he takes a step forward and kicks the bucket beneath Roger's frame, making the old, fat rapist of a man flinch and start to weep. "Noooo," he moans out. "Nooo not a-a-again."

What had they done to him while I was out? I flick a look between the three of them. Braxton's slowly disintegrating smile. Abel's cold, calculated look. And Dean, with his face covered in nothing but disgust and rage. I decide I don't actually give a shit.

My finger burns from where one of my nails has been partially stripped back as I place it against the side of the gun in my grip. I round the chair and stand next to Brax. I don't know why—I don't understand it myself. Even with his strange smile and even more disturbing hardness at the torture he's obviously been dealing out—and how it kind of creeps me out—I don't feel afraid of him. Despite how they clearly have no qualms about hurting someone they don't know just because of what they found him doing and how so very evident it is that they've done this before, I don't feel afraid of any of them. They're sick and depraved and they're most certainly not normal. But that makes them more secure in their own way. A haven for someone like me. Someone just as messed up.

Roger blubbers, sobbing, as his chest shakes. There are blackened marks on his skin. I wanted to do this all myself, but now I'm just tired. So fucking tired. And irritated.

My stomach rumbles.

"P-please—" Roger stutters.

"Please what?" I ask.

He lifts his head until I can see the clouded fear in his eyes. "P-please make it stop," he says. "Please don't kill me."

I lift my gun. The barrel presses against his forehead and big fat tears begin to fall down his dirty cheeks.

"N-no, no, nononononono. P-please! I'll d-do anything!" The scent of urine leaks out as he pisses himself, yellow water running down his inner legs and dripping into the bucket. Brax rounds me and reaches for the jumper cables. "*No!*" Roger begins to rock back and forth, away from my gun, into my gun, away from my gun, into my gun. "Not again!"

Brax holds them up and eyes me as if waiting for my command.

I only have one to give and it's for myself.

I press the gun back into Roger's forehead and then, I pull the trigger.

EPILOGUE

DEAN

"Is she asleep?"

At Abel's question, I look down. Sure enough, her eyes are closed. I smooth my thumb down one cheek, noting the dark purple circles beneath her lashes. The bruises on her jawline make me want to go back to that shithole and set it on fire all over again.

"Yes," is all I say.

Brax is silent in the passenger seat, but I know what he's thinking. I know what they're both thinking. Abel's the one who voices it. "Are we going to tell her?"

I lift one single tendril of dark hair from her temple and smooth it back, careful not to wake her. She needs to sleep. Hell, I hope she dreams of nothing as she does. Not me. Not the world. And certainly not the man that she just killed. I glance back through the plastic of the soft top of the Mustang. I can barely make out the tail end of the car's trunk where the fucker's body lies, wrapped in plastic and duct tape.

She hadn't even blinked when she saw what we'd done. And when I'd given her the choice—to remain innocent in

EPILOGUE

at least this one way or to grab the bastard by the throat and end his miserable existence—she'd taken the gun and pulled the trigger.

To say it was sexy would be underscoring how fucking dangerous this woman is to me. Whether she realizes it or not, she's mine, and whether she wants it or not, I'm hers too. I'd known it when I'd felt my entire gut sink at the image Kate had sent me. I'd known it when she'd fought me—kicked my fucking balls into my body cavity and grabbed me by my throat. How long ago had that even been? A day? Two? Didn't matter.

I'd known what she would choose even before I presented the option. I knew she could handle it. But could she handle what we'd found out in the hours before she'd woken and the choice to end him had been given?

In all honesty, it wasn't so much that she couldn't handle it—it was more that I wasn't ready to let her.

My gaze lifts and meets Brax's in the rearview mirror. His lips curl back in the facsimile of a smile. It's not. It's a baring of teeth—an animalistic urge inside of him that he recognizes in the woman in my arms.

I shake my head. "No," I say. "Not yet."

"She's going to be pissed," Abel says.

I know she will be. The fact remains, though, we don't have more information than what Brax had managed to beat and torture out of the worthless small town drug dealer. The reminder makes me grit my teeth and hold back a snarl.

Abel pulls the Mustang into a very old cemetery. It's off the beaten path, to say the least. Far enough away from Plexton for this to feel comfortable. I gently nudge Avalon's sleeping body over and then, one by one, the three of us climb out of the car and head for the back end of the car. I

EPILOGUE

pop the trunk and look down at the white plastic package. Brax reaches for the first shovel.

"Go see if there're any fresh graves," I order. "I'll have someone pick up the SUV." He nods, before taking the shovel and heading up the hill. Abel and I stand there in silence for several minutes after I finish sending the text to one of my father's men, waiting until Brax is out of earshot. Only then do I turn to him and ask the question I've been needing to since we left. "How far did he take it?" I ask.

Abel crosses his arms and turns around, leaning his lower back on the bumper of the car. "Far enough," he says vaguely.

I growl. "Don't fucking bullshit me," I snap. "I need to know how far he went and what we're looking at in the coming weeks."

After a moment, he lowers his head and blows out a breath. "He's going to want a fight when we get back," he admits. "Probably sex too. Not from the girls at school, though. Hookers. Prostitutes. Ones we can pay off to not say anything."

"Think he'll kill anyone?" I ask.

Abel shakes his head. "No, but he'll be on edge for a while. He didn't take it too far, but he..."

Braxton's figure appears back over the top of the hill and Abel closes his mouth, his lips pinching shut. The shovel is gone from Brax's hand. He lifts his arm and waves it our way. He's found a grave. "Alright," I say. "Let's fucking do this."

Together, Abel and I each take an end of the body and haul it out of the trunk. "Fuck, I'm going to need my car detailed on the inside after this," he snaps as we steadily carry the load up the hill and over, following Braxton as he leads us to a lot in the far back of the cemetery.

EPILOGUE

"It didn't even touch the inside of your trunk," I say. "Quit your bitching."

"But the smell," he replies testily. "I don't want the smell of dead drug dealer in my car—trunk or not."

"Drop him there," I say as soon as I spot the semi-fresh mound of dirt clumped in front of a brand new tombstone. As soon as the word 'drop' leaves my lips, Abel releases and I jerk as the body falls at my feet.

"What?" he asks when I shoot him a glare. "You said drop it."

I ignore him, laying my end down and moving to the grave. I stomp on the dirt. "A couple of days old, but it should be fine," I say. Abel heads back to the Mustang to grab the rest of the shovels and I turn and look at Brax.

"Don't start," he says quietly.

"Just checking on you." I reach into my back pocket and withdraw a cigarette pack, slapping it on my palm once, twice, three times before I rip it open and dig out a smoke.

"You shouldn't do that here," he says as I put the end between my lips.

"I'm not going to smoke it yet," I say. Though I want to. Real fucking bad. This night has been a fucking shit show. In the nearby distance, I can hear Abel cursing softly to himself as he climbs the hill again. The clang of metal banging against metal echoing after him.

"You should tell her," Brax says.

I look at him. "Tell her what?"

He glares.

I sigh. "It won't do any good. She can't do anything about it. I want more details before we say anything."

"She deserves to know."

"I never said she didn't."

"Someone called that motherfucker." Braxton's voice

EPILOGUE

deepens with his anger, a note of something slightly unhinged entering his tone. "Someone warned him that she'd be coming back. He was waiting for her in that house."

As Abel makes it to the top of the hill and heads our way, I slowly turn and look at Brax. "Let her sleep tonight, man," I say. "Just give her that much. We'll figure the rest out in the morning."

"We're going to make them pay," he swears, keeping his eyes level with mine.

I pull the cigarette out of my mouth and stick it into my back pocket. If it gets crushed, it gets crushed—I just needed something for a moment. "Yes," I tell him, "we will."

Because he's right; before Roger Murphy died by Avalon's hands, he'd told us the truth. He hadn't acted alone. Someone had known she would be coming back. It was also the reason why any and all lingering anger at Avalon had dried up. Because someone had fucking set her up. I'd let myself be overtaken by my jealousy. I'd been more than stupid—I'd been the trigger for her latest trauma and I wasn't dumb enough to think that it was the only or even the last. Oh no. This wasn't over by a long shot.

Someone had known exactly what buttons to press to piss me off and I'd known exactly what to do to send her running. All of that had only ensured that she would be set up, drugged, raped and, if things had gone Roger's way, murdered.

Avalon Manning has someone on edge that is willing to do whatever it takes to get rid of her, and we're going to find out who. Starting with Luc Kincaid and Kate fucking Coleman.

ACKNOWLEDGMENTS

I keep hoping with each book I publish that I'll see a rise in readers who love to hear the stories in my head. Unfortunately, with each book I publish, I can't help but forget—though only momentarily—that I already have amazing readers who listen and love me. So, this one is for you guys. Thank you for reading.

Thank you to all of the people who have been eternally supportive. Who listened to me cry, rant, and rave over Avalon being such a fucking bitch and Dean being a stupid asshole. You know that this book wasn't easy by any definition of the word, but you stuck through it with me, and for that, I will be forever grateful.

To my editors, Heather and Kristen—seriously, without y'all, I do not want to think of where I'd be. Probably locked up in an insane asylum. To my proofreaders, Ellen and Jean. To my lovely assistant, Allison. To all of the alphas who helped me work through the early issues of this manuscript, especially Cassie. You're all babes. To my author friends. And last, but certainly never least, to my chosen family. I'm so lucky to have your support. You have never made me feel less than beautiful and perfect. You've never made me feel ugly or unworthy and you're always there for me. Thank you, truly, from the bottom of my heart.

ABOUT THE AUTHOR

Lucy Smoke, also known as Lucinda Dark for her fantasy works, has a master's degree in English and is a self-proclaimed creative chihuahua. She enjoys feeding her wanderlust, cover addiction, as well as her face, and truly hopes people will stop giving her bath bombs as gifts. Bath's get cold too fast and it's just not as wonderful as the commercials make it out to be when the tub isn't a jacuzzi.

When she's not on a never-ending quest to find the perfect milkshake, she lives and works in the southern United States with her beloved fur-baby, Hiro, and her family and friends.

Want to be kept up to date? Think about joining the author's group or signing up for their newsletter below.

Facebook Group
Newsletter

ALSO BY LUCY SMOKE / LUCINDA DARK

Contemporary Series:

Sick Boys Series
Pretty Little Savage
Stone Cold Queen (coming soon)

Iris Boys Series (completed)
Now or Never
Power & Choice
Leap of Faith
Cross my Heart
Forever & Always
Iris Boys Series Boxset

The *Break* Series (completed)
Study Break
Tough Break
Spring Break
Break Series Collection

Contemporary Standalones:

Expressionate
Wildest Dreams

Criminal Underground Series (Shared Universe Standalones)

Sweet Possession

Scarlett Thief

Fantasy Series:

Twisted Fae Series

Court of Crimson

Court of Frost

Court of Midnight

Barbie: The Vampire Hunter Series (completed)

Rest in Pieces

Dead Girl Walking

Ashes to Ashes

Dark Maji Series (completed)

Fortune Favors the Cruel

Blessed Be the Wicked

Twisted is the Crown

For King and Corruption

Long Live the Soulless

Nerys Newblood Series

Daimon

Necrosis

Resurrection (Coming Soon)

Sky Cities Series (Dystopian)

Heart of Tartarus

Shadow of Deception

Sword of Damage

Dogs of War (Coming Soon)

Printed in Poland
by Amazon Fulfillment
Poland Sp. z o.o., Wrocław

89988236R00242